CALL IN THE CANYONS

CHAPARRAL HEARTS
BOOK SIX

KATHLEEN DENLY

To the traumatized and ostracized.
You are not alone.
You are loved.

A new heart also will I give you, and a new spirit will I put within you: and I will take away the stony heart out of your flesh, and I will give you an heart of flesh.

— EZEKIEL 36:26 KJV

CHAPTER 1

September 29, 1875
Lupine Valley Ranch
Eastern San Diego County, California

Sweat soaked Virginia "Ginny" Baker's bodice and made her linen trousers stick to her legs as she studied the formidable path to the cliff top. Scattered boulders and loose gravel dotted by prickly cacti formed a treacherous maze. Reaching the stranded calf by horseback would be impossible.

Ginny dismounted and tethered her chestnut gelding, Mr. Darcy, to a mesquite tree. With deliberate movements, she clambered up the steep, slippery slope.

The young cow bawled as if impatient with her cautious steps.

Ginny tossed her twin blond braids over her shoulders and glared up at the big brown eyes watching her. "Quit your cater-wauling. I'm coming." She shook her head as she continued upward. "If you're hungry, it's your own addle-headed fault for wandering so far from the herd. Again."

As if the scrub calf hadn't been born runty enough, the creature had wandered away from its mama no less than four times in the three weeks it'd been alive. When she'd first realized it was missing again, she'd sent the rest of her all-female crew back to the ranch, countering their protests with assurances that she'd be careful and would soon join them for the evening meal.

Watching them ride away and feeling the silence of the desert settle in around her had been the highlight of her day. Much as she loved her younger sister, Biddie too often acted as though Ginny was made of glass. She squawked like a cranky hen whenever Ginny wanted to head anywhere alone and sent the others with her as if she couldn't even tie her own boots. Normally, she tolerated the nuisance because Biddie would worry otherwise. But today, she'd wanted a moment to herself, and the missing animal had provided the perfect excuse. The day Ginny needed help wrangling a reedy calf would be the day she traded her horse for a rocking chair.

An hour later, she'd spotted the calf standing in the difficult-to-reach spot, and a part of her had been tempted to leave the cow to the elements. As scrawny as it was, it surely wouldn't bring enough at market to be worth so much hassle. But despite the rumors she knew circulated about her, even Ginny wasn't that cold-hearted.

So here she was, risking her neck for a foolish, measly, worthless critter that would no doubt run off again just as soon as Ginny dragged her back to the herd. Feeling ornery as a scorpion pestered by an army of ants, she stomped onto the next ledge.

The rocks beneath her shifted, sending a shudder through the ground. The earth gave way. She threw her hands out, searching for purchase. But it was too late.

She tumbled down the cliff in a chaotic whirl of dust and stones. Flailing, she tried in vain to halt her descent. Her ribs bounced off a two-foot boulder. She wrapped her arms around her head just in time to avoid a skull cracker on the next.

Sliding on her backside, she shoved her heels into the earth as she barreled toward another pile of rocks.

Her left foot disappeared into a crevice. Wedged. Yanked her to a stop. Fire surged from her ankle up her leg.

She cried out.

Heart pounding and chest heaving, she lay still against the nearly vertical slope, her foot firmly trapped in the narrow space between two boulders. Struggling to catch her breath, she took stock of her injuries. Her arms would surely be black and blue, but they were otherwise unharmed and had spared her head from worse than a throbbing headache. Her ribs smarted something fierce, but a deep breath seemed to prove they were bruised, not broken. The stinging in her raw palms and torn fingernails was nothing compared to the gnawing sensation in her left leg.

Gingerly, she lifted onto her elbows and inched up the slope to ease the pressure on her trapped ankle. The movement sent bolts of pain shooting up her limb. She resisted the urge to air her lungs—a habit gained through her childhood spent among gamblers, thieves, and worse. Biddie had cajoled the "indelicate language" out of her since planting herself on Ginny's Lupine Valley Ranch more than two years ago and refusing to let Ginny rebuild alone. Biddie, adopted by a well-to-do family twenty years ago—after their father took Ginny and their brother away in the night and their mother died a year later—had more refined sensibilities than Ginny was used to. Not that Biddie was here to care.

Ginny sucked in a breath, clamped her lips tight, and tried moving her left foot. As expected, the limb shouted its protest, but it obeyed. Barely. There was less than an inch to wiggle it in the tight confines between the rocks. Somehow, her foot had crammed itself into a diamond-shaped gap between three sandstone boulders that should be too small for such a possibility.

It seemed the smaller rock had slid from the ledge where she'd stomped, and the stone had stopped just behind her heel, ramming itself under her leg. Whatever the case, it looked far too heavy to move.

Bracing against the pain, Ginny planted her palms and right heel into the dirt and tried to tug her left foot free. Agonizing pain forced a cry from her lips, and she collapsed, the rocks still holding her foot as captive as the closed jaw of a bear trap. She brushed sweat from her brow with the back of her wrist. At least her boot and stocking protected her skin from the rocks' tiny, sharp teeth.

Ginny forced herself into a sitting position, then sucked in a breath and leaned forward. Her ribs screamed, but she ignored them, trying desperately to shove her fingers between her boot and her leg near the ankle. If she could widen the gap enough to wiggle her foot free, the greedy stone could keep her boot.

After a full minute of painful wriggling with no progress, she was forced to give up.

She lay back and stared at the cloudless sky. Now what? No one was close enough to hear her shout, and her rifle was still tied to her saddle. Along with her canteens. Ginny let loose a long groan. How could she have been so careless?

She looked for the scrub calf, but it was gone. Probably frightened by the loud noises of her fall. She'd have to track it down all over again.

Resting her head against the dirt, she glared at the deepening hues of a red-and-purple sky. If she didn't find a way home before her crew came searching, she'd never live this down. Worse, Biddie would insist on someone shadowing Ginny everywhere she went. The notion grated worse than the coarse gravel beneath her. She wasn't a child that needed coddling. Never had been. From her earliest memories, it had been her job to care for herself and everyone around her. And she'd done a fine job. For the most part. She hadn't needed help then, and she didn't need it now. Accidents like this could happen to anyone. She'd been in worse scrapes and found her way through. She'd figure her way out of this too.

Ginny scanned her surroundings for anything that might help set her free. A stick the thickness of her thumb and as long as her forearm lay within reach. She snatched it up only to have it crumble in her grasp, dry as the desert sand. She tossed it away.

The only other objects in reach were cacti and more rocks. Ignoring the plants more likely to hurt than help her, she eyed the rocks and settled on a black-gray-and-white speckled one about the size of her hand with a sharp edge. Plucking it from the ground, she turned the sharp edge away from her stinging palm and sat up again. With a grunt, she leaned forward and scratched at the sandstone boulders above her stuck ankle. Bits of sand and pebbles rained down on her leg and the rock beneath it.

After a few seconds, she examined her tool. It appeared no worse for the rubbing. She grinned. This would work. It would take time. A long time. But eventually, she'd get free. She swallowed, but her thick saliva moved like glue, getting stuck halfway down her throat. How long had it been since she'd taken a drink from her canteen? She couldn't remember.

After a glance at the last sliver of sun hovering above the horizon, she lifted her speckled stone and got to work.

Hours later, she'd scraped away enough of the sandstone to tug her foot free. The boot stayed behind as she crawled through the dark down the slope. Exhausted, she rolled onto her back and lay panting at the base of the hill staring up at the stars. She gave herself a full minute to recover, then lifted onto her elbows.

That's enough lollygagging. No doubt her crew was already

searching for her, and the last thing she needed was to be found helpless on her backside.

Thankfully, she'd trained Mr. Darcy to respond to her whistle. One sharp note was all it took to bring him to her side. Reaching up, she grasped a stirrup and hauled herself to standing, carefully keeping her weight on her uninjured foot.

She popped the cork out of a canteen and drank greedily as she pondered how to get into the saddle. A nearby waist-high boulder seemed her best bet. Getting on top of the stone and then into the saddle without placing weight on her injured ankle made her ribs scream, but she ignored them. Pain was temporary, and home awaited.

Ginny grimaced. Heading home meant chaos, but at least there'd be a warm meal. Much as she admired her sister's gumption to keep cooking and baking despite being with child, Ginny half wished Biddie would take to bed. Then maybe Ginny would have a hope of dodging the fuss her younger sister was bound to make when she saw Ginny's injuries.

~

September 30, 1875
Alameda, California

Sheriff Heath Monroe fought the urge to let his shoulders sink along with the sun's last rays as he and Deputy Jeb Reed made their way down Alameda's bustling main street. They'd spent four grueling days chasing the transient gambler who'd shot Charles Barlow over a card game in a local saloon. But yesterday, all trace of the murderer had vanished as surely as if God Himself had plucked the man from the face of the earth. Like Enoch. Except Heath was confident the man they'd pursued hadn't walked with God a day in his life. Not that it mattered. With no way of guessing where the killer had gone, Heath and Jeb were forced to return to Alameda empty-handed. Again.

The tense silence he and Jeb had shared since breaking camp this morning and setting out for home was broken only by the clatter of horses' hooves, the creak of passing carriage wheels, and the murmur of townsfolk going about their business.

Heath tipped his hat, shielding his eyes from the setting sun as he studied his closest friend. Jeb looked as defeated as Heath felt. Should he say something encouraging? It wasn't Jeb's fault they'd lost the tracks, but knowing his friend, he was probably still blaming himself.

"All that for nothing," Jeb muttered before Heath could decide. "Four days of hard riding, and the rotter slips away."

Heath clenched his jaw against the sting of truth. "We did all we could, Jeb. That's just how it goes sometimes. We'll catch him eventually. Or God will. You know that."

Jeb gave a tiny nod but said nothing.

As they neared the jail, people paused their conversations, casting curious and sympathetic glances their way.

Tom Barlow, the father of the murdered gambler, stormed into the street. His face was contorted with rage, but Heath saw the grief in his eyes. "You call yourselves lawmen?" His shout sounded raw, no doubt from bouts of crying. "You let him get away! My boy is dead, and you two couldn't even catch the man who did it."

Jeb cast Heath a resigned glance and dismounted.

Heath followed suit. "Tom, I know you're hurting. But there wasn't anything more we could do once—"

"Anything more? It's only been four days, and you've already given up. Slinking into town with your tail between your legs. Just like last time." Tom's voice rose to a fever pitch. "You're incompetent! This is Valadez all over again. Months on his trail, and you didn't even bring him in. It was the Los Angeles sheriff who captured him, not you."

A crowd began to gather, whispers spreading as fast as wildfire. Doubt flickered in their eyes, their trust wavering.

Tom spun to face those watching. "We need a new sheriff! One brave enough to stick to a criminal's trail and bring him to justice no matter the sacrifice."

Jeb stepped forward, his fists clenched. "Wait just a minute, Tom. It's Heath's information that led to Valadez's capture. That sheriff in Los Angeles tricked him, then took his lead and the glory."

Heath held up a hand, stopping Jeb. "Let him be, Jeb."

Tom advanced, his eyes wild with anger. "You aren't fit to wear that badge!" He jabbed his finger against the star pinned to Heath's shirt.

Heath took a deep breath, then spoke in the calmest tone he could muster while holding Tom's gaze. "I understand you're angry, Tom. Losing a child...there's no pain like it. But a windstorm blew off the man's tracks, and no one in the area had seen him. There wasn't anything else we could do. I'm sorry we couldn't bring him back."

"You're sorry?" Tom sneered. Then his shoulders slumped, the fight draining out of him. He turned away, shaking his head. "Your best isn't good enough." He pressed his way through the gathering, head low.

The crowd began to disperse, the tension slowly ebbing away. Heath watched Tom retreat, his heart heavy with the weight of his failures.

Jeb placed a hand on Heath's shoulder. "You did right by him. Even if he can't see it now."

Heath shook his head as several of those who'd witnessed the confrontation and heard Tom's demands for a new sheriff regrouped in clusters scattered along the street. He couldn't hear their words, but the frowning glances his way spoke volumes. "Problem is, Tom isn't the only one questioning my abilities."

Deputy Ross Kendrick emerged from the jail, grinning. "Hey, you're back." He glanced around, noted the lack of a prisoner, and his smile dimmed. "I can take your horses to the livery for you."

With thanks, Heath and Jeb handed over the reins, removed their belongings from the saddles, and strode into the jailhouse.

The familiar scent of tobacco and gun oil wafted through the air as Heath dropped his bags beside his desk and settled his weapons in the wall-mounted gun rack. A groan escaped him as he sank onto the creaky wooden chair and reached for the top paper in the pile that had grown in his absence. The late-afternoon sun casting long shadows through the barred windows did little to illuminate the words on the page in his hands. He lit the gas lantern on his desk. Revealed by the flickering light, a flyer reminded folks of the upcoming election. It wouldn't be held until November of next year, but the campaigning had already begun in earnest. At least this paper encouraged people to reelect *him*. He'd seen plenty more supporting his opponents, Deputy Ross Kendrick and Seth Whitaker.

Jeb peered over Heath's shoulder. "See, you've still got plenty of friends in this town."

"Not sure that'll be enough." In any case, he didn't want to be chosen based on loyalty. If he was reelected, he wanted it to mean the people had faith that he was the best man for the job. "A lot of folks resent that I was gone so long without reward."

"That's not fair, and you know it."

Heath shrugged. Fair or not, he and Jeb had been on Valadez's trail for months, leaving the good people of this town in Ross's capable hands. While they'd gotten used to Ross meeting their needs, they'd expected Heath to return with

Valadez in cuffs. Or draped across a saddle, ready for the undertaker. Instead, Heath had been tricked into returning home under the belief that his last lead was false testimony, only to see the headlines, along with everyone else, that Los Angeles Sheriff Raymond had captured the state's most notorious bandit leader. What the papers hadn't reported was that Raymond had done so by acting on the tip he'd convinced Heath was no good.

Jeb picked up the next sheet from the pile, scowled, then crushed the page in his fist and tossed it into the bin beside Heath's desk.

"Hey!" Heath retrieved the balled paper and smoothed it out. Then immediately regretted his action. The words *Whitaker for sheriff!* were blazoned across the top, followed by impossible promises of peace and prosperity if he won and vague warnings of the city's doom if he lost. Seth Whitaker owned a saloon three blocks from the jailhouse and was about as shady as they came. Heath tossed the paper back in the bin. "How can anyone be fool enough to vote for a man like that? He hasn't exactly hidden his darker dealings."

Jeb shrugged. "Some people see what they want to."

Heath studied the details of a few new *wanted* posters before another flyer came up—this one endorsing Ross Kendrick.

Unlike Whitaker, Ross was a good man. Heath had met him following an attack on a stage station by Valadez. The young man had been at the station at the time of the attack and not only managed to keep his head and keep everyone safe, but he'd mounted up and ridden to where he'd heard Heath and his posse were resting.

Ross had provided enough information to get Heath the closest he would ever come to capturing Valadez—not counting the lead the Los Angeles sheriff had convinced Heath was false. Truth of the matter was, Heath had offered Ross the position as a deputy two years ago purely because of his strong moral compass and unflinching courage in the face of danger. He hadn't even betrayed Heath by throwing his hat into the election. He'd been nominated by some families who were grateful for his protection in Heath's absence.

Ross would make a fine sheriff—if he could win. Heath had his doubts considering Ross refused to campaign on his own behalf. Meanwhile, Whitaker had found ways to convince several local officials to endorse him. Heath tried not to think how.

Even if Ross could win, Heath wasn't ready to step aside. He'd been Alameda's sheriff for nearly ten years and loved the work. Despite the toughness of the job and his regular brushes with death, he couldn't imagine anything as satisfying as protecting the good citizens of his bailiwick and seeing criminals served justice. Besides, with Susannah gone, what else was there to provide meaning in his life?

Jeb sank into a nearby chair. "Maybe it's time to change tactics." He leaned forward, resting his elbows on his knees. "What about Claudio Chavarria? Word is, he's still lurking around the hills east of here, still threatening to kill every American in California as revenge for Valadez's 'murder.'" Jeb rolled his eyes so hard with that last word, they about fell out of his head. They both knew the trial and hanging Valadez had received after capture was no more than the robber-murderer deserved. "The governor has issued a two-thousand-dollar reward for his capture. If you could bring Chavarria in, it might just be the break you need."

Heath's eyes narrowed as he considered Jeb's words. "Chavarria... He's a slippery one too. But if we could get him, it might remind folks that I know this job better than anyone."

"Exactly." Jeb slapped his thigh. "I figure the governor might even be willing to finance the manhunt. You get the state's backing, you can put together a posse strong enough to track him down."

Heath sat back, eyeing his best friend. "I don't suppose you'd be willing to stay behind and keep this chair warm?"

Jeb laughed loud and hard, as Heath had known he would.

The memory of their numerous close calls while hunting Valadez gnawed at him. Law work of any kind was dangerous, but hunting this particular group of ruthless criminals was far worse. He hated putting Jeb at greater risk again—the Lord knew Heath couldn't stand to lose another person he loved in pursuit of justice—but the thought of letting his town down, of losing his job... What was the point of losing his wife if he also lost this job? What would he do without his badge?

With a deep breath, Heath withdrew a sheet of stationery from his desk and dipped his pen in the inkwell. "All right, Jeb. Let's see if we can make this happen."

Jeb whooped and jumped to his feet, doing a little jig. "We'll get him this time, Heath. Just you wait."

Heath bit back a grin at his friend's sudden mood shift and wished he could recover as quickly from life's disappointments.

A few minutes later, Heath signed his name and slid his request into an envelope. As he sealed the letter and addressed it to California's governor, he couldn't stop the worry that he'd just sealed their fates. He had no idea whether this decision would save his position as sheriff or cost him everything and everyone he cared about.

CHAPTER 2

October 7, 1875
Lupine Valley Ranch
Eastern San Diego County, California

*B*elly full, Ginny leaned back in her chair at the head of the long makeshift table in the yard outside her home. As usual, her younger sister, Biddie, dominated the conversation among the rest of the ranch's residents. She sat beside her husband, Gideon Swift, at the opposite end of the table. Being seven months pregnant had barely slowed her down. Their three female ranch hands—Lei Yan, Esther, and Carmen—and two giggling girls occupied the rest of the chairs. The general mood was one of tiredness but contentment, as chatter filled the deepening twilight settling into their desert mountain valley.

The conversation at the table shifted as Biddie leaned back in her chair, resting a hand on her growing belly. "Hard to believe it's been more than two years since I received your letter that Pa was dead and you needed help."

"I needed *money*." Ginny tightened her grip on her cup, her eyes fixed on her dinner plate. Oliver—their pa—had died in a terrible bandit attack that had left Ginny the sole survivor and owner of Lupine Valley Ranch. Two months later, Biddie, Biddie's best friend Lucy, and Gideon had joined her in the desert—much to her consternation. "You weren't supposed to come, let alone stay."

"I promised to leave as soon as Preston showed up."

Ginny snorted softly. It'd taken longer than any of them expected for her and Biddie's younger brother to arrive. "Yeah, I remember that promise. You were all supposed to leave after a couple of months. Next thing I knew, you two were getting hitched." She waved a hand between Gideon and Biddie.

Her sister grinned. "I still can't believe you gave us part-ownership of the ranch as a wedding present."

"Well, I couldn't seem to get rid of you." Ginny's smile softened her teasing words. "So I figured that if you were determined to work the ranch alongside me, and since you brought me new ranch hands, it was the right thing to do." Even if trusting Gideon—a man—with any portion of her precious land had been a less than comfortable decision.

Biddie waved her fork toward Carmen, Lei Yan, and Esther. "I'll never forget the looks on your faces when Gideon and I brought y'all to Lupine Valley almost two years ago."

Even Ginny—whose heart beat for her home—recognized that working on a desert cattle ranch in the middle of nowhere was a far cry from living at the women's and children's charity home in San Francisco that Biddie's adoptive parents, the Davidsons, owned. Ginny had been impressed by how well the three women and two young girls had adjusted.

Biddie settled her gaze on twenty-nine-year-old Carmen. "You probably thought we'd brought you to the ends of the earth."

Carmen's rich brown hair spilled over her shoulders, framing her tawny face and sparkling brown eyes as she leaned her elbows on the table. "I'd never been pelted by so much sand in my life. Thought I'd be rubbed raw before we even arrived."

Eighteen-year-old Esther tucked a stray lock of her strawberry-blond hair behind her ear. "And now you wouldn't trade the desert for anything." She tossed Carmen a knowing grin before wiping food off the face of her three-year-old daughter, Deborah.

"I guess you could say the charm of this place has won me over." Carmen tipped her head toward Ginny. "Even if this one still bosses us like she owns the place."

Ginny smirked and crossed her arms. "That's because I do own the place." She glanced at her sister's raised brow. "Mostly."

Chuckles spread down the table.

Biddie's expression sobered. "For a while, I thought you'd need to share another piece of this land."

Ginny didn't need to ask to know her sister was thinking of when their brother, Preston, and Biddie's best friend, Lucy, decided to get married.

Gideon took his wife's hand. "This life isn't for everyone."

"I know." Biddie's chin dipped, as she was clearly missing the couple that had left last year to return to Preston's career as a trick-shot sharpshooter in a traveling variety show.

Lei Yan's yelp shattered the somber moment. One of Biddie's cats had leaped onto Lei Yan's plate, scattering beans and biscuits.

Before anyone could react, another cat followed, and together they raced across the table, knocking over Gideon's coffee cup. Plates rattled and food flew as the animals left a path of chaos.

"Shoo! Get out of here, you little rascals!" Gideon waved both hands at the offending creatures.

"Those retched cats!" Ginny grabbed for her tipped cup.

"They're just having fun." Josie laughed, hopping up to chase the cats off the table.

"You can't say they aren't earning their keep." Gideon began collecting the bits of scattered food onto his plate. "No rats in the barn, no chewed-through flour sacks. Worth a little trouble at the table, if you ask me."

"Maybe." Ginny shook her head as the spilled water from her cup poured off the table edge, just missing her leg. "Josie, grab me a rag, will ya?"

Deborah giggled as she clutched a spoon. "Kitty naughty!"

Ginny couldn't help grinning at the little brunette. "You like them troublemakers, don't you?"

Biddie chuckled, brushing crumbs from her lap. "Oh, leave them be. They're just keeping things lively."

Josie darted over with a cloth, handing it to Ginny. "Here ya go, Ginny." She glanced nervously in the direction the cats had disappeared. "You aren't going to get rid of them, are you? They didn't mean any harm."

Guilt pinched Ginny that the girl would even ask. Ginny must have sounded angrier than she was. "Of course not." She winked at the girl. "But your question reminds me that those cats belong to Biddie. So I'd say the mess belongs to her too. Wouldn't you agree?"

Josie laughed while Biddie made an expression of mock offense. "Hey, now! I'd say I did my share cooking all this food." She turned to Deborah. "And what about you, little miss? Are you going to help me clean up?"

Deborah beamed, holding up her spoon proudly. "Help Miss Biddie!"

"Good girl," Ginny said, reaching across Esther's empty chair to ruffle the girl's curls. "Now let's see if we can get this table back in one piece before the next disaster." Ginny tidied as much of the table as she could reach from her seat, glancing around at the bustling yard. The constant activity, the clutter of people and animals—it all wore on her nerves in ways she wouldn't admit aloud. Her once quiet and solitary life was now filled with noise and chaos—nothing at all like she'd planned. Even farther from any life she'd known before.

Gone were the days of ducking Oliver's drunken swings and dodging his ranch hands' unwanted advances. When her pa had been alive, each night had been a gamble. Sometimes, the men would drink themselves into a stupor, leaving Ginny to clear and wash their plates in peace. On other nights, they'd strike up a card or dice game, someone would lose, and a fight would break out. In those days, her only comforts had been Preston's sporadic secret letters and the spunky friendship of Gabriella Hernandez, whose unexpected and bright presence in Ginny's life had been ruthlessly cut short.

Ginny surged to her feet, grabbing the table edge as her weak ankle screamed in protest. Chewing on the past was a waste of time. More work awaited.

"Careful," Carmen admonished as she rushed to Ginny's side, holding out the crutch Gideon had fashioned for Ginny.

Esther appeared on Ginny's left a moment later and reached for her plate. "Here, let me take that."

Ginny accepted the crutch but jerked her plate out of reach. "I can manage."

Esther's cheeks reddened, and her eyes lowered.

Ginny huffed, mad at herself for being rude and hurting the young woman's feelings. "Thank you for offering, though."

A small smile returned to Esther's expression as she reclaimed her chair and wiped sauce from her three-year-old daughter's face. Deborah squirmed under her mother's efforts.

"I'll take your plates." Carmen's thirteen-year-old daughter, Josie, stood and reached across the table for Esther's and Deborah's plates. The girl was a dab hand at minding the younger girl. Despite Ginny's initial concerns that having children on the ranch would be a dangerous distraction, the girls—despite one alarming rock-climbing accident—had proven to be mighty helpful. Even little Deborah aided with the domestic tasks around the ranch.

Her plate in one hand and the crutch in the other, Ginny hobbled toward the dish tub as everyone else finished cleaning the mess.

Biddie caught her eye with a knowing look. "Don't even think about washing that. You know I'll come out to take care of it later."

With a grunt, Ginny let her plate plop into the waiting soapy water. She turned toward her house, but Biddie stepped into her path.

"Why don't you come over to our house tonight? Gideon and I would love your company."

Ginny shook her head, wincing as she shifted her weight. She knew from experience that accepting the invitation meant listening to the Bible being read, and tonight, she wasn't in the mood. "I'm tired and planning to turn in early." The others were listening in. "The rest of you go on. I'll see you in the morning."

Biddie nodded and joined everyone else, heading toward her half-stone, half-wood house behind a large juniper bush several yards away. Dark smoke puffing from its chimney stood out against the gathering dusk. No doubt Biddie had something delicious baking in her oven. She was always baking, whether it was for the ranch, their neighbors, or the store in Campo—the nearest town, built and run entirely by the Gaskill brothers, Luman and Silas.

Despite Ginny's protesting taste buds, she faced her own home, just ten feet away. Made entirely from rock and adobe mortar except for its thatch willow roof and the wooden door, it blended almost seamlessly into the rugged landscape. Unlike the glass windows Biddie and Gideon had installed in their house, Ginny's house bore more practical slot windows, just wide enough to slide her rifle through. Even those were covered on the inside with wooden shutters. She could light sixteen lanterns inside, and no one spying from the valley's rim would have a clue she was at home.

She hobbled inside and shut the door. Pitch-black silence greeted her. From habit, she found the box of Lucifers she kept on a small table near the door and lit the lamp hanging from a hook above it. Dim light spread across the room, highlighting the empty table and single chair with three empty beds at the back of the room. When they'd built this house a little over two years ago, two of those had been occupied by Biddie and her friend Lucy. Now, it was just Ginny who lived in this too-big house.

Lifting the lantern, she limped around the table and reached for the curtain hanging from a rope dividing the room. She gave the empty space one last disgusted look before tugging the fabric across. "I never should have let Biddie talk me into building something so big." After hanging the lantern from a hook beside her bed, she leaned her crutch against the wall and teetered on one foot as she undressed.

She washed up using the cold water and soap in her washbasin, grumbling as she scrubbed the sweat from her skin with a clean rag. "Too much house just makes for wasted space that still needs cleaning." Not that she cleaned the room herself. Soon after their arrival, Carmen had insisted Josie take over cleaning each of the ranch's residences as part of earning her keep. As Ginny wrung water from the cloth and hung it up to dry, she chuckled over the image of little Deborah tagging along to "help" Josie.

Ginny moved slowly but deliberately, setting out clothes for tomorrow and double-checking that her knife, guns, and canteens were ready for the next day. Her every move seemed to echo off the stone walls, shouting that she was alone.

"Which is exactly as I want it," she loudly declared to no

one. Then she shook her head. "It's a sad state of affairs when you're arguing with yourself, Ginny."

Finally, she slid her pistol under her pillow and dropped onto her tick mattress, her dully throbbing ankle an angry reminder of her stubbornness. She glanced around one last time, the empty shadows glaring back at her.

"I'm better on my own," she told herself firmly, though the words rang hollow in the empty room. She closed her eyes, willing herself to sleep, knowing that tomorrow would come too soon. But as she shifted around, trying to get comfortable, the soft sounds of the others singing in Biddie's home pushed their way through the stone walls she'd built to keep people out. She sat up and glared into the dark. Could she never have peace?

⁓

OCTOBER 13, 1875
ALAMEDA, CALIFORNIA

*H*eath gripped the arms of his chair on the porch of Jeb's sister's house. The laughter and shouts of a half dozen of Jeb's cousins playing in the yard filled the air with a lightness he couldn't reach. The governor's response to Heath's letter crinkled in his pocket as he shifted in his seat. He'd received and read the message just as he was locking up to join the celebration of Jeb's cousin Sally's eighteenth birthday, and the governor's words tugged Heath's mind in too many directions for him to focus on the festivities. His request for funds to pursue Claudio Chavarria had been approved.

Heath's gaze followed Garret Lawson, Jeb's nephew, as the young man chased after the children, his hazel eyes sparkling with amusement. Garret's youthful energy and enthusiasm were a stark contrast to the burden Heath carried. This mission was his chance to finally bring Chavarria to justice and prove Heath still had what it took to be this town's sheriff, but it would mean putting men like Jeb and Garret at significant risk. Jeb's brother-in-law had been robbed and killed on his way back from Oakland four years ago. Jeb's sister depended on her brother and eldest son for the money to feed and clothe her five younger children. It was the only reason Heath had agreed to hire Garret as a deputy. So far, Heath had managed to keep Garret safe from the worst risks of the job by assigning him plenty of desk work and sending him out for lower-risk things such as tax collection and distributing *wanted* posters— including the flyers that had helped catch Garret's pa's murderer. But ever since Jeb had let slip about Heath's plans to hunt Chavarria, the nineteen-year-old had been after him to be named part of the posse.

Jeb was leaning against the porch railing, a smile on his face as he watched the scene unfold. His best friend had been no help, filling the kid's head with wild stories of their pursuit of Valadez. It didn't matter if the stories were mostly true. Jeb had a bad habit of glossing over the miserable, boring parts and making the dangerous parts sound fun.

Heath checked that no one else was in earshot before admitting in a low voice, "Got some news, Jeb."

Jeb turned, his smile fading slightly as he took in Heath's serious expression. "Good news, I hope?"

"The governor approved our request for funds to hunt down Chavarria." Heath tugged the paper from his pocket and held it out. "We can assemble a posse and set out as soon as we have the necessary resources."

Jeb grinned, a spark of determination lighting his brown eyes. "Have you decided who to bring along?"

He knew Jeb was actually asking whether Heath had finally caved to Jeb and Garret's pressure to include the younger man. "Bringing Garret will only hurt his chances with Cole." Cole

Harris, Heath's father-in-law—Heath couldn't think of him as anything else, even if his wife, Susannah, had been dead for five years—was a caring but tough man.

Garret had been in love with Susannah's much younger sister, Agatha, since they were children. Determined to court and marry her as soon as possible, he'd been working on earning enough to purchase his own home since he was eleven. Unfortunately, giving his ma half his earnings to support his siblings since their pa's death meant that goal was still a ways off. Worse yet, after Susannah's death, Cole swore he'd never allow Agatha to marry any lawman.

Cole and Heath each had urged Garret to consider another profession, but the young man had a passion for seeing justice served that refused to be satisfied through any other endeavor. He insisted Cole would eventually change his mind. Heath had his doubts.

He rubbed his palms across the thighs of his trousers. "This is going to be a dangerous mission. Taking both of you with me isn't right. What'll your sister do if something goes wrong?"

Garret leaped up the steps. "Things could go wrong here in Alameda. At least if I'm with you, huntin' real criminals, I can die knowin' I made a difference."

Heath opened his mouth to argue that Garret was making a difference right here, but the boy jabbed a finger at him. "And don't try to tell me collectin' back taxes and solvin' who's goin' to pay for the fence Mrs. Gray's cow knocked down is makin' a difference. It isn't the same, and you know it."

"What about Agatha? Have you thought what your death would do to her?"

"Agatha understands." Garret leaned against the rail. "We've talked over the risks. She'll mourn me, of course, but she supports my need to leave this world a better place than I found it."

Jeb's sister stepped onto the porch. She laid a hand on

Heath's shoulder. "I appreciate what you're trying to do, Heath, but my boy's got a mind of his own. He's bound to find trouble either way. I'd rather you be around when he finds it. I trust you'll do your best to keep him safe. The rest is in the good Lord's hands."

A lump clogged Heath's throat as the memory of his wife's words on the day he'd first been elected sheriff came back to him. *"I trust you'll keep us safe."*

He swallowed hard and yanked his hat from his head. Running a hand through his hair, he looked from face to face. Not a one was going to budge. "Fine. Garret can come, but"— Heath jabbed his own finger at the young man—"you've got to do every single thing I tell you to, immediately and without question."

Garret straightened to his fullest height and nodded gravely. "Yes, sir. I promise."

Jeb clapped his hands together and rubbed his palms. "Now that's settled, who else we going to take with us?"

"I've been thinking on that." And praying for wisdom long into each night since mailing his request. "I'll ask Cole, of course." Cole may have graying hair, but his valuable experience as a former sheriff and unbending loyalty made him an obvious choice. "Then there's Enrique Flores. He's only twenty-two and as skinny as they come, but he's no stranger to long days in the saddle as a cowboy. He's also a skilled grizzly hunter, so he can track, and we don't need to worry about him turning tail in the face of danger. Plus, he's got a reputation for being reliable."

"I agree, they're both good choices if they'll agree to join us." Jeb folded his arms across his chest. "What about Alejandro? I don't think he'll want to leave his new wife so soon."

"You're probably right." His mood lifted with the memory of their former guide's joy at his wedding last week. "We'll still need someone who can speak Spanish, knows the terrain, and has connections to the Mexican families we'll encounter, which is why I've been considering asking Miguel Padillo. What do you think?"

Jeb nodded, his eyes thoughtful. "I don't know much about him, but the little I've heard paints him as a quiet man who mostly sticks to his uncle's ranch outside town. I know he speaks Spanish, and I've heard he makes regular trips to visit family east of Los Angeles."

"I've heard the same, which is why I'm considering him. He should have a good feel for the land down there and maybe some connections that can help us. If you don't have any objections, I'll ride out to his ranch tomorrow and see if he'll join us."

"You want me to track down Enrique and see if he's interested?"

Heath shook his head. "No, I want to speak to each man myself." It'd take longer to get their posse together, but if he was going to ask men to risk their lives by following him into danger, the least he could do was personally ensure they understood the peril they were agreeing to.

CHAPTER 3

NOVEMBER 11, 1875
LUPINE VALLEY RANCH
EASTERN SAN DIEGO COUNTY, CALIFORNIA

inally back in the saddle after recovering from her sprained ankle, Ginny rode tall and confident through the desert, leading Biddie and Carmen. The midmorning sun lit up the dry land, shining down on the scrubby mesquite and brittle creosote bushes. The sand of the empty creek bed they rode through muffled the clop of their horses' hooves.

Carmen glanced over at Biddie, whose rounded belly was unmistakable even under her loose bodice. "I can't help but wonder how Gideon agreed to let you ride this far from the ranch. You're eight months along, after all. I'd think he would be worried about you being out here."

Biddie chuckled softly, patting her belly as her horse side-stepped a rock. "Oh, he's worried, all right. He always worries. But I'm caught up on my baking, and I'll have to stay home for a long while once our baby is born. I told him I wanted to get out while I still can—feel the sun on my face, the wind in my hair. It's good for the soul."

"It sure is." Ginny tipped her face toward the sun. "Besides, women are tougher than men like to think."

Carmen shook her head, though a smile crept onto her lips. "Well, I hope the baby doesn't decide it's time to come while we're out here. I don't fancy delivering it in the middle of the desert."

Biddie laughed, the sound echoing lightly in the stillness. "Don't worry, Carmen. This little one's not due for another few weeks. Besides, from the stories the women at church have shared, if my pains start, I'll have more than enough time to ride home before I need to push."

Ginny chuckled. "If there's one thing I've learned, it's never to underestimate Biddie. She's as stubborn as they come—and that's saying something, coming from me."

Their shared laughter startled songbirds and jackrabbits from the sparse vegetation. The latter were fast, but Preston would've dropped them with a single shot.

Too bad her sharpshooting brother had returned to his traveling variety show last year and taken his new wife with him. Not that she could blame him for leaving after what had happened at the ranch while she'd been away. She still couldn't believe her nearest neighbor, Clyve Rowland, had nearly shot her brother. She squeezed her eyes shut against the fury-making memories and reopened them to focus on the task at hand.

With the sun hovering just above the horizon, it was warm but not yet blistering—the perfect time to check the cattle and search for the best place to build a rain catchment. Soon, though, the summer-like heat would go back to trying to sear her skin as if she were a steak on the fire.

Biddie rode beside her sister, her sharp eyes scanning the

cattle scattered among the sparse vegetation. "Is this the area you were thinking of?"

Ginny studied the slope to their right where the hard-scrabble mountain met the baked desert floor. "We need a spot high enough to catch the runoff but close enough to where the cattle graze."

Riding a few paces behind, Carmen called out, "When I was at the Rowland Ranch yesterday, Clyve offered to bring his hands and help with the construction. Maybe we could—"

"What did I say about mentioning that name in my presence?" The barely suppressed memories shoved forward again, igniting a ball of fire in Ginny's chest. Clyve had been one of two exceptions to her no-men-at-Lupine-Valley-Ranch rule. He'd earned her trust through years of sneaking letters between Ginny and Preston while Pa had been alive. Not to mention helping save Biddie from the bandits that had kidnapped her two years ago. But Clyve had tried to kill Preston last year and would've succeeded if Gideon hadn't intervened. The thought of how close she'd come to losing her brother still gnawed at her.

She swiveled sharply in her saddle to face Carmen. "I had one condition for allowing you to accept the courtship of that no-good snake belly of a man. I expect you to keep to your word." She turned back to their surroundings, seeking out the perfect spot. "Anything we need, we can handle ourselves."

Carmen's previously hopeful voice hardened. "He's trying to make things right. You can't stay mad forever. He wants to help."

"I don't care what he wants." She whipped her gaze back to Carmen's. "And if you can't be trusted to keep your word, you can ride on back to the ranch and pack your things."

Carmen's hands tightened on the reins, her knuckles pale. "Fine." She whirled her horse around and urged the gelding into a gallop toward Lupine Valley Ranch, sand and dust rising in her wake.

Biddie slapped one hand onto her hip. "Great work, Ginny. What are you going to do if she does pack up and take off? I know you were hoping she'd become our foreman, even if you haven't said it out loud."

A niggle of guilt mixed with worry nipped at her, but she shoved it away. Carmen had broken her word. Ginny had no patience for anyone who couldn't be trusted. "I'll figure things out like I always do." Ginny nudged Mr. Darcy into a trot.

They rode side by side in silence until Biddie reined her horse to a stop in front of a yucca plant, its tall stalk adorned with the dried remains of spring blooms. "You know, people are like this plant."

Ginny swallowed a groan. She recognized the signs that her sister was working toward a point. One Ginny probably wouldn't like. "If you say so." She pointed toward a cluster of boulders. "What do you think about—"

"They have parts that might nourish you and parts that might hurt you." Biddie kept talking as if Ginny hadn't spoken. "Their prickly parts don't make them bad or evil. You just have to understand them and know how to approach them to get to the good parts without getting hurt."

Ginny scoffed, her eyes narrowing. "A plant can't move or think. You can't blame a plant for folks too dumb to steer clear of its sharp points. But people can control whether or not they hurt others."

"I understand what you're saying, but it's only partially true. We're all different, Ginny. Sometimes, we don't know when something we're doing is hurting someone else. Still, we can learn from our mistakes and try not to hurt people the same way twice."

Ginny squeezed the hot leather reins in her hands. "You

have more faith in humanity's desire to be good and kind than I do."

"I suppose so. But I also recognize that I'm no more perfect than the next person. If I didn't forgive those who've hurt me and repented but expected those same people or others—even God—to forgive my mistakes, what kind of person would that make me?"

A hypocrite. Ginny cringed. She'd known she wouldn't like whatever Biddie was getting at. She scowled. "Trying to kill someone is hardly a mistake."

Biddie's sad blue eyes held hers. "Have you even spoken to Clyve since it happened? The regret is eating him up inside. He knows God has forgiven him. Even Preston has forgiven him for jumping to conclusions about what happened to his brother. Clyve's mind was addled with shock and heartbreak, but he knows now how close he came to a mistake he couldn't take back. And he's grieving the loss of your friendship and trust. You need to forgive him, as much for your sake as for his. I know a part of you misses him, even if you refuse to admit it."

Ginny harrumphed and walked Mr. Darcy toward the base of the slope. Her sister's words pricked at her conscience, but she brushed them away. They needed to focus on finding the best place for the rain catchment.

Biddie followed behind. "The Bible says it's not good for us to be alone. God designed us to need fellowship."

On closer inspection, a large, wide rock stretched across most of the land at the bottom of the hill. Digging a foundation there would be impossible. "If you're done preaching, I've got work to do." Ginny urged Mr. Darcy into a canter, leaving Biddie and her irritating words behind.

*T*he next morning, Ginny led the Lupine ranch hands and Gideon in digging a twelve-foot-wide by six-inch-deep circle as the basin for the new rain catchment system. It was grueling work that took more than half the day.

As the sun edged closer to the horizon, she wiped sweat from her brow with the back of her hand. Murmured conversation mingled with rocks thudding against wet clay as Gideon and the women worked to line the circle.

A five-foot-tall by five-foot-wide corrugated iron A-framed roof stood on four metal legs in the center of the circle, ready to direct the next rainfall into the basin. A pile of additional clay and a barrel of water waited nearby to make mortar for the gaps between the rocks.

Once the bottom of the reservoir was finished, they'd build a one-foot-tall wall around its edge. After a few days of baking in the unusually hot November sun, it would be ready to catch rain for the cattle. Assuming a storm obliged.

Carmen—who'd packed her bags, but ultimately not left the ranch—was flushed red with exertion and paused to catch her breath. "Did you hear the latest news about that gang of bandits?" The question was the first unnecessary word she'd spoken to Ginny since their disagreement the day before, and her testy expression made clear her reluctance to talk now. She must think the news, whatever it was, was important and urgent.

Gut sinking, Ginny slopped another layer of clay on the ground and squinted at her as Lei Yan plunked a large rock onto it. "What now?"

"Cly—er, the report says that Claudio Chavarria is making good on his threat to exact revenge on American settlers for Valadez's death."

Relieved it was nothing new, Ginny shrugged and spread another scoop of wet clay on the ground. "He's been making trouble up north for months. Nothing we need to worry about."

Carmen hefted a rock and plopped it onto the layer of clay. "That's just it. The article claims they've been seen moving south."

Ginny straightened. "How far south?"

"Some say they're headed for Mexico to avoid the posses hunting them."

Located as close to the border as Lupine Valley Ranch was, that path might send them right through her land or that of her neighbors. Even if the gang didn't pass through on their way south, they'd made a habit of harassing Lupine Valley Ranch on their return trips from Mexico.

A heavy silence fell over the group.

"Should we reinstate round-the-clock guards for the ranch?" A warble shook Biddie's voice.

It was something they'd done for months following the gang's initial attack on the ranch. Ginny chewed the inside of her cheek. Could they manage such vigilance while keeping up with the ranch's needs? Most ranches around here didn't resort to such extremes. They just went about their business with a weapon nearby and prayed for the best. As if God would stop a bullet. Well, maybe He could, but in her experience, He usually didn't.

Carmen placed her hands on her hips. "We'd be exhausted within days. We don't have enough people to keep that up for long."

Gideon, leaning on his shovel, spoke up. "We could combine forces with the Rowlands. They've got more hands to help with patrols. Maybe if we worked together—"

Ginny shook her head firmly. "The Rowlands' land and Lupine Valley Ranch together are too much for the same hands to patrol. Besides, depending on anyone who don't live at the ranch—especially men—is downright foolish."

Carmen shot her a pleading look. "But, Ginny—"

"No," Ginny interrupted, her voice steely. "When it comes down to it, most people are only out for themselves. Fact is, I have more confidence in the women working this ranch to keep us safe, even if they have less experience with weapons and keeping watch. I know not one of you'll turn tail and hide in the face of danger or get caught sleeping on patrol. That's more than I can say for any man." She caught Gideon's scowl and grudgingly added, "Present company excluded."

Gideon nodded slowly. "All right, then. We'll set up a shift rotation. It's not perfect, but it's better than nothing." He looked at his wife. "But you won't be on the list."

Biddie opened her mouth to protest, but her husband cut her off.

"I know you're willing to put yourself in danger—again—to protect our home, but you've got to think of the baby right now."

Biddie's mouth closed as her hand came to rest on the full mound of her belly. She heaved a loud sigh. "All right. I'll stay inside."

"And sleep," Gideon gently insisted.

"And sleep," she glumly agreed. Then she brightened. "But I'll cook extra during the day so you have something nourishing to eat during your shifts."

Gideon hesitated, then—no doubt seeing the same spark of determination Ginny saw in Biddie's eyes—relented. "Sounds good."

Satisfied with the plan, they resumed their work, the tension easing slightly as they focused on the task. By the time the sun dipped below the horizon, casting long shadows across the desert landscape, the bottom of the basin had been completed. Tomorrow, they'd return to build the wall.

As they gathered their tools and mounted their horses, the

sky deepened with the encroaching shadows of night. An unsettling quiet replaced their earlier chatter, and Ginny couldn't ignore the chill creeping into her bones that had nothing to do with the swiftly dropping temperatures. She glanced at the slumped shoulders of the riders around her. Despite clear exhaustion, their heads swiveled constantly, on guard for any danger. Gideon's rifle sling hung empty from his saddle, the weapon laid across his lap.

The ranch buildings, a two-hour ride away, suddenly felt impossibly distant. Had she made a mistake refusing to consider asking the Rowlands for help? Their neighbors had proven right handy in previous skirmishes with Valadez's *compadres*. Or perhaps they were Chavarria's bandits now? From the little she'd heard of his attacks up north, Chavarria held even less care for human life than Valadez had.

She checked that the pistol holstered at her waist was loaded and moved her own rifle onto her lap.

Gideon's grim gaze caught and held hers. She knew him well enough now to know he disapproved of her stance regarding the Rowlands, but he'd stand by her decision as head of the ranch. Not many men would respect a woman in her position. That he did and was good to her sister was why he'd not only been allowed to remain on Lupine Valley Ranch but had also earned a grain of her trust. She hated to admit it, but having him on her side was a comfort. Still, each hoofbeat in the fading light echoed the uncertainty of their future, gnawing at her resolve.

~

November 17, 1875
Eastern San Diego County, California

*R*ifle at the ready, Heath crouched behind a cluster of short boulders. He squinted against the late-afternoon sun to scan the rock-strewn mountains split by a skinny trail and bordered by sandstone rocks and sparse vegetation. No movement nor anything out of place caught his eye. Each of his men was well hidden at key spots on either side of the narrow valley.

Heath pinned his attention to the farthest point of the trail. Chavarria and his gang would be coming around that bend any time now.

If Miguel's source was true.

And *if* reporter Wesley Turner's latest article for the *Daily Alta California* hadn't tipped off the bandits that Heath had led the posse south of Los Angeles.

He tightened his grip on his rifle. Letting the bandits believe his posse was still following cold leads up north would have been far better. But the newspaperman's wording, though vague, had hinted too strongly at the posse's next destination— something Heath hadn't known until he'd seen it in the paper along with the rest of the world.

He'd immediately given Turner a tongue-lashing, but the ginger-haired, pasty-white, freckle-faced man who smelled constantly of sun cream just shrugged and insisted that readers had a right to know how their tax dollars were being spent. It was the same reasoning the governor had used in the letter Turner had brought with him when he showed up on Heath's doorstep two days before the posse had set out.

When Heath had demanded the right to read Turner's accounts before he submitted them, the newsman had cried "freedom of the press" and refused to comply. Later, Heath had demanded to see his first report before it was submitted, but it had been written in some sort of code Turner had refused to explain. There'd been no doubt Heath would regret bringing a journalist along for the hunt, but the governor's orders had left him little choice.

Heath rechecked the valley, his gaze catching the faint glint of sunlight off Garret's rifle barrel among rocks north of the trail. To the south, Jeb's hat blended almost seamlessly with the shadow of a scraggly mesquite tree, while Enrique, Miguel, and Cole crouched in the dense scrub, their positions invisible except for the occasional twitch of a boot or sleeve. On the far ridge, their newest member—their Southern California guide, Alberto—remained concealed behind a cluster of boulders.

Even Turner was managing to stay out of sight behind a bush. Heath said a prayer that the chuckleheaded man wouldn't do something foolish—like stick his head out for a better view while bullets were flying—and get himself killed. Heath was genuinely surprised the tenderfoot was still with them. Judging by his fancy duds and naively optimistic outlook, Heath had expected Turner to quit within the first week. Unfortunately, Turner had proven hardier than Heath had given him credit for. They'd been on the trail for nearly a month, and the man remained unyielding. Too bad he hadn't also proven smart enough not to give their plans away to the world. That was why he'd kept details of this ambush out of Turner's earshot until the last minute.

Southern California's deserts had become a mocking torment in the past two weeks—dusty, unrelenting, and treacherous. Each time they'd seemed close to catching their prey, Chavarria and his bandits would elude them. Although just as tired and worn as the horses they'd left hidden beyond the crest of the hill, Heath's men hadn't yet let the weight of exhaustion and frustration press them into quitting. But how much longer could he ask them to continue traversing this desolate land far from the comforts of home?

Heath adjusted his hat to shield his eyes from the late-afternoon sun. It had been a grueling chase, with little sleep, fewer supplies, and false leads testing their resolve. But the latest tip had come from a wary rancher's wife, her hands shaking as she recounted the bandits' last sighting. Heath's gut told him she was trustworthy, and the fear in her eyes had strengthened his resolve. Claudio Chavarria and his gang were a terror to the good people of California. Heath's job was to restore their sense of safety and bring these bandits to justice.

He glanced over at Jeb, who nodded silently, confirming that he was ready for whatever came. Each man Heath had approached to join him on this perilous hunt had agreed. They were smart, seasoned, and reliable. He trusted them with his life. Yet only a fool would underestimate the threat of confronting men like those Chavarria had surrounded himself with. The thread of fear tensing Heath's shoulders assured him he was no fool.

Heath returned his gaze to the still-empty trail. A slip of his boot across the sandy ground echoed as loud as a gunshot in the silent desert, making him cringe. Near the head of the trail, a rabbit burst from a bush, startling Heath into a quick jump. He chuckled soundlessly as the furry critter bolted over the opposite hill and out of sight. He sucked in a deep breath and let it out slowly. Healthy fear was one thing. Jumpy nerves could get him killed.

This spot was perfect for an ambush—the only feasible ambush point for miles. Heath prayed the bandits were either too arrogant or too rushed to realize the danger.

The faint sound of approaching hooves reached his ears. His heart quickened, and he adjusted his grip on his rifle. Without taking his eyes off the bend in the trail, he signaled to Jeb with a hand barely raised above the ground.

The first two bandits trotted into view. They spoke loudly and laughed as if they hadn't a care in the world.

Perfect.

Heath's pulse pounded in his ears, time stretching as he waited for the rest of the bandits to enter the valley and pass Heath's first hidden man. Once the posse encircled the unwitting group, he'd drop his hand—the signal to attack.

But no more men entered as the seconds passed.

Alarm shot through him just as a voice behind him shouted, "¡*Ahora*!"

Whizzing bullets forced his posse to scatter. Caught off guard by the rear attack, they scrambled for new cover.

A shot bounced off the boulder mere inches from Heath's head, and he spun.

Above a rock near the crest of the hill, a slouch hat popped up. Chavarria!

Heath's shot knocked the felt from the bandit leader's head.

Return fire hissed past Heath's ear, as he dashed behind another boulder.

Hidden from Chavarria's view, Heath was now exposed to the two bandits still shooting from their jittery mounts on the trail. He whirled just in time to avoid a bullet in the back. With the boulder deflecting Chavarria's shots, Heath opened fire on the two riding up and down the narrow passage taking reckless shots at Heath's pinned-down men. He clenched his jaw. Surviving this ambush was going to take a miracle.

NOVEMBER 17, 1875
LUPINE VALLEY RANCH
EASTERN SAN DIEGO COUNTY, CALIFORNIA

*G*inny signaled to Esther and Lei Yan to spread out among the crowd of cattle gathered around the new water source. The three women walked carefully through the grazing cattle, keeping an eye out for any signs of distress. Ginny didn't expect to find anything concerning, but a ranch owner could never be too careful. Last year's battle with Texas fever proved the caution necessary.

A cacophony of gunshots rang out, sharp and loud. No shots were aimed at the women or their cows, but the battle was close. Too close. The cattle began to surge.

"Mount up!" Ginny's heart lurched as she raced for Mr. Darcy amid the startled cattle. She grabbed the saddle horn and swung up, immediately checking whether Esther and Lei Yan had escaped the stampede unharmed.

Both women sat safely atop their mounts. Ginny's posture relaxed even as her heart continued beating at a pace to match the retreating cattle.

In a blink, the herd had vanished into a nearby canyon. There should be enough feed there, but no water. She'd have to check on them later.

Echoing gunfire continued ringing across the desert, reminding her of the reports that Chavarria's gang was headed their way.

She exchanged a worried glance with Esther and Lei Yan. "That sounds like it's coming from the northern section of the Rowlands' land." As furious as she was with Clyve, she didn't wish him dead. She checked that the pistol at her waist was loaded as she continued. "I need to see what's happening. If the Rowlands are in trouble, I aim to help." Satisfied that her pistol was ready, she eyed her companions. They seemed steady despite the scare they'd just been through. Though both were less than twenty years old, their harsh childhoods had left them tougher than cowhide—something she completely understood and respected. "Are you with me?"

Both women nodded, and they all raced toward danger.

If Biddie were here, she'd be praying. Were the other two women praying? They faithfully attended Biddie's nightly Bible readings and rode with her and Gideon into town to attend the new church each Sunday. So probably, they were. Before she could decide how she felt about that, she spotted a group of horses tied to a desert ironwood tree near the bottom of a slope. From the sounds of things, the battle was happening just past the crest of the hill.

She reined Mr. Darcy back to a trot, studying the waiting horses. Judging by what she could see of the tack and lack of decoration, these weren't Indian horses. Nor did she recognize any of the gear as being from the Rowland Ranch. She hesitated. Was the risk of getting involved worth it for men she didn't know? The image of a traveling family possibly trapped by bandits on the narrow trail that ran through the valley just out of sight clinched her decision.

Not sure whether the bunch of horses was owned by friend or foe, Ginny directed Esther and Lei Yan to follow her to a mesquite tree hidden behind a boulder, well away from the unknown beasts. They dismounted, tied their mounts, and sprinted up the slope with their loaded rifles.

As they drew closer, the sounds of the skirmish grew louder, the crack of gunfire mingling with shouts and curses.

Slowing near the ridge, Ginny signaled for Esther and Lei Yan to stay low.

Peering over a rocky outcrop, Ginny scanned the chaos below. A group of close to a dozen men were engaged in a fierce exchange of bullets. Their identities were unclear from this distance, but it appeared half were pinned down at the far east end of the valley, their heads popping up from behind a line of large boulders, while the rest closed in from the west—their backs toward the women.

A man in a brown hat and faded blue shirt lunged forward, dragging a ginger-haired man by the collar into the cover of a boulder just before a volley of bullets peppered the brush where the hatless man had been hiding.

Ginny's breath hitched as the sunlight glinted off a sheriff's badge pinned to Blue Shirt's chest. He was part of the cornered group. "There's a sheriff," Ginny whispered and pointed at Blue Shirt, whose shadowed face bore a close-cut, light brown beard and a thin mustache. She glanced at Esther and Lei Yan. Uncertainty was painted on their expressions and rightly so. The three of them were far outnumbered. But if a sheriff was involved, those pinned men were likely part of a posse seeking justice. Ginny couldn't stand idly by and let them be slaughtered.

"We have to help. I have an idea, but first, check your weapons." Ginny double-checked that her pistol, rifle, and knives were ready for battle while the other women did the same. Quickly, Ginny explained her plan to make the attackers believe there were more of them than there were. "It's risky," she admitted. "But I think it'll work. So long as they never see us."

When neither woman protested, Ginny gave the signal, and they parted ways. Esther stole north, while Lei Yan skirted south, and Ginny advanced straight ahead, her path taking her along the southern edge of the trail, so as not to be completely exposed. Each used the desert's scant cover to remain out of sight. Thankfully, their prey seemed too intent on their quarry to notice them.

As soon as each woman was in position, Ginny took a deep breath and fired at the back of the man nearest the center of the attackers. Unfortunately, he moved just as she pulled the trigger, and her bullet struck his arm. He dropped behind a rock as the man beside him whirled, squinting in her direction. Hidden behind a bush and with the sun at her back, she was little more than a shadow as she readied her next shot.

Esther and Lei Yan each fired on different men. One cried out in pain, and the skirmish momentarily faltered, heads turning toward the unexpected interruption.

"¡¿Quién está ahí?!" the man who'd been searching for Ginny yelled. *Who's there?*

The familiarity of his accented voice sent a river of ice across her skin. Chavarria. It had to be.

Bile climbed her throat as she aimed at his heart. This was for Gabriella.

CHAPTER 4

*H*eath popped his head around the boulder as a bullet whizzed past Chavarria, who'd swiveled just in time to avoid being shot. Taking advantage of Chavarria's distraction, he took aim, but a bullet zipped past his face, forcing him to duck before he could get his shot off.

At the same moment, another volley of shots rang out from the mystery shooters behind the gang.

"¡*Es una trampa!*" one of the mounted bandits shouted, his voice tinged with panic. "¡*Estamos superados!*" He and his companion spurred their horses out of the valley.

Chavarria returned fire, alternating his aim between the posse and the unseen shooters while dashing wide around Heath's men. "¡*Vámonos!*" The last three bandits followed him into the cover of nearby scrub brush, their footsteps rapidly fading. "¡*Lucharemos otro día!*"

"Come on!" Heath vaulted over the boulder he'd been hiding behind. "We can't let them get away!"

"Alberto's shot!" Jeb's shout halted Heath's pursuit.

A glance behind revealed Jeb was working to staunch the bleeding from a wound in Alberto's shoulder.

From both sides of the trail echoed more shots, forcing the gang into a hasty retreat. The bandits scrambled through a cluster of boulders near the valley's northeastern rim.

Coiled with tension, Heath waited, every muscle poised to react to any sound of the bandits' return. Several tense seconds later, rapidly retreating hoofbeats marked the end of his hopes for the day.

Chavarria and his compadres had evaded capture.

Again.

Heath swallowed words his Ma would disapprove of. Not only had they not captured the gang, but another man in his care had been injured. Lowering his rifle, Heath ran a hand over his face.

Forgive my ingratitude, Lord. I know it could have been much worse. Thank You for sending help.

He studied the surrounding hills but caught no sight of their saviors. With the gang gone, why hadn't they revealed themselves?

"I'm Sheriff Heath Monroe," he called out. He pointed at the badge on his chest, then at the men emerging from the rocks behind him—everyone except Jeb and Alberto. "These are my men. You have nothing to fear from us. We're grateful for your assistance. But I'd be obliged if you showed yourselves now."

Movement near the western end of the trail caught his eye first. A dark silhouette separated itself from the brush.

Squinting against the sun setting behind the man, Heath strode forward, his hand extended. "Your timing couldn't have been better. I'm not sure we'd have—" The rest of his words died as he got a clearer view of the figure walking toward him—the very female figure. In trousers.

He rubbed the back of his hand across his eyes and looked again.

A beaten brown leather hat not much different from his

own topped a sun-tanned, dirt-streaked face with gray-blue eyes and rosy cheeks framed by twin blond braids. The strange woman's filthy blue bodice was tucked into a loose-fitting pair of brown men's trousers. A pistol hung from a well-fitted holster around her trim waist, and the butt of a rifle poked up from where the weapon hung behind her back.

Never in his life had he seen the like.

Strange as her appearance was, her confident strut and satisfied smirk lured a responding smile to his lips.

Two more silhouettes emerged from the lengthening shadows, one from the north and another from the south. Both clearly wearing skirts.

Heath whipped the hat from his head and scratched the back of his neck. They'd been saved by a bunch of women? That couldn't be right. He glanced around, but no one else made themselves known. He looked back at the first woman. "Where're your men?"

The odd-but-pretty blonde stopped in her tracks, and her smug expression turned colder than the ice he kept in his icebox back home. She made a noise akin to a bobcat's snarl. "We're the ones that just saved your sorry hides." She pivoted away from him with a wave for the other two women to follow. "You're welcome."

Heath searched the slopes again. No one else was there. The three women striding away had saved their lives, and he'd just insulted them. He slapped his hat on his head and hurried after them. "Wait. Please."

The young redhead and Chinese girl stopped to look at him, but the blonde in trousers and braided pigtails kept stomping.

He broke into a jog until he passed her. Stopping in her path, he held up his hands, palms out. "Look, I—"

"Heath!" Jeb's yell forestalled Heath's apology. "We need a doctor."

"It's that bad?" He yelled back as he sprinted to where Jeb tended their guide.

Blood soaked the groaning man's shoulder, shirt, and the ground around him.

Jeb glanced up from cinching a knot over the thick bandage covering Alberto's wound. "I think the bullet's lodged in his shoulder blade."

"But he's not...?" He gave Jeb a look that finished the question of whether their guide's life was at risk.

Jeb shook his head, relieving Heath's worst fears. "But I can't get the bullet out myself, and I'm worried leaving it in will make things worse."

Heath squinted at Alberto. Miguel's expertise lay east of Los Angeles and northward. When the gang had unexpectedly retreated farther south after their last robbery, Heath had hired Alberto Warren to be their Southern California guide while Miguel continued as their translator. No one else in their posse knew much about this far south portion of their state. "Do you know where we can find you a doc?"

"No." Alberto's face, redder than the setting sun, broadcasted his pain. "Sorry, boss. Last I heard, they didn't have one in these parts."

"I know where the doc lives." A female voice surprised him from behind.

He turned to find all three women looking on.

The redhead continued. "Lei Yan and me can fetch him." Lei Yan must be the Chinese girl's name.

"Absolutely not, Esther," the blonde protested. "You are not riding off alone while Chavarria's gang is still roaming these parts."

Heath jolted. How had she recognized Claudio Chavarria? Had she known who the bandits were before joining the fight? And who was she that she issued orders as confidently and comfortably as he did? Shock and admiration filled his chest as he stared at the mysterious, courageous beauty before him. He belatedly jerked his hat from his head. "You're right, Mrs....?" He lifted his brow, silently requesting her name.

"*Miss* Baker. And of course, I'm right." She crossed her arms with a look that almost dared him to challenge the unspoken insinuation that she was usually—if not always—right.

Why did his lips want to curl upward with her emphasis on *Miss*? He smothered the urge, sensing a grin would not be well received. "If you'll tell us where the doc lives and direct us to the nearest home likely to provide rest for Alberto while Cole and Enrique go after the doc, we'd be most appreciative."

"The doc lives about three hours' ride that way." She pointed southwest, then recrossed her arms.

He waited for her to direct him to the nearest welcoming home.

The other two women exchanged a cryptic look.

When Miss Baker didn't continue, he prompted, "And the nearest home?"

She opened her mouth, then closed it again with a sour look. Her gaze inspected each of his men in turn before she crossed her arms with a sour look. "Lupine Valley Ranch is the closest."

Why did she seem reluctant to share that information? "Do you think the owner will agree to let Alberto rest there?"

"I will. So long as you and your men are well-behaved and do exactly as I say without question. There ain't no alcohol, and gambling ain't allowed neither. No exceptions."

He blinked. She owned the nearest ranch? By herself? That would explain her familiarity with giving orders. And the trousers.

Another look passed between the redhead and the Chinese woman, this one filled with what seemed to be relieved surprise.

The leader's eyes narrowed when he didn't immediately agree to her terms.

He cleared his throat. "Uh, yes, ma'am. That shouldn't be a problem."

"We got plenty of food, and we can make space for Alberto inside, but the rest of you'll need to pitch camp."

Heath swallowed his disappointment and nodded. Finding a home with eight spare beds was rare, but it sure would have been nice to spend a few nights off the ground for a change. At least they'd be enjoying home-cooked meals from the sound of it. Although, if the women of Lupine Valley Ranch were out tending cattle and joining shootouts, who was home doing the cooking?

Arms still crossed, she widened her stance and lifted her chin. "You'll also need to hand over your guns."

Heath straightened. "Now, hold on—"

"You ain't no more than strangers to me, and I don't tolerate armed strangers prowling my land." A new spark lit her gaze. "If you don't like my terms, you can ride on to the Rowland Ranch not too far past mine. You're just north of Rowland land now."

Esther gasped. "Ginny, their home is another hour's ride, and you know it." She gestured at Alberto, still lying on the ground. "Look at this poor man. Every mile is going to be agony for him."

Miss Ginny Baker appeared not to be swayed.

Tempted as Heath was to accept her suggestion that they ride on to the next ranch, the redhead was right. Alberto would be hard pressed to make it through the ride without fainting. Glaring at Miss Baker, Heath jabbed a finger in the direction the bandits had run. "Those were the most ruthless men in the state. If they return and track us to your ranch, you'll be glad to have us and our weapons 'prowling' your land."

The stubborn spitfire glared right back. "It wouldn't be the first or even second time I've defended my land from such, and I'm still standing here, ain't I?"

Lei Yan stepped between them, facing Miss Baker. "You say need more guards. He sheriff. Let him come. Keep his guns. Protect us."

Miss Baker's glare could melt steel as Esther nodded in agreement with Lei Yan.

"You know Biddie would agree." Esther tipped her head to one side, a knowing gleam lighting her eyes. "And she'll be madder than a gambler caught cheating if she finds out you turned away a posse with an injured man."

"I ain't turning no one away. Just setting the terms, as is my right." Miss Baker's words were tough, but they'd lost most of their fire.

Who was this Biddie that could soften Miss Baker's iron will without even being present?

Heath moved to redirect Miss Baker's cold blue gaze and tapped his badge. "You may not live in my bailiwick, but I've sworn an oath to protect the good people of this state." He gestured to the men behind him. "So have they. I promise you have nothing to fear from us."

Miss Baker huffed. "Fine. You can keep your guns on one condition."

Heath crossed his arms. "What's that?"

She glanced at Esther, who nodded and pulled something from her pocket.

Heath stiffened when Miss Baker pivoted sideways and hovered her hand over the pistol holstered at her waist.

Esther tossed a small brown disc into the air.

Miss Baker drew and fired, shattering the object before returning her weapon to its sheath as small brown pieces plummeted.

Esther dashed over and plucked the chunks from the dirt. She gave them to Miss Baker, who held out what he could now see were the remains of a homemade clay target. Her triumphant grin lit her gray-blue eyes and stole his breath as she explained her condition. "You and your men remember that I'm never unarmed."

~

*G*inny kept her eyes trained on the boulder-strewn ridge ahead, beyond which lay the high desert mountain valley she called home. She had no desire to look back at the eight men following her with Esther and Lei Yan in their midst, especially not Heath. His commanding presence chaffed more than she cared to admit.

She, Lei Yan, and Esther had saved his posse, but he'd assumed only men could do such a thing. Typical male. And she was leading him and his armed companions straight to her ranch. She must have forgotten hitting her head and addling her brain. Why else would she have agreed to something so foolish?

She pictured Chavarria's furious expression as he demanded to know who had joined the shootout. A chill traveled down her spine. Nearly two-and-a-half years had passed since he'd been part of the gang led by Valadez in attacking Lupine Valley Ranch. Two-and-a-half years since the day the Valadez gang had slaughtered her father and her only friend, along with the rest of the ranch hands, leaving her alone in a land of blood and ash. But she'd never forget the sound of his voice shouting during the raid.

After Valadez's trial and lawful execution in the spring, she'd heard rumors that Chavarria had taken up leadership of the gang and vowed revenge against all Americans for Valadez's "murder."

Lei Yan was right—they needed more guards. But could she trust the men following her?

She glanced over her shoulder to Heath. Trail dust clung to his worn and faded clothes, but he sat tall in the saddle, projecting strength and confidence despite having been bested by the bandits. His sharp hazel eyes constantly scanned their surroundings, assessing every moving creature, every shadow, every shift of branches in the wind.

He caught her looking and lifted a brow.

Ginny frowned and faced forward. The way he spoke with the other men left no question about who was in charge of their posse. Yet he didn't bark orders. He didn't need to. Their swift obedience demonstrated an earned respect.

But to her, he was a stranger. One with a badge whom she'd watched risk his life to save another man, but a stranger just the same. He'd better not try giving her orders. Round here, folks answered to *her*.

"There it is. Lupine Valley Ranch." Esther's voice cut through Ginny's thoughts as they crested the ridge and everyone paused to take in the view.

With the sun now set, Ginny's land was blanketed by the shadow of twilight, but there was still enough light to make out the many structures, corrals, and fences they'd worked hard to build over the past twenty-nine months. A smile tugged at the corners of her lips, and her chin lifted.

Esther pointed north. "At the far end, you can see our corrals surrounded by stone fencing that won't burn. In fact, nearly everything is made of stone. That was Ginny's idea to keep out bullets and make them hard to set ablaze. Plus the rock and mud mortar keeps the buildings cooler in the summer and warmer in the winter like adobe houses."

"Clever." Heath said, his eyes surveying her valley. "And there are plenty of boulders here but not much wood." He tipped his hat toward Ginny. "Sounds like you're a wise woman."

Well, what was she supposed to say to that? Ginny avoided his gaze by nudging Mr. Darcy onward and leaving Heath to follow behind.

Esther continued her self-appointed tour guide role. "Then there's the spring house, the barn, and the chicken coup near the center of the structures. That long, skinny building is the bunkhouse, and the small stone building with slits for windows is Ginny's house. The building closest to us that's made of half stone and half wood and has all those glass windows is Biddie and Gideon's house. Ginny's brother-in-law, Gideon, is the only man living at Lupine Valley Ranch."

"What about the hands?" one of the posse members asked. Ginny didn't know which one since she didn't look back and hadn't bothered paying attention when Esther and Lei Yan had blathered through introductions to all eight men. They wouldn't be staying more than a day or two at most. What was the point in learning their names?

"All women." A strong dose of pride colored Esther's voice.

Ginny straightened in her saddle.

"Didn't you say this was a cattle ranch?" another man asked. "I don't see how a bunch of females can handle that kind of work."

Ginny deflated with a snort. "Of course not. Men are always underestimating women."

"So your brother-in-law lives here"—Heath brought his horse alongside hers—"but you're the one in charge?"

Irked that he continued to underestimate her, Ginny just nodded.

Esther filled the awkward silence. "Ginny's sister, Biddie, is our cook and baker. No one leaves the table hungry. If you're lucky, she might even make one of her special desserts while you're here. She bakes extra so she can sell her bread, and sometimes cakes, to our neighbors and the Gaskills."

A deeper voice asked, "Who're the Gaskills?"

"They're the brothers who built and own our nearest town, Campo. Silas is a blacksmith, runs their hotel, and was the closest thing we had to a doc until recently. In addition to running the general store, Luman is our postman, Judge of the Plains, and Justice of the Peace."

Heath whistled and glanced back at Esther. "They sound like busy men."

"About the only thing they don't do is run the telegraph. That's Mr. Kelly's job." Esther chuckled. "But as I was saying, they can't get enough of Biddie's baking—not just for themselves, but for their store. Folks know to come every Saturday to purchase her fresh-baked goods."

The trail descending into the valley squeezed between two boulders, forcing Heath to move behind Ginny. She glanced past him to see the rest of the group sliding into a line with the gray-haired posse member at the rear.

"That sounds like a lot of work." The man who appeared to be the youngest posse member fell in behind Esther. "I remember when my ma was carrying my youngest brother. She couldn't make it through a day without taking a nap."

"Biddie's tougher than she looks. Wait and see. Plus, she has the biggest heart of anybody I know." Esther exchanged a grin with Lei Yan, who rode in front of her. "And you'll meet Carmen too. She's got a daughter named Josie. She's only thirteen but as tough as they come. She watches my little girl, Deborah, when the rest of us are working away from home. She also feeds the animals, tends the garden, and helps with mending and washing. Don't underestimate her just because she's young."

Flashes of her own childhood made Ginny snap, "You keep clear of Josie."

"You have nothing to fear from me and my men." Heath's promise rang with sincerity.

She patted the handle of her holstered pistol. "Just remember my condition."

"Ginny doesn't let many men on the property," Esther said with a nervous wobble to her voice. "Not any men, really. Not since—"

"That's enough." Ginny whipped around to pierce Esther with a warning look.

These men didn't need to know anything about Ginny's past. All she'd promised was a doctor for Alberto, and a safe place to shelter while they filled their bellies and got some rest. Heath's selflessness in rescuing his posse member and the commanding yet respectful way he spoke to his men didn't change the fact that he was a stranger. They all were.

A knot formed in her stomach. Would she regret trusting them enough to let them stay even a few nights? What if Chavarria found out where they were and came to finish what he'd started? He'd had only five men with him this afternoon—his most loyal *amigos*—but she'd heard reports of him attacking towns with more than a dozen raiders at his side. Had her choice to let the posse recover on her land opened the door to making her home a battleground once more?

Ginny's mind raced with unanswered questions as they entered the ranch yard. She'd made her choice, and she was a woman of her word. There was no going back now. Whether Heath and his posse would be the help she needed or the threat that destroyed everything she had left, only time would tell.

~

*S*everal hours later, Ginny stood outside her house, watching the doctor mount up in the golden light of a lantern hanging from a hook on the outer wall of her barn. It'd taken longer than expected for Heath's men to return with the doctor, who'd been busy with another patient, and still more hours to perform the surgery needed to remove the bullet and stitch Alberto's wound closed.

Ordinarily, Biddie or Ginny would help with the doctoring on Lupine Valley Ranch, but Jeb had insisted on taking that role. That suited Ginny just fine since it left her free to tend to her evening duties and Biddie free to cook all the extra food they needed to feed eight extra mouths.

Ginny pressed one jagged nail into the palm of her left hand. What had she been thinking to allow so many strange men onto her land—and armed? Softhearted foolishness is what Oliver would've called it.

The low murmur of the posse members settled in the chairs around her outdoor table drew her attention. Their faces were weary and serious as Lei Yan and Biddie filled their cups and bowls.

Jeb spoke in a low tone. "Doc says it'll be weeks, maybe months, before Alberto's ready to travel."

Ginny ground her teeth. So much for a short stay.

"Maybe we ought to pack up and go home," the gray-haired man they called Cole suggested. "We've been at this for weeks, and they keep slipping away."

Garret protested. "We can't give up. People are countin' on us to stop them."

Cole puffed on a pipe. "We aren't the only ones looking for these men."

Heath tipped his hat up and scratched the side of his head. "True, but I'm not ready to leave the fate of our citizens in the hands of greedy bounty hunters."

A Mexican-looking man widened his stance. "But where are we going to find another guide?"

Lei Yan, normally the next thing to silent, spoke her mind for the second time that day. "You take Ginny. She smart, tough, and very brave. She know the desert."

Nine pairs of eyes turned her way.

She lifted her hands as if to ward off a blow. "No, no, no. I've got a ranch to run." Not to mention there was no way she would ever willingly travel alone with a group of strange men. Pigs would sooner fly.

Biddie shifted the pot she was holding to one hand and set the other hand on her hip—never a good sign. "The rest of us are perfectly capable of keeping this ranch running in your absence."

"Maybe." Ginny stiffened her spine. "If you all weren't so busy making cow eyes at the men around here."

Biddie gasped, her wide gaze flying to the men around the table, as her face turned red and a scowl formed.

Ginny waved her hands in the air. "No, not them." She pointed at Biddie first. "You've got a husband distracting you. And they"—she pointed at Esther and Carmen, who'd just stepped out of the barn—"are both busy being courted by our neighbors, not to mention tending to their own children." She turned to Lei Yan. "You may not be distracted, but one woman can't run this place on her own." Not anymore. Though that had been Ginny's original plan, she'd let Biddie talk her into adding more buildings and cattle and sheep and...well, just far more than any one person could maintain on their own. "Who knows how long this hunt might take?" She shifted her attention to Sheriff Monroe. "Sorry. I can't go."

He nodded. "Of course not. Hunting bandits is far too dangerous for women."

~

*T*he moment the words left his mouth, Heath knew he'd made a mistake. Ginny Baker's firm expression turned mutinous. Biddie set her pot down and rushed past him to her sister. She began murmuring something to Ginny in a soothing tone.

Rather than wait for the ranch owner's sputtering to turn into words, Heath twisted in his seat to address his men. "There must be at least one man in these parts brave enough to join us. Tomorrow, we'll set out for Campo and put the word out that we need help. Someone's bound to answer the call."

Although his men's gazes bounced nervously from Heath to a point behind him and back again, he refused to check over his shoulder, as they all nodded their heads. A moment later, every man was focused on eating his late supper as though it was his last meal. Heath followed suit, despite the tension keeping his body ready for an attack.

He couldn't argue that Ginny's skills with a pistol were remarkable. Nor would he attempt to describe her actions during the shootout as anything but intelligent and courageous. Nevertheless, it was bad enough he risked his men's lives in pursuit of Chavarria and his gang. His conscience wouldn't bear risking another woman's life. Not after what happened to his wife.

His hand settled over his chest, finding the locket beneath his shirt. Susannah may not have had Ginny's level of skill, but she'd known how to handle a weapon—her pa had seen to it—and she'd been brave too. Still, that hadn't been enough to save her when he'd failed to protect her.

He set his spoon in his empty bowl and pushed away from the table. "I'm glad we're all agreed." He stood and met each man's gaze. "Get a good night's sleep. We leave at dawn." Finally, he turned.

Ginny and her sister were gone.

He scolded the irrational sinking in his gut that their absence was good. Ginny had accepted defeat. No matter how uniquely qualified to be their guide she seemed to be, she was still a woman. A beautiful one. Though nowhere was truly safe as long as Chavarria's gang ran free, Ginny was safer here at home, surrounded by people who cared about her.

Heath strode away from the table, his boots crunching against the packed dirt. Finding another guide could take days they didn't have. Tomorrow's stop in Campo might turn up someone willing. Maybe. But willing wouldn't be enough—not with Chavarria slipping farther out of reach by the hour.

CHAPTER 5

*G*inny stood in the barn stall, gently stroking Mr. Darcy's muzzle. Despite the silly name his prior owners had saddled him with, the chestnut-colored gelding had proven himself faster than most horses and calm amidst the chaos of agitated cattle and gunfire. She ran her fingers through his dark-brown forelock. The white star on his forehead seemed bright despite the barn's dim interior. He dipped his head and nuzzled her pocket, making her laugh.

"All right, all right." She withdrew the carrot she'd brought for him and held it up on her flat palm. He made short work of the treat. "You did well today," she whispered, keenly aware of the two posse members talking quietly in the opposite corner of the barn as they oiled their tack in the gentle glow of a single lantern. The last thing she wanted was to be forced into more conversation with the men she already regretted inviting to her ranch.

The young man they called Garret spoke with increasing enthusiasm, his words carrying over the stall walls. "...certain it was the bandit leader because he was wearin' a ring with a jaguar head."

Ginny went still, her entire body tightening. A jaguar ring? It couldn't be the same one. Could it? She inched closer, careful not to draw attention as the other man—Jeb?—responded.

"I saw the sun glint off a large gold ring on his hand." His tone was grim. "The same ring I've seen in Chavarria's picture."

What picture? Ginny's stomach turned. The description of the ring was too familiar. She had to know. Exiting the stall, she stepped into their light. "Was the jaguar's mouth open or closed?"

Both men turned and looked at her, surprise flickering across their faces. Jeb hesitated. "I couldn't get a good look today, but in his photo, the jaguar's mouth is open, its teeth showing."

"What picture?"

Jeb exchanged a glance with Garret, then set his tack aside and reached into his pocket. He withdrew a folded paper and handed it to her, his expression curious.

She unfolded the small page and barely swallowed a gasp. The paper bore a photograph of Chavarria posing in front of an adobe house. His thick mustache couldn't conceal the scowl he aimed at the camera while holding two pistols crossed in front of his chest. There, on Chavarria's right hand, was Gabriella's ring. The one she'd cherished. The one she'd been wearing the day she died.

Ginny threw the image back at Jeb and whirled away.

"How'd you know about the ring?" he called after her.

Ignoring him, she fled the storm of grief and rage threatening to shatter the stoicism that had kept her together through the worst days of her life. But the suddenly freed memories chased her past her house, through the darkened valley, and beyond the large juniper bush, into the secret gem mine it had long concealed.

She placed a hand against the cold stone wall, her breaths sounding loud in the long black tunnel. Though no fire now burned, the smell of smoke filled her nostrils as gunfire and screams filled her mind.

This was where she'd been that terrible day. Alone.

The bandits had destroyed everything, killed everyone, leaving only ash and pieces of bones.

Only Ginny had survived to bury what was left of the dead.

She pressed her fingers harder against the cold rock wall of the tunnel and focused on breathing slowly in and out. As the memories gradually released her, her gaze refocused on the blackness around her. What was she doing hiding in here?

The men hunting the very gang responsible for the horror that changed her life needed help. Help she was more than capable of providing. How could she stay safe on her ranch while the man who murdered the only true friend she'd ever known continued his acts of terror, all while wearing Gabriella's ring? Biddie was right. She and Gideon and the other women had proven their ability to keep the ranch running when she'd twisted her ankle. Maybe things wouldn't thrive as well without her here, but the ranch wouldn't fall apart.

Unless Chavarria returned a third time.

Which was all the more reason she should join Sheriff Monroe's posse and make sure they caught their prey.

Ginny stalked out of the tunnel and toward the flickering glow of lantern light near the tents the posse had set up. Sheriff Monroe's silhouette ducked into a tent, and she paused. She was about to commit to spending an untold amount of time alone in the desert with a bunch of men she knew little about. Could she really do that?

She straightened her spine. Of course, she could, for Gabriella and for the safety of everyone living on her ranch. Not to mention her neighbors. Everyone would be safer once Chavarria and his men were behind bars. Or dead.

She took another step forward, then stopped again. Sheriff

Monroe had been pretty adamant earlier that she was safer at home. He wouldn't like her change of heart.

Ginny pivoted toward the house. Tonight, she'd pack and plan. In the morning, she'd wait until they were ready to head out and simply ride along with them. No doubt a man used to being in charge like a sheriff would be displeased, but he'd better get used to it. As his posse's guide or not, she had no intention of taking orders from any man.

~

*A*s the pale gray of dawn spread farther into the sky, Heath surveyed his men's progress. From the look of things, they'd finish loading their gear and be ready to ride in under five minutes. Good. The delay of needing a new guide was already grating on his nerves. They didn't need dawdling to make things worse.

The creak of the barn door split the otherwise quiet rumble of his men's preparations. Heath turned just as Ginny emerged from the barn leading her saddled gelding loaded with trail supplies.

"No." The loud word slipped from his lips before he realized he was thinking it, but his protest rang out with the effect of a gunshot. All movement and quiet chatter behind him ceased.

Ginny, however, didn't falter in her advance. She strode straight up to him, head held high, spine straight. "I've decided to join you, after all."

He opened his mouth to remind her that he didn't want her help, but she held up a hand.

"No need to thank me. I ain't doing this for you"—her determined blue eyes moved past him, and her voice rose—"or any of you. That ring Chavarria's wearing was stolen two years ago."

Her gaze returned to Heath. "When we catch him, I want it back."

For a moment, the terrorizing thought of Ginny encountering Valadez and Chavarria captured his voice. Where had it happened? Had she been alone? Was the ring the only thing she'd lost? He studied her expression to no avail. It was like steel shutters covered her eyes. Still, her connection to the ring explained the strange reaction Jeb had said she'd had to Garret's mention of it the night before. She must have an emotional attachment to the ring. Yet no piece of jewelry, no matter how sentimental, was worth her life. "It isn't safe. You should stay here—"

"I ain't asking." In one swift move, Ginny mounted her horse. "I'm telling you, I'm coming."

Heath resisted the urge to kick the low stone wall of the horse corral.

Jeb came to his side. "You said yourself that looking for a new guide will give the bandits more time to disappear, possibly even slip across the border into Mexico."

Heath's gut twisted at the thought of losing their quarry.

Gideon, who had risen early to help, approached with a steady stride. "Ginny knows these lands better than just about anyone. She's good with guns, and she's calm under pressure. You'll be lucky to have her."

Of course, Heath knew all that. He'd witnessed those things himself. But the idea of bringing another woman into danger filled him with cold dread. Panic squeezed his throat. "What about her reputation? Traveling with a group of men, none of whom are married, could—"

"Ginny's reputation is solid with those who matter," Gideon replied, as calm as a dog gnawing a bone. "Besides"—a spark of humor lit his expression—"it's well known Ginny sleeps with a pistol under her pillow and one eye open. She'll be fine."

The implication that anyone who tried bothering Ginny

might not live to regret it was clear. Not that Heath had any concerns about his men in that regard. Still, gossip didn't need a whisper of truth to spread like echoes in a canyon. Too bad the unperturbed expressions on nearly everyone's faces confirmed most of his men had accepted Ginny's decision. Cole and Miguel were the only ones who still appeared displeased. But neither man would speak up. They'd leave the decision to him.

As if he could force the stubborn woman to stay home.

He yanked the hat from his head and smacked it against his thigh. Raking his fingers through his hair, he spun toward the western rim of the valley, searching for anything that might stop Ginny from joining them. But there was nothing. He couldn't think up any new reasons to keep her on her ranch. He slapped his hat on his head and drew in a deep breath, letting it out slowly. "Fine," he ground out through clenched teeth. "She can come." He turned back to hold her gaze. "But you have to promise to hide at the first sign of danger and stay out of sight when we're questioning witnesses and homesteaders."

Ginny glared down at him. "I ain't hiding when there's trouble."

"If my men are focused on protecting you instead of catching the bandits, we'll fail at capturing them again." Heath crossed his arms. "You need to stay out of sight."

After a tense moment, Ginny jerked her head in what he took for a nod.

Turner whipped his notepad from his vest pocket, pulled the pencil from behind his ear, and wrote furiously.

"Stop." Heath snatched the notepad and ripped out the page the reporter had been scribbling on. He crumpled the notes in his fist. "If so much as a hint that a woman is traveling with us gets printed in your reports, I'll send you home faster than you can blink, governor's orders or not."

"But my orders are to report the truth—the whole truth—

and if she's helping guide the posse, that's too big to leave out. Besides, it'll make a great story. Think of it. 'Beautiful woman leads posse to victory.'" When Heath continued to glare, Turner looked to Ginny for support. "Don't you want to inspire other women with your skills and bravery?"

To Heath's relief, Ginny shook her head. "All I want is justice and that ring."

Heath crossed his arms again and stared down the recklessly ambitious reporter. "I want your word."

The ginger-haired man hesitated another moment before begrudgingly agreeing.

Heath returned the notepad.

Then he gave the signal to mount up and led the posse, plus Ginny, out of the desert mountain valley just as the sun crested the eastern horizon. Even the beautiful pinks and golds streaking across the cloud-speckled blue sky couldn't erase the doubt gnawing at his resolve as they traversed the rugged terrain back to the location of the shootout.

Ginny rode tall in her saddle, scanning their surroundings. He'd never doubted she was bright and capable, but too many of the best lawmen had met their fate while in pursuit of justice. What if his decision to let her join them led her to an early grave?

CHAPTER 6

*S*weat and dust coated Ginny's skin, and her muscles were a bit sore from the day's ride, but that wasn't what bothered her. She was used to spending long days in the saddle, and though the sun had done its best to bake them as they'd followed the bandits' trail, November's temperatures had nothing on a desert summer. Rather, it was how thoroughly the gang's tracks had vanished with the wind, leaving the posse with no clue which way to turn that had her scowling.

Shortly after sunset, Heath ordered them to make camp in a small area surrounded on three sides by boulders and shrubs. The half circle opened onto the wide, flat desert floor. By the time they'd settled in and gathered around the small campfire, evening's chill was starting to creep in, and night had blanketed the landscape.

"Hey, Ginny." Enrique grinned at her. "How 'bout you cook us up some dinner? Bound to be better than what any of us could fix." The dark-haired, skinny man rubbed his belly and licked his lips for emphasis.

Ginny barely suppressed her growl. Of course, they assumed she would be better at cooking just because she was a woman. Cooking and cleaning had been her primary duties when Oliver was alive. She hadn't missed the domestic duties one bit since the other women at the ranch had taken them over so she could be free to focus on the cattle.

Now, she wanted to knock the smug look right off Enrique's face and remind them all that she was here to help track the bandits, not to be their cook. Next thing would be an expectation that she wash their laundry. She snorted. Over her dead body.

Enrique frowned. "What?"

Heath stepped forward. "Miss Baker's here to share her knowledge of this terrain, not—"

"No, it's fine." On second thought, men were swayed best by their stomachs, and some of them still seemed unhappy about her joining the posse. Especially Heath, despite his unexpected defense just now. "I don't mind cooking. Just don't expect nothing like what you ate at my place." Her sister was the one with the gift for making ordinary food taste like heaven.

She strode to where their supplies had been removed from the pack horse and set on the ground.

"Didn't your ma teach you the same as your sister?" Turner asked.

Ginny pressed her lips against the pain of Mama's memory. When Oliver had spirited Ginny and Preston off in the middle of the night, leaving Mama and Biddie behind twenty years ago, neither of them had realized they weren't coming back. Mama had died less than a year later, and Ginny hadn't seen Biddie until she'd shown up at Lupine Valley Ranch a little over two years ago.

The continued silence pressed Ginny for an answer. She shook her head. "Biddie was raised by our mama before she was adopted and kept Mama's recipes, but my brother and I were raised by our pa, who didn't know a lick about cooking. So I figured things out for myself." As she had most things in life.

Stooping low, she rummaged through the supplies and pulled out the raw steak and potatoes Biddie had given them. "How do steak strips and pan-fried potatoes sound?"

Most of the men made noises of agreement, but Garret just stared at her.

"What do you mean?" he asked. "Didn't you all live in the same house?"

Jeb smacked him on the back of the head. "Quit being so nosy." He sent her an apologetic smile.

A few minutes later, she had a decent sear on the potatoes. Using a stick, she nudged a few hot coals away from the flames. Then she set the pan of tubers on the pile to keep them warm while the steak continued to cook and the men quietly conversed about life back home.

Jeb lifted his voice. "I know we told Miss Baker our names yesterday on the ride to her ranch, but it seems to me that since she's one of us now, more thorough introductions are in order."

"Call me Ginny." She hated that her name tied her to Oliver even after his death. "It's simpler. And..." Her cheeks warmed. "I have to confess, I don't remember most of your names." More like, she'd ignored that information when it had seemed irrelevant, but they didn't need to know that.

"Understandable." Jeb nodded with a smile. "A lot happened yesterday." He turned to the rest of the men. "Who wants to introduce themselves to Ginny first?"

Turner spoke up first, hooking his thumbs in the pockets on his vest. "Name's Wesley Turner. You've no doubt heard of me. I'm a reporter for the *Daily Alta California*, and I cover the most sensational, most read, best front-page stories in the country."

"And he's modest too." Garret tossed a pebble at the ginger-haired man, who ducked.

The others guffawed as Turner's face mottled. "I'm just stating the facts. My articles have been reprinted all across our great nation. The president himself reads my reports."

"Of course." Enrique chuckled. "How else would he get to sleep?"

Most of the men enjoyed a good laugh at Turner's expense, as the reporter scowled and pulled out his notebook. Plucking the pencil from behind his ear, Turner appeared to focus intently on whatever he was writing, clearly dismissing the rest of them.

Ginny wasn't sure insulting the man responsible for their printed reputations was wise, but since he'd promised not to mention her in his reports, she kept her mouth shut. Not her problem.

The short gray-haired man with a thick mustache and bushy eyebrows caught her attention with his kind blue eyes. "My name's Cole Harris. I was the sheriff of San Joaquin County for eleven years before returning to harness making, which is what I do when I'm not busy keeping these fools alive." Half-hearted protests erupted from those around him as he pinched the brim of his hat, eyes twinkling. "Pleased to make your acquaintance, Miss...er...Ginny."

"This youngster's my nephew, Garret Lawson." Jeb wrapped one arm around the shoulders of the youngest posse member and ruffled his light-brown hair. "He's Alameda's newest deputy and hopelessly in love with Cole's youngest daughter, Agatha."

Garret's face reddened as he pulled himself out of Jeb's hold and cast a glance at Cole, whose eyes no longer twinkled. "Not that I've been given permission to court her."

Cole grunted. "I've told you my terms."

Garret crossed his arms and stood tall. "And I told you, I'm not—"

"That's Enrique Flores," Heath interrupted, gesturing at the skinny, dark-haired man sitting beside Garret, "our state's most famous grizzly hunter."

"And not-so-famous—or skilled—cowboy," Garret added with a smirk.

Enrique gave Garret a shove. The younger man shoved back, and the two began to wrestle.

Ignoring them, an olive-skinned man with a thin mustache, dark-brown eyes, and a guitar settled in his lap nodded to her with a smile. "I'm Miguel Padillo, a wheelwright. *Encantado de conocerla, señorita.*" He idly strummed a few chords that sounded like part of a song.

Also ignoring the two men now rolling about in the dirt and exchanging blows, Jeb continued his introductions. "Miguel speaks the best Spanish of the lot of us and has a knack for getting people to trust him with sensitive information."

Enrique, with a wriggling Garret pinned beneath him, called out, "Except with these Southern Californios, eh, Miguel?"

"I haven't any friends this far south." Miguel shook his head. "But don't forget, I got us close to Chavarria and his gang once, before we came south. Both times, you let them slip away."

The others protested the insult to their efforts. They began boasting of their prowess, leading to off-color remarks and crude language.

Garret took advantage of Enrique's distraction and shoved him off, while calling out, "Yeah, Miguel, these southerners must have better noses that can smell your—"

"Hey!" Heath interrupted. "Watch your language around the lady. That goes for all of you." He directed a stern gaze at each man in turn.

"Don't worry about it." She waved off his concern. "There ain't nothing any of you can say that I ain't already heard."

Heath aimed his stern gaze at her. "Just because you've heard something before doesn't mean you should hear it again." He glared at his men. "So settle down. No need to show off just because there's a woman in our midst."

The men fell silent, and Miguel began playing a song she didn't recognize.

Ginny returned to her cooking, her neck hotter than the flames beneath the pan. There'd been no call for Heath to make such a scene. She'd been surrounded by men most of her life, and not one had ever bothered to change his behavior around her. Well, not many. Before Oliver had died, the number had been less than she could count on one hand. Since then...well, she wasn't quite sure what to make of the mostly civil behavior she'd encountered since then. To be honest, a well-behaved man made her more nervous than a wild one. It wasn't natural, and she was forever waiting for the act to stop.

Once the meal was ready, she handed out portions to the men. The crackle of the fire, the soft munching of their grazing horses, and the tiny skittering feet of unseen desert creatures scurrying by seemed loud in the relative silence as everyone ate.

Finished eating, Heath stood and dumped his plate and fork into the waiting dishpan. Then he walked around, collecting everyone else's dishes. When he reached Ginny, he paused. "Dinner was good. Thank you." Then he held his hand out.

She stared at him. No man except her brother, her brother-in-law, or one of the Rowlands had ever thanked her for anything. And was he asking for her dirty plate and fork? What was the point? "I can carry mine over since I got to wash—"

"No. You cooked. Tonight's my turn to clean up. Tomorrow it'll be Garret's turn to cook and Enrique's turn to clean. You can join in the cleaning rotation once all the men have taken their turn."

Without waiting for her response, he stooped and plucked the plate with its fork from her hand. Back at the dishpan, he mixed a small amount of water with some sand and scoured everything clean. The men retrieved their dishes and stowed them away.

Heath kicked sand onto the fire, putting out the flames. "Time to bed down. We've got another long day ahead of us."

Ginny found a spot slightly away from the others and laid out her bedroll. She stared up at the star-filled sky. Heath Monroe's actions reminded her of Gideon and her brother. Was it possible there were more men worthy of trust?

She closed her eyes to the beauty above. She didn't have time for such silly questions. Her job as guide required a clear head and attention to detail. As a member of this posse, she needed to stay on guard. None of that could happen if she didn't get a good night's sleep.

The low rumble of two men's snores disrupted the quiet, and she rolled over, turning her back to the sound.

A soft *shhh* sounded close by, and her eyes flew open. A snake slithered within arm's reach, traveling across the dirt away from her, its rattle quiet. Unmoving, she watched until it was too far away to see in the dark.

A quiet click from behind startled her.

She rolled onto her back to see Heath propped on one elbow five feet away, returning his pistol to its sheath.

His gaze met hers with a reassuring nod. He'd been watching, ready to shoot if the creature proved a threat.

Although she'd come to accept Gideon's protective nature, having another man concerned with keeping her safe was strange. But not altogether unpleasant. Something fluttered in her chest as she returned his nod. His face was etched with worry and something else she couldn't quite place. The firelight cast shadows that made him look older than the mid-thirties she guessed him to be, more haunted. She turned away, determined to find sleep. Tomorrow, they would find a lead and capture Chavarria. Tomorrow, Gabriella would finally have justice.

~

The next day, Ginny's impatience grew as the posse combed the desert, stopping at every homestead and questioning every traveler who crossed their path, hoping for some sign of the Chavarria gang. At places where folks were likely to speak mostly Spanish, Miguel went ahead alone while the rest of them stayed back, out of sight when possible. Miguel insisted more people were willing to gossip than to help a posse hunt a dangerous bandit who might learn of their betrayal before he was caught.

The strategy made sense, but Ginny hated sitting still while others got things done. Every time Miguel came back shaking his head, it set her teeth on edge. He had to have missed something, not asked the right questions. The gang couldn't have just disappeared into the desert dust.

On the second morning after leaving Lupine Valley Ranch, Ginny woke while it was still dark and began preparing their morning meal. A minute later, Heath rose and silently joined her. Working together in the gray of dawn, they kept their voices to a whisper so as not to wake the others earlier than necessary. It was strange having a man help her with something Oliver would have scorned as women's work. Yet Heath seemed as at ease with the task as he did commanding his men. By sunrise, everyone had eaten, the dishes had been scoured and packed, and they were ready to break camp.

Turner paused beside his horse and addressed Ginny. "Where's the nearest telegraph office? I need to send my report of the ambush and Alberto's injury."

"You kept Ginny out of it, right?" Heath cinched the strap on one of his saddlebags.

Turner nodded.

Ginny answered. "The only telegraph office in these parts is almost forty miles southwest, in Campo. "But I'd planned on taking us north to another homestead."

"You know the folks there?" Jeb asked.

"No, but I've passed by many times, so I know where it is. And I've heard there's a couple running the place who only speak Spanish." She shrugged. "They may not know anything about the gang's whereabouts, but it's the closest place to where we are."

Heath nodded. "Worth a try." He looked at Turner. "We've got no reason to ride south."

"That's fine. I'll go on my own and meet up with you afterward."

Ginny couldn't read Heath's expression as he agreed to Turner's plan, but she knew Heath considered the man a nuisance. No doubt he was pleased as punch to have the man out from under foot for a few days. If they got a lead and rode hard, it could take quite a while for the reporter to find them again.

Turner mounted up and rode south, and Ginny led the rest of the men north.

Heath brought his horse alongside hers.

Squinting against the rising sun, she smirked at him. "Finding us again may not be so easy for Turner."

Heath's smile widened to a grin. "That's what I'm counting on."

"I'm surprised you didn't demand to see his report. You don't seem to trust him much. How can you be sure he didn't write about me?"

Heath's grin faded. "I tried that the first time he wanted to submit a report. He writes in some sort of code to save money on telegraph costs. According to Turner, only the men at the *Daily Alta California* office in San Francisco have the decoder."

"That don't make sense. How's he know what he's writing?

Don't he need some sort of key? Couldn't you use whatever he uses to figure out what he wrote?"

"He has it memorized. Nothing in writing."

"Oh." Ginny let the topic drop, and they rode on in silence.

Eventually, they entered a wide, sandy wash whose tall walls hid the posse and their horses from view of the nearby homestead. She looked at Heath. "We're almost there. The house should be just a quarter mile or so from here."

From behind her, Miguel responded before Heath could. "Sounds good." He guided his horse past hers and up a crack in the wall that formed a slope to the top.

Ginny nudged her horse to hurry after Miguel, but Heath reined his horse to a stop. "Wait, Ginny."

Swallowing her frustration, she slowed and turned to face him, already dreading what he would say. "Yes?"

"You said this couple only speaks Spanish. Let Miguel go ahead and speak with the homeowners privately."

"Again?"

Heath nodded and dismounted. The rest of the men followed suit. With a groan, Ginny slid from her horse. They watered their horses from the extra canteens they carried, then settled in the sand, their backs against the dirt wall.

When more than an hour had passed, she jumped to her feet and paced up and down the wash through the cool morning air. "What's taking so long?" she demanded of no one in particular.

No one bothered answering. She suspected Garret and Enrique were napping. Heath, Jeb, and Cole had broken out a pack of cards and started a friendly game. They'd invited Ginny to play, but she'd declined. She'd seen too much growing up— paid too high a price for Oliver's gambling. She appreciated that the men weren't betting on the outcome, but she wasn't sure she could ever hold a playing card without wanting to lose her stomach.

Seconds later, the clip-clop of a slowly approaching horse broke the near silence. Standing on tiptoe, she peeked over the top of the wash wall and spied Miguel making his way back from the small adobe house. The slump of his shoulders told her everything she needed to know—another dead end. This was the third day since they'd left Lupine Valley Ranch, and they were no closer to finding the bandits. Frustration made her want to punch something, but she kept her hands relaxed and expression neutral.

"Nothing," Miguel said as he dismounted and joined them in the meager shade of the wash. "The family hasn't seen anything suspicious."

Ginny studied Heath's expression. The set of his jaw, the way his eyes narrowed slightly betrayed his own frustration. They couldn't afford to keep coming up dry like this. There had to be another way.

She searched her mental map for the part of the desert they were now in and remembered the family she'd traded cowhide for pottery with last year. "I know another ranch." She faced Heath. "The people there might have seen or heard something. They travel regularly to visit family scattered all over the desert and might have useful information. They're good people. I've traded with them many times when they've gone south to visit family. I think we can trust them to tell us if they know anything."

Miguel protested. "If they travel so much, how do you know they'll be home?"

"I don't, but I think it's our best option."

Heath didn't hesitate. "Lead the way."

They mounted up and rode on. The miles passed slowly as the landscape shifted from the board-flat valley floor to the gently sloping hills with rocky outcrops and stretches of sagebrush. Enrique and Garret's conversation about mutual friends in Alameda was drowned out by Ginny's nagging fears. How were Biddie, Gideon, and the others getting on without her? Was there any chance the bandits had circled back to attack Lupine Valley? What if she'd left them to chase bandits, only for them to be attacked in her absence?

The sun hung straight overhead as they approached the ranch she remembered. It was a modest spread, the adobe house and outbuildings weathered but well-kept. Several hundred yards behind the house, a small herd grazed in a fenced, irrigated meadow. Ginny signaled for the others to wait as she dismounted in the yard and approached the house. Everything was so quiet. The stillness gnawed at her. What if the owners weren't home? This family was her last hope for a solid lead. If no one answered, the posse might waste another day chasing shadows in the desert, every passing hour giving the bandits more time to slip away.

CHAPTER 7

*H*eath shifted in his saddle. To avoid intimidating the occupants, he and the other men had agreed to wait at the edge of the packed-dirt clearing about one hundred feet away from the front of the adobe house and small barn as Ginny approached the dwelling. But something wasn't right. The flutter of an Indian blanket covering the home's front window caught his eye, the bright colors stark against the sun-bleached walls. Three large native-style pots stood beside a weathered bench, with two Indian baskets on its seat. One was unfinished, with reeds sticking out from its edges. His gut clenched, the decades-old echo of war cries filling his ears.

She lifted her hand to knock.

"Ginny, wait!" His voice came out sharper than he intended.

She turned to look at him, confusion clouding her features. "What is it?"

He waved for her to return to where he and the others waited, still mounted.

As she strode back, he took a deep breath, trying to slow his racing pulse while he wiped his damp palms against his trousers. Then he straightened and pulled his rifle from its holster, praying the actions hid his slight trembling. He checked that there was still no sign of the home's owners before sliding from his saddle to meet her beside his horse. He kept his voice low. "What kind of family lives here?"

Her face screwed up, and she looked at him as though he'd been out in the sun too long. "I told you, they're good people." She gestured at his weapon. "Why are you—"

"That's an Indian family in there, isn't it?" His breath quickened. Why would she bring him here?

Ginny's spine jerked ramrod straight, and she smacked her hands onto her hips. "And what if they are?"

His grip on the rifle tightened, memories clawing their way to the surface. Hiding for hours amid the tall sagebrush. The sight of his parents' lifeless bodies sprawled across the blood-stained yard of their Texas homestead. Five Indians in warpaint galloping circles around the yard, their triumphant shouts mixing with his little sisters' screams from inside their burning home. The taste of his own bile as he heaved into the dirt. He shook his head, trying to push the reminders away.

"Indians can't be trusted." They needed to ride away. Fast. He clenched his teeth against the cowardice. "They're dangerous, and this is a waste of time."

The sting of Ginny's slap burned his cheek. Her eyes flashed with fury. "How dare you judge a person's character based solely on their heritage?" She whirled away, and as she stormed back to the house, he heard her muttered words. "You're an even bigger fool than I am."

⁓

*G*inny stomped toward the door, her palm smarting. She was a fool. After everything she'd been through, she knew better than to believe any man was different. They all thought the same way. If Heath knew about her father, he'd never have let her join the posse. He'd have judged her the same as Oliver, just like the others who'd turned their backs and gossiped. Which made him an even bigger fool than she was.

She was nothing like her father.

And these Indians were good, kind, hardworking people. She rapped hard on the door. Imagine ignoring a potential lead just because the people with the information looked and lived differently than yourself. The notion was plain simpleminded.

She glanced back and noted that the rest of the men had dismounted but moved no closer to the home. Jeb wore a concerned expression as he spoke quietly to Heath, while Cole and Miguel stood silent and somber as ever, their gazes passing between her and Heath in clear curiosity. But Garret and Enrique wore wide grins as their shoulders shook with laughter. Thankfully, none appeared likely to punish her for slapping Heath.

The door creaked open, turning Ginny back to the house. A weathered face framed with thick dark-brown hair gazed up at her. Sinfora's sable eyes reflected a mixture of caution and curiosity.

"Good afternoon, ma'am." Ginny shoved Heath's hateful words away and offered her warmest smile. "Do you remember me? I live down south on Lupine Valley Ranch, and we've traded a few times. Last year, I traded some of my cowhide for your beautiful pottery."

Sinfora's eyes lit with recognition. "Ah, yes, I remember you." She looked past Ginny with a frown. "I do not remember them."

"They mean you no harm."

Her expression still wary, Sinfora confided, "My husband is not here, and my children are sleeping."

"I understand. Would—" Ginny's question was interrupted by the soft cry of a toddler waking from sleep, swiftly followed by the distinct sound of a wailing infant. Ginny winced as Sinfora whirled away from the door. "I'm so sorry," Ginny called after her. "Is there anything I can do to help?"

Sinfora scooped up her infant strapped to a cradleboard and sat beside her toddler on a reed mat in the far corner of the one-room house. She handed something to the older child before gently rocking the cradleboard and murmuring softly.

Ginny shifted her weight from one foot to the other. She cast a glance at the impatiently waiting men behind her. Should she leave? She'd caused this poor mother enough trouble. But what if Sinfora knew something that could lead them to the gang?

Ginny waited helplessly as the infant's cries continued. The toddler sat cross-legged on the packed-earth floor, fixated by a string adorned with shells, bones, and stones. He poured the necklace as though a waterfall into one small palm, then watched intently as he transferred it to the other.

She'd had a necklace once. A few months after Oliver had forced Preston and Ginny to sneak away with him in the night, she had woken early on her tenth birthday to prepare their morning meal over their campfire.

"Hello, daughter." Oliver appeared, stretching the first word long enough to confirm he'd yet to recover his senses after another night of drinking, gambling, and who knew what else. But his jovial tone let her relax. His luck must have been better than usual.

His glossy eyes twinkled as he fished around in his pockets before finally lifting out a beautiful string of abalone pieces. "For you, Ginny."

When she didn't immediately reach for the gift, he frowned and jiggled it. "Go on, take it."

She snatched the shimmering strand.

He grinned and stroked her scraggly locks with a rare look of affection. "Happy birthday, Ginny."

Ginny swallowed, afraid to move. He'd remembered? Oliver had never remembered her birthday before. It had always been Mama who did her best to make the day special with what little they had. Without Mama, she'd expected the day to pass as any other. Never had she imagined Oliver would not only remember but bring her a present.

Oliver's cheek pat was a bit clumsy. "That's a good girl." His watery gaze remained fixed on her, emotions she couldn't understand flowing through them. "You're always my good girl, ain't you, Ginny? So smart. So strong." He jerked her into a bone-crushing hug. "I love you. Don't you ever forget that."

Just as quickly as he'd grabbed her, Oliver loosed her and stumbled toward their tent.

She stared at his broad back, stunned. He'd hugged her. Said he loved her.

She lifted the necklace and let it dangle from her fingers. The tiny pieces of abalone shimmered in the light of the campfire, their iridescent colors mesmerizing. Where had he gotten it? Had he won it in last night's game, or was it possible he'd spent some of his winnings on something just for her?

It didn't matter. Oliver had remembered her birthday and given her a gift that would forever remind her of his shocking words of praise and affection. It'd been more than enough. It'd been more than she'd ever dared hope for.

Ginny blinked hard, pressing the memory back. That one kind moment had ruined her life. Not until after the attack on the ranch that killed Oliver and burned the necklace to ash had she realized she'd lived the next eighteen years of her life hoping and waiting for one more moment like that. One more glimpse of a father who loved and valued her. But that father had never existed. That memory, that night, had been an illusion brought on by too much drink.

She clenched her teeth. Oliver was gone, along with her foolish hope. She needed to focus on the here and now.

The infant finally quieted, and Sinfora fixed questioning eyes on Ginny.

"Why have you come?" Her gentle tone matched her calm, curious expression.

Ginny didn't think she'd be nearly as forgiving if someone had woken her children. Not that she ever planned to have any. Goodness, what a thought. Children required husbands, and she had zero desire for one of those. Besides, both would be a distraction from her ranch.

Ginny quickly wrangled her thoughts back to the matter at hand. "One of the men outside is a sheriff. We're tracking a group of men who might have passed through here recently. Six men, mostly Mexican, though one is French. They're very dangerous. Have you—"

A shout from behind made Ginny whirl just as Heath and his men charged the house, weapons drawn.

CHAPTER 8

*B*efore the posse could reach the house, an angry-looking man thundered into the yard atop a brown steed. Ignoring the armed men behind him, the stranger leaped from his horse, pistol drawn.

Ginny's hand flew to her holster, her weapon out and aimed in a heartbeat.

Sweat dripped down the sides of the stranger's sunburned face as he stormed toward her, his gaze fixed on something—or someone—behind her.

"Stop right there!" Ginny widened her stance, blocking the doorway.

The man skidded to a halt, his eyes wild and bloodshot, lip curled in a sneer. "Those thieves stole my cattle!" He directed his words at the darkened home behind her. "Get out here and face your fate, you—" The man hurled nasty words at the kind mother and her children.

Ginny resisted the urge to pull the trigger. Men like him weren't worth hanging for. Besides, Heath's posse was quietly surrounding the man from behind. This would be over soon.

"That's a lie!" Sinfora shouted over Ginny's shoulder. "We

bought our cattle from the Herndon Ranch, and you know it. Stop threatening us. It's not our fault you're too lazy to keep track of your own herd." Sinfora, arms empty, squeezed into the doorway beside Ginny. The infant's cries filled the room behind them, though the toddler remained blessedly silent.

The man's eyes narrowed as he lifted his pistol, the barrel glinting in the sunlight.

"Lower your weapon." Heath's commanding voice split the air.

The stranger froze. Then, with his gun still aimed at Sinfora, he slowly looked over his shoulder and saw that every member of the posse had their pistol aimed at his chest.

He glared at Heath. "What're you pointing your guns at me for? You're a sheriff, ain't you?" He nodded toward Heath's badge. "I figured you were here to hang these animals for rustling'."

Ginny's heart pounded as she recalled Heath's words from before she entered the house. Her gut told her this man's accusations were wrong, but Heath had said Indians couldn't be trusted. What would she do if he sided against the family behind her?

Heath didn't budge. "I said lower your weapon." When the man hesitated, Heath took a step forward, his aim unwavering. "Now. Or I'll order my men to fill you full of lead."

The man glanced around and finally lowered his pistol. He spit into the dirt. "What kind of fools are you? Can't you see—"

"What I see is an armed man threatening to kill an unarmed woman and her two small children." Heath lowered his pistol but didn't holster it. The rest of the posse did the same, but Ginny remained ready.

"They stole my cattle! They're rustlers. They're nothing but—"

"What's your proof?" Jeb demanded.

It was a good thing he cut the man off. Ginny's trigger finger was getting twitchier the more the rat talked.

The stranger's jaw hung open a moment. "Proof? Just look at them! They're Indians. Everyone knows Indians are thieves and murderers. They can't be trusted."

Heath flinched, then gestured past the house toward where Ginny remembered seeing the small grazing herd. "What's your brand? Perhaps I can take a look and see if any of those cattle match." He glanced at Sinfora. "With your permission, ma'am."

She nodded, but the stranger sputtered. "Her—her what?" He took a step aimed at going around the house. "I'll show you—"

"No." Heath's command brought the man to a stop. "You tell me your name and show me your brand, then wait here while I inspect the herd."

The man clearly wanted to protest, but a look around at the hardened men still surrounding him must have convinced him to cooperate. "Name's Hank Simmons. My brand's like this." He holstered his pistol and used the heel of his boot to draw a symbol in the dirt.

"Thank you, Mr. Simmons. I'm Sheriff Heath Monroe." Heath put away his own weapon, strode closer, and studied the mark. "I'll be back in a few minutes." He speared the man with a sharp look. "You wait here."

Mr. Simmons huffed, puffed his chest, and shuffled his feet, but he didn't argue. And his gun remained holstered.

A look passed between Jeb and Heath before the sheriff mounted his horse, nodded at Enrique, and rode past the house. Enrique trailed after him.

Ginny waited another beat before finally holstering her pistol.

Jeb engaged Simmons in conversation about the challenges of ranching in the desert, and gradually, the man's demeanor relaxed. Some. Every few seconds, he'd look toward the corner of the house Enrique and Heath had rounded. Then he'd aim a glare at Sinfora still standing beside Ginny.

Eventually, Heath and Enrique returned, their expressions grim.

Ginny's gut tightened. Had she been wrong? Had he found Simmons's cattle among the family's herd? Could it be an innocent coincidence? Without fences, most herds were free to wander where they would, but Sinfora's herd was fully fenced in. No doubt their fence had been built specifically to avoid situations like this.

Heath dismounted and approached Simmons. "I inspected the brand on every cow out there. Not one bears the mark you showed me."

"They're there!" The man jabbed a finger toward the herd, his voice rising with indignation. "You must've missed them. I'll find them myself." He took a step forward, but Heath moved into his path.

"It's time for you to leave. There's nothing here that belongs to you." His voice was steady, a rock against the stranger's tide of anger.

Ginny moved her hand to the pistol at her waist. Simmons's eyes were wild again, darting between Heath, the distant herd, and Sinfora. As if sensing the tension, the infant began squalling again.

No one acknowledged the sound.

Simmons's hand jerked toward his holster.

In the same moment that Ginny drew her pistol, Heath caught Simmons's wrist. "Not a good idea."

The rest of the posse had also drawn their weapons.

Simmons wrenched his arm free but kept his fists away from his body. "I'm not leaving without my cattle."

Heath stared him down for several long seconds before speaking. "My men and I will follow you to the last place you saw your herd. We'll look for tracks. If there are any signs of your cattle, we'll find them."

Ginny's breath caught. What about the bandits? She still hadn't gotten the information they needed from Sinfora.

Why was Heath offering to find this man's cattle when Chavarria and his men were still out there threatening harm on every American in the state? Searching for missing cattle would take hours, possibly days.

"I'm telling you, they're right there." Simmons swung his arm toward the herd once more.

Heath's quiet voice grew cold as steel. "You calling me a liar?"

Simmons's mouth opened and closed twice. "Fine. But you're wasting your time. And when you don't find my cattle"— he speared Sinfora with another glare—"I'm coming back."

Heath silently motioned for Simmons to mount his horse before mounting his own. Ginny followed suit, and the posse fell in behind her.

Simmons urged his horse ahead of Heath's, and Ginny nudged Mr. Darcy to close the gap, until she rode beside Heath. "Shouldn't you just notify Luman Gaskill? He's our Judge of the Plains. Why not let him deal with this?"

"You heard Simmons. He's convinced those people stole his cattle. If we don't find his herd, he's likely to murder them."

Ginny jerked her head back. "You're the one who said they can't be trusted. Just like Simmons." She swatted at a fly buzzing around her face. "You don't make no sense. Why go to such lengths to protect them?"

Heath cringed. "I know what I said, and I had my reasons, but..." His jaw worked side to side as he appeared to mull over his next words. "Hearing my words from Simmons's lips, I...the ugliness of it..." He clamped his lips shut, then ran a hand down his face. "Indians or not, they're still people, and as sheriff, it's my job to protect them."

Ginny studied his profile. Something was clearly eating at him, and his words still didn't make sense. She held nothing but respect for the people who'd been forced from their way of life, bullied at every turn, and yet somehow managed to survive —sometimes even thrive—despite it all. But there were those who argued that the intelligent, talented, resilient Indians weren't even human. Which made as much sense as trying to brand a cow with a cold iron.

When he didn't elaborate, she pointed out, "Plenty of folks would say they ain't really citizens and so ain't your responsibility."

"I answer to a higher authority than the law." He gave her a sideways glance. "I believe that God gave me this"—he thumbed a point on his badge—"and He expects me to do my best to protect His people. All of them."

Big words. How far did they go? "What about Chavarria and the men riding with him? Are they 'God's people'?" She couldn't keep the sneer from her tone as the smell of smoke and charred flesh filled her mind.

Heath scratched the stubble along his jaw. "I suppose God made them too."

"What kind of God creates evil men?" Memories of fighting in vain against Lieutenant Colonel Atkinson's attack, alone in the shack in Oregon, flared to life. At sixteen, she'd been no match for the full-grown man. Without thought, she tried to push down her skirts, but her palm met the rough fabric of her trousers, bringing her back to the moment.

Heath was shaking his head. "In my experience, defining a person by one part of who they are is dangerous—especially, when that part is something we disapprove of, such as sin. Labeling someone by their sins—real or imagined—makes it easier to deny their humanity and helps you justify treating them however you like." His voice lowered in pitch as if he were quoting someone else. "'He murdered my foreman. He doesn't deserve a trial.'" With an agonized expression, Heath's voice dropped to a whisper. "'Those children were being raised by barbarians. Killing them now spared the world from their future sins.'"

Ginny felt sick. How could anyone justify killing children?

He twisted to face her. "Did you know Valadez had a mother who loved him and, by all accounts, was a devout Catholic? His four siblings all grew up to be law-abiding citizens. Her youngest son's choices broke her heart. Chavarria grew up across the street from Valadez's family and called him *tío*, though they weren't related by blood."

"That means uncle, don't it?" It was strange thinking of Valadez caring about someone other than himself—of having a family. *Had* he cared about Chavarria? She couldn't quite wrap her mind around the notion.

He nodded. "Though not all, most of the gang are related to one another or were neighbors or have some other bond outside their criminal activities. Many of the places the gang hides out are run by friends and family who genuinely care for these criminals. It's one of the reasons they're so difficult to catch."

She'd never considered any of the bandits' families before now. The idea that anyone would mourn the loss of a bandit— whether through arrest or death—was uncomfortable. But if what Heath said was true, weren't those same family members guilty of aiding these criminals? Maybe they deserved to hurt the same as everyone who'd been hurt by the bandits. "None of what you're saying changes the fact that they've murdered and robbed and terrorized good people."

He sighed. "No, it doesn't. Which is why I do what I do." Heath's gaze focused on Simmons's back. "The truth is, I have no idea why God creates boys who go on to do vile things. But I have faith that God loves us. And I have faith that His ways are wiser than mine, and someday—in the hereafter—we'll find the answers we need."

Jeb rode up beside them and addressed Heath. "How long are we going to search for Simmons's cattle?"

Ginny let Mr. Darcy fall behind, but Heath's words stayed with her, circling through her thoughts as she rode. Never had she met a more confusing man. One minute he seemed as vile and untrustworthy as others she'd known. But in the next, he'd say or do something to buck down the fence she'd corralled him in. Which man was the real Heath Monroe?

~

The sun dipped low over the western horizon by the time Heath and his posse finally tracked Simmons's stolen cattle to a narrow canyon on a ranch several miles away from the angry man's house. There'd been no question the brands had been altered. Ropes at either end of the canyon kept the cattle penned. Thankfully, Ginny was familiar with the land and knew where to find the owner's house.

The heat continued to drain Heath as he followed her directions through the hilly desert terrain, but he was determined to see this through. He couldn't leave that Indian mother and her children at the mercy of Simmons's blind hatred. Each repetition in Heath's mind of Simmons's angry accusations—an echo of Heath's own words—stung with conviction.

As a lawman, he knew better than to judge people on their appearance or by their family. He'd arrested a finely dressed man for murdering his own wife and seen the church-going, kindly librarian's son sentenced to ten years in San Quentin for violating a woman. He'd seen men and women of every race behaving in the best and the worst of ways. Yet the nightmare he'd survived at just eight years of age continued to haunt his decisions—the fear distorting his perception of anyone who reminded him of those who'd attacked his family. What must he do to be rid of this cowardice?

Before he could find an answer, he crested a ridge, and a ranch house came into view.

On her horse beside him, Ginny adjusted the thong holding her hat in place. "That should be it."

Heath glanced right as Jeb joined them.

His deputy nodded toward the house with a mischievous grin. "What story do you think they'll try?"

"Story?" Ginny's questioning gaze hopped from Jeb to Heath and back as they continued toward the house.

Jeb chuckled. "Oh, yeah. Rustlers have always got a story. My favorite was when they claimed a bear must've chased the stolen cattle onto their land."

Ginny's mouth dropped open. "Seriously? Someone actually claimed that?"

Heath grinned. "Yep. But the most popular is just plain ignorance."

"Stolen cattle?" Jeb slapped a hand to his chest with a loud gasp. "On our land? There couldn't be!"

Heath played along, assuming a serious expression. "So you claim no knowledge of the three hundred cattle with altered brands grazing in the meadow right outside your back door?"

Ginny's laugh was full and deep, with no effort at restraining her amusement the way some women were taught.

"Well, of course not. Why, I've never even seen a cow." Jeb clutched dramatically at his collar. "Are they dangerous?"

Tears leaked from Ginny's eyes as she held her stomach.

Heath let loose his own chuckle. "And if it's not ignorance, it's the new cowboy they recently hired who mysteriously disappeared just before we arrived."

Jeb sobered. "Assuming they don't start shooting the second they spot our badges."

Heath nodded and looked at Ginny. "Which is why I want

you to fall back. Wait out of sight until we're sure it's safe to approach the house before you join us. In fact, you could—"

Ginny scowled. "Will any of the others be falling back?"

Heath resisted the desire to roll his eyes. He'd known she wouldn't obey his orders without question, the way the men did. He'd never met a woman so determined to put herself in harm's way. "No, but I was hoping—"

"I didn't think so." Ginny kicked her horse into a canter, leaving Heath and the others to catch up.

He closed the gap just as she entered the ranch yard.

The house stood isolated amidst the arid expanse, its wooden structure weathered and bleached by relentless sun and wind. Open windows framed with the torn edges of old oil paper coverings and sagging roof shingles testified to years of neglect. An overgrown creosote bush engulfed the southern corner, and tumbleweeds piled against the rotting support of the crumbling porch.

Heath and Ginny dismounted and tied their horses to a nearby mesquite tree before approaching the house. The rest of the posse trickled into the yard, tethering their steeds to bushes with quiet efficiency. Since intimidation was likely to be helpful in this case, the men formed a semicircle just a few steps behind Ginny and Heath.

Heath bumped Ginny, forcing her to stand just left of the door as he knocked—placing himself between her and the potential danger waiting inside.

Thankfully, the ranch owner, a burly man with a weather-beaten face, greeted Heath with the usual veneer of indignant surprise rather than lead. "Who're you?" He wobbled in the doorway on one booted foot and seemed reluctant to put weight on the bandaged one. "What do you want?"

Heath hooked his thumbs behind the lapels of his coat—a practiced move that drew attention to both his badge and his holstered pistol. "I'm Sheriff Monroe, and I'm afraid I need to talk with you about the stolen cattle I've just found on your land."

"I don't know nothin' about no stolen cattle." He leaned against the splintered doorframe and rubbed his eyes, as if their arrival had interrupted his afternoon nap. Unfortunately for him, the holstered pistol at his waist ruined the act. "Are you sure they're on my land?"

"Yes." Ginny's grim expression left no room for argument. "They're in a canyon on the northeast quarter of your stake."

The man's eyes widened. "Then they must've just wandered in. I do have a good spring. Maybe they—"

"They're roped in." Jeb stepped forward to stand just behind Heath's right shoulder.

The man sputtered. "Well...well...I don't know what to say. Seems I've got trespassers takin' advantage of my poor health." He gestured to his bandaged left foot. "I haven't been able to get around as much lately. Who knows what's been going on without my knowledge?"

He was a decent actor, but Heath had seen better.

Ginny's response confirmed his suspicions. "Last time I came through here, I heard it was your right foot that was injured."

The man's face darkened. "What're you trying to say?"

"That you're a—"

Heath cut Ginny off before she riled the man into pulling the pistol at his waist. "In that case, you won't have any objection to our returning the herd to its rightful owner." Heath was outside his jurisdiction here, and with no solid proof to arrest the man, he had no choice but to go along with the pathetic ruse.

"Of course." The man shot another glare at Ginny before turning his false smile on Heath. "Please do. I certainly wouldn't want to deal with the owner myself. Angry men have a tendency to blame innocent people."

Jeb coughed in the way he did when trying not to laugh.

"You sound parched." The man stepped backward into the house. "Let me get you some water for your long journey."

Heath followed him inside to be sure he wasn't going for a hidden weapon, but the man bent over a table with three tin cups and a small bucket of water. He scooped the cups through the water one at a time while Heath surveyed the space.

A fireplace occupied the wall opposite the door. Inside, a small pot of boiling potatoes warmed amid a bed of hot coals. Above the hearth, a wooden shelf held a plate, a fork, and a knife. Beyond the table, a pallet that seemed larger than the short man required filled the far corner. No box or cabinet existed to hold a pantry. Were the potatoes in the pot the man's only food?

Heath turned back toward the doorway and stilled. A photograph nailed at eye level to the right of the door fluttered in the breeze. He narrowed his eyes at the sight of his own image looking back at him. Beside Heath's photograph was one of Los Angeles's sheriff and one of the sheriff of San Diego. There were three more he didn't recognize.

Judging by the state of the man's house, Heath had thought —hoped—the man had fallen on desperate times and his theft wasn't a regular activity.

Those photographs told a different story.

Criminals often collected such images to aid them in avoiding lawmen. This was no ordinary rancher facing hard times.

He spun back to the man now holding two filled cups. "I'll be reporting this situation to Campo's Judge of the Plains and San Diego's sheriff. So I suggest you keep a closer watch on your cattle and your land. If anything like this happens again, you'll be facing charges for rustling."

"You'd best be careful about threatening my reputation,

Sheriff." The rancher's face darkened. He dropped the cups and reached for his pistol.

In an instant, Heath's hand was on his own gun. Rustling sounds indicated his posse drawing their weapons.

Before Heath could take aim, a bullet whizzed past the man's ear, lodging into the wood behind him.

"The next one won't miss." Ginny's hard voice came from the doorway behind Heath. She must have moved when his back was turned.

The man froze, his fingers clasping the handle of his still-sheathed weapon.

"Let it go nice and easy," Heath ordered.

In the same moment, high-pitched voices erupted in the yard, mixed with the patter of small running feet. Two young girls pushed through the wall of armed men too stunned to stop them but found themselves lassoed by Ginny's arms. Tears streaked their dirty faces as they fought for freedom. Ginny moved the smaller one to her hip while attempting to keep hold of the older girl.

Heath kept one eye on the rustler, who eyed him back, seeming hopeful for a moment of Heath's distraction. Heath was determined to disappoint the man.

Though she could be no more than eight, the elder girl fought as fiercely as a wildcat. "Let me go!"

While the rest of the men kept the rustler in their sights, Enrique sheathed his gun and relieved Ginny of the crying toddler. Stroking the girl's greasy hair and whispering something in the child's ear, he strode away from the danger, disappearing from Heath's view.

Both girls released ear-piercing screams. "Bring her back!" the older one demanded.

"Shh, now," Ginny said. "He's not going far. He's just trying to get your sister away from the danger your pa's caused." Unappeased, the girl tried to bite Ginny's arm, but she adjusted her grip on the child to avoid her teeth. "Calm down, now. I ain't going to hurt you."

"Then let me go." She jabbed her elbow hard into Ginny's stomach.

With a grunt, Ginny dropped to the ground just inside the doorway, taking the girl down with her. Ginny twined her long trouser-clad legs around the youngster's skirts, halting her kicks to Ginny's shins, and wrapped both arms around the girl's torso, pinning her arms in place. "Can't let you go and get in the middle of things," she huffed. Though her face was pink with exertion, Ginny showed no signs of straining the limits of her strength. No doubt that impressive strength came from her cattle work. "You'll get yourself hurt right along with your pa."

Unfortunately, Heath's admiration was exactly what the rustler had been waiting for. He jerked the pistol from its holster, but a shot to his arm forced him to drop his weapon immediately. He grabbed at the wound, howling in pain.

The girl's screams increased until Heath thought his ears might explode. "Papa! Papa! Don't shoot him! Please, Papa!"

The girl's distress tore at Heath's heart, but he couldn't regret the fast action of whichever posse member had just saved Heath's life.

Heath kicked the gun to the far corner of the room, then yanked his bandanna from his neck and tied it tight around the man's arm, slowing the blood pouring from the wound. "There." He caught the older girl's wild eyes and pointed at the makeshift bandage. "See? He'll be fine. Your pa isn't going to die." Today.

Even if the man avoided infection and the wound healed well, it was only a matter of time before he found himself at the wrong end of a noose if he continued rustling. Then what would happen to these girls?

Heath motioned for Jeb to come wash the man's wound but couldn't take his eyes from Ginny, who scooted farther inside and to the left of the door so Jeb could squeeze by. Anyone else might have grown angry with the thrashing girl, but Ginny remained calm. She continued body-hugging the distraught child and crooning soothing words in the her ear until eventually, the house fell silent. Only then did Heath realize he could no longer hear the younger girl's wails. Enrique had also managed to calm his charge, or he'd carried her beyond earshot. Either was a blessing.

Still, Heath watched Ginny with awe. She'd loosened her hold so she now cradled the girl's shoulders in one arm and gently stroked her long, dark hair with her other hand. The child watched Jeb with wide, watery eyes, shuddering breaths, and trembling lips as he cleansed and re-bandaged her father's wound.

The defeated man slumped in their lone chair, seeming to have lost all fight. Thank the Lord. Rustler or not, the last thing Heath wanted was to be forced to kill a man in front of his children. He knew too well the pain of witnessing a parent's violent death, and he wouldn't wish it on his worst enemy.

Through the open door, Heath sent a questioning look to each of his men until Cole gave him a silent nod, letting Heath know that it was Cole's shot that'd spared Heath's life. He'd need to speak his thanks once they were away from the house.

When Jeb was finished, he stepped back, and Ginny released the older girl. She ran to her father, clinging to him as if he were her last hope. "Papa! I thought you were going to die!"

Enrique appeared in the doorway and set down the younger girl, who promptly mimicked her elder sister's behavior.

As the three comforted each other, Garret stepped inside, retrieved the dropped pistol, unloaded it, and tossed the bullets and the empty weapon into the yard.

Heath remained on guard as Garret, Ginny, and Jeb exited

the room. When only the man holding his two girls remained, Heath paused in the doorway. The man looked at his girls with a spark in his eyes that said they were his world.

"Those girls need you to do better. Keep on as you are, and their fears will come true." Heath held the man's resentful gaze. "If you love them as much as you seem to, quit this." He ripped the photographs from the wall and crushed them in his fist. "Find an honest way to make ends meet."

"Easy for you to say." The man sneered.

"Maybe." Heath nodded. "But I know for a fact that if you don't, those girls will find themselves alone in the same world you're facing now. Is that what you want for them?"

The man didn't answer, but his gaze fell to the floor.

Satisfied he'd done what he could to persuade the man to change his ways—and that the man wasn't considering stabbing him in the back—Heath strode outside and rummaged through his bags until he found his meal sack. He marched back to the house with it and dumped the contents on the rickety table. Then he spun on his heel and left the rustler alone with his children.

He refilled his canteen at the well and was about to reclaim his saddle when Ginny caught his eye with a confused look. "Did you just give that man your food?"

"Of course, he did," Jeb answered as he mounted up. "That's who Heath is."

Her surprised expression was less than flattering, but it was better than the glare she'd given him outside the Indian family's home. One he'd fully deserved.

As she and the rest of the men refilled their canteens and mounted up, Heath's focus remained on Ginny. A woman who wore trousers and could outshoot, outride, and probably outwork most men he knew. Yet she still had the gentle touch he remembered his mother and his wife possessing.

"She can shoot, cook, and soothe babies." Jeb's whispered imitation of a peddler's call caught Heath by surprise.

When had his best friend ridden so close?

Jeb winked. "And she ain't bad to look at neither."

Heath's face warmed. "Shut up." He whirled his horse around and trotted away from the yard.

Jeb's laughter followed him. The man needed to grow up. He knew well and good that Heath had no interest in remarrying, yet Jeb loved nothing more than causing a bit of mischief. Normally, Heath didn't mind, but he hoped his friend would obey his order to drop the subject. The last thing he needed was Ginny getting the wrong idea because of Jeb's baseless teasing. Heath might not want to marry her, but neither did he want to hurt her. He'd need to speak with Jeb. As posse leader, it was his job to protect those following him—their bodies and their souls. And when it came to Ginny, that went double.

CHAPTER 9

*T*he full dark of night blanketed the land as Heath led the posse into the canyon where the stolen herd waited. Driving the animals through the night posed too great a risk of injury, so he ordered Enrique to take first watch and everyone else to set up camp near where the animals had been corralled. The delay made his skin itch, but they'd make better time tomorrow. The cattle may move slowly, but at least they'd have a clear destination, unlike the wandering the posse had done in search of the beasts.

Cole prepared a quick meal, which they ate before bedding down, leaving Enrique to stand guard.

Rather than sleeping, though, Heath lay awake, guilt gnawing at him as Simmons's hateful words echoed in his mind, uncomfortably close to his own. Heath had told Ginny the truth—that Indians were people made in God's image, deserving of protection—but his earlier accusations painted him a hypocrite. Worse, he'd set a poor example for his men, letting prejudice overshadow justice. He shifted on the hard ground, irritation flaring at the thoughts that kept circling when he needed sleep to lead tomorrow's cattle drive.

Three hours later, Heath gave up attempting to sleep and stomped over to Enrique. "I can't sleep, so you may as well get some rest."

Enrique gave him a concerned look. "Something bothering you?"

"Nothing I want to talk about." Not yet. He needed to choose his words carefully, and the right ones still eluded him. Besides, what he had to say should be said to all the men and Ginny.

Enrique nodded and strode to his bedroll. Soon, the young man's heavy breathing joined with Cole's snores.

By the time Heath was satisfied with his plan, the gray of a coming dawn had lightened the night sky. He smothered a yawn as the rest of the posse began to rouse. It was going to be a long day.

Hours later, with the sun already sunk below the horizon and twilight settling in, the Simmons homestead finally came into view. Heath's horse snorted, and he gave the reins a tug, slowing to a halt in the yard. Behind him, the cattle, dusty and restless, bawled as Simmons's ranch hands corralled them into a pen. The rancher appeared, his boots thudding the packed earth as he stormed toward Heath.

"Who took them?" Simmons demanded, his face flushed despite the dropping temperature. His hand hovered near the revolver strapped to his hip. "I got a right to know."

Heath waved to where a gate was being closed behind the last cow. "The cattle are back where they belong. That's what matters."

Simmons stepped closer, his eyes narrowing. "Not to me it ain't. A thief needs justice."

"He'll get it." Heath kept his voice calm but firm. "By the law, not by a bullet in the dark."

Simmons clamped his lips tight, his glare as hot as a cattle brand.

Heath held his gaze. "I won't tell you again, Simmons. Let the law handle it."

For a long moment, the only sounds were the shuffling cattle and the creak of leather saddles as the rest of the posse waited behind Heath. Finally, Simmons stepped back, muttering under his breath as he turned toward the pen.

Heath watched the angry rancher until he disappeared into the deepening shadows. Finally, Heath exhaled and turned his mount around. "Let's go."

~

By the time they returned to Sinfora's home, the night was deep and quiet, and Ginny slumped in her saddle beneath a sea of stars. Her breath fogged the chilly air as they rode into the yard.

The door flew open, and the young mother emerged holding a flickering candle. "You found the cattle?" she called, her voice trembling with cautious hope.

Heath swung down from his saddle, his boots crunching against the dirt. "We did. They're back on Simmons's land, and he won't trouble you again."

Sinfora pressed a hand to her chest, and her shoulders sagged. "Oh, thank you. How can I repay you? My family does not have much, but—"

With a weary smile, Heath laid a gentle hand on the woman's shoulder. "All we ask is that you share anything you know or have heard about the whereabouts of the Chavarria gang. I believe that when we were here earlier, Ginny explained who they are and what they look like."

Sinfora looked at Ginny. "You said six men. Mostly Mexican but one is French. Yes?"

"That's right." Ginny slid from her horse.

Sinfora's eyes lit. "While you were gone, my cousin came to

visit. So I asked him about the men you seek. He said he saw a group of five or six men three days ago, riding north along the stage route. They weren't close enough for him to tell if any were French, but it's possible."

Heath yanked the hat from his head and muttered, "Three days is a long head start."

Ginny's breath caught mid-yawn, and she grinned at Sinfora. "Thank you." This was the first lead they'd found since she joined the posse. And it had come from her contact. She straightened, a new energy filling her as she turned to Heath. "So we head north?"

Heath's gaze fixed on the darkened trail as he squeezed the life from the brim of his hat.

"No." Sinfora raised a hand. "You must be exhausted. Please, stay here tonight. My home is not large, but"—she stepped back and waved toward the barn—"I moved the animals and put in fresh hay and blankets in case you returned." She smiled appealingly at the rest of the posse who'd also dismounted. "I have food to share. It isn't much, but it's warm."

Jeb set a hand on Heath's shoulder. "You know it's too late to set out."

Heath raked a hand through his hair, then slapped his hat back on. "Yeah, I know."

Sinfora led the group toward the barn, but Ginny hesitated. This family worked hard for every scrap, and the thought of taking their food didn't sit right. But refusing might hurt Sinfora's pride. With a sigh, Ginny trailed after the rest.

Before long, the group had settled their things in the barn, and Sinfora returned with bowls of thin broth and slices of bread. As Ginny accepted hers, Sinfora whispered, "You're welcome to join me in the house, but I must warn you that my baby is getting new teeth and does not sleep well."

Ginny looked around the small barn. While the rest of the

men had paired up to share a pile of hay, they'd quietly left one mound entirely to her. She smiled at their host. "Thank you, but I've already spent three nights under the stars with them. They won't bother me." Ginny startled. She'd actually meant what she said. When had she begun trusting these men?

The thought gnawed at her as she ate her meal and spread her bedroll across the fresh hay. Ginny checked that her pistol was loaded and placed it under the coat she used as a pillow. But the routine felt more like a comforting habit than a necessity.

What was wrong with her? She knew better than to trust men. Lips pressed tight, Ginny forced herself to lie down. She spread Sinfora's blanket across her legs and chest, then tossed more hay atop that. Despite her worries, the resulting warmth soon lulled her to sleep.

Sometime later, ribbons of pale morning light filtered through the cracks and gaps in Sinfora's barn as Ginny rose to one elbow to survey the rest of the posse. All still asleep.

She released her disheveled braids. Running her dusty fingers through her filthy hair, she removed tangles, bits of plant, and tiny clumps of dirt. Then she split her tresses in two and wove each side into tidier plaits. As she finished, movement caught her eye.

Heath was watching her from across the barn. The intense look in his gaze made her jump to her feet and stride toward the door.

Heath matched her energy and caught her arm in a gentle grasp. "Wait. I didn't mean to upset you. Your hair is just..." His voice was husky—from having just woken up or something more? She couldn't tell. Wasn't sure which she preferred.

And that scared her most of all.

She shook free.

He ran a hand down his face. "What I mean is—"

"I need privacy." Without waiting for his reply, she rushed from the barn.

Sinfora stooped over a pot hung above a fire in the yard, her back to the barn. She must have heard Ginny's hasty exit because she straightened and spun. "Are you well?"

Ginny slowed, despite hearing Heath's bootsteps behind her. "Of course. I've just got to..." She didn't bother finishing her sentence as she rushed toward the outhouse. Safe inside, she listened, but Heath hadn't followed her.

What was wrong with her? Of course she didn't want Heath feeling anything more than friendship for her. Not even that, really. Partners? No, that was still too intimate. What was the word? How did he view the other members of the posse? Allies? Yes, that seemed right. She and Heath were allies united against evil men. Nothing more.

She took a deep breath and let it out slowly. Stupid morning mind fog. That's all it had been. The sluggishness of sleep had addled her thoughts for a moment. She was better now.

Voices in the yard let her know more of the men had woken and left the barn.

Heath's voice carried over the rest. "Glad to see you back in one piece, Turner."

Ginny snorted at the blatant fib. Of course Heath didn't wish ill on the hapless reporter, but he sure as fire wasn't glad to see the man. She pushed open the door and joined the rest of the posse in the yard near Sinfora's cookfire.

Turner, Enrique, and Miguel held steaming bowls of broth while Heath, Jeb, Cole, and Garret opened envelopes.

Turner spotted her and set his spoon in his bowl with a frown. "I've got news for you, too, but not a letter."

Ginny tensed. "What happened? Who's hurt? Was there another attack?" What if Chavarria had somehow learned she was with the posse and set upon Lupine Valley Ranch as revenge? It was exactly what Heath had warned her might happen. If anyone had been injured or—her stomach clenched into a hard rock—been killed, it would be her fault.

"No one attacked." Turner raised his free hand in a calming motion. "But the cattle are sick, and—"

"Is it Texas fever?" Not again. The herd had been decimated by the disease not eighteen months ago. She'd barely managed to hang on to the ranch, thanks to the gems her brother's now-wife had mined from Ginny's land. But those gems were gone. If the same thing happened again—

"Not Texas fever."

"What, then?" There were dozens of other reasons her cattle might be sick, none of them good.

"I don't know. Gideon did say, but I'm afraid I've forgotten the term he used. He didn't seem very concerned, though. Not about that."

Ginny relaxed. Almost two-and-a-half years of working with her brother-in-law had forced her to admit he knew how to manage a cattle ranch. And she trusted him...mostly. If he wasn't worried, then...wait. "Did you say Gideon's worried about something else?"

The way Turner cringed poured cold dread through her. "It's your sister." He flinched as though expecting a blow.

Ginny stepped forward, ready to throttle him if he didn't spit out the message quick. "Biddie? What's wrong with her? Is she hurt?"

"Not exactly. She has headaches and mild swelling of her extremities. So the doctor has ordered her to stay in bed until the babe comes. Gideon was in town in search of more fruits and vegetables, since the doctor has recommended them and forbidden your sister to eat any meat."

"No meat?" Enrique sounded horrified.

Ginny ignored him and turned to Heath. This was the last thing she'd expected—the last thing she'd wanted—but caring for her living sister had to come before justice for her dead friend. "I'm sorry. I have to go—"

"No." Turner cut her off. "Gideon specifically said for you not to return."

"What?" That couldn't be right. The dullard must not have listened carefully. "Don't be mutton-headed. Of course I got to go home."

"Gideon said that having you hovering will only make Biddie less likely to comply with the doctor's orders to stay abed. If she sees you working—especially trying to take over Biddie's usual tasks—she'll insist on getting up and working alongside you. Plus, she'll feel guilty for pulling you away from something that means so much to you." Turner nodded firmly. "He wants you to stay with the posse. He just thought you should know about your sister's condition and that..." Again, Turner hesitated.

She gritted her teeth. "And what?"

"Well, he thought you should know that if Biddie's condition worsens, the doctor has threatened to send her to the hospital. But if that happens, Carmen is prepared to keep things going at the ranch. So you shouldn't worry."

Right. As if the possibility of her sister being sent to the hospital wouldn't worry her. How was she supposed to focus on tracking the bandits with her sister so sick? "I don't care what he says, I'm going home."

Heath lifted a hand as if to touch her, then lowered it and stepped closer. "Is he right, though? About your sister trying to work if you're there working?"

Something fluttered inside at his nearness. Ginny scowled and moved back. "Maybe." All right, fine. So Biddie hadn't stopped working since she arrived at the ranch. And maybe that did have something to do with Ginny's own drive to work from sunup to sundown and often later. "So I won't work." Even as she said it, a sick feeling filled her stomach. "I can just take care of Biddie."

Cole rubbed his jaw with the back of a knuckle. "If it were my wife, I'd want to be the one taking care of her."

"Besides," Heath added, "could you really just sit at her side reading a book to her while there were gardens needing weeding and cattle needing fed and—"

"Of course." She cringed. "Well…"

"Listen." Again Heath moved as if to touch her, but she stepped back.

He shoved his hands in his pockets. "I know this sounds selfish, but I think your brother-in-law's right. I think you should stay with us."

Ginny wanted to argue. Oh, how she wanted to defy these men. And she could. They couldn't stop her if she chose to ride out of here right now. But…fly on a biscuit, they were right. She clamped her jaw shut, not yet ready to admit defeat.

Seeming to sense this, Heath faced Turner. "Did Gideon say anything about Alberto?"

With everything else happening, Ginny had nearly forgotten they'd left the posse's injured guide at Lupine Valley Ranch.

Turner swallowed a spoonful of soup before answering. "He fought infection for a while, but he's doing fine now. Doctor expects him to recover, but they're not sure how well his arm will work once it's healed."

"Thanks." Heath nodded, then waved his envelope toward Jeb. "Did you get a letter from your sister?"

Sinfora brought a spoon and a steaming bowl of broth to Jeb.

"Who else would write me?" Jeb handed the opened letter to Garret before accepting the food. "Here, there's something for you in here too."

Garret accepted the paper but slid it under the letter he was already reading, barely seeming aware of the conversation that continued around him. His pinched brows hovered over a concerned expression. If the letter Jeb had handed him was from Garret's mother, who had written the letter that seemingly held the young man captive?

Sinfora retreated to the pot over the fire once more before returning with another steaming bowl.

As Heath slipped his letter back into its envelope, Ginny caught a glimpse of the signature. Fancy lettering made it impossible to read. Not that she should be reading his mail. She wrinkled her nose in irritation. Who had written to Heath? Was it professional or personal? Male or female? More to the point, why did not knowing bother her so much?

Fortunately, Jeb was curious too. "Is that from the governor?"

"Uh-huh." Heath accepted the soup as if in a daze, his unfocused gaze fixed on some point in the distance as he stirred his broth.

She could only think of one reason California's governor would be writing to Heath—complaining that the hunt for Chavarria was taking too long. Heath's somber expression seemed confirmation of the message's sour contents. He wandered to the edge of the yard, Jeb on his heels. The two men talked quietly as they ate, their conversation too low to make out.

Cole folded the paper he'd been reading and tucked it under his arm. The noise drowned out any sounds from Heath and Jeb. She glowered at Cole's back as he crossed to the cookfire.

After getting his food from Sinfora, the older man strolled behind Garret while blowing across a steaming spoonful of broth.

Was he attempting to sneak a look over Garret's shoulder at what the younger man was reading? Ginny smirked. Apparently, she wasn't the only one battling curiosity.

Seeming to sense Cole's interest, Garret shifted, blocking the older man's view.

A look of irritation replaced the feigned innocence in Cole's expression, and he strode through the barn's open door, disappearing into its shadows. Strange. Why would he—? Oh, right. When the posse members were introducing themselves, Jeb had said Garret was in love with Cole's youngest daughter. Was the message from her? That would explain Cole's attempt to read the message, though it was no excuse for snooping.

A minute later, Sinfora approached Ginny with two hot bowls and two spoons in her hands. Ginny accepted one set with a murmured thanks. Then Sinfora offered the other to Garret, who finally looked up from his letter.

"Oh." He folded his papers and tucked them into his pocket before relieving Sinfora of the broth. "Thank you." Though he smiled at Sinfora, it vanished the moment their hostess returned to her cookfire.

"Bad news?" The second she asked, Ginny wished the words back. The situation was none of her business. She started to hunch over her bowl, but the ends of her braids threatened to dip themselves. She gave a toss of her head, flicking the plaits over her shoulders and out of harm's way.

"Hey." Garret's expression lit up. "You're a woman."

Ginny snorted at his expression of discovery. "Very good," she said slowly, lacing her voice with mock encouragement, as if talking to a child. She gestured with her empty spoon toward a desert bunny huddling in the nearby scrub. "Now, can you name that creature? I'll give you a hint. It rhymes with *funny*."

He laughed. "No, I mean, I need a woman's advice. Normally, I'd talk to Ma, but she isn't here. So I thought..." He plopped his spoon into the bowl, splattering himself with broth, then tugged the papers from his pocket. "Here. Read this." He shoved the letters into her hand before taking back the bottom paper. "Just that one. From Agatha." He crammed the other paper—the one from his ma—into his pocket.

An infant's wail erupted from the house, and Sinfora swung the hook holding the pot so it no longer hung over the fire before rushing toward the sound.

Ginny frowned at Agatha's letter. Her writing was almost as fancy as the governor's. Finding the letters among all those extra loops and curves was like trying to track a herd in a sandstorm. She looked up at Garret. "Why don't you just tell me what the problem is?" Not that she was likely to have much advice. Ginny's expertise lay in cattle, guns, and navigating the seedier side of society. She doubted Agatha's letter contained any of that.

Garret scanned the yard, then glanced toward the barn, the door of which was still open. He leaned close and kept his voice low. "Agatha wants to elope as soon as I return. She's tired of waitin' for Cole to come around."

Ginny nodded. That made sense to her. Not the marriage part—she'd never understand giving a man that much control over her life—but the idea that a woman wouldn't let anyone, especially a man, stand in the way of what she wanted. She waited for Garret to get to the problem. When he didn't say anything else, she matched her volume to his and prompted, "And? What's the trouble? I thought you wanted to marry her."

"I do. I'd marry her tomorrow if Cole gave his blessin'." Garret looked at the barn again. "But I know Agatha. Not having her father at the weddin' will break her heart. She's mad right now, but in a month or a year, she'll regret leavin' him out. And I'm not even sure our pastor would marry us without Cole's blessin'. Which means we'd need to find someone else who was willin'. And that would mean not having the ceremony in our church, where she's always dreamed of being married. She's been plannin' our weddin' for years and has everythin' figured out, down to the last flower placement. But without Cole's blessin', she'd have to give it all up."

Ginny tipped her head, studying him, but found no sign of deception. His wide hazel eyes were earnest. Garret seemed genuinely ready to sacrifice his own desires for what he believed would make Agatha happiest. He reminded her of Gideon and Preston—two men she believed were rarer than diamonds. Was it possible she'd been wrong? Could good, trustworthy men be more common than her life had led her to believe? She shoved the confusing question away.

"Why don't Cole want you to marry his daughter?" Outside of the unspoken tension she'd sensed between them now and then, they seemed to work well together and otherwise get along. Cole's disapproval made no sense.

"It's not me, exactly. He won't let Agatha marry *any* lawman. Not that Agatha wants to marry anyone else. I mean—"

Ginny waved his fumbling words away. "I know what you mean. But why? He's a lawman himself. Or he was. Why don't he want his daughter marrying one?"

Again, Garret looked toward the barn where Cole and Enrique could be heard discussing their plans for the day. "Agatha's eldest sister, Susannah—" His words cut off abruptly as Heath and Jeb passed them on their way to the washbasin, where they used a bucket of soapy water to clean their bowls.

His expression inscrutable, Garret glanced between Heath and Ginny a few times before continuing in a voice barely above a whisper. "Well, let's just say Cole is worried Agatha wouldn't be safe or happy married to a lawman."

What had Garret been about to say about Agatha's big sister? And why did Heath and Jeb's nearness stop him from saying it? Before she could ask, Heath and Jeb had dried their dishes and were walking toward her and Garret.

Heath gestured toward their untouched broth. "Better eat

up. We need to head out." Without waiting for their reply, he continued on to the barn.

Jeb gave them an appraising look, clearly sensing their interrupted conversation, but he said nothing as he followed Heath.

With a new urgency in his tone, Garret whispered, "What do I do?"

"If you think waiting for Cole's blessing will make Agatha happier, then wait."

"But what if she thinks I've changed my mind about marryin' her? What if she gets mad at me for wantin' to wait?"

"I don't know." Ginny flapped her arms up in exasperation, then presented him with the fingers of her left hand. "Do you see a ring here? What makes you think I got any clue about these things?"

Garret slumped, and she immediately felt bad.

"Look, I want to help. You seem like a nice enough man. But I don't know anything about getting married." Too bad Biddie wasn't here. She'd no doubt have a bushel of sage advice for Garret. "My own pa didn't know the first thing about staying loyal to a woman, let alone making her happy. And my ma died when I was very young." She shrugged. "Now if you got questions about cattle or shooting or..." She wasn't about to teach him how to gamble or pick pockets. "Well, if you've got those kinds of questions"—she jabbed a thumb at herself—"I'm your gal."

He nodded, still looking glum. "Thanks anyhow." He shuffled toward the washbasin.

She swallowed a groan. "Wait." She caught up with him. "Look, here's what I do know. Women are usually smarter than men give them credit for, and most got a clear notion of what they want. I hear your concerns about Agatha giving up her dreams, and they make sense. But don't you think she's clever enough to realize she's doing that by asking to elope?"

Understanding sparked in his gaze. "Of course. Agatha's one of the smartest people I know."

"Exactly." Ginny smiled. "So instead of worrying about making the wrong decision for her, why don't you wait and talk to her about your worries when you get home? Let *her* decide what she's willing to sacrifice to marry you."

Garret straightened. "You're right." He slurped a spoonful of the now-cooled broth. "Thanks." Dropping the spoon into the bowl, he set his lips to the brim and gulped his meal down. When the bowl was empty, he wiped his sleeve across his mouth and plunked his dishes into the soapy water. Then he pulled them out, dried them with the hem of his shirt, and headed toward the barn. His quickened steps and expression seemed to reflect a renewed purpose.

Ginny hurriedly finished her own broth, her thoughts returning to Biddie and the sick cattle. What if staying with the posse was the wrong decision? What if Biddie got worse? Then again, what could Ginny do to help? For all she'd ever learned about healing, she knew nothing about pregnant women. Except that they sometimes didn't survive the birth. But surely someone as devoted to God as Biddie wouldn't die so young. Would she?

∽

The next day, Heath swallowed uncivil words and thanked the couple who'd just shared that they had seen a group of men matching the description of the gang pass through the area three days before. It wasn't their fault Heath and his posse were just as far behind now as when they'd set out from Sinfora's home. Nor could they know the burning sense of urgency the governor's words had lit inside him with his refusal to increase the amount he'd promised to fund their pursuit of Chavarria. Funds were running low, and when the money ran out, that was it. He'd be forced to return to Alameda empty-handed. Again.

The smiling woman looked past him to where his men waited in the yard. "Would you and your men like to rest here a while? I'm happy to prepare a meal and—"

"No." He forced a smile. "Thank you, but we'd best be on our way if we hope to catch those men." He turned on his heel, stormed back to his horse, and swung into his saddle. "Let's move out."

The others fell in behind him without question.

His horse ate up the miles as his mind churned with frustration. Maybe he should be grateful that Sinfora's information had been valid and they weren't falling farther behind, but he was tired of chasing the bandits' tails. He wanted to be ahead of the gang, ready to attack when Chavarria least expected it.

Remembering the failed trap that had nearly gotten them all killed chafed at him. Worse than his failure to stop the dangerous gang was the nagging notion that Chavarria and his men had somehow known about the ambush in advance. Yet that was impossible. None of his men would betray him in such a way. Even if they would, there'd been no opportunity. They'd been together from the moment they'd received the tip that led them to that valley to the moment they'd taken position around the ambush point. No, he and his men must have done something that gave away their position. Though for the life of him, he couldn't figure out what.

He reached the crest of the nearest small hill and glanced behind him. The couple still stood in the yard, watching them ride away. A young child had joined them and must have noticed Heath's regard because he lifted his arm and waved vigorously.

With a grimace, Heath raised one hand in return as the rest of the posse rode past him, over the hill. The image, though, was seared into his mind, reminding him of that dark day nearly three decades prior.

Ginny's voice cut through the memory. "What is it?" She kept her mount beside his at the back of their group.

"That family—homesteading so far from anyone else. Their vulnerability reminds me..." He hesitated. The event that changed his life wasn't something he usually talked about. But after the way he'd acted outside Sinfora's home, maybe Ginny deserved to know. "When I was very young, an Indian war party attacked our home. They k— " Guilt tightened his throat, cutting off the rest of what he'd meant to share.

Ginny gasped. "How awful! You don't have to say anymore. I can't imagine..." She didn't finish her sentence. She didn't need to.

He pressed his eyelids closed against the gathering moisture and took a long deep breath. He may never understand why God had chosen to spare him and not the rest of his family, but the choice hadn't been Heath's. He wasn't responsible for their deaths. He swallowed hard. "When it was over, I ran for our closest neighbor's house, but they'd been attacked as well. It took three days to find someone to help me."

He'd refused to be left behind when a posse set out to exact justice for his murdered parents and sisters. "I was so angry, so determined to see those five men hang." He let his head fall. He should have known better. Should have guessed...but he'd been too young, too innocent. "Instead, I watched the posse surround a small Indian encampment and murder everyone in it—men, women"—his voice cracked in anguish—"children."

From the corner of his eye, he saw Ginny's hand fly to her mouth. Would she hate him now?

"Afterward, the white men whooped in triumph just like the Indians as they plundered the burning village." Heath had been sick in the bushes.

It had taken years in the care of Pastor Jim and his wife before Heath had finally accepted that those deaths hadn't been his fault. But the horrific experience had taught him two things. First, no good came from men acting on their rage instead of allowing the rational wheels of justice to proceed as the law dictated. That calm commitment to carrying out the law was what separated lawmen from vigilantes, order from chaos. Second, he'd learned that evil existed beneath all skin colors.

Though it seemed that lesson hadn't quite stuck. Not if his response to Sinfora's home was anything to go by. He squeezed his reins tight as his horse pounded across the wide, flat desert valley. Why, after all these years, had he allowed irrational fear to seize him?

Jeb called for Heath from the front of the group. Unable to look Ginny in the eye, Heath silently nudged his horse to close the gap.

It turned out Jeb just wanted Heath to verify the tall tale he'd been telling Miguel. In a tone no one would take seriously, Heath assured Miguel that the black bear really had been as big as a grizzly. Miguel and the rest of the men burst into laughter over Jeb's indignant protests.

A glance over his shoulder revealed that Ginny had ridden into the middle of the posse, as at home in her saddle as any of the men. Though she smiled while the others laughed, when her eyes met his, they conveyed sadness, compassion, and...was that...understanding? Heath faced front. How could she possibly understand?

By nightfall, there was still no sign of the bandits, so Heath ordered everyone to make camp. As they settled in for another night under the stars, the need to apologize refused to let him sleep, even though the perfect words still hadn't come to him. After tossing and turning in the increasingly cool air for several minutes, he sat up and assessed the others. Miguel slept soundly, but the rest appeared awake. Perfect or not, he needed to get this off his conscience.

He cleared his throat, and six heads turned toward him. "I owe you all an apology."

Jeb's face screwed up. "Whatever for?"

"My..." He couldn't get the word *fear* off his tongue, so he tried another tack. "I should have listened when Ginny said Sinfora's family could be trusted. If I had, we might've had our lead and been on our way before Simmons arrived to cause trouble. We wouldn't be so far behind Chavarria now."

"Maybe." Garret's thoughtful voice floated across their circle of bedrolls. "But that would've left Sinfora alone to defend her little ones."

The kid was right. Heath frowned. He was bungling this. "Yes, but I still shouldn't have..." Why was this so hard? "I know better than to judge a person by their race."

A derisive snort punctuated the night.

Heath clenched his jaw. The sound had come from where Miguel, Enrique, and Cole lay. Which was responsible for the noise? "Evil and deceit are present in all races. I set a bad example, and I'm sorry. You deserve a better leader."

"'Course we do." Jeb tossed an acorn-sized rock that thudded against Heath's chest. "But we're stuck with you. So quit yer jawin' and let us sleep."

He faced Ginny, who studied him with an expression he couldn't discern. "Where does this trail lead to? Any guesses for where they might be headed?"

She tipped her head. "I've got one or two ideas."

"Are there any shortcuts that might get us closer?"

Ginny crawled out of her bedroll, found a stick, and began drawing a map in the dirt near the remains of their small cookfire. Still using the stick, she pointed out two different possibilities for attempting to catch up with the gang. "Either way is a gamble. If we guess wrong..."

Heath rubbed the back of his neck, contemplating their choices. "Which one seems more likely to you?"

"Well, if we go this way and we're wrong, we'll be farther off course than if we try this one." There was hesitation in her tone.

"But?"

"But my gut says they're more likely to head along this path that has more water and eventually leads to a bigger town."

"I think you're right. First thing after breakfast, we'll head that direction." He caught her gaze. "Thank you."

She shrugged and turned to leave but stumbled.

He caught her shoulders, drawing her close to steady her. "Easy there." The unexpected tingling of awareness in his hands lowered the timbre of his voice. "I've got you." His heart pounded against his ribs as though he'd just missed being shot.

Wide blue eyes glanced up at his for less than a blink before she jerked away. "I'm fine."

Without another word, she slipped into her bedroll and immediately turned her back to him.

He pressed the jagged points of his broken fingernails into his palms. *Get it together, Heath. There's no place in your life for a woman. Especially not one who owns a ranch hundreds of miles from your bailiwick.*

He climbed into his own bedroll and rolled onto his back. He focused on counting the stars until his heartbeat slowed and his vision grew blurry. Yet her image lingered, a vivid painting on the inside of his eyelids that refused to fade. And one question plagued him. When their pursuit was over, how would he find the strength to let her go?

*G*inny held still as stone, her heartbeat thundering as fast as a spooked stallion. Not that she was scared. Stunned was all. Her faint memories of feeling attraction for a man were so few and so distant that she almost hadn't recognized the sensation when it shot through her at Heath's touch.

She ground her teeth as though the action could grind the feeling out of existence. Only fools entertained notions of attraction. Ginny was no fool. She counted her breaths until her heart rate slowed and her muscles relaxed—the foreign sensation evicted from her body.

Her mind finally clear, she turned to apologize for her rude response to Heath's help.

His eyes were closed, his breathing slow.

Her gaze lingered on his pale-pink lips. She flopped onto her back and stared at the vast canopy of stars. When had she become so witless?

The call of nature prevented her from digging too deep into her thoughts, and she rose. There'd be time enough to think tomorrow.

She refastened her holster to her waist before wandering away for some privacy. Several minutes later, she returned. Out of habit, her gaze traveled across the fire's embers and sleeping men—then froze on an empty bedroll. She quickly identified each sleeping form.

Miguel was missing.

She scanned the shadows surrounding their camp. Movement by their tethered horses caught her attention. Someone was messing with the reins of a horse. With the large animals in the way, she couldn't see who it was. What if the bandits had found their camp and were attempting to steal their horses before attacking? Hand poised to draw her pistol, she searched the shadows once more but saw no other figures lurking. Muscles tight as a coiled rattlesnake, Ginny crept across the camp.

The tiny glow of a cigarette pierced the night as it fell to the ground. The light was stomped out, and the figure turned. "Ginny?" Miguel's accented voice was laced with guarded surprise. "What are you doing?" His tone turned to alarm and his hand went to his own holster. "Is something wrong?"

She stiffened, but he didn't draw his weapon. Of course he didn't draw his weapon. This was Miguel. She'd clearly startled him with her stealthy approach. "No. Nothing." She lowered her hand and exhaled. "Sorry. I couldn't tell who you were in the dark."

"Ah." His wide grin shone like silver in the moonlight, and he relaxed his stance. "Don't worry about it. Easy mistake. Especially with Chavarria and those *rufiánes* who ride with him still running free, *sí*?"

"Sí," she agreed and turned to go.

"Ginny?"

She faced him, keeping her voice low so as not to wake the others. "Yes?"

"I'm glad you decided to join us. You're beautiful, smart, and good with your gun. The men are...happier since you joined us."

Miguel was usually quiet when the others were joking and trading stories. This was the most he'd spoken to Ginny since he'd introduced himself shortly after she joined the posse. She struggled for a response. "Um...thanks."

Still grinning, he waved toward her bedroll. "Better get some sleep. It's going to be a long day tomorrow."

She nodded, bid him goodnight, and returned to her bedroll. Slipping off her holster, she laid it and the pistol beside her under her blanket.

A moment later, rustling let her know Miguel had also returned to his bed. Less than five minutes passed before his snores filled the night air.

She stared at the stars, willing sleep to come, but she couldn't release the compliments Miguel had given her. He must have meant them. Why else say them? Yet something about them bothered her. In the past, the only men who'd called her beautiful had done so in hopes of using her. Were his words meant to soften her for an improper proposal? If so, why not ask her tonight? They'd been alone. No one to witness her rejection.

She pulled the holster closer. Had her pistol deterred more primitive inclinations? She hadn't sensed his interest or attention before tonight. Surely, Heath wouldn't have a man on his posse capable of the evils Atkinson had forced on her. Surely, Miguel had meant only to compliment her and make her feel welcome.

Still, it was a long time before Ginny closed her eyelids.

Morning came far too soon, and with it, Ginny's discomfort around Miguel returned. Yet he paid her no attention. He simply went about preparing for the day, same as every other morning.

By midmorning, it was clear that any strangeness in Miguel's compliment had been entirely in her head. Ginny resolved not to allow the evils of her past to keep her from enjoying her present. She nudged her horse forward until she rode beside Miguel. "Did you sleep well?"

He grinned and opened his mouth, but Enrique beat him to a response. "Didn't his snores keep you awake? I don't think I got a wink of sleep thanks to *El Chachalaco*."

Garret piped up. "He's not as bad as the miner Uncle Jeb and I shared a room with at Galt Station. That man snored louder than a steam engine, and we worried he'd shake the house down around us."

The men carried on, sharing stories of different noises that had disturbed their sleep over the years, until Cole's story of a bleating goat turned the conversation to strange encounters with animals.

By noon, Ginny's face hurt from laughing as she rode at the back of the posse, her eyes scanning the hilly desert landscape for signs of the bandit gang. As the men grew quiet, her smile faded.

The route she'd suggested had seemed like a good idea last night, but what if she'd been wrong? Heath had agreed, but would the others blame her if they wound up farther than ever from the quarry they sought?

Her gaze drifted to Heath's broad shoulders. Again. He rode at the front of the group and, aside from necessary communication, hadn't spoken a word to her since dawn. Nor would he meet her gaze.

She replayed his heartbreaking childhood story and apologies to the posse the night before. She'd never known a man to be so vulnerable. Then to admit to other men that he'd been wrong... She hadn't thought men were capable of such humility. Maybe Heath regretted his display.

She shook her head. No, that wasn't it. He'd not acted oddly with the others. Only her.

Did he regret sharing his story or... Was it possible he'd sensed the jolt of attraction that had shot through her when he had stopped her from falling after she'd tripped over her own two feet? Had her emotion shown in her expression? Heaven forbid. The notion made her squirm in the saddle.

What was it about him that could bring to life feelings she'd believed long dead? Feelings she hadn't experienced since before Oregon. Before Atkinson. When she'd informed Biddie over two years ago that she planned to live a life of solitude, she'd meant every word. More than a decade of being flirted with and propositioned by dozens of men without the slightest hint of a response on her part—well, not one that didn't involve violence—had convinced her she was incapable of such feminine feelings as she'd heard other women discuss. Which had been fine with her. A life without a man was a life with less trouble.

Yet Heath had stirred something in her. She couldn't deny it. Wouldn't deny it. There was no sense in lying to herself. Still, she didn't like it.

She caught Heath glancing back at her for the seventh time since they'd set out after breakfast. What did he see? She looked down at her filthy blue bodice buttoned to her neck. She'd grown irritated with the tall collar's chafing yesterday and had undone the top two buttons. Sand stuck in the folds of the sweat-drenched garment. She didn't have to dip her nose to know the stench of days without a bath clung to her. A leather ammunition belt and holster hung at her waist where the bodice tucked into loose-fitting brown trousers. Though she couldn't see much of them, the men's brown boots she wore had seen better days. As had the wide-brimmed brown leather hat she'd cinched over her frazzled blond braids with leather strips.

A snort escaped at the mental image of herself. From the waist down, could she be distinguished from the rest of the men? Even if so, from the waist up, she probably looked like a woman with no care at all for personal hygiene. Yes, sir. She was a rare catch. She gave in to a chuckle. Rare, indeed.

Good thing she wasn't hoping to get caught.

At the front, Heath's fist rose in the air, then pointed toward the horizon. She squinted ahead and barely made out the shadowy figures of a group of riders a mile or two farther up the trail. Goosebumps rose across her sweaty skin. Was it Chavarria and his men? Heath's horse broke into a gallop, with the rest of the men right behind him.

Ginny leaned low over Mr. Darcy's mane, loosening the

reins and squeezing his sides with her legs. "Let's go, boy!" Excitement pumped through her veins, and her breath burned in her lungs as Mr. Darcy's hooves pounded the earth beneath her. The wind whipped her hair back, stinging her cheeks, but her wide-brimmed hat, tightly tied beneath her chin, stayed firmly in place. She barely noticed the sting of the breeze against her face, her eyes locked on the riders ahead.

As her posse closed the distance, tension coiled in her gut. This was it. They'd catch Chavarria, and she'd finally have justice for Gabriella's death.

As she drew closer, the blurry silhouettes slowly sharpened into focus. The riders appeared dusty, their mounts tired, movements slow and unhurried—until the thunder of the approaching posse startled them into whirling around and drawing their weapons.

"Hold up!" Heath's voice cut through the air, his horse pulling up sharply. The rest of the posse followed suit, a cloud of dust lifting and then settling around them.

Ginny clenched the reins, heart sinking as everyone came to a halt.

The armed men, now less than a hundred yards away, looked nothing like Chavarria or the other bandits Heath had shown her pictures of.

A lanky man raised one hand in greeting, the other retaining a firm grip on his rifle. "Afternoon, folks," he called out, tipping his hat back. "What can we do for ya?"

Heath's shoulders dropped a fraction before he straightened. "Afternoon. Sorry to startle you. I'm Sheriff Heath Monroe." He carefully moved his jacket to reveal his badge. "We're following a lead on some bandits and from a distance thought you might be them. But clearly, you're not."

The men across from them returned their weapons to their holsters and rode close enough for easy conversation.

"I'm Ham Franklin, head foreman at the Chamberlin

ranch," the lanky man said. "I'd say I'm sorry to disappoint, but I can't honestly say I'm sorry I ain't looking down your barrel right now, Sheriff." He chuckled.

Heath joined his laughter. "I don't suppose you've seen a group of strangers pass through here recently?"

CHAPTER 10

*G*inny dismounted, dust from the trail clinging to her boots as she led Mr. Darcy to a water trough in the Chamberlin ranch yard. She let him drink for a few minutes before guiding him inside the barn where a ranch hand was busy mucking a stall.

She waited a few seconds, but the man didn't appear to have noticed her entrance. So she cleared her throat.

He quit shoveling and looked up. "Who're you?" He stuck his finger under his hat and scratched as he stared at her. "You can't be part of the posse Ham brought back."

Ginny bit back a growl. "And why not?"

He opened his mouth but she waved him off.

"Forget it. Like it or not, I am part of the posse. I came in here looking for a comb I could borrow."

Mouth gaping, he pointed at the tool she needed hanging on the wall behind her, near the door.

"Thanks." She plucked the item from its hook and led Mr. Darcy back outside to a corral.

She removed his saddle and tack, then brushed the sweat from his coat while checking for any sores from the long, hard ride. Finding none, she offered him another bucket of water and some hay before following the aroma of stewing meat and fresh bread toward the cookhouse.

Ham Franklin's group of ranch hands hadn't seen the bandits, but they had been heading home for the noon meal and generously invited the posse to join them. Her shoulders slumped. This wasn't the lead they'd hoped for, but at least they'd leave with full bellies, their mounts rested, and their canteens refilled.

Ginny's gaze drifted across the sprawling ranch. Several split-rail corrals surrounded a large yard encircled by several buildings, including an impressive two-story house, a long bunkhouse, a horse barn, a dairy barn, a chicken coop, a smokehouse, a cookhouse, and at least three other outbuildings she couldn't identify the purpose of. No less than fifty calves occupied one of the corrals, while a gorgeous remuda ambled within another. She loosed a long whistle. This outfit was easily three times the size of Lupine Valley Ranch and bigger than any place closer to home.

The bustling activity of men tending to horses, mending tools, and doing all the things she'd planned to manage alone on her ranch—before Biddie, Lucy, and Gideon had insisted on staying—drove home Biddie and Gideon's point that growing her ranch without more men to work it was next to impossible.

Yet the sight of so many men at work resurrected haunting memories she'd managed to keep buried for nearly two-and-a-half years. Would she lose her sister like she'd lost Gabriella? The backs of Ginny's eyes stung, but she curled her fingers into fists and bit down hard on the inside of her cheek. She would not cry.

Pivoting on her heel, she changed course and stalked toward the shade of three broad oak trees growing on the banks of a dry riverbed far from the house. The coolness of the shadows enveloped her, a stark contrast to the relentless sun.

Her back to the busy yard, she leaned against the rough bark and stared out at the remote mountains. The sound of the men's work was quieter here, but the stillness brought no comfort. Instead, memories surged in a flood she couldn't hold back.

About three months after Gabriella had ridden into Lupine Valley Ranch with her boyfriend, Angel, who joined the crowd of lazy, drunken gamblers playacting as Oliver's ranch hands, she and Ginny had stumbled across the gem deposit. By then, Gabriella had seen the truth about her sweet-talking man and eagerly planned with Ginny to use the gems as a means of escaping their miserable lives. For weeks, they'd managed to keep their discovery secret by working only in the mornings when the men of the ranch were too crapulous to notice the two women missing.

But Gabriella had been sick with fever the morning of the attack and remained in bed, leaving Ginny to continue working their hidden mine. She'd been mid-swing with her pickaxe when a thunder of hoof beats filled the valley, followed almost immediately by shouting and gunfire.

"No! Please, stop!" Gabriella's pleading cries spurred Ginny into motion.

She dropped her tool and raced toward the house, silently raging at Oliver for forbidding women to carry firearms and demanding that they wear cumbersome skirts.

Chaos filled the ranch yard as mounted bandits exchanged shots with the men of the ranch. Flames rose from the wooden structure they called home. Her friend's screams filled the air. *Gabriella!*

The memory of Gabriella's screams echoed in her ears. Gabriella, the only friend Ginny had ever had, and Ginny had failed to save her.

Ginny blinked rapidly and sucked in long breaths. Tears blurred her vision. She squeezed her eyes tight and clamped her lips to stop a sob from escaping. Still, tears escaped, trailing down her cheeks and dripping from her chin. Her hands trembled, so she clasped them together, squeezing.

The sound of boots crunched across dry ground and grew louder. She swiped angrily at her face, wishing there was cold water in the empty creek bed that she could splash her face with to hide her distress. As it was, keeping her back to the intruder was her only hope of saving her dignity.

The footsteps stopped close behind her. "What are you doing out here?" Heath's question was laced with a touch of concern.

She couldn't trust her voice not to betray her. So she said nothing, only shouted silently for him to go away. At the same time, she braced herself, anticipating his demand for an answer. Most men grew belligerent in the face of silent defiance.

She should have known better. Heath had already proven himself different. Instead of commanding her to respond, he waited. After several seconds, he tried again, his gentle tone holding an added layer of wariness. "Is everything all right?"

Ginny nodded, but the dam had already cracked. She couldn't keep the words in any longer. The truth of her failures needed to come out.

"It was my fault. I should have stopped them. I should have saved her." Her raw voice shook, her words barely above a whisper. The trembling in her hands spread to her whole body. "I was in the mine when it all started. Stupidly unarmed. I heard the gunshots. Heard Gabriella scream. I ran out. I tried to help, but he...he saw me and..."

The rider had galloped into Ginny's path.

She skidded to a stop and hurled curses at the man grinning wickedly down at her. She didn't recognize him, but the look in his gleaming eyes was far too familiar.

He'd holstered his pistols and slid from the saddle.

Ginny dug her fingers into her hair, knocking her hat loose. "I had to go back...had to find something, anything to fight with."

She'd burst through the juniper bush and into the mine. Smoke followed her inside. If she could just reach the pickaxe—

"But he caught me with his rope." A lasso had flown over her head and cinched around her shins. With a cry, she toppled to the ground. Her lungs burning, Ginny dragged her body toward her abandoned tool.

A yank on the rope jerked her backward across the gravel floor of the shallow tunnel, scraping her face and palms. The man above her laughed as he bent to grab her.

"He was so strong." She'd rolled onto her back and shoved the heels of both boots into his gut.

Groaning, he covered his stomach with his hands and stumbled backward.

"But I got free." She'd tugged the lasso off her legs and scrambled for the pickaxe. Her fingers wrapped around its wooden handle.

A large hand grasped her long braid and yanked.

She whirled, the blade finding its mark. The man fell with a sickening thud. The sight of what she'd done had bent Ginny double as the meager contents of her stomach exited her body.

"There was only my pickaxe. So I..." Her knees buckled.

Before she could hit the ground, Heath's strong hands caught her shoulders. He pulled her back against his chest, wrapping his arms tightly around her. For the first time, she had no urge to pull away. Instead, she felt...safe.

"What about your father? Why wasn't he helping you?"

"When the bandits attacked, he was still passed out in the house. As drunk as he'd gotten the night before, I was surprised he managed to grab his gun and stagger into the yard before they shot him. But that's where I found him. After."

"Then you were forced to kill that bandit on your own." Heath's words were a statement, not a question.

She shuddered. The brutal memory of the bandit's face, twisted in surprise, still visited her nightmares. "I didn't have a choice."

"You did what you had to." Heath tightened his embrace and dipped his head so that the stubble on his jawline scratched her temple. "You did nothing wrong."

His reassuring words bathed her in a warmth as soothing as sunshine breaking through a storm, but the cold memories refused to stop playing. "When it was over, everything was on fire. Everyone was dead. The cattle and the bandits were gone."

The yard had been littered with bodies, and only the crackle of burning timber broke the sudden silence.

In the time she'd been fighting for her life, the walls of their house had collapsed. Had Gabriella still been inside? A frenzy of flames had devoured what was left.

Ginny had screamed Gabriella's name as she sprinted toward the remains of her home.

Not a soul moved in response to her shout.

Quickly, she checked the corpses. Several were burned beyond recognition, but she found Oliver face down in the middle of the yard, his back blackened. She swallowed hard against the lump in her throat, denying the tears freedom until she'd found her friend. She kept searching, but as best she could tell, none of the unmoving figures had worn skirts. A quick count confirmed the number of bodies matched the number of men who'd been sleeping off last night's revelry when she'd sneaked out that morning.

Where was Gabriella?

Slowly, Ginny turned back to the now-smoldering pile of lumber. A few patches of flames still licked here and there. She was too late.

She fell to her knees as the sobs overtook her. The smell of charred flesh seized her stomach, and she heaved fruitlessly into the dirt

"I was too late." Her fingernails dug into her thighs.

Heath stroked her shoulder. "Shh. It wasn't your fault."

"You don't understand." Unable to bear the sights around her, Ginny had forced herself to her feet and stumbled away from the carnage in a daze. She'd wandered to the far end of the valley and sank down against a boulder.

Heath clasped Ginny's shoulders and turned her to face him. "Then explain it to me. Because all I hear is how an incredibly brave woman did what was necessary to survive a brutal attack and somehow found the strength to move on and rebuild her life."

"No, I didn't." She dropped her chin . "The Rowlands saw the smoke and came looking for survivors. They called for me, but I didn't answer." She hadn't been able to make herself reply. She hadn't been able to move or think. "I just sat there, hiding until they rode off. I did nothing while the bandits who'd murdered my pa and my only friend took everything and got away." She clenched her fists. "I should've done something. I should've got a posse together and chased after them."

Long after the Rowlands had left, she'd sat, watching the sun cross the sky and gradually sink below the horizon. The moon and stars had appeared, then faded away into the gray of dawn. And slowly, slowly, her mind had returned to her.

She'd buried the bodies. Then she'd found a usable canteen, filled it, and started the long walk to town.

Despite her body in motion, Ginny realized now that she'd still been in shock by the time she reached Campo. It was the only explanation for why she'd begged two sheets of paper and postage from Luman Gaskill, then used those supplies to mail a request for help not only to her trusted younger brother but also to the little sister she hadn't seen or heard from in eighteen years.

Although she'd since repaid her debt to Luman, that day still registered as the lowest point in Ginny's life. Never before had she begged for anything. Not even the day Oliver's gambling debts had robbed her of her innocence.

She straightened, holding her chin level, but still unable to meet Heath's gaze. "If I'd been stronger, braver, none of the people the gang has hurt since then would have suffered. And Gabriella would have justice."

～

*H*eath stared at Ginny, her words weighing him down like a river current trying to drag him under. Valadez hadn't just waylaid her on a trail somewhere and taken her ring, as Heath had assumed. The murderous bandit had attacked her home.

Heath recognized that haunted look in Ginny's eyes. He'd seen it every time he looked in a mirror for the past twenty-eight years, and it had only intensified in the five years since his wife's murder. His failure to catch Valadez had already gnawed at him. But to know his failure had cost Ginny so much... He swallowed hard.

"No." Heath turned Ginny to face him, and when she kept her head down, he stooped to look up at her. "You are not responsible for Valadez's crimes. *I'm* the one who failed to capture him before he hurt you and your loved ones." Though he'd never been told of the raid on Lupine Valley Ranch, the timing she mentioned must coincide with the weeks when Heath had lost track of the gang only to later learn that they'd spent the time in Mexico resting from the chase before returning north. Now he knew they'd also paused in their journey to wreak havoc on Ginny's home.

She shook her head and pulled away. "Gabriella would've

hated me for giving up. She was the only person who ever believed in me, and I failed her."

He knew that feeling too well, understood the futility of others' attempts to convince him otherwise. Still, he prayed for something, anything he could say that would make a difference. The silence between them felt fragile, as if it would snap under the wrong word. But he couldn't leave her here alone drowning in memories.

"Ginny—" He had to clear his throat. "What you went through...it wasn't your fault." He hesitated. No amount of reassurance or claiming the blame for himself could erase what she'd seen, what she'd done. But maybe—just maybe—sharing his own demons could ease the burden she carried. "I know because...because I also watched my family die."

Ginny's tear-streaked face turned toward him, her jay-blue eyes wide with shock and something else—empathy, maybe. "When the Indians attacked your home?"

"I was eight." The words were rough as sandpaper scraping against his throat. "We had a homestead in Texas. Hadn't been there long. Less than a year. It was just me, my parents, and my two little sisters, so progress was slow, but we'd all been working so hard..." He squeezed his eyes shut. "I was coming back with an armload of wood for the fire when I heard my mother's scream. I dropped the wood and ran as fast as I could. Five Indians on horses filled the yard. Father lay on the ground, an arrow in his back. Mother knelt at his side weeping, but she looked up and saw me coming. She waved at me to stop, and I dropped to my knees in the bushes. But they shot her too. My sisters... The Indians...they set the house on fire. My sisters were still inside." He should open his eyes, should have the courage to face Ginny, but he couldn't. "I did nothing. And they died."

Heath's fists clenched at the memory, the helplessness of that moment, the terror that had rooted him in the bushes where he'd hidden. "I was too scared to move. Too scared to help. I just... I watched. And when the flames took everything, I ran. I've spent years trying to outrun what I saw, what I did—no, what I failed to do—but the pain hasn't gone away."

She laid her hand on his arm, and he jumped. The touch was light, almost hesitant, but it was enough to ground him. He didn't realize how much he needed it until that moment.

Jeb's long-ago words challenged the guilt he couldn't shake. *"It wasn't your fault, and even if it was, nothing can separate you from God's love."*

He ran a hand over his face and opened his eyes. "Part of me knows that what happened was the fault of those Indians and not my cowardice. But like you, I've battled against blaming myself. Too many nights have been lost to wondering what might have happened if I'd found the courage to act. But a long time ago, Jeb pointed out that the most likely outcome was my own death added to the others." He grasped her hands and held her gaze, praying she truly heard him. "A pickaxe is no match for a group of men armed with guns. There was nothing you could have done to save your friend."

She trembled in his grip but didn't protest.

"Jeb also reminded me that God's love isn't conditional on us always making the right choices. Sometimes we're foolish or stubborn or too afraid, and we do something wrong—or fail to do what's right. But God forgives us and loves us regardless."

Ginny's mouth tipped up on one side. "You sound like my sister."

His return smile faltered. The memory of Susannah flickered like a ghost he couldn't quite shake. He wanted to tell Ginny—wanted to confess that his past bore more darkness. But the words stuck in his throat. Speaking of Susanna's death would undoubtedly lead to confessions he wasn't ready to make. And that Ginny might not be able to forgive.

He let himself stare into the shimmering, blue-gray eyes

that reminded him of a scrub jay a moment longer before releasing her and turning away. Beautiful, tough Ginny had enough to carry without adding his darkest sins to her load.

He drew in a deep breath and let it out, his gaze fixed unseeing on the activity in the distant ranch yard. "You're stronger than you know, Ginny. And you're not alone in this. We've both seen the worst of what the world can throw at us, but we're still here. Still fighting. You left your home and joined our posse to find justice for Gabriella. That's got to count for something."

From the corner of his eye, he saw her nod and square her shoulders. "Thank you."

He exhaled, though the needle of unspoken secrets still pricked his conscience.

Walking back to where the others were gathering in the yard with plates of delicious-smelling food, Heath tried to shake the tension from his shoulders. He'd shared what he could. He prayed it was enough.

CHAPTER 11

*T*he posse lingered over their meal, letting their horses rest and taking the opportunity to bathe. Eventually, it was time to get back on the trail, so Heath gathered Ginny and his men in the yard.

Mr. and Mrs. Chamberlin and Ham Franklin moved onto the porch to bid them farewell.

Heath tipped his hat. "I can't thank you all enough for letting us rest and get ourselves in order before we head out again. Your hospitality has made a world of difference to my men."

"And me." Ginny nodded with a smile, all evidence of her earlier distress gone.

"You're more than welcome." Mr. Chamberlin slid an arm around his wife. "You're risking your lives to keep folks like us safe. We were pleased to offer you what we could."

"As he said." Ham Franklin hooked his thumbs in his suspenders. "It was the least we can do."

The rest of the posse expressed their thanks, then mounted up. Their complete silence as they rode through the desert for the next several hours spoke volumes about their lowered morale. When the sun set without any sign of the bandits, Heath found a likely camping spot and ordered a stop for the night.

Weary to the bone, he settled on the ground and leaned back against a rock. He silently worked over the choices he'd made, second-guessing his past decisions and toying with new ones.

The others tended to their belongings, and Ginny stirred something in a pan over the fire about a dozen feet away from him. His heart stopped as her braids dipped close to the flames, but she jerked back before it was too late. Mumbling something he couldn't make out, she yanked her hat from her head, tied her braids in a knot on top, then crammed her hat back on to keep the hair in place.

Jeb's teasing laughter rang out behind him. "Looks like you've got your eye on something soft and pretty, Sheriff." Jeb plopped himself on the ground beside Heath. "Haven't seen you look at a woman that way since Susannah."

The comment settled as comfortably as a splinter. Heath widened his eyes at Jeb in a look that he hoped shouted, "Shut your reckless mouth!"

Not that Jeb was wrong. Well, maybe he was wrong about Ginny being soft. That word just didn't fit her. But the rest of it... He couldn't deny the pull he felt when she was around, the way her presence seemed to shift something deep within him. Still, he didn't need Jeb making Ginny uncomfortable with his careless teasing.

Heath stared at the horizon, where the desert met the darkening sky. Was it possible to fall in love twice in a lifetime?

The idea gnawed at him, bringing with it a knot of emotions he wasn't sure how to untangle. He tugged at the thong around his neck until the double-sided locket hidden beneath his shirt pulled free. He popped open one side, revealing a tiny lock of Susannah's fine brown hair. He stroked his thumb twice over the glass enclosing it, then closed it and opened the other side. Susannah's brown eyes and fair complexion looked up at him.

When he'd proposed, Heath assumed Susannah, as a sheriff's daughter, understood the rough edges of his life. He'd underestimated how sheltered she'd been by her finishing school upbringing, She'd been kind, loving, and hardworking, but until she married him, she'd had no reason to recognize the evil in this world.

In hindsight, Heath realized his bride's confident refinement had masked her naiveté and lack of preparation for a life with a man who angered dangerous men and was often away for long stretches. Despite her love and efforts to adjust, he'd watched helplessly as his lifestyle drained the joy from her. Then, two men, seeking revenge for the hanging of their murderous friend, killed Susannah while Heath was away chasing a false lead on Valadez. Cole had never blamed Heath for Susannah's murder, but the guilt had torn Heath apart, twisting him into someone he didn't recognize. Until God got hold of him.

Ginny, with her grit, resilience, and stark, unyielding determination, had proven her ability to survive the world's worst and keep moving forward.

Heath drummed his fingers against his thigh. Since Susannah's death, Heath had avoided women. No female deserved the loneliness and dangers of a lawman's life. But Ginny was different—independent, self-sufficient, and always alert to danger, especially around men. If he married her, he might worry less about leaving her alone while he was away. Maybe. He tugged off his hat and ran his fingers through his sweat-matted hair, still watching Ginny by the fire. Was it possible he could have both his career and a happy marriage?

"No protest?"

Heath frowned. "Protest about what?"

Ginny chopped onions and added them to the pot, her movements quick and confident.

"Ginny. The way you're looking at her."

Heath jerked his attention back to his friend "What?" He looked back at Ginny, but if she'd heard, her expression revealed nothing of her thoughts. He glowered at Jeb and whispered, "Keep your voice down!"

Jeb stole Heath's hat and spun it on his finger. "Seems like this is more serious than I thought. You do realize her ranch is several hundred miles south of our bailiwick, right?" He hadn't lowered his volume one bit.

Cole returned from collecting kindling for the fire. He glanced in their direction with an expression Heath couldn't decipher before turning to set out his bedroll. Had he heard Jeb?

"You shut up, or I'll tell Mary Alice that you want to court her." He wouldn't. The poor woman had nurtured a crush on Jeb since they were children, and Heath would never be so heartless as to encourage her affections knowing Jeb wasn't interested. His deputy had a strange aversion to cats, and Mary Alice housed six of them in her small house. Nevertheless, the threat worked.

Jeb's mouth snapped shut, and his eyes narrowed as his face turned red as a rooster's wattles. "Have it your way." He stood and tossed the hat at Heath, then stalked to the other side of camp and engaged Garret in a conversation Heath couldn't hear.

Of course. *Now* he chose to speak quietly. Heath gripped the wide brim of his hat in both hands. Jeb did have a point. The distance between Ginny's ranch and his home in Alameda was a chasm he couldn't easily bridge, but the idea of leaving his post as sheriff felt like a betrayal of everything he stood for.

As popular as Ross had grown as a deputy, he was still considered new to town. Folks didn't trust newcomers easily.

Besides, Heath suspected Seth Whitaker held too many persuasive secrets for the election to be a fair fight. But if Heath could capture Chavarria, he was almost certain to keep his position. If he failed to capture Chavarria or didn't run at all... Well, the thought of leaving his town under the thumb of a corrupt saloon owner churned his stomach. The chaos that would follow was something he couldn't bear to imagine.

Like two cats fighting, his opposing desires went round and round in an endless battle. Maybe he should speak with Ginny, see if she held even the slightest affection for him, ask if there was any chance at all that she'd relocate to Alameda. Her answer might settle his struggles one way or another.

So get up and go ask her.

He didn't budge.

Coward.

Maybe. But was it fair to broach the subject with her if he hadn't yet settled in his own mind exactly what he wanted? He didn't think so.

Instead of crossing the distance to speak with her, Heath did the only thing he could think of to stop himself from watching her. He tipped his head back and set his smelly hat over his face.

~

*G*inny kept her face impassive as she tended their meal. Jeb's voice had carried easily on the quiet desert breeze when he teased Heath. Was it possible he'd seen Heath holding her at the ranch earlier and misinterpreted what he saw? Should she clarify? No. Heath clearly hadn't wanted her to hear them. Acknowledging that she had would only make things awkward.

But who was Susannah? The way Jeb had mentioned her made it seem as though she was someone from Heath's past. Yet

Ginny couldn't remember Heath ever mentioning someone with that name.

And had Jeb called Ginny "soft and pretty"? She snorted at the notion she was soft, but...pretty? Did he really think so? She resisted the urge to look over her shoulder and check whether Heath was looking her way. Instead, she gave the beef stew another stir to keep it from sticking to the pan. Jeb must have been joking, as usual. *Soft* and *pretty* were words people used to describe her sister. Not her.

How was Biddie faring? Had bed rest and the new diet helped? Or had Gideon taken her to San Diego's hospital? How would any news find Ginny way out here?

She shook her head. There was no point worrying over something she could do nothing about. What she needed to focus on was figuring out how to fix her obvious mistake in suggesting this route. They'd seen no sign of the bandits, and neither had the homesteaders and ranchers they'd stopped to ask. But Jeb's laughter pulled her thoughts from that problem and back to what he'd said to Heath.

Did Heath agree with Jeb's notion that she was pretty? Did she want him to?

Of course not.

Although...

No. She was perfectly content with her own appearance. She didn't need a man calling her pretty to make her feel good. In her experience, expressions of admiration were swiftly followed by presumptions beyond propriety.

But Heath wasn't like other men she'd known.

He was an honest lawman far from home, risking his life to capture a gang of bandits terrorizing the state. He wasn't above getting his hands dirty to pitch in wherever help was needed, and he'd gone above and beyond to ensure the safety of Sinfora's family. After he'd accused them of being untrustworthy liars. Though he'd apologized for that and seemed to really mean it. He could have gone on as if he'd done no wrong. He could have apologized privately to her. Instead, he'd humbled himself before the men he felt responsible for leading.

What if Heath did think she was pretty? Was there any chance he liked her and maybe wanted more from her than her skills as a guide? Was he worth taking the same risk the other women on her ranch had taken in agreeing to courtships?

She finally gave in and cast a peek over her shoulder.

Heath leaned against a tree with his hat over his face.

When she turned back, Jeb was looking straight at her. Catching her eye, he grinned.

Ginny jerked the pan from the fire and began filling bowls. She clenched her teeth against the disappointment that Heath hadn't been watching her.

What was she thinking? Jeb had rightfully pointed out that Heath's bailiwick would usually keep him hundreds of miles from Lupine Valley Ranch. She certainly wasn't willing to consider leaving her home. Nor was she willing to hand over ownership to any man. And that's what marriage was, after all —a legal agreement that gave a man complete control over the woman foolish enough to marry him, including any property or finances she brought into the marriage. No, thank you.

Heath might be different from other men, but she wasn't about to give that kind of power over her life to anyone. Ever.

No matter how his touch affected her or left her yearning for more.

～

*F*or two more days, they trailed along Ginny's shortcut, winding through dry washes and rocky hillsides with nothing to show for it. Each bend in the path promised a sign of the gang—tracks, smoldering ashes, anything—but delivered only more empty stretches of desert.

Ginny had gone to bed early last night, unable to meet the men's gazes.

Now she crouched by the dying embers of the campfire and rolled up her bedroll as the first light of dawn crept over the horizon. The crisp morning air carried the scent of sage and smoke as the men around her broke camp. She carried her bedding to where Mr. Darcy waited and strapped it to the back of her saddle.

No one spoke as they prepared for another long day on the trail. Heath kicked sand over the remnants of their fire, lines of worry creasing his face.

She looked away. Though no one had said a word, their aimless wandering was her fault. Why had she thought she knew better which route to take than the lawmen who'd made their careers chasing criminals? She checked the straps on Mr. Darcy's saddle. She should have kept her mouth shut and let Heath make whatever decision he thought best.

Miguel's voice broke the silence, his tone thoughtful. "We need to change our approach."

The rest of the men stilled, their attention on Miguel.

Heath gave a final jerk to one of the straps holding his saddlebag. "What do you suggest?"

"I think..." Miguel stroked one side of his thin mustache. "Maybe instead of hunting them down, we find a way to make them come to us."

"Sure, we'll just post an invitation in the newspaper." Jeb chuckled and assumed a high-pitched voice Ginny assumed was meant to imitate a high-society matron. "Dear Señor Chavarria and companions, the pleasure of your company is requested for a special gathering on Saturday evening, the thirtieth of November, 1875, at the renowned San Quentin Hall. Festivities will commence sharply at eight o'clock, featuring the most riveting music of lively gunfire followed by jingling keys. A modest repast shall be served. Gentlemen, come attired in your finest—or your worst—and join us for an evening of unforgettable company behind secure walls. Admission is free, and a stay is guaranteed."

"Not bad. You could write for our paper, Jeb." Turner sounded half amused, half serious.

The rest of the men chuckled. All except Heath, whose serious expression remained on Miguel. "Did you have a plan in mind?"

"I thought maybe if we spread a rumor about a stagecoach transporting gold..."

Before he'd finished the sentence, Heath was shaking his head. "Too obvious and too complicated. It'd take weeks to set up something like that—even if we could convince a coach to participate—and we've no guarantee Chavarria would take the bait."

"I like the idea, though." Cole stroked his horse's mane. "What about a big rancher instead of a stagecoach? An outfit like the one that fed us a few days ago might need a large cash cargo to pay its crew."

Heath nodded slowly. "That might work. But again, we'd have to coordinate with one of the big ranches. I don't like the idea of putting more people at risk."

"They're already at risk." Enrique threw his saddle onto his horse and adjusted the straps as he spoke. "So long as Chavarria and his gang are loose, places like that are going to be targets for rustling, robbery, or worse. I spoke with those ranch owners, and they were very grateful we're out here chasing Chavarria."

"That isn't the same as actively participating in a trap." Heath secured his rifle in its sheath.

This was her chance to make up for choosing the wrong trail. Ginny cleared her throat, drawing the men's attention. "I've got a better idea." She caught Heath's gaze. "And it won't put anyone else in danger."

Heath lifted one eyebrow with clear skepticism.

"Chavarria and his gang have already held up several shipments from the mines up north. So we know they're interested in raw treasure. I say we let it be known that a garnet miner in this region has struck a new vein and is preparing to transport the riches to a jeweler in San Francisco. Alone."

Cole gave a mirthless laugh. "No one's foolish enough to transport gems that far by themselves."

At the same time, Heath crossed his arms and said, "I thought your idea wouldn't put anyone in danger."

"I said it wouldn't put anyone *else* in danger. I'm already in danger just by being here." She smirked. "I'm the miner."

Heath uncrossed his arms. "Sorry, but no one will believe you're a miner. Everyone who's recognized you has identified you as the owner of Lupine Valley Ranch. We can't just make up a garnet mine and—"

"The mine's real, and it's on my land. Plenty of folks know all about it, thanks to a man being murdered in my barn last year. We had to tell about the mine's existence during the trial. Since the murderer was so well known, the news was in *The San Diego Union*, a couple of San Francisco papers, and even a Chicago paper." The loss of secrecy still clung to her nerves, as stubborn and aggravating as burrs caught in a horse's mane. "We pulled about two thousand dollars' worth last year, but the mine seems mostly played out now. That's the part no one knows yet. So I've got no doubt people will believe the lie that a new vein has been discovered."

"I still don't think anyone would believe such a large amount was being transported by a lone miner." Cole lifted one of his horse's forelegs and studied its hoof.

Ginny quirked her lips to one side. "You're forgetting one thing."

"And that is?" He set the first leg down and lifted another to repeat his inspection.

"I'm a woman. Men always underestimate women. And that goes double for me, thanks to my pa. He may have been dead for over two years, but I'm still fighting to escape the shadow of his sullied reputation." She scowled. "Trust me. There are plenty who'll believe I'm foolish enough to try it."

Heath's expression darkened. "And the rest?"

She lifted one shoulder. "I've got a reputation for being 'unreasonably independent.'" Not that it was true. Most people just couldn't understand the difference between blind stubbornness and a wise determination to ignore foolish suggestions. Fact was, too many people had a habit of thinking they knew best and spouting off their ideas without considering whether they had all the facts. Especially men. Nor did they seem to notice she'd never asked for their advice to begin with. "It's also well known that men ain't generally welcome at Lupine Valley Ranch. Even if Chavarria suspects I ain't alone, he'll expect another woman to be riding with me—another easy target. The opportunity will be too tempting to resist."

"Aren't you worried this will put another target on your ranch?" Jeb's usual joviality had been replaced with clear concern. "What if the gang decides to head straight for the ranch rather than wait for you to transport the gems?"

"Of course I'm worried about that. That's why we've got to be choosy about what we say." The last thing she wanted was a gang of bandits stirring up trouble when Biddie's rest was so important for her health. Ginny rubbed her palms down the sides of her hips. "The exact location of the mine ain't known. So we've got to let slip that the mine is a couple miles north of the ranch buildings—"

"Is it?" Garret asked.

"Of course not. But Chavarria can't know that." Ginny shook her head. As if she'd tell anyone the mine's true location, which was just a few hundred yards from her house. "We also need to say I've already headed north on the stage route. That should be enough to convince Chavarria his only chance of catching me is on the trail."

Enrique frowned. "What if they've already heard you're riding with us?"

"I..." She hadn't considered that, but he was right. A woman riding with a posse was likely fodder for gossip. "Then we can say the discovery was made by my brother-in-law and that once I heard the news, I hightailed it back and demanded to transport the gems myself. While we're at it, we can remind folks how little I trust people with anything important to me."

The silence that followed was thick with consideration. Would they agree to her plan? Did she want them to? It had seemed so perfect in her mind, but the longer she spoke, the more doubt pushed through the cracks. What if the gang did decide to attack her ranch rather than wait to catch her on the trail? What if the trap didn't work and the gang somehow figured out it had all been a lie? Would they attack Lupine Valley in revenge?

"It's too dangerous, Ginny." Heath's low voice, filled with concern, finally broke the silence. "Too much could go wrong." He shook his head. "We can come up with something else." He turned toward his horse, clearly considering the conversation over.

"I need to do this, Heath." She strode after him and, grabbing his shoulder, turned him to face her. "For Gabriella." The name slipped out on a whisper. "We can't keep chasing the wind. She deserves justice. So does every other person Chavarria and his men have hurt." And Ginny needed this chase to be over so she could head home and see for herself how Biddie was faring. She glanced back at the men, and their expressions seemed in agreement. "This plan is our best chance. We've got to take it."

Heath's jaw muscles flexed, his hazel eyes intense with

conflict as he studied her. Several long seconds passed. "Fine. But you follow my instructions. No arguments. Agreed?"

She hesitated. Unquestioning obedience wasn't something she'd ever promised anyone. And her word was her bond. If she agreed, she'd have to follow whatever order he gave.

"I need your word, Ginny, or this isn't happening." His expression was unyielding.

Still, she couldn't force the words past her lips.

His gaze softened just a fraction, and his voice quieted. "It's the only way I can keep you safe."

The sincerity in his look shifted something deep inside, and a weight lifted, as though a boulder had rolled free from a cave entrance, letting sunlight pour in. "I promise."

CHAPTER 12

*W*ith the plan settled, Ginny, Heath, Jeb, and Garret took one route while Miguel, Cole, and Enrique followed another. Each group was tasked with spreading rumors of the gem transport at different stage stops and nearby homesteads. They agreed to rendezvous just outside the nearest town in two days.

Later that afternoon, Ginny sprawled on her belly to peer out from behind a large outcropping of sandstone that tugged at her sleeves.

Almost a quarter mile away, Garret strode across the dusty yard toward the stagecoach waiting outside Carrizo Creek Stage Station, his confident gait making her almost believe the lie he was about to tell.

"Think he'll pull it off?" Jeb muttered, shifting beside her. He tilted his hat lower to shield his face from the slanting afternoon sun.

"He better." Her attention stayed locked on Garret's figure nearing the stagecoach driver. "Word needs to spread fast." The desert breeze tugged at a strand of hair, and she brushed the lock from her face.

"I still don't like it," Heath murmured from where he leaned against a boulder at her right. "If that gang catches wind—"

"They will catch wind." She turned her gaze toward him. The tension in his jaw betrayed the calm he tried to project. "That's the point. And when they do, we'll be ready."

The stagecoach door slammed shut, and the driver climbed into his seat. Garret said a few more words to someone inside the carriage, then stepped back. A moment later, the driver snapped the reins, and the coach lurched forward, rolling down the dusty road.

When the vehicle was out of sight and the stationmaster had gone inside, Garret sauntered toward their hiding spot, a mischievous grin playing on his lips. "Well, that's done."

"Let's hope so." Heath straightened, and his gaze turned toward the horizon where the stagecoach had vanished. "Now let's see how many houses we can visit before sundown."

~

Two days later, Ginny adjusted her crouch amid the branches of the desert ironwood tree concealing her and Turner from folks wandering the lone thoroughfare that divided the small town below. Despite the sparse shade, the afternoon sun baked her hat as steadily as one of Biddie's loaves in the oven.

The faint murmur of distant voices mingled with the creak of a farm wagon as it rumbled out of the livery, led by a pair of horses whose hooves clip-clopped along the dirt road heading east and faded into the distance. A moment later, Miguel emerged from the livery's shadows beside a man who must be the owner. Their translator said something that made the other man laugh and clap him on the back. It seemed Miguel's role, at least, was going as planned. The two continued chatting as a couple strolled past.

When the husband held the general store door open for his wife, Ginny caught a glimpse of Garret and Enrique inside, where they'd been sent to whisper loudly in front of the clerk. Now they'd have the couple added to their audience. Perfect. The more people who "accidentally overheard" of Ginny's plans to transport gems tomorrow, the better.

Her gaze darted back to the blacksmith's shop. Jeb was somewhere in the shadows behind the glowing forge. Hopefully, he was as skilled at subtly sharing gossip with the owner as he was at making smart remarks.

A man exited the back of the saloon. It wasn't Heath. Nor was it Cole, who'd gone with him to play cards and help spread their concocted story.

She snapped a twig from the branch at her right. Two long hours had passed since the rest of the posse had left her with Turner on the outskirts of town. If only the men would hurry so they could move to the next step—when she'd have something helpful to do.

Of course, playing a single game, spouting their story, and dashing straight off would arouse suspicion. Many men spent the better half of a day or more playing cards and getting drunk —life with Oliver had taught her as much. And her trips to Campo had taught her most folks took advantage of a visit to town to linger and learn the latest news. An inclination Ginny couldn't relate to. And after spending the last two days doing nothing but hiding, obeying Heath's instruction to stay out of sight until the rest of the men returned was about as easy as ignoring a cholla cactus needle stuck in the tip of her finger.

Only the knowledge that being recognized would ruin their plans kept her in place.

Another hour passed before Jeb finally exited the blacksmith shop and strolled casually through town, stopping to chat with whomever crossed his path before finally gathering his horse and making a show of heading west. It was another twenty minutes before she heard him ride up behind her, dismount, and join her behind the bush.

Ginny studied his pleased expression. "So you think they believed you?"

"'Course they did." Jeb winked as he removed his deputy's badge from the pocket he'd hidden it in while in town. "I'm a believable fellow."

His wink made her stiffen, and she gritted her teeth. This was Jeb. He was harmless. Still, undoing instincts honed through years of winks followed by unwanted attention wasn't going to happen overnight. She forced herself to relax and turned back toward the town. "Any clue how Heath or the others are getting on?"

"I heard Enrique's laughter as I passed the general store, but otherwise, nothing."

Turner backed out of the bush. "I'm heading into town. As an impartial observer, I can't help spread the rumors, but I'll be able to tell a better story if I see some of the others in action."

Jeb scowled. "Heath ordered you to stay put. If you draw attention to the others—"

"I answer to my readers, not the sheriff." Turner walked away, tossing over his shoulder, "But don't worry. I'll be discreet."

"That man's about as subtle as a rockslide," Jeb muttered.

She nodded, then turned her glare on the back of the saloon below. If only she could see through its walls. Were Heath and Cole doing what they'd promised? Or had the lure of drink, women, and "easy" money distracted them from their cause?

Jeb chuckled softly. "Is that a flame licking the back side of the saloon?"

Her heart stuttered, and she squinted. "Where?"

He leaned close, pointed one finger at her eyes, then

pretended to trace a straight line from there to the saloon's back door. "I'd guess right about there."

She scowled at the twinkle in his mischievous brown eyes. "What nonsense are you on about?"

"That glare of yours is hot enough to start a fire. For a second, I thought it had."

"You muttonhead." She smacked his shoulder.

He laughed, then sobered. "I'm guessing there's a history there."

She didn't bother replying to his cryptic statement and returned her attention to the town. Encouraging him with questions would only lead to more foolishness.

"Want to tell me about it?" His gentle tone drew a response against her will.

"About what?"

"Why you hate saloons." He cleared his throat. "I mean, I know all the usual reasons, but you seem to have a particularly strong hatred for that building."

"Not that one in particular," she admitted. "If I could, I'd burn every saloon in the world to the ground. Nothing but misery and heartache wait inside."

"And not just for the men who enter." Jeb spoke with a knowing tone.

Ginny refused to meet his gaze. They needed a change of subject. "Have you considered whether your sister may be helping Chavarria avoid us?"

"What?" Jeb's high-pitched squeak made it hard for her to keep a straight face.

"Sure. The longer it takes to catch him and his men, the longer you're gone from home." She crossed her arms. "I figure that's got to be a relief."

His belly laugh loosed her grin.

Long seconds passed in comfortable silence.

"She actually hates when I'm gone this long." His tone was

quiet, serious, the words spoken almost to himself. "She worries. She prays constantly and has a strong faith that God watches over me... But I know she still worries." He scuffed his boot in the dirt. "This kind of work...well, it's dangerous. Always hanging over us is the question of whether we'll make it back. If we'll see our families again." He rubbed the back of his neck. "Having family who rely on me...knowing how much they'll hurt if I don't return, makes these jobs harder."

Her chest tightened. Had Oliver ever worried for her like Jeb did his family? "Then why do it?"

"Because of my sister and her children." Jeb's voice filled with passionate conviction. "I want to make the world a better place—safer for everyone, but especially women and children." He gave a mirthless laugh. "My sister's not the only worrier. Every time I think about what happened to Heath's wife..."

Ginny spun toward him. "His what?" Heath was married? The memory of how she'd let him hold her beneath the oak trees filled her throat with bile. She clamped her lips tight, fingers curling into her palms. She'd known better.

Jeb paused, his eyes unfocused and pinched at the corners, as if seeing the memory in his mind's eye. "Two criminals looking for revenge after Heath's arrest of their friend led to the man's execution. They found Heath's house and his wife alone inside while we were away chasing someone else." He closed his eyes. "We found her body in the bedroom. Buried her the same day."

Ginny blinked. Heath was widowed. Not married. She released her fists. Then Jeb's words sank in, and she crossed her arms over her middle. Had they—? Ginny shut down the question before it reached her lips. Atkinson's face flashed in her mind. No. She would not think of him now. Nor ever again.

Yet what about the women of Lupine Valley Ranch? They'd come to work for her in good faith, seeking safety from their troubled pasts. Was she putting them in greater danger by spreading rumors about their mine like this? The idea had seemed like their best option when she'd convinced Heath to pursue it, but had her desperation to gain justice for Gabriella blinded her? She'd been so certain the gang would follow the easy target rather than search for the hidden mine. What if she were wrong?

Oblivious to her warring thoughts, Jeb continued. "That was five years ago. Heath took it hard. He'd never had a problem with drinking before, but after Susannah's death, it nearly cost him everything—his position, his reputation." He shook his head. "Took him a long time to move on with his life."

Heath was a drunkard like Oliver? Ginny turned away as fire chased ice through her veins. She should have known. No man—no matter how good he seemed—could ever be fully trusted. He may not be married, but she'd still been a fool to let him see so much of her heart.

Jeb absently plucked bits of scale-like leaves from the branch in front of him. "Heath's a fighter. But it's not just Susannah's death that hurt him. There's the whole mess with the Los Angeles sheriff. Heath had a tip about where Valadez was hiding. But that Sheriff Raymond tricked him, took Heath's tip, and stole the glory and reward. Heath's been trying to redeem himself ever since. He needs to catch this gang to secure his reelection next year."

Then this chase was about Heath's pride, not the safety of the people he was supposed to serve. And if he failed? If someone on the posse were killed? Heath would turn to drink again for solace. She'd seen it before—men claiming to have given up drink, only to start again with the first hardship or loss. Oliver had made the claim more than once. She kicked a small rock, sending it skittering out of the bush and down the slope. Once a drunkard, always a drunkard.

Jeb shrugged in her periphery. "I try to put it all in God's hands, though—my family, our jobs. I mean, it's all in His hands, anyway. Worrying is just our way of trying to pretend we have some control over this world. Which, of course, we don't. We can make the right choices and do our best to make this world a better place, but in the end, what happens is up to God."

Ginny's fingers dug into her sides. "Seems to me He's fallen asleep on the job."

"God never sleeps." Jeb's tone turned stern. "He's always watching, always guiding. Just because things don't go the way we think they should doesn't mean He's turned His back or stopped loving us. It just means we don't yet understand His wisdom well enough to perceive His love. And He does love us. I've seen too much of His handiwork to ever doubt that."

Ginny held her tongue, knowing from her many conversations with Biddie that a believer couldn't be reasoned with. Any argument from her would be wasted breath. Instead, she kept her attention fixed on the town's saloon.

When Heath had first explained his plan to spread their fake story while playing cards in the saloon, Ginny's instinct had been to protest. But, she reminded herself, Heath and Cole weren't like Oliver or the men who'd been drawn to him. Neither of them had swallowed so much as a drop of alcohol in all the days she'd been with the posse. Oliver had never gone more than two days without getting drunk. She'd thought she could trust Heath. Now she wondered what condition he and Cole would be in when they returned.

A shiver shook her, and she rubbed the handle of her pistol in its holster. She was no longer a young defenseless girl. This time, she'd be prepared to defend herself.

∾

*T*he curly wig beneath Heath's bowler felt secure enough, but the fake mustache he'd glued to his upper lip threatened to come loose. He checked that the other players at the table were preoccupied with their cards before catching Cole's eye across the table and lifting his brows. Then he glanced pointedly downward, hoping Cole would understand the question. He did. A subtle rub of Cole's hand across his mouth and a tiny nod let Heath know the mustache remained convincing.

A smoky haze hung heavy in the air, mingling with the warm scent of sweat and whiskey. One man sat at the bar, two flirted with women at a table near the back, and three played cards with Heath and Cole at a table in the center.

They each added a few coins to the pile at the center of the table. The cards were dealt with a practiced flick, and Heath let himself be swept into the rhythm of the game, playing the role of the indifferent gambler.

After another two rounds left him with only a little left to risk, he forced himself to keep his face neutral. Losing money was part of the act, though the weight of his losses made him clench his jaw in an effort to stay composed. Hopefully, his frustration added to the credibility of what they needed to say.

As discussed, Cole reassured him. "Don't worry. We'll get that back and more in two days."

Heath speared him with a practiced glare. "Shut up."

Cole said no more, and the game went on in silence.

Just as Heath was worrying the other players wouldn't take the bait, the burly man with a thick mustache won a round and called for drinks all around. When the barkeep brought the glasses, Thick Mustache immediately pushed one toward Heath and another toward Cole. "Drink up." He leaned in with a grin that was more of a sneer. "Unless you're too weak."

Faking insult, Heath grabbed the glass and caught Cole's gaze. "To success."

Taking his cue, Cole jumped to his feet in an overly enthusiastic cheer that drew the eyes of everyone in the room. As Cole downed his drink, Heath dumped his own on the floor beneath the table. By the time the others turned back, Heath had the empty glass in front of his chin as though he'd just downed the amber liquid the same as Cole.

The game continued, and the drinks kept flowing. Four more times, Cole created a different diversion, allowing Heath to discard his drink. When the fifth round arrived, Heath was about to take a pretend sip when the man who'd won his money in the first round gave him a hearty slap on the back. The unexpected force made the liquor spill over his lips and into his mouth. With the other man's eyes on him, Heath swallowed.

Heath's stomach churned as the fiery liquid burned its way down. He forced himself to laugh as he wiped at the alcohol splashed across his shirt.

Finally, Thick Mustache must have believed them sufficiently inebriated and began questioning Cole about their plans for tomorrow. Slowly, in bits and pieces, so as not to arouse suspicion, Cole and Heath shared the agreed-on rumor about a foolish female miner planning to transport garnet gems to San Francisco. Cole was clever, leaving the man to tease out every important detail. He made sure to whisper loudly that she'd already set out from her mine and provided key landmarks for the detour route Ginny planned to take from the stage road after Carrizo Creek Stage Station. He laughed drunkenly over the foolish female's idea that straying from the main road would make her harder to waylay when her plan did the exact opposite. Cole even made it seem as though he'd forgotten some of the details and only remembered the section of Ginny's route they planned to ambush—thus narrowing the distance the posse would need to monitor.

As they spoke, a man in a gray hat sitting at the bar glanced over his shoulder toward their table. Initially, Heath felt satisfaction that their efforts seemed to be working. But the longer they played, the more that satisfaction turned to unease. There was something strange about the man at the counter.

Gray Hat swiveled to fully face them with a smirk curving his dark beard. "What are the odds both beauty and bounty would deliver themselves together?"

The man's raucous laughter brought Heath to his feet. They needed to leave. Now.

Every player, including Cole, stared up at him.

"Sorry. I just remembered there's somewhere..." Remembering at the last moment that he was meant to be drunk, Heath deliberately slurred his words. "S-somewheres, to uh... I...let's go." He swayed on his feet and waved widely at Cole. "Come on." Without waiting, he pivoted and shuffled toward the door, ignoring the protests of the other players.

This had been a terrible idea. He'd known it the moment Ginny suggested it. Why hadn't he listened to his gut? He glanced over his shoulder to check that Cole was following.

Someone slammed into him from the front, sloshing alcohol across his shirt once more. Wonderful. At least Cole had followed his lead and was making his way toward the exit.

He pushed through the door, the cool night air hitting his face like a balm. They'd been inside longer than he'd realized. Despite knowing better, he glanced toward the ridge where he'd told Ginny to hide. Was she still there? Was there any way to convince her to forget this foolishness and return to questioning locals for leads? There must be. Because he couldn't risk losing another woman he cared for. And despite his best efforts, Heath cared far more for Ginny than was wise for either of them.

CHAPTER 13

*T*he nearly full moon slipped behind a layer of clouds as the cold bite of a late-November wind sliced through the sparse desert brush and threatened to steal Ginny's hat. She gripped the brim tightly as she peered over the ridge for any sign of Cole and Heath.

The rest of the men, including a tipsy Turner, had long since returned from their missions. Garret and Enrique gleefully reported that the couple who'd entered the store were later overheard gossiping with the blacksmith about the "foolish female miner." Since it was too risky to light a fire this close to town, the rest of the posse lounged on the ground behind her, eating the cold bread, jam, cheese, and apples Garret and Enrique had purchased at the general store. She knew better than trying to eat with her stomach clenched tight.

Where were Heath and Cole? Had they given in to the lure of alcohol, money, and women?

A light flickered in the upstairs window of the saloon.

She was going to be sick.

"What's that?" Miguel leaped to his feet and glared into the darkness, one hand on his holstered pistol.

The crunching of gravel met Ginny's ears. How had she missed it?

Unable to make out anything in the cloudy night, she palmed her own weapon as the rest of the men scrambled to alertness. "Who's—"

"It's me and Cole."

Heath's calm, sober voice drained the tension from her body like the cork pulled from a washtub. About time.

Jeb grinned, his teeth a pale gray amidst the black, as everyone else reclaimed their previous relaxed positions. "How'd it go?"

Heath's and Cole's figures finally separated themselves from the blackness as they drew within a few feet. The unmistakable odor of whiskey came with them.

Ginny stiffened.

"Change of plans." Despite his obvious indulgence, Heath's gait was steady and his words clear as he lifted a woman's dress in the air. "Enrique, you'll wear this so Ginny can stay behind."

"And Mr. Darcy's going to dance a polka." She crossed her arms. "Our plan's good. We stick to it. No matter what your whiskey-soaked brain says is better."

Heath's eyes widened. "My wh—"

"She's right," Miguel interrupted. "That won't work. The bandits will never buy Enrique as a woman."

Heath peeled his fake mustache free with the hand not holding the dress. "He's got the skinniest build of all of us, and we don't need them close enough to see his face. Just close enough to spring the trap."

Jeb shook his head. "I'm not sure that'll work. I know you want to protect—"

"I can protect myself." Ginny straightened her spine, meeting Heath's gaze with a narrowed stare. "I'm going ahead with the original plan, with or without your approval."

"Interfering with a lawman's duties is grounds for arrest." Heath's nostrils flared. "You gave your word to obey—"

"I promised a sheriff." She scraped the lingering taste of betrayal from her mouth and spit at his feet. "Not a drunk."

Heath recoiled as though she'd gut-punched him.

Good. Served him right for fooling her.

Jeb stepped forward, hands raised toward each of them in a calming gesture. "I'll ride with Ginny. One male escort won't be enough to scare off the bandits, but it'll give her a little more immediate protection."

"Whoever's with her will be at the greatest risk." Heath squared his shoulders. "It should be me."

Jeb shook his head, his voice firm. "You're too recognizable. The bandits will know it's a trap."

"You were both in town today," Ginny said. "What if they recognize you?"

"The only people we have to worry about recognizing me are the bandits." Jeb smirked. "And if any of them had been in town, we wouldn't be having this conversation. Remember, Chavarria's cousin owns the livery, not the blacksmith shop. That's why we sent Miguel there to speak Spanish with the livery boy and make sure the owner overheard."

Miguel smiled from his seated position on the ground. "Which he did."

Heath ripped the bowler and wig from his head. "Dogs-eat-it, Jeb. I don't want you down there either. I wasn't even sure using Enrique was smart." He paced two steps forward, then back again. "This whole thing is a bad idea. I never should've agreed to it." He stopped and slapped his hat onto his sweat-matted hair. "Forget it. The whole thing's off. We'll come up with—"

"It's too late for that." Ginny glared him down despite his superior height. "Rumors are already flying. You can either back me from a distance as we agreed or, better yet, go do something else and leave us grownups to handle it. But I'm moving forward with the plan." Fury crackled and flashed within her like lightning slicing through the parched desert sky. She pivoted on her heel and marched into the darkness, too livid to remain without taking actions that really would land her in jail.

~

The next morning, Heath resumed his protests, but the rest of the posse agreed that the plan they'd already set in motion was worth seeing through. While the men talked in circles trying to convince Heath, Ginny ignored them all and prepared to set out. The one change she'd agreed to was that when she left the rest of the posse behind, Jeb went with her. So while the rest of the posse rode ahead to scout the trail she and Jeb would follow the next day, the two of them rode south to Carrizo Creek Stage Station.

The fact that she felt safer with him at her side wasn't something she cared to examine. Instead, she'd spent the four-hour ride encouraging Jeb to entertain her with tales of his exploits as a deputy. Not that he'd needed much encouragement. If words were cattle, his herd would fill the state.

In keeping with the story they'd sold in town, they made a wide circle of the stage station and waited until dusk before riding in from the south—the direction her ranch was located.

Ginny entered the Carrizo Creek Stage Station ahead of Jeb. She tugged off her hat and brushed dust from her sleeves. The adobe structure offered a welcome break from the relentless wind outside. Standing by the large hearth with a wooden spoon in hand was the wiry station master they'd spied on two days prior.

"Evening." Ginny stomped the dirt from her boots before

moving farther into the room. "We'd like supper and a place to bed down for the night."

He squinted, studying them a moment before nodding. "Fifty cents apiece for a meal and a pallet. If you don't mind sharing the space with other travelers, I can clear a spot in the next room."

"We'll need *two* pallets." Ginny reached for the coins in her satchel. "But sharing the room with others is fine."

The station master's brows rose, but he nodded his agreement and accepted her payment.

Jeb leaned his rifle against the wall and stretched his back. "Got any coffee to go with that stew?"

"Of course." The station master chuckled. "Help yourselves to the pot while I fill your bowls."

A few minutes later, Ginny settled at the long table, spooning stew into her mouth. "I'm done in," she muttered, stifling a yawn. She glanced at Jeb, who was already leaning back in his chair, cradling a cup of the station's thick brew.

"You turning in already?" Jeb's eyes twinkled over the rim of his mug. How did he still have so much energy?

She pushed her bowl aside. "Sun'll be up before we know it, and I'd rather face it rested." Rising, she offered a polite nod to the station master. "Thanks for the meal."

"Room's through there." He pointed to a door behind her.

As she left the room, she heard Jeb say, "Have you heard the rumors that Chavarria's gang is somewhere in this region?"

There was only one other person in the sleeping room. The man appeared sound asleep, but she still spread her bedroll across the pallet farthest from the stranger. Then she checked her pistol and tucked it under her folded coat before lying down and letting sleep take her.

Shortly after dawn, the two of them set out on the northerly detour route Cole had given to the men at the saloon. Their horses kicked up a plume of dust as they traversed the wide sandy wash which led up a gradual slope onto a vast sunbaked desert mesa. Pancake-flat land scarred by jagged gorges stretched out around them, an ocean of tan, sage, and cinnamon speckled with cacti and overlaid with pale streaks of shimmering gold cast by the rising sun.

A strong, chilling gust rustled the dry brush and flapped Ginny's unbuttoned coat. Guilt nipped at her for spending a warm night indoors while the rest of the posse—minus Jeb—had slept outside in the blustering wind. No doubt a fire had been ruled too great a risk and they'd shivered through the night.

She squinted toward the east, but detecting Heath and the rest of the posse watching them from the hills beyond the mesa was impossible. Were the men still there, or had they moved on to the narrow sandstone gorge that awaited Jeb and Ginny just three or four relatively low hilltops and one sandy wash away?

In discussing their plans, it had been agreed the sandstone canyon would make the most likely ambush point. So Cole had purposely blurted out its description in his drunken ramblings, and the others had made sure to mention enough key details in their gossip—including that she would be staying the night at the Carrizo Creek Stage Station—for the bandits to follow the clue. It'd been a gamble that the gang wouldn't be able to organize fast enough to strike the station, but as she rode beside Jeb, it was clear that risk had paid off. But what if the rumors hadn't reached Chavarria yet? She scanned the desert surrounding them, but the only unusual movement was that of the gliding gray clouds that seemed to be chasing them across the valley.

"Did we move too fast?" She broke into Jeb's chatter about his family—his sister, deceased brother-in-law, and a seeming multitude of nieces and nephews, who apparently never sat still. "Maybe two days wasn't enough time for Chavarria to hear about my so-called gem shipment and take action."

Jeb's gaze searched the land as hers had done. "If we waited any longer, he'd have had a chance to dig deeper, find holes in our story, and get suspicious. Two days gives them just enough time to catch wind of the opportunity and scramble into place without time for too many questions."

Jeb resumed his storytelling, this time launching into a tale of how his nephew had fallen after climbing a tree. The story reminded her of the time Josie had fallen while climbing boulders. The resulting head injury had scared them all, but she'd recovered just fine.

Had Josie gotten into more mischief since Ginny had left? How bad was the cattle illness Gideon had mentioned to Turner? Were the cattle still fattening themselves on the last pasture near the new rain catchment, or had Carmen decided to drive them to the pasture closer to the spring? Ginny had expected the grass to hold out until December, but if the cows had eaten faster than she'd predicted or if Gideon suspected the field had become contaminated somehow, the herd had probably been moved. That was, if Gideon was still on the ranch. The question of whether Biddie was better, worse, or the same continuously circled in her head, as persistent as a hawk over its prey.

Jeb's story of his own sister's attempts to copy their mother's favorite cake recipe interrupted Ginny's worries.

She laughed at the sour face he made as he described her accidentally swapping the powdered sugar for the baking powder. "That sounds like something I'd do."

He chuckled. "I'm no daft hand with cooking, either, but our mother thought men should know their way around a kitchen—to help them get by until a wife came along. So she tried teaching me..."

He went into detail about a cookie-baking disaster, but somehow, his story stirred in her a yearning to return home. Not to check on the cattle or take up the reins of her operation...but to see Biddie and Gideon and all the others who'd claimed her ranch as their new home. Did she really miss the lively conversations that spilled over their evening meals? Ginny blinked. She did. What was wrong with her? She shifted in the saddle and glared at Mr. Darcy's mane. When had she gone soft?

The sandy desert valley narrowed to an arroyo barely wide enough to fit two wagons traveling abreast. Towering sandstone walls guarded both sides, and long, cooling shadows covered the trail as she and Jeb rode into the canyon's mouth.

Heath's signal—a soft, birdlike call—drifted through the canyon, her only reassurance they weren't alone.

The sky was fully consumed in dark gray, and gusting winds whipped stinging sand against any exposed skin. She glanced behind them as a curve erased sight of their entry point. There was no turning back now. Were the bandits waiting somewhere along this trail as the posse had hoped they would be?

Another bend several yards ahead concealed what awaited them. She clamped a hand on her hat and peered way up to spy the high cliff rims. She could stack her house on top of itself at least five times without reaching the lip. Wavy, horizontal lines ran along the sandstone walls, interrupted here and there by cracks and gaps where a cave-in must have occurred years prior. A few hearty plants had found ways to cram their roots into narrow gaps and grow from the cliff face.

After a little while, the canyon widened, and smooth sandstone walls gave way to tall, rugged cliffs as wrinkled and worn as an old woman's skin. Her gaze darted to the numerous dark crevices. Could a man climb into one? Were the bandits hidden amid the canyon's crags?

She shook her head. Surely, the climb was too much effort, and the bandits were most likely farther along the canyon in one of the places where the cliffs gave way to less intimidating slopes. Or even more likely, they were lying in wait along one of the multiple gorges that connected with this canyon.

Had Heath and his men spotted the bandits yet? Must not have, or she'd hear gunfire. She pressed her lips tight. What if Heath had brought a whiskey bottle or some other drink back from the saloon? She hadn't seen him with one, but that didn't mean he couldn't have a flask under his coat. A drunk man with a weapon was as dangerous as any bandit. Would the other men stop him from drinking while on the hunt? Had she been foolish to continue with the plan, knowing she couldn't count on Heath?

If Heath and the others didn't find Chavarria before the bandits made their move, she and Jeb would be at the center of the gunfight. What if something went terribly wrong? She'd never see Biddie, Gideon, Carmen, or any of the others again. At least not "this side of heaven," as Biddie would say.

She tightened her grip on the reins. Was heaven real? She'd seen enough in life to know God was real. What He thought of her—if He thought of her—she still wasn't sure. Biddie had quoted enough Scripture for Ginny to be confident that the Bible said God loved her—no matter her past mistakes. But she still struggled to see the evidence of that claim in her life.

The shadowed gorge narrowed again and seemed to close in around them. Acutely aware of Jeb's oddly silent presence beside her, Ginny inspected the narrow strip of blackened clouds overhead. The impending storm had swallowed the morning sun, leaving them to follow the canyon trail through gloom and thunder. One fat drop splatted on her sleeve. Then another. Then the rain fell quick as a stampede of cattle, crashing to the earth in a sudden, chaotic rush.

∾

*H*eath huddled against his horse's neck, keeping as much distance as he could from the edge of the canyon. Dark clouds had blocked out the sun, and cold rain hammered down, turning the world into a blur of gray and black. The already treacherous mesa above the trail Jeb and Ginny followed turned slick. More than once, his horse slipped, but he pressed on, with Garret not far behind him.

Turner had tried to insist on remaining with the posse so he could "authentically report the details of the action." But when Heath threatened to tie him up and leave him behind if he didn't stay away of his own accord, the chucklehead had reluctantly agreed to wait at their rendezvous point beyond the canyon's end.

Through the curtain of rain, Heath caught occasional glimpses of Cole, Enrique, and Miguel searching the opposite side of the narrow gorge. They were all far enough back so that Jeb and Ginny, riding down the middle of the canyon, couldn't see their fellow posse members but were close enough to spot any trouble brewing. If the bandits had caught wind of the rumors Heath and his posse had spread two days ago, they'd be hiding somewhere along these canyon edges, waiting for their chance to strike.

Heath's gaze darted over the muddy rocks and scrubby brush, searching for any sign of movement. The canyon and its surroundings remained eerily empty.

After nearly two hours, the downpour eased to a sprinkle, and Heath reached the end of the canyon, where the narrow gorge opened up into a wider valley. Still, there was no sign of the bandits. If the enemy had come and gone, the deluge had erased all traces. Heath let out a slow breath, his fingers curling tighter around the reins as he surveyed the valley. All this effort for nothing. Then again, the bandits' failure to take the bait meant Ginny and Jeb had remained safe.

Thank You, Lord.

Heath signaled to Garret with another birdlike trill. He worried his call might be lost in the wind and rain, but he prayed Jeb's nephew would catch enough to understand. They'd have to regroup and consider their next move. Something that wouldn't put two of the people he cared about most in such great danger.

At the agreed-upon point, Ginny and Jeb left the valley, climbing a small hill that led to the rendezvous location out of sight from the main trail.

Heath scanned their drenched surroundings one last time to no avail. The bandits hadn't appeared. He led Garret across the small valley and over the ridge Ginny and Jeb had disappeared behind.

Cole and Enrique joined them, out of view from the trail through the canyon.

Heath searched the direction Cole and Enrique had come from. "Where are Turner and Miguel?"

"Miguel needed to..." Enrique, looking as damp and grim as Heath felt, glanced at Ginny, his cheeks reddening. "He'll be right here."

Heath nodded and addressed the group. "Well, I think it's clear th—"

A volley of gunfire cut through his words.

Garret's horse reared up with a terrified whinny, eyes rolling wildly. The young man clung desperately to the saddle horn as his mount wheeled and bolted, thundering away across the muddy ground.

"Garret!" Heath's shout was lost in the chaos. His spooked gelding pranced sideways, tossing its head. He struggled to control the animal while pulling his revolver from its holster. "It's an ambush! Go, go, go!"

Cole and Enrique galloped from the clearing after Garret.

But Mr. Darcy reared with a shrill neigh. Ginny threw her

weight forward, wrapping her arms around her horse's neck. Her lips moved, but Heath couldn't hear whatever she said to her gelding.

Beside her, Jeb's mount bucked, nearly unseating him. Clinging to the reins, he fought to control the panicked animal.

A brown hat popped up from behind a boulder, and Heath fired. Unfortunately, his shot went wide thanks to his unsettled steed.

More gunfire rang out from bushes at his left. Heath returned fire just as the thunder of hooves grew on his right. A trio of riders burst from behind a set of boulders and charged after Cole, Enrique, and Garret.

Heath fired two shots after them, but they were too quickly out of range.

Finally, Ginny got Mr. Darcy under control and thundered away. A moment later, Jeb and his horse followed suit. Heath brought up the rear, sending more shots into the brush and rocks behind them until the clearing was out of sight and his weapon clicked empty.

"Fan out!" He shouted as the rain increased again. "It'll make us harder to shoot."

Ginny moved right, and Jeb drifted left as they raced across the muddy ground ahead of him, their horses kicking up sprays of water with each stride.

Slick fingers frustrated Heath's attempts to reload.

From behind, more gunshots boomed, and the pounding of hooves grew louder.

With his revolver finally full, Heath twisted in the saddle. Four more bandits were chasing them. He jerked his rifle from its sheath and fired back as he rode.

Jeb did the same. Where were Cole and Enrique? Had Garret managed to regain control of his horse?

Ginny joined the exchange of bullets with the bandits behind them. He wanted to shout at her to quit shooting and just ride away—leave the fight to the men. But it'd be a waste of breath. Instead, he let her cover him as he reloaded.

Far ahead, the terrain opened up into a winding, sandy valley sparsely dotted with scrub brush and large rocks. Heath caught glimpses of Cole, Enrique, and Garret weaving between the obstacles, still being pursued by the three mounted bandits.

He urged his gelding faster, desperate to catch up and protect them from the shots their pursuers continued to fire.

Without warning, Garret toppled from his horse. He must have been shot. But how badly? *Please Lord, let him still be alive.*

With the bandits right on their heels, Cole and Enrique had no choice but to continue on, leaving Jeb's nephew in the wet sand.

Shots echoed before and behind. A bullet whizzed past Heath's shoulder, but he couldn't drag his gaze from the scene ahead.

Enrique jerked forward, slumped across the neck of his horse. His body appeared as limp as a rag doll as his horse carried him around a bend.

God, no! Please, no!

A loud bang rang out to Heath's left. He whipped his head around to see Miguel gallop from behind an outcropping fifty yards beyond Jeb. Their translator was firing his rifle at the outlaws pursuing Cole, Enrique, and Garret. *Thank the Lord.*

He scanned their surroundings, but Turner was still nowhere in sight.

As the five riders ahead made a wide turn around a tall mound of dirt, it suddenly became clear that Miguel's aim wasn't on the bandits. It was on Cole. Before Heath could react, Miguel pulled the trigger.

Heath's father-in-law slumped to one side, barely managing to keep his seat as he disappeared around a curve in the valley with the bandits closing in behind him.

"No!" Heath's shout drew Miguel's attention. The traitor had the gall to smirk as he turned his weapon on Jeb and pulled the trigger.

With a shout, Heath's best friend fell from his saddle.

Rain and tears blurred Heath's vision as he fired three times before he managed to clip Miguel's forearm, making him drop his weapon. Fury burned in his veins as he took aim at Miguel's chest.

"Heath!" Ginny's shout stalled Heath's trigger finger. Never had he heard such fear in her voice. A chill ran down his back. Holding his aim steady, he slowly turned his head just enough to spot her.

With her hands on Jeb's wound, she knelt on the ground beside Heath's friend, who lay sprawled on his back with Sebastian Debert aiming a rifle at his chest. At the same time, Cesar Landa—Chavarria's right-hand man—pressed his pistol to the back of Ginny's head.

⁓

The unmistakable click of a revolver hammer being pulled back echoed in Ginny's ears as the hard metal of what could only be a gun barrel pressed against her skull. Behind her, a man's thickly accented voice growled low. "Now you watch her die."

"No!" From twenty feet away, panic flashed in Heath's eyes. Miguel took advantage of his distraction and knocked Heath's weapon to the ground.

"Wait!" Bile surged up her throat. "If you shoot me, if you shoot any more of us," she shouted, her voice strong and steady despite the trembling inside, "you'll never know where my mine is! There's thousands of dollars' worth of garnet ore still waiting to be processed."

The man behind her laughed. "You think we don't know that's a lie, Ginny Baker? Your mine is played out."

So she'd been right to think these men knew whose ranch they'd been terrorizing for nearly three years. "No. That's the lie I've been telling to keep men like you from trying to find it." The gun barrel dug deeper into her skull.

With the shooting stopped, two other bandits dismounted and moved in closer, weapons still in hand. None of them Chavarria. Was Chavarria the man behind her? The voice didn't sound like his.

Whoever it was scoffed. "You expect us to believe you lied to this posse too?"

How did they know what she'd told the posse?

Ginny exhaled a slow breath, keeping her expression impassive, her posture confident. "If you know who I am, you know I don't trust any men. Even lawmen."

The barrel of the gun slid around to her temple as the man came to stand in front of her. Cesar Landa. Her stomach clenched at the gleeful evil in his dark eyes. "Yet you work with them to trap us, and now while your hands try to stop his blood, you bargain for their lives."

She lifted one shoulder, forcing herself to hold his glare. "I said I don't trust them. Don't mean I want them dead. Do you want the gems or not?"

CHAPTER 14

eath held his breath as Landa studied Ginny's unflinching gaze. Would he buy her lie? No matter what she'd told the gang's most violent member, Heath knew she hadn't lied to the posse. If Landa didn't believe her, he'd have no reason to keep any of them alive.

Except Ginny.

Fire roared through Heath at the thought of what would become of her if Landa killed them all and took her captive. It took everything in him not to hurl himself at Landa. Any defensive move on his part would only speed his death, leaving Ginny alone.

After several tense seconds, Landa asked, "*¿Qué opinas, Miguel? ¿Está mintiendo?*"

Alvio Monteres shifted his aim toward Heath, allowing Miguel to lower his weapon and approach Ginny.

He studied her, his brow furrowed. "*Es astuta. Tendría sentido que ocultara la verdad sobre la mina. Si yo estuviera en su lugar, no confiaría en nadie con algo tan valioso como una mina de granates.*" He shrugged. "*Tal vez esté mintiendo, pero seríamos unos tontos si la matáramos antes de comprobarlo.*" He smirked and switched to

English as he looked Ginny up and down. "Besides, if it's a trick, we can still make her pay." Had the traitor ever looked at Ginny that way before, Heath would have knocked him flat and sent him back to Alameda. As it was, with weapons pointed at Jeb, Ginny, and himself at close range, he could do no more than pray.

The distant rumble of hoofbeats made everyone turn. Heath's gut twisted as three riders came into view, leading three familiar horses—Garret's Palomino, Enrique's chestnut, and Cole's dun.

As the bandits approached, Heath's stomach sank at the sight of empty saddles, rifles missing, and streaks of dried blood marring the horses' flanks.

"*¡Ya era hora!*" Landa snapped as if he were the leader. Where was Chavarria? "*Donde estan los demas?*"

The front rider was a bearded man with a jagged scar running through one brow. Something about the man's face tugged at Heath's memory, but the connection remained frustratingly out of reach. He caught Heath's gaze. "We left them bleeding out in the mud." With a smirk, he dismounted and tossed a bloodied hat to the ground.

Heath's breath caught. It was Enrique's.

The wiry rider swung off his horse holding a pistol that Heath recognized as Garret's. He offered the revolver to Landa.

Landa made sure Miguel had Ginny covered, then put his own pistol in its holster and accepting Garret's. He glanced at the weapon before tucking it into his pants at his back. "Did you search their pockets?"

The last rider dismounted, his cold, flat eyes sweeping over the group before he deposited coins and papers into Landa's waiting hands.

"Good. Now check them." Landa's chin jerk encompassed Heath, Ginny, and Jeb.

The bearded stranger rummaged through Heath's pockets

first. He took Heath's knives and his money pouch before he found the leather thong holding Susannah's locket and jerked it over Heath's head. "That's mine!" Heath's rage drove the shout from his lips.

"*Déjame ver eso.*" Landa gestured for the bearded man to come.

He gave Landa Heath's locket.

With a wink, Landa slipped it on.

"Give it back!" Heath roared as he lunged toward Landa.

Landa stepped back but kept his pistol against Ginny's head. "Stop or she dies!"

Heath swallowed hard and forced himself to remain still even though every ounce of him wanted to snatch up his pistol and start shooting. Especially when the bearded man searched Ginny.

A matching fire blazed in her gaze, though her hands didn't budge from pressing against Jeb's wound. Thankfully, the bandit didn't linger over the job or take liberties. Heath wasn't sure he'd have been able to control himself otherwise.

By the time Jeb's pockets had been cleaned out, Heath's knuckles ached in his clenched fists.

Landa grinned. "Now tie their wrists so we can get going. *Hemos perdido suficiente tiempo.*"

Heath's throat thickened. Cole, Enrique, and Garret were gone—or as good as—and it was his fault. He'd brought them here. They'd trusted him, and now their horses and gear were trophies for the men who'd killed them. How would he tell Agatha that neither of the men she loved most would be coming home, or Garret's mother that her eldest son was dead?

Jeb grunted as the bandits forced him to his feet with Ginny at his side, and Heath shook himself. Getting lost in guilt would have to wait. He couldn't save the dead, but he could still fight for the living.

~

*T*he following night, Ginny stumbled forward as Miguel gave her a rough shove into an old crumbling adobe home in a canyon at the eastern base of the San Ysidro Mountains. Their translator's betrayal burned as sharp as acid in her gut as she staggered, her feet catching on the uneven dirt floor. She barely managed to keep herself upright. Her wrists, bound tightly in front of her, were rubbed raw from two days of trekking roughly northwest through the desert.

She'd had no clue where the gang was driving them. This decaying structure was far from any trail. She'd only been grateful their march was in the opposite direction of her ranch. Why the bandits had driven them so far from where she'd claimed the mine was, she didn't know. Nor did she care. The farther they went from her mine's fake location, the longer she'd have to come up with a plan to save her, Jeb, and Heath. Not that she could think clearly. The lack of food and the minimal water Miguel and the bandits had allowed her left her mind fogged.

She shouldn't count their former guide as separate from the gang holding them hostage. His betrayal of the posse's plans and assistance in herding her, Heath, and Jeb across the desert made it plenty clear where his loyalties lay.

She glanced at Heath beside her. A muscle ticked in his jaw as his sharp eyes took in their surroundings, no doubt searching for any way out—a way back to the injured men they'd been forced to leave behind. Was there any chance that Cole, Garret, and Enrique were still alive? What about Turner? There'd been no sign of the reporter at the rendezvous point or during the chase that followed. Had he betrayed them the way Miguel had? But if he had, why wasn't he with the gang now?

On her other side, Jeb grunted with each shuffled step. Beads of sweat dotted his pale brow from the strain of walking with the gunshot in his left arm. At least she'd been allowed to bind his wound to slow the bleeding. With the amount of darkened blood staining his shirt, she wasn't sure how he remained upright. Possibly it was determination to return for his injured nephew that kept him moving, thin as that hope might be. Whatever drove him, Jeb's silence since the shootout shouted the severity of his pain and suffering.

Lord, if You're listening, Jeb's a good man who says his faith is in You. It'd sure be nice if You could prove his faith justified and keep him alive. If You wouldn't mind rescuing the rest of us while You're at it, that'd be appreciated too. Including Mr. Darcy, please. Thank You. Um, amen.

She'd heard too many stories of bandits riding their stolen horses until the animals died beneath them not to include Mr. Darcy in her prayer. Not that she'd be foolish enough to wait on divine intervention. Her life had more than proven that getting out of this fix was up to her. Still, she felt better after giving prayer a try. Biddie would be pleased if she knew. Thoughts of her sister brought a lump to Ginny's throat and strength to her spine. She would see Biddie again. They just needed some way to escape.

~

*H*eath followed Ginny and Jeb into the derelict structure.

"If you try anything"—Cesar Landa's dark eyes flicked between the three of them—"you won't live to regret it. Tomorrow, you take us to the mine"—he pointed his pistol at Ginny—"or your friends pay the price."

He slammed the door, kicking up a thick layer of dust. The sagging adobe walls shuddered, and tiny rockfalls cascaded to the floor. The light of a full moon poured through the gaping roof, and at the front, firelight from the campfire they'd passed flickered through holes in the bricks.

Heath swallowed uncivilized words. Landa had no intention of letting them go, even if Ginny led the bandits to the mine. Not because she was lying about the gem ore, but because men like these couldn't be trusted. Killing this posse was the safer bet for these criminals than leaving her, Heath, and Jeb alive to try again to capture Chavarria and his gang. Especially now that they knew the location of this hideout. Landa had made no effort to blindfold or otherwise disorient them.

Where was Chavarria? For the past two days, Landa had barked out orders as if he were in charge. Was it possible Chavarria had been arrested or killed and the posse hadn't yet learned the news?

Beside him, Ginny glared at the walls enclosing them as she flexed her wrists against her tight bonds. Heath wanted to punch Landa. Her skin had to be chafed raw. Heath's certainly was.

Jeb sank to the floor, his back against an unstable wall.

"We need to come up with a plan." Heath clenched his fists, too angry to sit despite his fatigue. "There's no telling how long the others can last without help."

Jeb winced, shifting his wounded arm as if seeking a more comfortable position. "I can't tell my sister I let her firstborn die." His voice was tight, rough from dehydration and worry.

Ginny pressed her lips together. "You won't need to. We're going to get out of here."

Heath stared at what was left of the darkened adobe ceiling, frustration and regret tangling up inside him as cutting as a ball of barbed wire. He'd made a fool's choice letting Ginny come along on this hunt at all. Letting her talk her way into playing bait had been even worse. And now because of his stupidity, he and Ginny were captured along with Jeb, who was also wounded.

Heath tried not to consider what had become of Cole, Garret, and Enrique. At the very least, they'd each been wounded in the gunfight, and it seemed none had been able to stop the bandits from looting their bodies and stealing their horse. Everything seemed to point to his friends being dead. But he would not give up hope until he saw their bodies for himself.

And if they were dead, he'd make sure Miguel hanged for his betrayal. If by God's mercy his men survived their wounds and abandonment, he'd still make sure Miguel spent the rest of his life behind bars. How had Heath so badly misjudged the man's character?

And where was Turner? He couldn't imagine the reporter in cahoots with Miguel, yet Turner should have been waiting for them. As wrong as Heath had been to trust Miguel, he had to consider that his assessment of Turner might have been equally as mistaken. But if it was, the governor had also been fooled. That seal on the letter Turner had presented to Heath had been real.

Heath's gaze drifted to Ginny. She stood, hands bound, in the center of the dilapidated room, her shoulders squared as she scanned the walls with a determined expression that layered a hard veneer over her natural beauty. He almost relaxed. If anyone was brave and clever enough to find a way out of this situation, it was Ginny. But she shouldn't be facing such a problem. This was exactly why the only way he could see a future with her was if he gave up his duty, his calling to protect the citizens of this state, and moved to Lupine Valley Ranch, where his only duty would be providing for and protecting Ginny—assuming she'd accept his help.

The image of such a future ignited a warmth deep in his chest.

But how could he walk away from his position as sheriff? This capture, this whole mess was a reminder that men like him were needed to keep the peace. To protect the innocent. Giving up his badge to chase after dreams of a quiet life with Ginny would be selfish. Foolish, even. The kind of decision that would leave good men and women vulnerable to gangs like Chavarria's.

He clenched his fists. There could be no future for him and Ginny. Not so long as men like Chavarria and Landa roamed California.

A soft gasp brought his attention back to Ginny as her face drained of color so fast that he reached out, certain she was going to faint. Panic flared hot in his chest. Was she hurt? Had she been hiding an injury from him this whole time? Fool woman! He ran his hands down each of her arms, scanning her clothes for signs of blood. "Ginny, where—"

Her hands slapped over his mouth, her eyes wide. "Shh!" Her fingers trembled against his lips.

What on earth had her so scared? He studied her in the silvery moonlight. Her gaze was unfocused. She was listening—straining to hear something beyond the walls surrounding them. The pulse in her wrist galloped against his cheek, matching the breakneck speed of his own heartbeat as he strove to discern what was being said.

What did Ginny hear or think she heard? He heard nothing but the raucous boasting of men confident in their victory mixed with the laughter of the lone woman Heath had spied just before they'd been shoved inside this sorry excuse for a home. She'd been lurking in the shadows as if hoping not to be seen, and making him wonder if she was here of her own free will. But her presence had been erased by the reality of being locked in for the night and worry for the fate of his posse.

He gently pulled Ginny's fingers from his lips. With everything they'd been through, he'd never seen her so shaken. What could possibly be worse than what they'd already faced?

He wanted to ask but forced himself to respect her command for silence.

After several seconds, she whispered so softly he barely heard her. "It can't be."

Before he could make sense of her words, she pulled away, moving toward the door, her bound hands reaching for the latch. He grabbed her arm, pulling her back. "Are you crazy?" He leaned closer. "They'll shoot you if you open that door."

She didn't answer, didn't even seem to hear him. Her gaze was fixed on the door as if she could see through it, see something—or someone—beyond. And then, as if on cue, the door swung open, held by a man who hadn't been among those who'd ambushed Heath's posse—a man in a the same gray hat he'd seen at the saloon. When he caught Heath's glare, the man's scowl turned to a smirk, and he winked.

From behind him, a feminine voice said, "*Sal de mi camino!*"

The guard stepped aside, and the beautiful Mexican woman about Ginny's age that Heath had noticed before strode inside, a grin spread across her face as though she'd just won a prize. She carried a bowl of water, a sliver of soap, and a rag, but her sharp eyes didn't match the joyous grin.

Ginny sucked in a breath, clearly about to speak, but in an eerie imitation of Ginny's own move, the woman slapped one hand over Ginny's mouth and wrapped her other arm around Ginny as if to hug her. The woman's grin momentarily vanished, replaced by the hard expression Heath was used to seeing on criminals. "Keep quiet. I'm here to help," she whispered. Then she grinned again and looked over her shoulder at the man guarding the open door, her body blocking his view of her hand on Ginny's mouth. "You see, they're so tired, they can barely stand. I'm perfectly safe."

On the slim chance the woman's claim of wanting to help was legitimate, Heath played along by sagging against the wall behind him as though his knees were threatening to give out.

The guard scowled. "I still don't—"

"Do you want to stand there watching me clean their wounds while everyone else feasts on my chicken mole? There will be nothing left for you if you do."

The door shut behind her with a thud that echoed in the small room. The woman's brown eyes darted between Jeb and Heath before returning to Ginny. "Promise you won't speak." Her voice was low and urgent.

Ginny's wide eyes had narrowed to a glare so intense, it threatened to singe the air between them. She struggled against the woman's hold, but her lithe body must disguise her strength because she maintained her hold.

Heath straightened, ready to pry the stranger off Ginny, but to his shock, Ginny stopped fighting and nodded. He hesitated.

The woman lifted a single, questioning brow. "I have your word?"

Ginny's impatient huff was loud enough to escape the palm over her mouth.

The woman studied Ginny another moment, then slowly pulled her hand away.

Ginny immediately whisper-shouted, "I buried you!"

CHAPTER 15

*G*inny glared at Gabriella. How dare the woman just stand there? Alive. Breathing. Perfectly healthy. What of the bone fragments she'd retrieved from the ashes of the original ranch house? Pieces she'd believed belonged to Gabriella. Before Ginny's brain caught up with her hands, the back of her left hand was stinging, and Gabriella's cheek bore a large pink mark.

Gabriella blinked, moonlight glistening off the tears filling her big brown eyes. "I deserved that."

Ginny barely managed to keep her voice low. "You were my friend!" She had mourned Gabriella, grieved her as a sister, buried her memory along with so many others from life at Lupine Valley Ranch before Oliver's murder. But there Gabriella stood, a face she never thought she'd see again. "I trusted you." The betrayal threatened to break her as nothing else had.

"I know, and I'm so sorry." Gabriella knelt beside Jeb, set down the bowl, and began untying the bandage around his wound.

Ginny lunged and clawed at Gabriella's arm. "Get away from him."

Her friend—no, *former* friend—shrank away. "I just want to help. If his wound isn't cleaned, infection will set in, if it hasn't already."

Heath came to Ginny's side. "She's right. It needs washing."

"Then I'll do it." Ginny ripped the rag and then the soap from Gabriella's hand. Then she knelt beside the bowl next to Jeb. She waited for Gabriella to leave, but the fake didn't move. As Ginny worked to clean Jeb's wound, part of her wanted to shout at Gabriella to leave. But the part of her that wanted answers won. Without pausing or looking away from her task, Ginny demanded, "Why?"

"My name is Gabriella Torres."

"What?" Ginny cast the woman she'd always known as Gabriella Hernandez a confused look. Memories crashed over Ginny like waves. Gabriella had shown up at the ranch years ago, young and scared, tethered to that no-good boyfriend, Ángel, as surely as a calf caught in a cougar trap. Recognizing the caged look in Gabriella's eyes, Ginny had done what she could—little as it was—to shield her from Ángel's unpredictable fury. In return, Gabriella had done her best to distract Oliver whenever his drinking turned angry.

They'd quickly become friends—something Ginny had never had, nor expected to have. Despite herself, Gabriella's wide, earnest eyes and dreams of a life free from the men who tried to control them had ignited a tiny spark of hope inside Ginny. And when Gabriella had found the mine, that spark of hope had flickered into a small flame, its light resurrecting her own long-discarded dreams of a happy future.

As the black of each night gave way to the gray of dawn, they'd dug their treasures in secret. While the men slept off the previous night's debauchery, they'd whispered dreams of escape, planning a future far from the likes of Ángel and Oliver. Giving up her last hope of earning Oliver's love had been painful, but Gabriella had convinced her she deserved a better life.

Then the attack happened. The gunshots. The fire. Ginny had been sure Gabriella was gone. Murdered like all the others. Their dreams turned to ash with everything and everyone else.

Ginny's heart twisted painfully as she stared at the woman she thought she'd lost forever. "What do you mean, your name is Torres?"

Gabriella wrung her hands, her eyes downcast, voice low. "After Ángel...after he beat me so badly that I thought I would die..." Her voice faltered, and Ginny felt a pang of empathy despite herself. She had nursed Gabriella through that beating, tended the bruises and cuts, set her broken arm, and seen the shattered spirit in her friend's eyes.

"I wrote to my brother, Fedorro Torres." Gabriella's voice was steadier now. "He was one of Valadez's men, Chavarria's now. I was desperate, Ginny. I had no other way out. I told Fedorro about the gems we had found, hoping it would convince him to come and free me from Ángel. I never thought...I never imagined they would kill everyone."

Ginny's heart slammed against her ribs. "But they did." She spoke through gritted teeth. "They did, Gabriella! They killed them all, and I thought they'd killed you!" Her voice cracked with the weight of her grief. "How could you do that? How could you tell them about our mine? How could you..." *Leave me?* The last two words caught in Ginny's throat.

Gabriella shook her head, her eyes glistening with tears. "No, I swear, I didn't tell them about the mine. I only said the gems were won in a card game, just to get them to come. After... after the attack, I tried to get them to leave quickly. I knew you weren't hurt. I'd been watching. I knew you had to be hiding

somewhere without a weapon, or you'd have joined the fight."
She reached for Ginny, but Ginny flinched, and Gabriella let
her hand fall. "I was so relieved—you have no idea how
relieved—that you didn't come out. I didn't know what I would
do. So I urged them to leave. Told them the neighbors would
surely see the smoke and ride to the rescue." Her voice faded so
that Ginny could barely hear her. "I didn't know you thought I
was dead. I thought... I thought you must have seen me ride
away and hated me for leaving with the men who murdered
Oliver. For all his faults, I know you loved him."

Ginny waited for the anger, the hatred Gabriella's actions
deserved. It didn't come. Instead, a cold numbness clawed its
way out of her chest and over her skin, filling her body with a
heavy stillness she couldn't shake.

Tears spilled down Gabriella's face, her voice breaking. "I'm
so sorry, Ginny. Please, you have to believe me. I never meant
for any of that to happen. I thought they'd be satisfied with the
gems—"

"Our gems." The words burst from her lips quick as a bullet
from a rifle.

"Yes." She nodded, wiping the tears from her cheeks.
"You're right. They were our gems, and I had no right giving
them away without your permission. I was desperate. But I
know that's no excuse. I only hope that someday, you can find a
way to forgive me."

Never. The angry thought spurred movement in Ginny's
limbs. She silently resumed cleaning Jeb's wound.

He placed his hands over hers, stilling her motion.

She looked into his gentle, pain-filled gaze. "I can see you're
hurting...but...everyone makes mistakes. That's why...God sent
His son to die for our sins. Just as we...have been forgiven
much, so we are called to...to forgive others."

Ginny jerked her hands free and dunked the bloody rag in
the water, then wrung it out with more strength than necessary.

"You forgive her, then. I—" *Can't.* Again, the word stuck in her throat. This time because she didn't want to be a liar like Gabriella. The truth wasn't that she couldn't forgive Gabriella, it was that she didn't want to. Same as she didn't want to forgive Clyve for trying to kill her brother—no matter his reasons. First, Clyve had betrayed her, now Gabriella. Who next? Her gaze flitted to Heath. Then back to Jeb's watchful eyes. No. Forgiveness softened a person, made them weak and vulnerable to more hurt.

"I ain't fool enough to trust no one who could do what she did." Ginny untucked her bodice and began ripping the hem off—a job ten times more difficult and painfully slow with her hands bound. The fabric really should be boiled and dried before applying it as a bandage, but she doubted the bandits would allow her access to fire and boiling water. So the sweaty fabric would have to do as it was. It was cleaner than any other part of her outfit.

"Forgiveness doesn't require you to trust her. Forgiveness is a...gift—a letting go of resentment and anger. It's a...releasing of the desire for revenge. Trust is a separate thing and must be earned."

"Says the man helping chase a band of criminals across the state."

"Justice is not revenge. My goal isn't to make these men suffer. It's to hold them accountable for the wrongs they've done."

Was this why Heath's posse had seemed so different from the ones usually rounded up right after the crime? From the beginning, she'd noticed their lack of hate-filled words. Heath's men held no respect for the men now holding her captive, but neither had she heard them express any desire for exacting pain or carrying out a swift execution. Instead, their focus had always been to capture first, kill only if necessary.

And now Jeb preached forgiveness. Maybe they were better people than she was. Or maybe they were fools.

Ginny finished tying the new bandage in place and stood without responding. What was there to say? Jeb asked her for something she couldn't give. Not now. Maybe not ever.

Gabriella retrieved the supplies she'd brought in. "Whether you forgive me or not, I want to help you now—help all of you escape."

Ginny's chest tightened. "You claim you ain't after my trust, yet you expect me to believe you're going to help us? I don't think so." She stabbed a finger toward the door. "Just go. I don't want your help."

Gabriella looked as though she might argue, her mouth opening, but Ginny glared her down. Gabriella closed her mouth, shoulders slumped in defeat as she turned toward the door and paused. With a loud inhale, Gabriella straightened and knocked on the door. It opened to reveal the scowling guard who must be her brother. The family resemblance was obvious now that Ginny was looking. With an energy to match her initial entry, Gabriella slipped from the room, and the door creaked shut behind her.

The room fell silent under the weight of Jeb's and Heath's stares.

Heath cleared his throat. "Was that wise?"

"We can't trust her," Ginny said, her voice hard.

"She seemed earnest to me," Jeb argued. "And the others are counting on us to return for them before it's too late."

"All the more reason we can't wait around for whatever scheme Gabriella thinks she can pull." Ginny shuffled to within a few inches of the back wall, running her hands over the bricks, searching for a weak point. "I'm getting us out of here."

If only she had a clue how to do it without alerting the bandits outside.

~

*H*eath's backside grew numb on the cold, hard dirt, and his wrists chafed against the rough rope, but he ignored the discomfort, focusing instead on the slivers of conversation filtering through the cracked wooden door. The bandits weren't exactly making an effort to keep their voices down. A sure sign they didn't plan to leave him, Ginny, or Jeb alive.

Ginny gave up her inspection of the back wall and turned toward the only other exterior wall on the left. What did she plan to do? Kick out a brick? With the state of the structure, she probably could, but the bandits were bound to hear any brute-force tactics. Without the weapons the bandits had stolen, she, Jeb, and Heath would wind up right back where they started. Or Landa would make good his promise, and they'd be dead.

Regardless, Ginny's jaw was set, lips pressed tight, and he didn't need the light of the full moon to know there was pain behind the determination in her eyes. Everything he knew about her told him she didn't let many people close. And tonight, she'd learned her friend—the woman Ginny had left her ranch to seek justice for—was not only alive but had betrayed her and joined up with the same bandits that had murdered Ginny's pa and burned down her home.

Heath had seen Ginny stick out the miseries of the trail without complaint and hold her own in a gunfight without flinching. But this was different. A betrayal like that cut deep, and he sensed this wasn't the first such betrayal Ginny had suffered. But for all he could tell of her suffering, he had no idea what to do about it. All he could do was keep her alive long enough to give her the chance to heal. Which meant trusting Gabriella to help them escape.

Despite her past, Heath's gut told him Gabriella was sincere in her remorse and her offer. He could be wrong, but he usually wasn't. Besides, he couldn't see any other way out.

Jeb slumped against the wall on Heath's other side, his bound hands twitching as he slept.

Heath sucked air through his teeth just loud enough to gain Ginny's attention.

She turned to stare down at him. "What?"

Heath jutted his chin toward Jeb and whispered. "He's got the right idea. We need to get some rest if we want to make good our escape."

"You rest. I'm figuring a way out of here." She turned back to the wall.

Sighing, Heath rested his head against the wall and let his eyes flutter shut.

A voice from outside filtered in. "What about them Gaskills? I heard they're hard men to kill."

Heath straightened at mention of the brothers who owned Campo, California, the tiny town closest to Ginny's ranch.

"You worry too much," another man answered. "With the men joining us from Mexico, we'll more than outnumber them."

Heath leaned closer to the door, catching more of the bandits' conversation. Some of it was in Spanish, and he made a silent vow to become fluent in the language once this was over. His limited understanding did help him discern that at least nine more men planned to join them for the raid. He also caught something about them already having a spy in place.

From what he could tell, they fully expected to take Luman and Silas Gaskill by surprise and capture the town with little fight. The bandits' laughter grated his ears as they plotted to raid Campo as soon as they were done locating and securing the ore from Ginny's mine.

He jerked his shoulders to yank the ropes around his wrists and flexed his hands as he pulled against the restraints. No way was he letting these devils hurt more people. The unyielding bindings mocked his efforts.

He looked up at Ginny, who'd grown still at the mention of her nearest town. "I won't let them do it."

"*We* won't." Ferocity snapped in her eyes. Then they closed, and she dug dirty fingers into her scalp with a frustrated groan. "But I can't find a way to loose these bricks that won't cause a ruckus."

He sucked in a breath, bracing for her protest. "Gabriella seemed genuine. I think she wants to help us."

"Then you're a bigger fool than I took you for." Ginny kicked the packed-dirt floor. "She lied to me for more than a year. Tricked me into thinking she actually cared." Her voice cracked on that last word. "And you expect me to believe anything that comes out of her mouth?" She barked a humorless laugh. "Not on your life. For all we know, this is another trick."

"To what end? If they want us dead, they've got us. There isn't much we can do on our own." Heath raised to his feet and stepped as close as he dared. "You must see she risked herself by speaking with us at all. She didn't have to do that." Keeping his words just above a whisper, he waved his bound hands toward the closed door. "She could've stayed out there where you'd never have known she was here."

"So what?" Ginny's expression remained unyielding.

"So"—he said a small prayer for patience—"we're out of options. You said yourself you can't find a quiet way out of here, and without our weapons, quiet is our only option."

Ginny looked away, but not before he saw the war raging in her eyes—anger, hurt, confusion, and just a glimmer of consideration for his words. But they didn't have time to sift through all of that. Not with the bandits planning to murder them and storm a town. He ducked to reclaim her gaze. "Ginny, they're not planning to let us go—they never intended to. Listen to how loud they are. They're not the least worried that we've overheard their plans for Campo."

"I don't want the Gaskills dead any more than I want my ranch raided again. But I can't trust her." Her lower lip trembled then firmed. "I won't."

You don't have a choice. Heath kept the words to himself, knowing they'd do no good. Ginny could be as stubborn as granite when she'd made up her mind. It was one of the things that made her so good in a fight, but right now, it made him want to shake her. Or hug her. Despite her tough exterior, he knew she spoke out of pain. What would she do if he tried wrapping her in his arms and holding on until she let her guard down?

Probably kick him where the sun don't shine. He huffed and retreated to his position on the floor. They still needed rest if they hoped to make it more than a mile without falling down. Food and water would be better, but rest would have to do.

Sometime later, the creak of the door jarred Heath from slumber, and he whirled toward the entrance as his bound hands went to his hip. And his missing holster.

To his relief, Gabriella slipped inside, her steps silent on the earthen floor. "Everyone's asleep," she whispered. "I slipped something in their drinks to make them sleep, but it won't last long. You need to go—now." She cut Heath's rope, then gave him the knife and gestured toward Ginny.

Moonlight glinted off the blade as Heath sawed through her binds and Gabriella freed Jeb.

When they were all released from the ropes, Heath stepped toward the door, but Ginny's arm flew out, blocking his path. "How do we know this ain't a trap and Landa ain't waiting outside to shoot us?"

With a look that reminded him of Ginny, Gabriella made a rude noise. "Don't be stupid." Then she spun on her heel and marched out of the room, leaving the door open behind her.

Jeb strode out behind her, the long rest clearly having done him much good.

When Ginny still didn't budge, Heath grabbed her upper arm and propelled her from the room. Once outside, she looked around at the snoring men scattered around a small fire burning at the center of the courtyard and finally relaxed beneath his grip.

"We should tie them up while they're still out." Ginny halted and pointed at Landa's sleeping form. "He's wearing your locket."

Heath's hands itched to yank the necklace from the bandit's neck.

"Shh!" Gabriella rushed back to whisper, "Come before you wake them!"

Ginny dug her heels in. "But—"

"No, she's right." Heath tore his gaze from his last connection to Susannah and tugged Ginny along. "There's six of them and three of us. Plus, Jeb's injured. Even if we could steal a weapon without them waking up, we'd still be outnumbered." As much as it killed him to say so. "Besides, Cole, Garret, and Enrique are counting on us. Maybe even Turner." Saving lives would always trump arresting criminals.

Finally, she nodded and quit dragging her feet.

He let her go, and they scurried with Jeb and Gabriella out the front of the U-shaped dwelling. The full moon and stars above provided just enough light to navigate the rocky terrain. Every rustle of the wind made him brace for a shot in the back.

With Gabriella leading the way, they hurried through the cool desert night to where their mounts had been corralled with the bandits' horses. Ginny darted straight toward her gelding, stroking its forehead and whispering something he couldn't hear.

Gabriella moved toward a nearby pile of gear and weapons and lifted Heath's empty leather holster. "I couldn't get all your weapons—some of the men had claimed them and were wearing them. I didn't dare try stealing them. But I was able to find these. I hope you can use them to stay safe."

Heath, Jeb, and Ginny rushed toward the pile.

Heath tucked his knife into his left boot, then claimed his holster and found Jeb's rifle. He handed the weapon to his friend, then considered the rest of the pile. Two more holsters and three lumpy pouches lay beside three old pistols he didn't recognize.

Ginny frowned. "None of these are mine."

Heath chose the best-looking pistol and shortest holster. He held them out to her. "Take these."

Tucking the pistol under her arm, she tried on the gun belt. It was far too large for her small waist and would have fallen to her boots if she hadn't held it up.

Heath dropped his holster and withdrew the knife. "Here, let me." He slid his finger between the leather strap and Ginny's waist, ignoring the feel of her warmth as he pinched the point where the leather crossed. Then he gently tugged the gun holder away and used the tip of the knife to stab a new hole. "That should work."

Her fingers grazed his, sending a shiver of warmth up his arm as she reclaimed the belt, then fastened it around her waist. It wasn't a perfect fit and still sagged a little, but this time, the holster stayed at her waist even when she added the weight of her new pistol. "Thanks."

As Ginny practiced drawing and returning her new weapon, Heath retrieved and fastened his own gun belt before loading it with the last two pistols.

Jeb snatched up the pouches and checked their contents. "Ammunition." He handed one to Ginny and another to Heath.

Weapons distributed, they returned to the horses.

"I'm sorry if I put the wrong saddle on the wrong horse," Gabriella apologized quietly. "One of the men was sleeping on your satchels, so I tied one of our bags with some food to that horse." She pointed to Ginny's horse. "I did take four canteens, though, and filled them. So—"

Heath held his hand up for her to stop. "You've done more than enough. More than I thought possible. We're in your debt."

"Yes, thank you," Jeb said in a low voice as he struggled to tie his rifle to his saddle. Gabriella stepped up and tied it for him. He thanked her again, then mounted up using only his good arm. Once seated, he glanced past her toward the house several yards away. "What about you? Will you be safe here? Won't they be angry you helped us?"

"They won't know." She smirked. "They'll just think they drank too much." Her smile turned into a grimace. "It's Alvio they'll blame, since he was standing guard."

Heath hesitated, his hands gripping the reins. "Still, maybe you should come with us."

"No." She backed away. "Thank you. But if I leave, they'll know I helped you, and they'll punish Fedorro for my betrayal." Her eyes sought out Ginny, who'd already mounted up and waited beside Jeb. "Just go. Be free. Be safe."

Ginny looked away without a word.

Heath mounted up, then froze at the sound of Ginny's voice.

"Thank you." Her eyes remained fixed on her saddle horn, the tense words clearly all she could offer her former friend.

Gabriella's smile returned. "You're welcome."

Without another word, Ginny nudged her horse into motion, and Heath and Jeb followed in her wake.

Once they'd reached a distance far enough not to alert the sleeping bandits, Heath urged his horse into a gallop. He made sure they'd put another two miles between them and the bandits before forcing himself to slow to a canter as they crested a hill. A wide desert valley spread out before them, dappled in splashes of moonlight reflecting off patches of sun-bleached sand. They'd walked nearly forty miles the past two days. Retracing their route by horse shouldn't be difficult. He'd been careful to note landmarks as they'd been forced to march. But what would they find when they reached the scene of the shootout? Was there any chance Cole, Enrique, or Garret had survived?

Lord, let us find them before Landa and his men find us.

CHAPTER 16

*T*he morning air chilled his skin as Heath finished sweeping away their tracks and tossed the broken branch far from their trail. His breath ragged with exertion, he squinted into the horizon and licked the salt of sweat from his lips. No sign of the bandits yet.

Jeb's horse shifted beside him. His breathing was loud and labored, but not so much as a grunt of pain escaped his stubborn lips. Blood had soaked through the bandage on his arm, a dark red blotch against the tan fabric. Ginny had done what she could to bind the wound, including strapping his arm to his chest, but the bullet had torn through muscle and bone. Nothing short of a miracle would keep Jeb from losing the use of that arm. Or worse.

Heath kept an eye on his friend, waiting for any sign that he was going to collapse. But Jeb was tough. Heath prayed the trait would be enough to see him through. He refused to contemplate the alternative.

Ginny lifted a hand, peering back to where their true path split from the false trail they'd created to convince the bandits the three of them were headed east to the nearest town. "Do you think it will work?"

"None of the men I recognized are skilled trackers, and they'll be in a hurry to catch us before we can report the location of the hideout." He adjusted his hat, tipping it down to shield his eyes, and remounted. "We've done the best we can. The rest is in God's hands." They couldn't spare any more time laying false tracks while his men might be bleeding out in the desert. He spurred his horse forward, and they rode on in silence.

Less than a minute later, Heath heard them. Hoofbeats. Pounding fast and growing louder. His gut tightened. He glanced at Ginny. Her stiff posture and hand rested on the grip of her revolver said she'd heard them too.

"Landa," Jeb rasped, his voice low, strained.

Heath nodded, taking in the terrain ahead. Flat and empty for miles, aside from a pair of bushy desert ironwood trees about a quarter of a mile off their planned route.

He checked over his shoulder. The bandits hadn't yet crested the last low rise, but they were close. "There's no way we'll outrun them, and we're in no shape for a fight. We've got to hide." He spurred his horse toward the trees.

Ginny and Jeb followed him.

They'd just ridden behind the wide, leafy branches when the gang raced into view.

Heath's pulse thrummed in his ears, and he barely dared to breathe.

Cesar and his men thundered across the desert floor, Miguel on their tail.

Heath's fingers tightened around the grip of his pistol. How could he have been such a fool as to trust that man?

Ginny's horse skittered sideways. She stroked Mr. Darcy's neck and murmured something in a soothing tone.

Silhouetted against the breaking dawn, the bandits' horses

kicked up a cloud of dust that rolled across the barren land the way a wave moves across the sea. They didn't stop. Didn't look right or left. Cesar and his men followed the false trail, heads down, eyes searching in the distance, too focused on their quarry's supposed direction to notice anything else.

Heath exhaled, the knot in his chest loosening just a bit.

The hammering hoofbeats faded, and the dust they'd kicked up settled.

When the silence was absolute, Heath guided his horse around the trees and back toward the southerly trail they'd been following. "Let's go. They might still turn back."

~

*G*inny's gaze swept across the desolate expanse, the midmorning sun casting shadows that stretched like dark fingers over the prickly cacti and restless sands of the desert. Mr. Darcy followed Heath's determined lead, with Jeb trailing a short distance behind her.

In the hours since their escape, they'd stopped once, and then only long enough to refill their canteens at a spring and distribute the food Gabriella had packed for them. They'd eaten as they rode, the heavy silence broken only by the rhythmic sound of hooves on sunbaked dirt.

Two days, two long brutal days as captives had left her sagging in her saddle, desperate for true rest. But the physical aches were nothing compared to the stabbing pain in her heart. She'd trusted Gabriella, believed in her friend's loyalty. And now...Gabriella's betrayal had left a wound far worse than any blade could inflict. Ginny had started this quest for her, to seek justice and retrieve her friend's precious ring. Her scoffing laugh remained trapped inside. Gabriella had no doubt given that ring to Chavarria. Ginny was a fool. All this time, energy, and risk for someone she'd clearly never known.

But she wasn't the only one struggling with betrayal. They'd left Miguel sleeping with the rest of the gang. Heath had chosen Miguel as their Central California guide and translator, someone they all depended on. He must have trusted him. Surely, Heath's focus on saving the others—if saving them was even possible—was what kept him from voicing his fury. He must want revenge.

They crested a hill and entered the valley where they'd last seen Garret, Enrique, and Cole. The expansive gorge carved a winding path toward the east and west. Already, the desert sun had erased any sign of the storm that had soaked the land on the day of the ambush.

Ginny drew a deep breath and held it as she scanned the terrain, searching for any sign of life—or death.

The landscape was a maze of cracked, baked mud hills, their barren slopes rippled like the surface of an ancient, petrified sea. Sparse scrub and scattered rocks disrupted the path of pale, windswept sand blanketing the base of the desolate ravine. Large, dark blotches in the sand drew her closer. Dried blood. Too much of it. But no bodies. She exhaled. Where were Cole, Garret, and Enrique? She checked again for signs of the missing men.

Heath rode past her, following the dark-red trail. "They should be here." His gelding snorted, tossing its head as he shifted in the saddle.

Jeb frowned at their surroundings. "Could be they crawled off somewhere."

Heath shook his head. "If they did, they wouldn't have gotten far without horses or supplies. And there'd be drag marks, which I don't see."

He was right. "There's nothing here. No bod—"

Her words broke off as her throat constricted. She'd been bracing herself to find them, lying here lifeless, but this emptiness was worse.

Scanning the gorge, Jeb twisted in his saddle and winced, his good hand reaching for his shoulder. "If they didn't leave on their own—"

"Someone else must have been here." Ginny's pulse quickened.

"They must be alive." Heath met her gaze with a cautiously wondrous smile. "Why take bodies?"

So they could be identified before burial? Ginny kept the morbid guess to herself as her heart thudded against her ribs. She wanted to believe the kind, courageous men she'd spent the last two weeks with were alive, wanted to believe they'd somehow managed to escape. But doubt crept in. Who had come? Why? How had they known where to find the injured men?

Ginny dismounted, her boots sinking into the soft sand. Her fingers trembled as she pushed back a strand of hair stuck to her face. Crouching, she inspected the ground near the spot where Garret had fallen two days ago. Aside from splotches of darkened blood, the sand was undisturbed, the telltale imprints of hooves and boots from the chase already smoothed away by wind. "No tracks."

"*Someone* moved them. There's no way they left here on their own." Heath slid from the saddle. "But I can't see the bandits putting in the effort. So who...?"

Ginny's pulse pounded in her ears. If someone *had* been here, they had to have left some trace. But where? She turned her attention to the dried mudstone hills surrounding the sandy valley bottom. Every brush of wind against the back of her neck sent a shiver down her spine.

Heath mounted again, his face set in determination. "Let's fan out. Call if you see anything that might tell us which way they went—tracks, blood, anything."

Ginny mounted her horse and ascended the northeastern

KATHLEEN DENLY

slopes of the valley, while Heath searched the southern side and Jeb headed west along the valley floor.

Several minutes later, Heath called out, and she turned back to see him kneeling on the ground, touching something in the dirt.

When she and Jeb were close enough to talk without shouting, Heath stood. "More dried blood." He pointed to a sporadic trail of dark dots no bigger than a half dime. "They're heading south."

Jeb wiped sweat from his forehead with a shaky hand. "That's not much blood."

Heath adjusted his hat, his gaze fixed on the southern ridge. "They must've been bandaged or..."

Or their hearts had already stopped because they had poured their life into the dirt before help arrived.

With his good hand, Jeb fumbled for his reins. "They must be headed toward the stage station. It's the only thing that makes sense."

Ginny sprinted to Mr. Darcy. Jeb was right. The stage station was the only real shelter nearby. If she'd found three injured men out here, that's where she'd take them—whether they were dead or alive. The station master would be the one to ask. He saw travelers come and go all the time and would probably be able to identify strangers. Hopefully, he'd be willing to send for a doctor too.

As she followed Jeb and Heath down the hillside, Ginny considered the sun climbing steadily in the sky, her gut twisting. They were running out of time to warn Campo about the raid. If Cole, Garret, and Enrique weren't at the station, she'd need to leave Heath and Jeb to continue the search and ride for Campo on her own.

*H*eath was out of the saddle before his horse had come to a full stop, his boots hitting the ground in a rush as he headed for the sun-bleached adobe stage station. Were his men inside? Were they still alive?

He heard Jeb and Ginny ride in behind him but didn't wait. He needed answers. He pushed through the door and was forced to pause as his eyes adjusted to the dim interior. The odor of blood mixed with medicinal herbs filled him with hope.

"Heath?" Garret's weak voice hit Heath with the force of a punch to the chest.

Jeb's nephew, pale as death, his upper leg bandaged, was laid out on a makeshift cot. Enrique sat propped against the wall, his arm wrapped in a sling, breathing shallowly but alive. Cole was stretched out nearby, his face coated with sweat and one hand laid over a wide bandage that covered his side. A pile of blood-soaked rags sat on the ground beside him. Only Garret appeared conscious, but all three were still clinging to life—barely.

Thank You, Lord.

The slosh of water drew Heath's eye to the back corner, where a man knelt beside a leather bag and a washbasin, cleaning medical tools. Heath crossed to the doctor's side and asked quietly, "Are they going to make it?"

The doctor paused his washing to consider Heath. Heath saw the moment the older man noted his badge and relaxed. "They were lucky. The bullets missed anything vital. So I'm hopeful they'll pull through. But it's too soon to tell. With wounds like these, infection is always a possibility. Even if their luck holds and they avoid infection, Garret's thigh will take weeks, if not months, to heal. Enrique's shoulder is shattered, and Cole won't be allowed to so much as sit up for a month. It'll be weeks before any of them can be safely transported elsewhere." The doctor's narrowed eyes pinned him. "If you're aiming to continue the hunt, you'll be doing so without them."

The front door opened, and Heath whirled, drawing his pistol. At the sight of Jeb draped as limp as a rag doll between Ginny and the station master, Heath jammed his weapon into his holster and rushed across the room. "What happened?"

He scooped one arm under Jeb's and shifted him so that he bore his friend's full weight. Jeb's chin flopped against his chest, his face flushed and dripping with sweat. He mumbled something Heath couldn't make out.

"I'll see to your mounts," the station master promised as he returned outside, closing the door behind him.

Ginny wiped a sleeve across her brow. "He's been slowly drooping lower in the saddle all day. When we reached the yard, he nearly fell off his horse. I managed to sort of catch him." She shrugged. "Kept him from hitting the ground, anyway." She nodded to the closed door. "Thankfully, the station master was coming out of the outhouse and rushed over to help."

The doctor's strong voice rose behind Heath. "His wound's infected. Bring him over here." He spread a blanket on the floor and waited for Heath to deposit his friend.

The doctor scowled at the makeshift bandage Ginny had applied. "No wonder. This bandage is filthy." He shook his head, muttering. "Fabric like this never should've been used. Dr. Lister's work clearly showed—"

"It was all we had." As much as he appreciated the man's help, Heath wouldn't let him condemn Ginny for doing the best she could.

"Yes, well..." Thankfully, the doctor left off finishing his sentence and focused on the task of removing pus and debris from Jeb's infected wound. Jeb's eyes flew open, and he moaned, but he seemed too weak to put up a fight.

Garret called from his cot, "Will he be all right?"

Ginny crossed the room to the young man and quietly informed him that she recognized this doctor as the one that lived nearest her home, and she'd heard he'd successfully patched bullet holes in several of her neighbors. She assured Garret that she was confident the doctor would do his best for Jeb.

Heath yanked his hat from his head and raked a hand through his hair. The doctor's best wasn't good enough. Jeb had to survive. They all needed to survive. He refused to consider any other possibility.

The back door opened, and a silhouetted figure stepped through. Again, Heath held his weapon until his eyes locked on Turner, standing as tall and healthy as when Heath had last seen him.

Turner's gaze took in the room, and he grinned. "You're alive."

Heath returned his pistol to its holster, though he was tempted to keep the weapon aimed at the man who'd somehow managed to evade danger while the rest of them were fighting for their lives. "Where have you been?"

Turner's grin changed to a wince. "I didn't head for the rendezvous right away." His posture was visibly tense as he eyed Heath warily. "I hung back, waiting to see if the bandits took the bait as you expected. When it seemed like they wouldn't, I tried to catch up with you—but before I got close, shooting started. I got close enough to see the bandits chasing you and knew I couldn't do a thing on my own, so I hightailed it back to the town we'd spread those rumors in and rounded up a new posse."

Heath stared at him, fists clenching. The man had disobeyed orders, put himself in harm's way, and gone off half-cocked. But the result...Heath couldn't argue with the result. "You're the one that saved them."

Turner ran a hand through his hair. "I led the men from

town back to the ambush site, but it was too late. You, Jeb, and Ginny were already gone. We assumed the bandits had taken you, and these three..." He gestured to Garret, Enrique, and Cole. "They were shot bad. We got them here as fast as we could, and the station master sent his son after the doctor."

Heath's gaze swept over his men again, their quiet breathing filling the heavy silence. "And then?"

"Then we tried following the bandits' trail, but the men I rounded up couldn't track to save their lives. If I hadn't seen the direction you ran, we'd never have found Cole, Garret, and Enrique. We lost your trail pretty quick and had to turn back. I came here, and...well, that's about it."

Heath nodded and reluctantly added, "You did good."

Turner straightened, his grin returning as he pulled his pencil from behind his ear and the notepad from his vest pocket. "I was sure you were dead. How'd you manage to escape?"

As Turner scribbled furiously, Heath gave a brief explanation of the ordeal they'd endured—careful to leave Gabriella out of the tale and only saying that they'd escaped while the bandits were sleeping after drinking too much.

A little more than an hour later, the doctor made Jeb drink some kind of medicine, then stepped away from his side.

Ginny left Garret and approached the doctor. "How's Biddie doing?"

"I'm pleased to inform you her condition has not worsened. However, bed rest continues to be the best course until the babe arrives."

Ginny let out a long breath, relief in her eyes. "I don't suppose you know anything about my cattle?"

"Sorry, no."

She glanced out the window, then turned to Heath. "We've got to get to Campo before the bandits. They'll need time to prepare to defend themselves."

Heath surveyed his friends laid across the floor of the station's main room—all seriously injured. Cole and Enrique hadn't even woken since he'd arrived. How could he leave them again so soon after finding them? But could he live with himself if good men were killed in the raid on Campo when he might have prevented the attack?

~

*G*inny hated asking Heath to leave his injured friends, but they were running out of time.

He ran a hand over his face. "Our horses need rest. We pushed them hard today, and it's over fifty miles to Campo from here."

"We're at a stage station. Surely, there are extra horses we can borrow." Much as she hated leaving Mr. Darcy, Heath was right. Her horse must be as exhausted as she was.

Heath shook his head. "Those animals are contracted. He couldn't loan them to us if he wanted to. Trust me, I've asked before."

Frustration drained what little energy had been keeping her upright, and she sank to the dusty wood floor. "We can't just sit here and do nothing."

"We won't. We'll rest too. That's not nothing."

"But the Gaskills—"

"Are tough men who won't be helped by us riding our mounts to death or collapsing ourselves before we reach them." He came and sat beside her. "Let's just take a few hours to rest. I'll make sure the station master gives our horses plenty of fresh water, some salt, and as much feed as they can handle. He should have already removed their tack and groomed them, but I'll go check."

She stood with him. "I'll come too." She'd rest better knowing for certain Mr. Darcy was being well cared for.

Besides, if they were staying a while, she needed to bring her saddle inside.

When they returned from caring for the horses, they set their saddles beside their pallets, checked on the injured men, then nearly inhaled the poor-tasting stew the station master kept warming over the fire. Since the bandits had stolen all their money, Heath promised to pay what they owed when he returned to check on his friends. The station master seemed unconcerned by the delay in payment and clearly trusted a sheriff to keep his word.

With their bellies full, Heath and Ginny spread out two more blankets beside the others. They shucked their hats, boots, and holsters, then lay down. With no folded coat to tuck it under, Ginny made sure her pistol was close to hand before falling asleep.

Sometime later, Ginny woke with a start, the faint creak of the door catching her attention. She blinked, trying to clear the fog of sleep from her mind.

Movement brought her gaze to the door, which was ajar just enough to reveal the faint outline of Heath's figure carrying a canteen and a saddlebag as he stepped outside. She jolted upright and checked the space beside his pallet. Sure enough, his saddle was gone. Where was he going?

The uncovered windows revealed the deep blue of twilight giving way to the dark of night as she tugged her boots on and fastened her holster. She snatched up her hat and surveyed the sleeping men. None appeared any worse or better than when she'd fallen asleep. Likely, that would remain the case for several days. At least she hoped none would take a turn for the worse. There wasn't anything more she could do for them. The doctor slept in the opposite corner and had promised to remain another day unless a greater emergency called him away.

Like victims of a gunfight in Campo.

Ginny hefted her saddle and rushed outside.

The light of the nearly full moon made it easy to spot Heath headed for his horse which was tied to a hitching post in the yard. Two canteens and a lumpy flour sack hung from the saddle. "Heath!"

He glanced over his shoulder at her but didn't slow. "Go back to sleep, Ginny."

She jogged across the distance between them. "You're leaving for Campo, aren't you?" And without saying goodbye. The idea struck as hard as a mule-kick to the gut. She swallowed hard. "I'm coming with you."

He finally stopped to scowl at her. "No, you're not. I've arranged for Turner to escort you back to your ranch first thing in the morning."

"Well, that was a waste of time." She strode toward the corralled horses, determined to collect Mr. Darcy.

Before she could release her gelding from the pen, Heath mounted up. "Just stay here. Wait for Turner and go see your sister." Without waiting for her response, Heath rode out of the yard, calling back, "It's safer this way."

Heat flared in Ginny's chest. How dare he make such a decision for her? As if his riding off alone in the same direction the bandits were likely traveling was safe? What would he do if he crossed paths with the undoubtedly vengeful gang before reaching Campo?

It took less than ten minutes to ready Mr. Darcy, fill her canteens, and obtain a small bag of food from the station master. Ready to ride, she shoved one foot into the stirrup and flung herself onto her horse. Then she kicked Mr. Darcy into a trot and followed in Heath's wake.

CHAPTER 17

*W*hen Ginny caught up with Heath, he didn't say a word, just kept riding in silence. He'd been simmering for miles. She could feel the storm brewing.

Ginny leaned forward, whispering encouragement in Mr. Darcy's ear as she urged him through the rugged desert terrain draped in the shadow of night. The steady clop of hooves and the occasional snort were the only things cutting through the heavy silence. The few stars peeking through the scattered clouds seemed cold and distant, but nowhere near as cold and distant as the man riding beside her.

"You should've let Turner escort you back to Lupine Valley as I told him to," he finally muttered, voice tight. "I had a plan, Ginny. You were supposed to be safe while I rode on to warn Campo. Aren't you worried about your sister? Don't you want to see for yourself that she's well?"

"Don't you dare use my sister's health against me." She didn't slow her horse. Didn't even look his way. "You've got no right making that decision for me. I ain't a child to be bossed about."

His silence told her she'd struck a nerve. She pressed on.

"Nor am I a helpless woman to be passed off to the nearest man for protection. Turner? He barely knows which way to point a gun, and you expect him to protect me in the middle of this desert with Chavarria's men prowling about?" She gave a sharp, humorless laugh.

"It doesn't take two to deliver a message. Is it so wrong not to want someone else I—" Heath hesitated before plowing ahead. "Another person I care about getting hurt?"

He cared about her? Silly question. Of course he did. Heath cared about everyone, especially the members of his posse. It should be no surprise that seeing Cole, Garret, Enrique, and Jeb so badly injured would make him even more determined to keep her safe. He'd feel the same about any posse member left standing after the last three days. She steeled herself against the genuine fear in his voice. "Because it makes more sense for you to risk running into Chavarria's gang alone?"

"And two against six is better?"

She refused to acknowledge his point. "It's too late now. We're miles away from the station." A coyote's howl punctuated their isolation. "Unless you'd rather I turn around and wander back? Maybe run into the bandits on my own and see how that goes."

Silence fell as solid as a wall between them. The minutes ticked by, with only the soft creak of leather and the continued thudding of their horses' hooves to keep them company. She almost wished he'd say something. Almost. But the silence was better. Silence didn't lie.

Had Heath actually lied to her?

He'd withheld the truth. First about his past, then about his plans for her. He'd truly meant to send her home without a goodbye. The no-good lout.

She kept her gaze ahead, teeth clenched against the cold creeping into her bones.

Finally, Heath broke the quiet. "You called me a drunk. We never had a chance to discuss it."

Ginny stiffened. "What's there to discuss?" He'd had a wife he loved enough that losing her drove him to drink. Ma had said Oliver's drinking started when his parents died in a mining accident back in England. She said he drank his grief away. That'd been when Ginny was still a babe. But for as long as she could remember, there hadn't been much Oliver wouldn't drink away—wins, losses, a beautiful sunset. Everything was an excuse to lose himself and his temper in liquor. "Once a drunk, always a drunk. I'm done trusting people," she said, her voice quieter now, the sharpness giving way to weariness. "It costs too much." Look at what had happened when she'd trusted Gabriella and Heath had trusted Miguel. Trust was a fool's choice.

Heath turned in the saddle to look at her, but she couldn't meet his eyes. "First of all, I'm not a drunk. Not anymore. Not for a long time. I've learned from my poor choices. Alcohol can't erase the pain. It only hides it for a while. But in the meantime, more pain is created. My own and that of anyone who cares about me. Jeb helped me see that." In her periphery, she saw him face forward again. "I'm sober now and intend to stay that way."

"Right." She scoffed. "That's why you smelled of whiskey when you returned from the saloon."

"That was an accident."

"Of course. Whiskey accidentally poured itself down your throat."

"No, someone bumped me, and I spilled some in my mouth while pretending to drink."

"Right. You were *pretending* to drink.'" She rolled her eyes. "Is that really the best lie you could come up with?"

He gave a frustrated growl. "I had to pretend so as not to

arouse suspicion. Stupid as it sounds, some men won't trust a man who doesn't drink."

"Well, that's backwards thinking if I've ever heard it."

"I agree."

There was a pause before he continued. "Not trusting *anyone* is a mistake, Ginny." He was looking at her again. She could feel his gaze. "You can't trust everyone, of course. But you can't just push people away because they made a mistake. No one is perfect. I didn't need the Bible to tell me that. But rarely are people purely evil either. Even Valadez had his moments. There's a claim that he once returned a watch he'd stolen when the widow he'd stolen it from said the piece was all she had left of her husband. Of course, with him, his bad choices outweighed the good. But you've got to look at how people handle their mistakes before tossing them away like garbage. Do they strive not to repeat the same offense? Do they express remorse and try to make things right?"

She thought of Gabriella sneaking back to the hideout after helping them escape.

As if reading her mind, Heath said, "Look at Gabriella. Yes, she betrayed your trust two-and-a-half years ago, but now she's risked her life to help us escape. To help *you* escape. There was nothing in it for her. No reward aside from your safety. You must see that proves her friendship was—*is*—genuine. Refusing to forgive her doesn't just hurt *her*. Bitterness eats at the one who holds it."

Ginny's heart thudded harder, anger and something else— something painful—fighting for control. She finally met his eyes. "Is that the excuse you'll use when you fall back into the bottle? 'Everybody makes mistakes'?"

Heath's expression darkened, and the muscle in his jaw ticked, but he didn't look away. "I'm not that man anymore," he said, his voice rough. "After all this time together, you've seen the real me. Either you believe the truth, or you don't." Pain cut through his gaze. "I can't force you to trust me." He urged his horse ahead of hers. Not far, but enough that she couldn't see his face anymore and talking would be difficult.

An ache filled her. Why had she said that? What was wrong with her that she pushed good people away? Because no matter his past, deep down Ginny knew Heath was a good man. He was right. She'd seen too much of his honesty, his selflessness, and his determination to do what was right no matter the cost. Yes, he'd made mistakes, but even in those he'd shown humility —a rare trait in her experience. As much as she wanted to deny it—to stop another person from having the power to hurt her— calling Heath anything but good and trustworthy was lying to herself. Even if what he'd said threatened to break the armor that had held her up and kept her moving through darkness no one should have to endure, he'd been trying to help.

"Heath." She called to him, but either he didn't hear her, or —more likely—he pretended not to. She gnawed her lip. He probably needed to calm down... But what if she'd gone too far? What if, when she tried to apologize, he refused to forgive her?

~

*H*eath heard her call for him, but pain kept him from responding. She didn't try again. So he kept his mount ahead of her, letting the silence grow between them for hours.

The frigid night air carried the faint scent of sagebrush and dust as dawn broke over the horizon to Heath's left, dappling the cloud-covered sky with patches of orange, gold, and pale yellow. Each breath he took seemed to cut through him, but the bitter cold was nothing compared to the sting of Ginny's words.

He and Ginny ascended a hill laden with pinyon pines, sage brush, and junipers as the first rays of dawn peeked out between the clouds, turning the sky from deep purple to soft pinks and oranges. Such a sight usually filled him with peace. But the glorious colors weren't enough to erase the slice of Ginny's accusation.

Heath tightened his grip on the reins. He would never return to the shadow of a man alcohol had turned him into. No temporary relief from grief was worth the damage his inebriation had caused. Why couldn't she trust him?

He thought of the little she'd shared about her pa—how he'd been drunk the day the bandits attacked her ranch. The surprise she'd expressed that Oliver had been able to reach the yard before dying seemed to imply that that morning hadn't been the first he'd spent sleeping off drink. And the story Gabriella had shared... If Oliver had been the father he should have been, Ginny's friend wouldn't have been desperate enough for rescue from her boyfriend to call on a gang of bandits to help her escape a man Oliver had hired. Heath's stomach churned as the full implication of what Ginny had likely lived through settled over him.

If his suspicions were right, the one man God had charged with protecting Ginny had done anything but. It was little wonder she struggled to trust anyone.

Still, hadn't Heath been steady enough, kind enough, honest enough to earn at least a sliver of her trust? If not her trust, he at least deserved more respect than her words had granted him. How could she believe he was biding his time, looking for an excuse to fall apart again?

He'd been a fool to think Ginny was softening, to think she might consider what he'd been trying to say. Instead, she'd wielded his past like a sword.

And maybe she was right.

Maybe there was no future for them, as friends or anything else. He'd known there wasn't room for a continued relationship before this ride, hadn't he? She had her ranch down here, and he had his calling up north. He was sheriff of Alameda. A life he'd chosen and that gave him purpose. Ginny was a proud ranch owner. Her passion for this rugged lifestyle was part of what he loved about her. She'd never be content as a mere sheriff's wife, no matter how much he might wish otherwise. And yet somewhere along the way, he had let hope creep in. A perilous thing, hope.

Thankfully, her harsh words had smothered that foolish flame. Love—especially that between a husband and wife—required trust. Something Ginny didn't seem capable of giving.

He let her catch up with him as he took a slow, steadying breath. "You don't have to worry about me making excuses, Ginny. Once we've warned Campo, you're free to return home. I'll find someone to escort you."

"But—"

"You've seen enough to know chasing these men is dangerous. Success and survival depend on trusting those who ride with me, and knowing they trust me in return." He squinted at a bat swooping through the early-morning light. "Trusting Miguel on so little acquaintance was a mistake that nearly cost lives. Might still. I can't afford to make another." He swallowed hard and flicked the reins, urging his tired horse to keep pace. "You've made it clear, you can't trust me. And I've made my peace with that."

The finality of his words hung in the air. Whatever future he might have imagined for them—it wasn't real. He could see that now.

He kept his gaze on the horizon where distant columns of smoke signaled the residents of Campo had begun their day and this ride was nearly at an end. His gut sank. *I've made my peace,* he reminded himself. But the ache in his chest told him that peace wasn't as close as he wanted it to be.

CHAPTER 18

"*Return home. I'll find someone to escort you.*"

Mr. Darcy skittered sideways beneath Ginny, as if sensing her tension. She patted his neck and murmured reassurances, even as the backs of her eyes stung with tears she refused to release. Heath wanted her gone. So much so that he wouldn't even escort her home himself. She wanted to shout at him, to rail against his hypocrisy. Hadn't he been the one to admonish her about forgiveness? Where were his big words now that she'd hurt him?

But the pain in her chest stole her speech.

She let Mr. Darcy fall behind Heath once more, half hoping he'd turn and take back his decision. Hoping he'd forgive her. A mirthless laugh shook her chest but made no sound. Was this how Gabriella had felt watching Ginny ride away? How Clyve felt each time Ginny refused to hear his apology?

The truth slammed down with the weight of a full-grown bull. She was a wreck. So broken and bitter, it was a wonder anyone ever cared for her at all.

Biddie's words replayed in her mind. *"If I didn't forgive those who've hurt me and repented but expected those same people or others—even God—to forgive my mistakes, what kind of person would that make me?"*

Ginny had known the truth even then, though she'd refused to admit it aloud. Biddie and Heath, even Jeb...they were all right. Holding on to anger, even hatred, in the face of sincere remorse did no one any good. It only caused more pain. And keeping people at a distance hadn't protected her. It'd left her alone.

And for the first time, Ginny admitted, she didn't want to be alone. She wanted to stay with Heath. More than that—if she were truly honest with herself—she yearned for the relationships she'd had with Clyve and Gabriella before their betrayals. Maybe that wasn't possible, but could Heath, Biddie, and Jeb be right that friendship didn't have to die because of someone's terrible choice? Could trust be repaired?

She wanted to ask Heath, but he still hadn't looked back at her. Her vision blurred, and she bit her cheek. Hard. She would not cry. Once again, she'd mucked everything up.

Jeb's words came back to her. *"I can see you're hurting. But everyone makes mistakes. That's why God sent His son to die for our sins."*

How many times had Biddie told Ginny that God had forgiven her sins, both past and future, and all she needed to do was believe it was true? Tears welled, and she tipped her face to the sky to keep them from spilling free. Two deep breaths and her vision cleared.

Where had the clouds gone? The last time she'd looked, there'd been nothing but dull gray overhead. Now, a clear blue sky filled her gaze, not a speck of cloud in sight. Hadn't she heard Biddie—or was it Gideon?—read Scripture about God washing away the filth of her sin?

A crack of gunfire shattered the silence.

"That came from Campo," Heath called over his shoulder

as he kicked his horse. "We're too late. Find somewhere to hide!"

Ginny leaned low over Mr. Darcy's mane, urging him to keep up with Heath as they raced toward town. Her poor gelding was far from prepared for such a burst of speed, but he gave her all he had.

As they neared town, two more gun blasts echoed from Silas Gaskill's blacksmith shop. Alvio Monteres and Sebastian Debert—two men she recognized from the long march to the hideout—came running around the south side of the building.

She reined Mr. Darcy to a halt beside Heath, who already had his pistol out and aimed at Debert. "Drop your weapons," Heath shouted.

Debert started to aim at Heath, but Silas Gaskill burst through the shop's back door, placing himself between Heath and the bandits. Silas's shirt was splattered with blood. A blast from his shotgun sent Debert to the dirt.

Monteres veered toward the gristmill.

Silas's gun clicked empty, and he ran for the barn.

Appearing around a corner in that same moment, Jack Kelly, the telegraph operator, unloaded his weapon in Monteres's direction.

Monteres returned fire.

Both Kelly and Heath fired at Monteres as he fled, still shooting. But Ginny's new gun and drooping holster slowed her draw.

Unharmed, the varmint dove behind a woodpile.

Heath and Ginny leaped from their horses as Kelly crawled under the store toward the creek the building straddled. Dark streaks marred the dirt behind him. The man must have been hit.

Heath sprinted toward the woodpile.

Ginny started after him, but movement in front of the store

caught her eye. Cesar Landa stood at the center of town, taking aim at Heath. Quick as a blink, she aimed and shot.

Blood spurted from the side of Landa's neck. He clamped his free hand over the wound just as two more bandits dashed out of the store, one carrying a can, likely filled with the Gaskills' cash. They spotted Ginny and raised their weapons at the same time Landa shot his.

Fire tore through her shoulder and side a heartbeat before it sliced through her thigh, and she fell.

Air. She needed air. Why couldn't she breathe?

~

*H*eath had just reached the woodpile when shots sounded behind him. He whirled and spotted Ginny on the ground.

Please, God, no!

He took aim at the men who'd shot at her. But when a man with blood dripping from his mouth and brandishing a shotgun crawled into the doorway of the store behind the bandits, Heath hesitated. Dark red soaked the left side of the man's shirt. Despite his condition, he shot one of the bandits, his true aim felling the man holding a can. Coins spilled into the dirt. Then the blood-soaked man with the shotgun fell backward into the store and out of sight.

Heath shot at the second bandit, but he lunged, and the shot missed.

Monteres rounded a building, gun firing wildly at Heath.

Unharmed, Heath returned fire, striking the man.

Hands over his gut, Monteres staggered into the head-high bushes.

Silas, still covered in blood, rushed from the barn, wielding another shotgun.

"*¡Retírense!*" Landa shouted as he followed Monteres into the bushes, the uninjured bandit on his heels.

Heath spared a glance for Ginny, who hadn't moved since she'd fallen, her face turned so he couldn't see her eyes. *Please, God, don't let her be dead.* Unwilling to trust that the bandits wouldn't return to finish what they'd started, Heath raced across the clearing after them.

Before he reached the bushes, the thunder of galloping horses met his ears and quickly faded. Bursting through the brush, weapon ready, he found only a trail of dust and the backs of three riders charging eastward. He lifted his pistol and fired his last three bullets, but the men were out of range.

For a moment, he watched helplessly as frustration roared inside him.

Ginny! He spun and rushed back through the bushes. He'd been every kind of fool not to accept the apology he'd sensed she wanted to speak.

Lord, forgive my unforgiveness. Please give me another chance to make things right.

CHAPTER 19

*G*inny lay on her stomach, her left cheek pressed against the dirt. She didn't dare move. Any sign of life might draw the bandits' attention, and with her shooting arm injured, she'd be helpless to defend herself. Worse, her movement might distract Heath and get him killed.

Better to let them all think her dead.

Blood pooled around her right shoulder, traveling across the dirt to puddle against her cheek. Moisture soaked her right side from her waist to her knee. More blood. Though she didn't dare shift her head to see how much.

After Landa had shouted for his men to retreat, boot steps had pounded away. Branches rustled. More thundering boot steps had passed her. *Heath?* More rattling, cracking brush.

And then horses' hooves had vibrated the ground, fading as they headed east.

Silence enveloped her. She tried to raise up, but her arm and leg wouldn't hold her. She collapsed with a cry.

The bandits had run, and Heath had chased after them.

Her vision blurred with tears. She was alone. Just as she'd always claimed she wanted to be. And she might be dying.

Her gaze returned to the clear blue sky. *Are You there, God? Biddie says You never leave us. No matter how stupid we act. She says You love us no matter what. I don't know if that's true. It's hard to believe You'd love someone like me, but if You do, I'd sure appreciate Your forgiveness. I missed the chance to ask Heath to forgive me —and Clyve and Gabriella, for that matter. Fact is, I probably owe apologies to a whole lot of folks. But right now, I'm thinking Yours is the one that matters most. I've done a bunch of things I ain't proud of —things Biddie says You wouldn't approve of, for sure. If you could see Your way to forgiving me, I'd be right grateful.*

The fire increased in her thigh, making her gasp long and loud. She shifted, trying to relieve the weight on it, but that only made her side scream. Yet for some reason, calm filled her. No, not calm. It was more like...peace. Wasn't that what Biddie was always saying God's forgiveness felt like? With a small smile, she let her eyes close.

Lord, if I am dying, could You somehow let Biddie know You forgave me? I know she'd like that.

Footsteps stampeded behind her, drawing closer. With her left arm, she reached for the pistol she'd dropped. But it was out of reach.

~

*H*eath crashed through the brush and emerged at the center of town. Silas was gone. The bodies of two bandits lay unmoving in the dirt. But it was the sight of Ginny reaching for her weapon that had his heart in his throat and his feet flying across the clearing.

"Ginny!" He skidded to a stop and knelt beside her. Mindful of her injuries, he pressed his cheek against the earth to meet her blue-gray eyes. He wiped the blood from her face. "Thank God, you're alive!" Without thought, he brushed his lips across her cheek, and her eyes widened. "You're going to be all right."

Straightening, he assessed her condition. Blood was slowly oozing from her right shoulder, and there was an exit wound on the back of her thigh, but more concerning was the blood coating most of her side. Gut shots were often a death sentence. The image of Cole barely clinging to life in the stage station turned his stomach.

Please, God, keep them both alive.

Gently as he could, he prodded Ginny's side.

She sucked breath through her teeth but didn't complain.

He found no rips in her bodice. No exit wound. Tension coiled in his shoulders. The bullet must still be inside. He knew from experience that would make things worse.

With a desperate glance heavenward, he silently begged, *Lord, help me.*

He looked down at Ginny. "I'm sorry. I have to roll you over."

She bit her lip and nodded.

He reached for her shoulders.

From the east came the growing thunder of pounding hooves. *No!* The bandits couldn't be back already. He'd taken too long assessing her wounds. Ginny was still in the open. It was too late to move her.

Heath whipped his pistol from its holster and stood as three riders galloped into town. The one in the middle bore a cream-colored hat, and a dark mustache over a full beard. On his left was a man with blond hair, and to Cream Hat's right was a Mexican-looking man with a long mustache.

None were Landa or the men who'd left with him. But could they be part of the group meant to join Landa from below the border?

Heath was about to demand they state their business when Cream Hat cried out. "Ginny!" Seemingly unfazed by the pistol Heath aimed at his chest, Cream Hat leaped from his horse and charged forward.

It took a beat for Heath to register the concern that had been in the man's shout and lower his weapon. Heath may not recognize the man, but Cream Hat clearly knew and cared about Ginny. That made him a friend.

Heath holstered his weapon as the man knelt in the dirt beside Ginny.

"What happened?"

"Clyve?" Ginny turned her head and tried to roll over, but a cry of pain stopped her efforts.

The man in the cream hat—Clyve, apparently—rolled Ginny onto her back and brushed the hair from her face as she moaned.

Heath clenched his jaw to stop himself from shouting at the man to keep his hands off her.

Aside from the pain-filled moan, Ginny wasn't protesting. Wounded or not, if she didn't like this stranger touching her, she'd have said as much. So she must not mind.

What did that mean? Who was this Clyve?

She squinted up at him. "How are you here?"

"Don't worry about that. What happened to you?"

"Bandits." Her voice was weak, clearly fatigued by the loss of blood. "They raided the town. Or tried to." She turned a faint smile toward Heath. "Heath stopped them."

Clyve glared up at him. "You're the sheriff she ran off with? Gideon said you promised to protect her." There was more than a hint of accusation in his tone.

Guilt nearly choked him, but Heath held his expression impassive. What mattered now was taking care of Ginny's wounds, and Heath was done being patient. He reclaimed his position beside Ginny and resumed probing her side. This time he found a tear revealing a diagonal wound that indicated a bullet had grazed her. He checked again, but found no other holes, no other wounds to her abdomen. Most of the blood had come from the shot to her thigh.

Thank You, Lord.

Heath pulled his shirt off, preparing to tear it into strips.

"Wait," Clyve ordered. Then he dashed into the store.

Heath scanned their surroundings. More riders were approaching at a fast rate. Once more, he stood and drew his weapon, letting his shirt fall to the ground. "There's no time to explain how, but we overheard Landa and his men talk of being joined by others from Mexico for this raid. I didn't see them during the shooting, but they could still be on their way."

Both of the men who'd ridden in with Clyve had their weapons drawn and took up defensive positions on either side of Ginny.

Clyve returned moments later with a bolt of clean calico. He took in the scene with a frown and tucked the calico under one arm to draw his gun. "I thought Ginny said you stopped the bandits." He nodded toward the dead bodies still lying where they'd fallen.

"Three of them got away, and there might be more coming."

"How many?"

"Not sure. From what I could hear, sounded like nine or ten. Maybe more."

As the riders drew close, Clyve returned his weapon to its holster. "I recognize those men. They live nearby and probably heard the shooting same as I did on my way into town." He unrolled some of the fabric and tore it into long strips. "Sure glad the tool I ordered was due in today."

Heath accepted the strips and folded them into wads.

The man with the long mustache stepped forward and helped roll Ginny onto her left side so Heath and Clyve could press the padding against her entry and exit wounds to slow the bleeding.

Ginny's eyes slammed shut, and she clamped her lips together, but she couldn't stop a heartbreaking moan.

Meanwhile, Clyve's blond friend greeted the newcomers

and explained the situation. The armed locals took up watchful positions around town.

With a guard now posted, Blondie turned his attention to tearing the rest of the fabric into strips, and the four of them worked together to tie the padding in place before lowering Ginny onto her back.

As they worked, more men poured into town from every direction, asking what was happening and who was hurt. The self-appointed guards filled them in. Some of the newest arrivals carted away the dead bandits' bodies, while others scoured the town, making certain no other bandits hid nearby.

Clyve called to a group of men near the store. "Where are the Gaskills?"

The grim expression of the tall man who answered foretold that his response would not be good. "We found Luman with Jack Kelly in the creek under the store. Kelly's arm was only grazed, but Luman's been shot through the chest, and it's bad. His wife's tending him, and two men are getting ready to search for the doctor, but I doubt Luman will make it."

Heath cringed as he focused on adjusting Ginny's bandages to apply the most pressure. Luman must have been the man he'd seen crawl from the store and shoot the bandit. *Lord, please save his life.*

Heath called over his shoulder, "The doctor's at Carrizo Creek Station." He hated the idea of the doctor leaving Garret, Enrique, Jeb, and Cole, but it sounded like Luman Gaskill needed him more. And Ginny would certainly be better off in properly trained hands. But what if one of Heath's men had taken a turn for the worse since he'd left? Heath shook off the worry. The doctor would need to make the decision whether to stay or travel to Campo. Heath needed to focus on Ginny.

"What about Silas?" Clyve asked, without letting up his pressure on the padding.

"Shot in the arm, but I think he'll be okay, so long as infection doesn't set in." The tall stranger nodded to Ginny. "You need any help with her?"

Heath tied the last knot on the bandages. "We need to get her inside and properly clean her wounds."

"Take her to the hotel. They should have an empty bed she can use." The man pointed toward a nearby two-story building that looked like a house with the word *Hotel* written on the wall beside the door in paint so faded Heath hadn't noticed it until now.

He slid one arm under Ginny's back and the other under her knees. Careful to cradle her head against his shoulder, he rose.

She groaned and her eyes fluttered open. "Wait."

Heath hesitated, looking down into her pale, blood-smeared face. "What is it?"

"Clyve," she whispered.

Heath tensed. Who was this Clyve person to her? Heath would have bet his life she had no beau, but he sensed an unspoken bond between these two. Had he been wrong in thinking her heart was free to be won? That she'd maybe begun to care for Heath before learning of his past?

Clyve stepped closer and peered down at her. "I'm here."

Her pained expression hardened into determination as she met Clyve's gaze. "I forgive you. Sorry it took me so long."

Clyve's laugh was choked with emotion as tears shone in his eyes. "You crazy woman."

Her expression remained serious. "Do you forgive me?"

He grinned. "Of course. Now let's get you fixed up." Clyve led the way and knocked on the hotel door before opening it.

Heath hesitated. "Shouldn't we wait—"

Clyve strode down the short hall. "Silas runs this place by himself. He won't mind us bringing her in. Not counting the doc, he has the most medical knowledge around these parts. He's used to folks making themselves at home. Besides, it sounds as though he's preoccupied with his own gunshot and his brother's."

Floorboards creaked as Heath followed him into a small room with a simple bed at the center.

Clyve threw back the quilt, revealing a stained but clean sheet. "I'll get some hot water and rags." He strode from the room.

Heath gingerly lowered Ginny onto the mattress. Her eyes were closed again, but thankfully, her breathing remained steady. It would take several minutes to heat water, and once the wounds had been cleared of debris and rinsed, most doctors used something stronger to fight infection. Should he search the hotel for alcohol or run to the store and see if they had carbolic acid or iodine? He hated the idea of leaving Ginny alone, but the sooner her wounds were cleaned, the better her chances would be.

Before he could decide, Clyve returned with an armful of clean-looking rags. "There's water heating on the stove. I'm headed to the store for some iodine. Here." He shoved the rags at Heath and left. Guess that meant he could stay.

He glanced around. There was a washstand in the right corner. A towel hung from a peg above the cream-colored porcelain bowl. On the left, several more pegs dotted the wall, and a single ladder-back chair sat in the corner beside a tiny table bearing a box of matches. Above that hung a single oil lamp, and blue gingham curtains framed a small window over the bed. He set the rags on the table and lit the lamp.

"Heath?"

He spun toward the bed and knelt on the wood floor. Ginny's eyes were open again, and he leaned over her. "What do you need?"

"I'm sorry. I know you wouldn't...that you weren't..." She expelled a frustrated sigh. "I'm sorry for the awful things I said." She lifted her left hand, and he clasped it in both of his. "I trust you."

His heart swelled as he gently squeezed her hand and smiled. "Thank you."

Her brow wrinkled. "Then you forgive me?"

"Of course." He cupped one hand against her cheek. "I'm sorry I wouldn't listen before."

A small smile curved her lips to match the light in her watery gaze. Something warm and special passed between them as they stared at each other. "Ginny, I..." The memory of Clyve interrupted his declaration. He withdrew his hands, straightened, and cleared his throat. "Who's Clyve?" His words came out gruffer than he'd intended.

Her expression turned confused. "He's my neighbor."

"Nothing more?"

She frowned. "He's my friend. Why?"

Her friend. Not her beau or her suitor. "You've never mentioned him, but just now you seemed...close. So I wondered..." He forced himself to voice his concern. "Are you in love with Clyve?"

CHAPTER 20

*G*inny's entire body hurt, and she could barely keep her eyes open. But Heath's stumbling words seized her attention.

"Me, in love with Clyve? Of course not." If she weren't so exhausted and certain the action would increase her pain, she'd laugh. "Clyve's like a second brother. Besides, he's courting Carmen."

Heath's posture relaxed, and his expression softened. "Oh, good."

"Is it?" Hope lifted Ginny's heart, but she pressed it down. She may have decided she wanted him in her life for longer than just this hunt, but that didn't mean he felt the same. His response could reflect anything.

"Yes." He stroked her hair and leaned close. "Because it means I'm free to tell you, I love you."

A covey of quail took flight in Ginny's chest, distracting her from the pain. "You do?" Was that what had been growing inside her—this feeling that she could really trust Heath and that she wanted him at her side for always—was that...love? The notion terrified her. Love destroyed women. Look at her mama. She'd loved Oliver, and he'd destroyed her life, then left her to struggle and die alone.

Look at Biddie, a small voice inside countered. *She's happier than ever with Gideon as her husband. And Lucy seems pretty happy to be Preston's wife, if her letters are to be believed.*

But Lucy's ma was beaten and left for dead by her husband —crippled for life.

Ginny couldn't imagine Heath doing such a thing. But surely her mama and Lucy's ma wouldn't have married their husbands if they'd known what those men would do to them. How could Ginny be sure she was a better judge of character? Was she willing to gamble her life on the feelings welling inside?

Before she could decide, Clyve burst through the door, his arms loaded with bottles and clean bandages. "Some of the men are discussing plans to go after the bandits that fled. Others will stay and take up defense positions in case the gang regroups and returns." He settled his load on the table. "I told them I'm staying with Ginny. They want to know if you'll go with the men heading out, since you're the only one who saw the bandits that are still standing."

Heath looked toward the empty doorway, the battle warring inside him obvious. His training was in catching criminals, not doctoring—though the first probably required experience with the other.

"You should go."

He turned back to stare at her. "Absolutely not. I'm staying with you."

"I'll be fine. I've got Clyve to take care of me. Besides, you're a sheriff, not a doctor." She fought the weights tugging at her eyelids. "And if you don't go after Landa now, there ain't much hope you'll ever get your locket back."

He shook his head, placing his hands on either side of her

face. "Don't you understand? You're more important than any keepsake."

The look in his eyes melted her, and she wanted to keep him at her side. Forever. But he'd never forgive himself if Landa and his men hurt someone else while he sat at her bedside. She firmed her resolve. "If not for yourself, then for me, and Jeb, and Cole, and Enrique, and Garret, and everyone else those men have hurt." She laid her left hand over his. "They got to be stopped, and the men outside will have a better chance at catching those varmints with you leading them."

~

*E*very clop of the horse's hooves that carried Heath away from Campo—away from Ginny—felt wrong. But she was right. Landa and his men needed to be prevented from causing more harm. After all this time chasing them, Heath couldn't ignore the best chance he'd ever had at catching what remained of Valadez's gang.

So far as he knew, one of them was uninjured, but Ginny had shot Landa in the neck, and Monteres had taken a gut shot. Those injuries would slow the trio down, and they had even left a trail.

So despite his heart crying out for him to turn back, Heath continued leading his new posse and silently begged God to keep Ginny safe. He also prayed for the safety and restraint of the men riding with him.

Before agreeing to lead them, he'd made it clear their purpose was to arrest Landa and his men if at all possible. Killing was to be a last resort. Heath wouldn't be part of vigilante justice. He'd waited on the word of each man before mounting up.

They'd been riding for nearly three hours when Heath spotted something out of place in the distance—a dark lump to one side of the trail. As they drew closer, he recognized the slumped form of a man. Eventually, they came abreast with Monteres's lifeless body propped against an ironwood tree. The scene suggested his compadres had decided he wouldn't survive his gut wound and had chosen to end his suffering.

"We'll collect him on our way back." Heath urged his horse onward.

No one else said a word, but they all fell in behind him.

The blood drops were smaller and farther between after that, but Heath managed to keep to the bandits' trail. A large blood splatter seemed to indicate Landa's wound had gotten worse. And it appeared fresh.

An hour later, the sun was dropping toward the horizon as the bandits' tracks veered off the trail, heading south—toward Mexico. They had to be within a mile or two of Mexico. If the bandits made it across the border, they'd be beyond Heath's reach. Though some posses had managed to successfully cross the border and return with their quarry, others had been imprisoned in Mexico for their efforts. That wasn't a risk Heath could afford to take.

Lord, let us catch them before they cross.

As they neared the crest of a boulder-strewn mountain, one of the townsfolk pulled up alongside Heath. "I may know where they're headed."

Heath eyed the older man he'd heard called McCain. "That so?"

"There's a cave in the valley just beyond this rise that's a known hideout for smugglers. It'd make sense for them to hole up there if Landa's hurt as bad as it seems."

Heath thanked the man and raised his fist, signaling the group to halt. Then he dismounted and approached the ridge, waving for McCain to come with him, while the others hung back.

Using the deepening shadows of the boulders to hide them

from watchful eyes below, Heath and McCain surveyed the valley. Heath saw nothing but more rocks and shrubs. Still, he kept his voice low. "Where's this cave?"

McCain pointed at a tan stone roughly five hundred feet below, settled at the base of the valley's boulder-strewn south-facing slope. The enormous rock was at least thirty feet wide, twelve feet across, and eighteen feet tall. "It's under that. From this side, it looks solid, but from the southeast, there's an opening tall enough for a man to walk in. Underneath, it's hollow, forming a large cave. If you look there"—he pointed to one side where a pile of smaller rocks leaned against the larger boulder—"you can see they've filled in some of the gaps to keep the wind out and block light from their fires."

The swiftly cooling wind chilled the sweat on Heath's brow as he surveyed the land around the boulder cave, a plan forming in his mind. He considered McCain. "Are you a good shot?"

McCain straightened. "I'd say so."

Heath nodded. "Good. Can I assume you're familiar with the men riding with us?"

McCain's expression turned curious as he nodded.

"Who are the three best shots?"

McCain listed off three names without hesitation.

Heath thanked him and strode back to the waiting men with McCain at his side. "McCain thinks Landa and his compadre are holed up under a boulder down there." He hooked his thumb back toward the ridge. "And I agree it seems likely."

He waited for anyone to object or suggest something different. No one did. Instead, they dismounted and waited for his instructions.

"It looks like there are two gaps near the back. Right now, they're filled with smaller rocks, stacked to keep wind out. But a good kick would probably knock those loose and let Landa and whoever's with him escape. Which means we've got to cover both the front and the back if we aim to keep them from running again." He glanced at the horses. "We'll need to leave our mounts here and advance on foot. So keeping the bandits out of their saddles will be key. We're only a mile or so from the border here. If they mount up and ride off, they'll be in Mexico before we can give chase."

He paused and searched until he found a fist-sized rock. He set it on the ground in front of the men. "This is the boulder cave." He broke off a brittle branch from a nearby shrub. "Here's what I have in mind." As he explained his plan, he drew in the dirt around the rock.

When he was certain everyone understood what was expected of them, they broke into two groups. One waited with McCain, while the others—the three best shooters McCain had listed—followed Heath in a wide, descending circle into the valley and around the cave. As the blue-and-gold sky slowly faded toward navy, they quietly darted from stone to bush, shadow to shadow until they reached the south side of the cave.

A three-quarter moon illuminated the uniquely shaped boulder. Another wall of stacked rocks covered most of the hollow's largest entrance. Firelight flickered through the gaps. Three sweaty horses stood saddled and waiting, tied to the thin branch of a bush just four strides from the opening.

Landa and the other man were definitely in there.

Heath crouched behind a short boulder and directed his men to fan out as the last whisper of twilight melted into night and stars appeared in the sky. Gritty sandstone bit into his palm as he waited for McCain's men to get into position. Images of Ginny lying pale and wounded back in Campo pushed their way into his thoughts. Was Clyve still at her side as he'd promised? Had the doctor reached Campo? What if Heath had misjudged her wounds and they were more serious than they'd seemed?

Heath's pulse pounded in his ears, the shadows around him deepening as night closed in. She'd seemed pleased by his declaration. Had Clyve's abrupt entrance stopped her from saying she loved him? Or was he a fool to hope she cared for him as much as he did for her? Was she truly worried about his locket, or had she been buying time to figure out how to tell him she didn't return his feelings?

A soft, birdlike whistle signaled McCain and his men were in place.

Heath shoved thoughts of Ginny away and focused on stopping the bandits. He aimed his pistol at the ground near the bandits' mounts and pulled the trigger. The horses reared and bucked, breaking the branch and galloping away—exactly as Heath had hoped they would.

Cursing erupted inside, and the light in the cave vanished.

Heath stayed low, his gaze locked on the cave's entrance. He fired again, this shot hitting the ground just outside the cave.

Landa's amused voice rasped from within. "You can't get us out that easy!"

"Come out now, and you'll see tomorrow's sunrise," Heath called back.

A shot rang out from the cave.

Heath ducked as the bullet ricocheted off a nearby boulder with a loud crack that sent shards of rock flying. He clenched his teeth. With night fully upon them, the bandits were firing blind, but one lucky bounce could still take him and his posse out.

"Hold your fire until I give the word," Heath hissed to the men. "Let's not get hit by our own bullets."

Heath fired another shot, aiming high to keep the bandits pinned without risking a ricochet. The bandits shot back, but their bullets careened off the rocks, whistling dangerously through the air. One bullet struck a boulder nearby, splintering off into the dirt near his boot.

"Stay low!" Heath shouted the ready signal, then darted behind a taller rock. He glanced right and left but in the darkness couldn't make out either of the men who should be there. He'd have to trust they were with him.

"Now!" Heath barked, standing up and firing three quick shots toward the cave entrance. The rest of his men followed suit, pouring fire toward the mouth of the cave in successive waves.

Landa and whoever was with him returned fire, their shots mostly flying harmlessly into the desert but occasionally bouncing off boulders, forcing Heath and his men to duck.

By the time the third man had emptied his chambers, Heath's weapon was reloaded. He fired more shots low into the gaping hole, hoping to strike a calf or knee that would stop the bandits while minimizing the risk of his bullets bouncing off the cave walls and ricocheting out.

When the last of his men emptied his weapon for a second time, they paused. Waited.

Silence dragged on, stretching every second into eternity. Then, from within the cave, came the scrape of shuffling feet. Three gunshots exploded in rapid succession, their sharp cracks mingling with the echo of tumbling rocks. An unfamiliar voice yelled something in Spanish. From inside came more cries and the muffled sounds of a scuffle.

"Let's go!" Heath shouted to his men as he charged the entrance, pistol loaded and ready. They followed him into the den, but it was empty. Heath strode straight through to the toppled wall near the northwest corner.

McCain met him with a grin and an offered hand. "Your plan worked."

Heath accepted his grip and was hoisted up and out of the opening, onto another, flatter boulder behind the cave. The bandit Heath didn't recognize lay unconscious on the rock, a bullet wound in his arm, his wrists and feet bound. Landa sat beside him, wrists bound behind him, a bloody bandage wrapped around his neck. His expression was that of a man clinging to consciousness by pure hate.

Ignoring Landa's dark eyes, Heath bent down and slipped his blood-soaked leather thong over the bandit's head. A slice of Heath's knife freed the locket. He stuffed the ruined leather into Landa's pocket, then pulled out a handkerchief and cleaned the locket, relishing its cool weight against his palm. For a moment, he stood still, his thumb brushing over its delicate surface. Memories of Susannah and the day she'd given him the jewelry surged up, but he pushed them down. There was still work to be done.

He met Landa's hateful gaze. "Who's your sleepy friend?"

The man spewed a slew of filthy words at him until one of the posse stuffed a rag in his mouth and tied it in place. "That's enough of that."

McCain eyed their unconscious captive. "Could be wrong, but I think I've seen him in town before. I heard him called Ignacio."

Heath studied the bearded man. That was why the man had seemed familiar before. The *wanted* poster for Ignacio Bicuna currently tucked in Heath's saddlebag showed a clean-shaven man, but the rest of the bandit's features matched up. "I think you're right."

Heath waited for satisfaction to fill him. He'd finally caught what was left of Valadez's gang. Minus Chavarria. He still had no idea what had become of that notorious bandit. But Chavarria's disappearance wasn't why gratification eluded him. Now that the danger had passed, all he wanted was to be at Ginny's side and see for himself that she was recovering.

Heath tucked the locket safely into his pocket. "Let's load them up and take them back to town."

McCain and the others hoisted the bandits and carted them back to the posse's waiting horses.

Heath spurred his horse down the northern slope of the hill, guiding the posse back toward Campo. If Ginny was well and awake when he arrived—which was by no means certain—did he dare hope she'd express a hint of romantic attachment, or should he be bracing himself for her cold look of rejection?

～

December 5, 1875
Campo, California

Ginny stirred, her eyes closed. What was...? Why...? Noise? Fractured thoughts and images whisked through her mind. Pain. So much pain. Flashes of a gunfight. Her face in the dirt. She'd been shot. Heath. Another hazy image. A doctor? Oh. The chloroform. He'd stitched her up. Must've finished. How long ago? Still so much pain.

Sleep lured her, but shouts from outside tugged at her attention. She forced her eyes open. The room was dim, a single lantern casting a soft glow that flickered against the walls. Clyve snored in the chair beside her bed, his hat pulled low over his eyes. The cheers of several men carried through the thin walls. She blinked away the haze, turning her head toward the window. She pushed herself up on her left elbow, clamping her lips against a cry of pain as her entire right side burned in protest.

Through the small window, Ginny watched the posse ride into town as dawn broke over the hills behind them. One bandit's lifeless body was draped over a horse, while Cesar Landa and Ignacio Bicuna rode with their hands bound in front of them and tied to the pommel of their saddles. Bicuna's arm was freshly bandaged. She didn't remember him being injured when he fled town. There must have been more shooting.

Where was Heath? She scanned the figures trailing into town but didn't see him. Sweat gathered on her brow, and her arm trembled beneath her, threatening to give way as her pathetic energy drained. She steeled herself, straining for any glimpse of him. But he wasn't out there. Her throat tightened. Had she missed her chance to tell him she loved him? Because she was certain now. The moment he'd ridden out of town, regret had filled her. If she could've called him back, she would have.

She closed her eyes. *Lord, please let him be safe. Don't let it be too late to tell him how I feel.*

The door creaked open, and Heath peeked through the crack.

He was safe. *Thank You, Lord.* She collapsed onto the mattress.

"She's awake," he said to someone behind him, as he widened the opening.

Biddie rushed past him to the bed, her large stomach leading the way. "Oh, Ginny. Thank the good Lord you're alive!" Her hands fluttered over Ginny like nervous birds. It was clear her sister wanted to hug her but couldn't decide how to do it without hurting Ginny. Biddie finally settled for smoothing Ginny's hair. "You poor thing. As if you haven't been through enough. What did those horrible men do to you?"

"How..." Ginny's voice came out in a croak, so she cleared it before trying again. "What are you doing here? You should be in bed."

Gideon joined his wife at Ginny's bedside. "After they caught Landa and Bicuna, Heath sent one of the posse members to the ranch to check on Alberto and tell us what had happened. I tried to tell her I'd come check on you, but—"

"Of course, I had to see you for myself." Biddie waved a dismissive hand. "Besides, I'm feeling just fine, and if I had to spend one more hour lying in that bed..."

As Biddie prattled on about the miseries of bed rest, Ginny forced a smile, but her eyes kept darting past Biddie's shoulder to Heath, who remained in the doorway watching her.

He looked just as relieved to see her as she was to see him. But the warmth in his eyes was shadowed with an unanswered question. The answer he needed bubbled up inside her—the one she'd been too afraid to speak before he left. But the room was too full. She couldn't say what she needed to with so many witnesses.

"Ginny? Did you hear me?" Biddie's tone pulled Ginny back to find her sister frowning. "I said the cattle are all better now. I thought you'd be happy." She laid the inside of her wrist on Ginny's forehead. "I don't feel a fever..."

"I don't think her health is the problem." Gideon's too-knowing look bounced between Ginny and Heath.

Ginny dropped her gaze to the quilt, her fingers fiddling with the hem. Were her feelings so apparent? The back of her neck warmed.

Biddie's tone turned confused. "Then what—?"

"Sheriff, what are your intentions now that Chavarria's men are all either dead or captured?" Gideon leaned against the wall, crossing his arms.

"Not all. Miguel and Fedorro Torres weren't among those who raided the town." He glanced at Ginny, and her heart twisted. He hadn't mentioned Gabriella. Would she be in his report to the governor? What had happened after Gabriella helped them escape? Had the Torres siblings left the gang, waited at the hideout, or...had Landa discovered Gabriella's betrayal and—

"And we haven't captured Chavarria himself," Heath continued, cutting off her fearful wondering. "I still don't understand where he went or why Landa seems to be calling the shots now. He refused to answer any questions on the ride back." Heath's voice held more than a hint of frustration.

Gideon shifted, making the floorboards beneath him creak as he glanced at Biddie, then back to Heath. "We thought you'd heard."

Heath stiffened, as if bracing for a blow. "Heard what?"

"Chavarria was killed by someone who recognized him in Arizona last week. He'd been working on a ranch there under a false name."

Biddie nodded. "At least, that's what the newspaper claimed three days ago. No one's verified the body yet."

Shock barreled through Ginny, as Heath sagged against the wall. Once again, someone had beaten him to capturing the man he was after. What would this mean for his career?

She peered up at him, but his attention was fixed on the opposite wall, his face lined with a defeated exhaustion that laced his words. "Someone still needs to take Bicuna and Landa to jail. I'll bring them in, collect the reward—which will be considerably less without Chavarria—distribute the shares among the rest of the posse. Then I'll stay to see that Bicuna and Landa both stand trial."

Ginny's stomach twisted with the thought of Heath returning to Alameda. He had a life there, a job he loved. According to Jeb, keeping his position as sheriff was a big part of why Heath had decided to pursue Chavarria in the first place. Surely, missing out on Chavarria wouldn't mean as much when he explained that he'd taken down the rest of the gang and saved a town in the process. What if he went back and realized how much he'd be giving up to join her on the ranch?

She blinked. Wait. Had he said he would join her? She searched her fuzzy memory but found nothing. He'd made her no promise. He'd only said that he loved her. Why had she assumed he'd be willing to give up his life up north for her? Other than Biddie and Preston, no one had ever given up anything on her behalf. And they were family.

Heath was...well, she couldn't put her finger on the right word, but he wasn't family.

"And after the trial?" Gideon prodded.

"I'm not sure." Heath turned his questioning eyes back to her. "The original plan was to stay in my own county for a good long while. I've been gone a lot these past few years. You said Alberto is doing well, but if the rest of my injured men are still at Carrizo Creek Station, I might return to help with their journey home. Or..."

She focused on a knot in one of the bedposts near her feet. Maybe he was hinting that he might come back for her. Maybe not. She was too afraid to ask. Because whatever his answer might be now, once the fame from capturing notorious bandits spread, his job would be more than secure. He'd be a hero. Why would he even consider giving that up?

She swallowed hard. The declaration she'd been so eager to give moments before now felt heavy in her throat. If she told him now—if she laid her heart bare and confessed her love— would it be too much? Would he feel obligated, pressured to choose her over the life he'd already built for himself? How long before that sacrifice grew into resentment? And resentment into anger?

Cattle ranching was far from the steady work of a lawman. Dangerous though his job was, it was guaranteed income. Cattle ranching was a gamble by comparison. Drought, disease, rustlers...any one of them could end her dreams in a blink. What if Heath gave up his life up north only to lose her ranch as well? As her husband, he'd feel obligated to stay with her no matter what.

She couldn't risk being the reason he spent the rest of his life miserable.

She let her eyes drift shut and pretended to fall asleep, focusing on slow, even breaths. *Please just leave, Heath. Before I lose the courage to let you go.*

CHAPTER 21

DECEMBER 8, 1875
CAMPO, CALIFORNIA

*T*he snoring from the next room rasped through Ginny's brain as loud as a saw. She sighed, staring at the cracked plaster above her hotel bed. Had Biddie always snored? Maybe it was a pregnancy thing. How did Gideon sleep through it? Whatever the case, at least her sister was finally resting.

Three days ago, Gideon had announced it was time to return to Lupine Valley Ranch, but Biddie refused to leave town. Her gift of persuasion swept aside his protests with the force of a flash flood. Since then, she'd been at Ginny's bedside day and night. This morning, Ginny found her sister asleep in the chair again. Convincing Biddie to take a nap had taken all day.

Had Ginny known it would come with such racket, she might have napped first. Instead, she lay awake, without a single thing to do but think. Worse than the stitches pulling tight with every shift was feeling as useless as a broken fence-post. How was she supposed to endure weeks of idleness when ranch life wouldn't wait?

The trod of boot steps in the hall yanked her from her thoughts. She stiffened, her breath catching. She knew that gait, the solid, confident thump. Heath.

Her heart raced. He must be here to say goodbye before leaving for Alameda. He'd stayed in town to rest up before his long trip home, and she'd managed to avoid talking with him by pretending to be asleep each time he stopped by. Biddie had played along, acting as a buffer, despite her disapproval. But now—

A second set of footsteps came down the hall.

Heath's low voice sounded outside her door. "How's she doing?"

Silas said, "She's about as well as can be expected, I'd say. No infection." Boot steps faded away, followed by the *whap* of the front door on its frame.

The knot in her chest grew tighter. Had Heath gone? It hadn't sounded like his gait, but—

Knock-knock-knock. Her door rattled beneath someone's knuckles. Silas had visited her earlier in the day. This must be Heath.

She squeezed her eyes shut, forcing herself to take long, slow breaths. *Please, just go away.* Every time he came, it grew harder to keep silent. Surely, this would be his last attempt. If she could pretend to be asleep again, maybe she could avoid the ache that came with his goodbye.

For a long breath, nothing happened. Then the door squeaked open. She swallowed, her body going stiff as a plank. Boards creaked, and the air in the room shifted as he moved closer. His presence was as comforting as a lantern in the dark. The urge to reach out and grab onto him nearly overcame her resolve. She clenched her fists beneath the blanket.

"Ginny." His whisper curled around her name as gentle as a plea.

She felt his warmth beside the bed, too close. Her breath hitched, but she didn't open her eyes. *Please, just leave.*

His hand landed gently on her uninjured shoulder. "Ginny."

He wasn't going to leave without talking to her this time.

With a soft groan, she cracked her eyes open, blinking up at him groggily, pretending she'd just woken. The sight of him clean, freshly shaved, and well rested nearly did her in. The unmistakable softness in his eyes made her swallow, but she couldn't help drinking it in like rain after a drought. Was she making a mistake, as Biddie said? Maybe she *should* confess her true feelings and let him decide their future. Her lips parted.

"I'm leaving," he said quietly, his voice thick as he brushed loose hair from her face. "Heading out for Carrizo Creek Station and then on to home."

Home. Her mouth clamped shut. He'd just referred to Alameda as home. Of course he had. Alameda was his home. That was why she needed to keep her feelings to herself. Keeping him here was just selfish.

Hope had broken free, but that word had roped it back in as surely as a calf at the end of a lasso. She nodded stiffly, forcing her throat to work. "Goodbye, then." Her voice sounded strange, brittle, as though she might shatter at any second. It wasn't a feeling she was used to. Heath needed to go. She shifted away from his touch.

Still, he lingered, his gaze locked on hers, as if searching for something. "I'll be ba—"

"Could you get Biddie for me?" She couldn't let him finish. If he offered to come back one more time, she might just let him. But giving up his life for her would never work. Losing him now was far better than losing him after they'd exchanged vows. It had to be.

She searched the room until her gaze fell on the bedpan sitting awkwardly on the nightstand. She waved her good hand toward it, the back of her neck growing hot as a branding iron. "I—uh—need her help."

He blinked, the words on his lips falling away as he glanced at the pan, then toward the door. "Sure." He stepped back, his expression filled with confusion—and hurt. She could see it in the set of his jaw, the way his shoulders sagged.

He turned toward the door, and the moment he was gone, she let out a shaky breath and squeezed her eyes against the tears. She'd done the right thing. It was better this way. For both of them.

The door opened again, and Biddie waddled in, her enormous belly preceding her. "I'm so sorry. I didn't mean to sleep that long."

Ginny tried to smile, but her heart ached too much.

Behind Biddie, Heath passed in the hall, catching Ginny's eye through the narrow gap in the door. His expression held questions she couldn't answer, then his eyes shuttered with frustration. And he was gone, the sound of his boots fading down the corridor.

Biddie reached for the bedpan, but Ginny waved her away. "False alarm. Sorry to wake you. You should go back to sleep."

"Don't be silly. It's almost time to eat." She shuffled toward the door. "I'll go check on the soup." A moment later, Biddie had disappeared down the hall.

Ginny's throat tightened as silence settled around her, the weight of what she hadn't said pressing in.

CHAPTER 22

JANUARY 11, 1876
LUPINE VALLEY RANCH
EASTERN SAN DIEGO COUNTY, CALIFORNIA

"*S*he's almost here." Ginny adjusted the clean cloth in her hands, ready to catch Biddie's baby the moment she slipped into the world.

Squatting at the end of the bed, with Gideon's arms supporting her, Biddie's breath came in shallow gasps, each one more strained than the last. A soft groan escaped her lips, signaling Ginny that another contraction was starting.

Ginny knelt on the floor, hands steady but her heart racing. She was about to meet her niece.

Biddie's face was flushed, beads of sweat glistening on her brow as she looked down at Ginny, her voice raw. "I can't—"

"Yes, you can," Ginny said in the same tone she used to order Deborah to stay out of the bull's corral. "Just one more push. You're almost there."

With a final, desperate cry, Biddie pushed, her body straining with the effort. Ginny's breath hitched as a tiny, perfect baby fell into her waiting hands. She immediately cleared the baby's airways, and a sharp cry filled the room, echoing off the walls. Ginny's eyes shone with tears of relief as she carefully wiped the baby's face, arms, belly, and—"Oh."

"What?" Biddie's concerned blue eyes peered down at her.

Ginny swallowed and forced a smile. "It's a boy."

Biddie chuckled and Gideon exhaled loudly, his eyes glistening with emotion as he leaned down, pressing a kiss to his wife's forehead. "You did it." He helped his wife onto the bed where she reclined against the sweat-soaked pillows.

As Ginny finished wiping her nephew clean and wrapping him in a cloth, her initial disappointment melted into awe. Her baby sister had created an honest to goodness human. And he was nothing short of perfect.

Ginny moved to the side of the bed, cradling the darling boy in her arms. "He's beautiful, Biddie."

Ginny gently placed the tiny bundle in Biddie's arms, watching as her sister's face lit with joy. "What will you name him?"

"Ezekiel Henry Swift." Gideon's hand rested on Biddie's shoulder, his eyes never leaving his wife and their newborn son.

"Ezekiel from the Bible"—Biddie traced a delicate finger along her son's cheeks—"and of course, Henry, after Father."

"I like it." Ginny had been reading the story of Ezekiel with Biddie and Gideon over the past few weeks, so that pick wasn't much of a surprise. And so far as she knew, Biddie's adopted father, Henry Davidson, had never been anything but kind to every person he'd ever met. "I just have one question."

They both looked at her expectantly.

"How do you feel about a nickname? Ezekiel's a bit of a mouthful."

Biddie returned to admiring her son. "We plan to call him 'Zeke' for short."

Relieved, Ginny watched her sister coo over her son. She had no doubt Biddie would raise him to be a trustworthy man. And for the first time, Ginny wondered whether *she* might make a good mother. Of course, that would mean having a husband. But she'd already pushed away the only man she'd ever considered trusting with that title.

FEBRUARY 4, 1875
ROWLAND RANCH
EASTERN SAN DIEGO COUNTY, CALIFORNIA

*G*inny adjusted her grip on the plate of food balanced in one hand, careful not to let the slice of apple pie slide into the pile of roasted venison. She nodded along as Mrs. Lathrop chattered about how lovely Carmen and Clyve's wedding ceremony had been, though it had ended hours ago. Even the racing and competitions had come and gone. The dancing was in full swing under the stars—not that Mrs. Lathrop seemed the least bit interested in joining the people skipping and swinging their way across the clearing in front of the Rowlands' home.

"They couldn't have picked a better day." The older woman's silver hair glinted in the lantern light. "And Carmen's dress—oh, didn't she look radiant? That shade of blue suits her so well."

"She did look beautiful." Ginny offered a polite smile. Her gaze drifted across the yard to where Carmen and Clyve stood arm in arm, laughing with a group of neighbors. Josie stood nearby, her dark curls catching the moonlight while Clyve bent to say something that made the thirteen-year-old giggle.

Ginny's chest tightened, though she wasn't certain why. Maybe it was the sight of Josie with a loving father figure.

Witnessing their father's murders was something Ginny and Josie had in common. Since Josie's arrival at Lupine Valley Ranch, Ginny had intended to talk to the girl about it, but the right time never seemed to happen. Now...well, now Josie would have the loving family Ginny had never had. Not that Ginny would begrudge the girl one moment of that.

Maybe the pinch in Ginny's lungs came from the way Carmen glowed with a happiness that seemed to light up the night. Ginny was glad for the new family, of course. She wouldn't wish anything less than love and happiness for her friends.

Still, the question gnawed at her—if Josie and Carmen could find a way to step out of their past into something new, why couldn't she?

"Of course, the horse races are always fun," Mrs. Lathrop went on. "Did you see that paint mare pull ahead at the last second? Clyve must be so proud."

"Mm-hmm," Ginny murmured, though she couldn't have named a single horse that had run. Carmen touched Clyve's arm, a small, natural gesture of affection. Ginny's own hand clenched her plate.

The scene felt like a glimpse of something she'd never known she wanted—a family, a partner, a chance to be loved as more than a sister or friend.

This morning, Carmen and Josie had moved their belongings from their room in the Lupine Valley bunkhouse to their new home on Rowland Ranch. Carmen had chosen to entrust not only her own life, but that of her daughter's in Clyve's hands.

But could Ginny do something so risky? She'd always considered herself brave, but if Heath returned and asked her to leave, would she have the courage to say yes? Did she have it in her to leave the ranch, to leave her independence and a life she loved, for something unknown?

"Are you all right, dear?" Mrs. Lathrop leaned forward, her brows knit.

Ginny blinked and smiled quickly. "Just a little tired. It's been a big day."

"It certainly has. But oh, what a wonderful way to celebrate," Mrs. Lathrop said, patting Ginny's arm before bustling away in search of another slice of cake.

Ginny exhaled, letting the smile fade as she turned her eyes to the stars above. Wondering what she'd do was pointless. Heath wasn't coming back, and she loved her life on the ranch. She wasn't leaving.

~

MARCH 4, 1876
LUPINE VALLEY RANCH
EASTERN SAN DIEGO COUNTY, CALIFORNIA

The sun sank low in the sky, bathing Lupine Valley Ranch in warm rays of reds, oranges, and golds. Ginny strode past the sheep corral and spotted a new little lamb lying beside its heavily breathing mama. Ginny hopped the fence and strode toward the ewe. That first-time mama looked too big for just one baby. Sure enough, a quick glance showed she was struggling to push out a fluid-filled sac.

Ginny knocked the ewe onto her side and placed the newborn near the head before kneeling in the straw beside them. "Come on, girl," she murmured, coaxing the ewe with gentle strokes. "Let's see what else you've got."

Reaching inside the sheep, Ginny felt a rush of warmth and moisture. She found two tiny hooves and waited for the ewe's next contraction, then pulled. "It's you and me now, partner," she whispered, gritting her teeth. "You're not alone."

With a mighty effort, the second lamb came tumbling into

the world. Ginny quickly wiped the fluids away and rubbed the little one to get it breathing. The animal shook its head, and Ginny grinned. "That's it, keep shaking." She placed the second lamb beside the first, and the mama started licking her new baby clean. "Welcome to the land of milk and hay."

Sheep rarely birthed more than two at a time, but Ginny reached back in to be sure. Her fingers found a single leg. Not good. "Oh, come on now," she muttered, pushing the baby deeper into the mother. "There's always one troublemaker." Carefully, she manipulated the baby until two legs reached forward. Then, with a slow but steady tug, she pulled the third lamb into the light, its yellow coat revealing a less-than-ideal start to life. "Well, at least you're breathing." She wiped, rubbed, and moved the little one next to its siblings.

After ensuring there was no fourth lamb, Ginny checked the ewe's teats, relieved to see milk flowing easily. "Look at you. Enough to feed a whole brood." She helped the mother back onto her stomach and gave her a pat. "Good job, girl."

Ginny stepped back and leaned against the nearest fence as the new mother nuzzled her lambs, then urged them upright with nudges of her nose and soft grunts.

These three new lives combined with their six ewes and two rams would make for a whole lot more wool. "Maybe we could ask Biddie's adoptive parents if any of the women in their charity home know how to spin and weave wool. Finished products would sell better than raw wool."

Satisfied the lambs were doing well, Ginny hurried across the corral and jumped over the fence. She scrubbed up to her elbows in the wash bucket by the barn, then scurried toward Biddie's house. Ginny's nephew woke his mama up at all hours, making it next to impossible to judge when Biddie would be awake. Hopefully, she was now and they could compose a telegram together. Ginny didn't want to wait to send a letter. They'd already sent one asking about replacements for Carmen and Josie. She needed to make her request for these additional skills known before the Davidsons made a decision about whom to send to the ranch.

As Ginny approached Biddie and Gideon's house, she caught a glimpse of the couple through the window. They were wrapped in a kiss that could make a grizzly bear blush. "Oh, no. No, ma'am. I ain't interrupting that!" Ginny spun on her heel, wishing she could unsee the intimate moment.

She contemplated running to tell Esther and Lei Yan about their new lambs instead, but they were out checking the cattle, and little Deborah was visiting Josie at the Rowlands'. A pang struck her as she surveyed the empty ranch yard. Even Alberto was gone, having received permission to travel home just after the New Year.

Had the former posse guide written Heath of his improved health? What was Heath doing right now? Was he happy?

She prayed he was happier than she was. Not that she was miserable. How could she be? Her life was going well. She'd been blessed with avoiding infection, her wounds had completely healed, and she was working on recovering her full strength. Her sister had successfully delivered a fine son. Everyone on the ranch was healthy and happy. The cattle had birthed a record number of calves, and even the sheep were producing in abundance. The legacy she'd said she wanted seemed within her grasp. Yet...

Standing in the middle of her yard, surrounded by the sights and sounds of success, she couldn't help but wonder. "Is the ranch really worth the price of living without Heath?" The weight of the question settled as heavy as a stubborn heifer on her chest. Most days, she was surrounded by the others who lived on her ranch—working side by side, sunup to sundown—yet she'd battled the sting of loneliness every day since she'd let Heath go.

Before he'd left, she'd held her peace to guarantee his. Her worry that giving up his calling as a sheriff would eventually embitter him toward her remained. "But what if I gave up this life for him?"

She shivered. How could she possibly consider such a notion? Without her land, she'd be entirely dependent on him —a man. She'd sworn on her life never to trust any man with so much.

As dusk settled over the quiet valley, Ginny's heart battled within, caught between the land that was meant to be her legacy and the man who made her believe in a future worth sharing. How could she possibly choose?

CHAPTER 23

*H*eath stepped out of the jailhouse and battled a gust of wind to shut the heavy wooden door behind him. He glanced over at Deputy Ross, who was busy hammering extra nails into the flyers posted on the wall. One was for Ross's candidacy, the other for Heath's, both asking the good folks of Alameda to vote for them come the election which was still eight months away.

He stared at the words urging his neighbors to reelect him, waiting for the excitement and determination that had fueled him in previous election years. Instead he found himself wondering what Ginny would be doing in November. Did she ever think about him?

"Don't worry." Ross drew two more nails from his pocket and stuck one between his lips. "You're sure to win."

Heath lifted an eyebrow at his friend. "That doesn't bother you?"

"Not really." Ross pounded in the first nail and pulled the second from his mouth. "I mean, would I like the job? Absolutely. But you're a great sheriff. I'm just honored to be nominated."

Uncomfortable with hearing the desire he lacked in the voice of his competitor, Heath tugged his hat lower and pulled his bandana over his face to shield against the sharp bite of the air. "Storm's coming in fast."

"Yeah, and it wants to tear these flyers right off the wall." Ross pounded in another nail. "It's a good thing they moved the big celebration indoors."

"I'm headed there now, if you still think you can handle things tonight." The gale whipped Heath's duster against his legs and stirred up loose dirt from the wooden sidewalk.

"I don't know." Ross made a show of looking up and down the street as he scratched his chin. The clatter of shutters and occasional slam of a door echoed down the near-empty road. Alameda was exceptionally quiet tonight, save for the racket of the incoming storm and the distant murmur of a saloon. "It's pretty wild out. I might need you, after all."

"You're probably right." Heath nodded thoughtfully. "Too bad, though. Staying means I won't be able to bring back that slice of berry pie I promised to save you."

Ross laughed and waved Heath away. "Oh, go on, and give Garret my congratulations."

"I will." Heath grinned and strode away, his boots thumping loudly down the boardwalk.

"And don't forget that pie!" Ross shouted after him.

"What pie?" Heath teased before turning the corner. The smell of salt from the bay mingled with the faint scent of wood smoke drifting from chimneys. With Landa and Bicuna locked up and awaiting their reckoning, the city had a different feel to it, despite Miguel still running free.

Heath's former translator and guide hadn't been among the men who'd raided Campo. He suspected Miguel had been with the bandits' reinforcements who were supposed to arrive from Mexico but never had. According to the men Heath had asked to keep watch on Miguel's uncle's home, the traitor hadn't returned to Alameda County. If he was smart, Miguel would spend the rest of his days south of the border.

Heath paused and took a deep breath, relishing the scent of home as he surveyed the calm streets. Satisfied that the night showed no signs of relinquishing its quiet spell, he continued on his way. A bit of pride lightened his step. So he hadn't captured Chavarria. But he had stopped the rest of Chavarria's gang. And maybe that wasn't much, but it seemed to him he'd helped make the state just a little safer. A little better for folks who deserved peace.

People like Ginny.

Every day since he'd returned, she'd been on his mind, as constant as the wind tugging at his collar. He'd told her what was in his heart—that he loved her, plain and simple. But she hadn't returned his feelings. The pain of that truth cut deep, even now.

The wind picked up again, a rushing whistle in his ears. Heath pushed his hands deeper into his pockets, his fingers brushing the rough wool of the gloves tucked inside. He pulled them out and shoved them on. Ginny had been through more than her share of trials and kept her emotions close. But he'd been certain he'd seen love in her eyes when he returned from capturing Landa and Bicuna. Yet she'd said nothing. Not one word of encouragement. No hint that she'd even like him to return or write letters. Nothing but a stiff goodbye when he'd told her he was leaving. How could he have been so wrong?

But then... Heath stared out at the darkened town. What if she *had* loved him? What if fear had kept her from speaking her heart? Heaven knew she'd been hurt by enough people she cared about to warrant the shell she hid behind. What if he hadn't done enough to break through? A part of him couldn't shake the feeling that he'd let go too soon. That if he'd just pushed a little harder, stayed a little longer, she might've found the courage to voice the words he longed to hear.

The wind pushed at him, reminding him that Jeb and the others were waiting. He hastened his steps. He had to believe he'd done right by her—by them both. But still, a small voice nagged at him.

What if?

~

*H*eath stood at the gate of Cole's house, lantern light spilling through the windows, casting a warm glow across the yard. The wind had died to a soft breeze, rustling the oak leaves. He pushed through the gate and headed for the porch, the sounds of laughter and conversation drifting from inside. The smell of roasted meat and fresh bread hit him, reminding him he hadn't eaten since noon at the jail.

Inside, nearly two dozen people crowded around a long makeshift table—some sitting, others standing with plates. Children filled the floor wherever space could be found. The warmth from their bodies and the fire at the far end pushed back the evening chill. Heath searched the crowd until he spied Garret leaning heavily on a crutch but grinning from ear to ear as Cole's daughter, Agatha, stood beside him, her eyes sparkling with happiness. Cole sat at the head of the table nearby, his face weary but content, watching the newly engaged couple with a mix of pride and surrender. Heath's father-in-law wasn't yet walking on his own, but the doctors were hopeful that would come with time.

Heath moved through the crowd, nodding at familiar faces. The room buzzed with voices, the clatter of cutlery, and chairs scraping closer to the table. The smell of venison stew mixed with herbs and fresh pie.

Garret spotted Heath and called him over before grabbing the back of his younger brother's chair. Garret all but dumped the young man out of it. "I told you this seat was for Heath."

Heath tried to protest that he was fine standing, but the younger Lawson boy had already disappeared into the crowd with his plate. Still, Heath hesitated, raising a brow at Garret. "Don't you need to rest your leg?"

Garret released the chair to wrap his free arm around Agatha's shoulders with a wide grin. "You couldn't pry me away from this beautiful woman."

Heath chuckled and gratefully sank into the seat. A fresh plate was set before him by arms he couldn't follow to a face before they disappeared. He'd just finished thanking God for his meal when one of Garret's cousins shouted for silence. It took a moment, but eventually, the din quieted, and all eyes turned expectantly to Cole.

Their host cleared his throat. "I wasn't always for this engagement." He gave a rueful smile. "Truth is, I had a lot of doubts about Garret and whether Agatha would be happy married to a lawman. But when we were holed up at the stage station, licking our wounds, Garret told me something I couldn't ignore."

A baby fussed somewhere in a nearby room, occasionally the fire popped, and a few people shifted in their seats, the ladder-back chairs squeaking beneath them, but no one spoke.

"Agatha wanted to elope." Cole glanced at his daughter, who smiled sheepishly, as a few people gasped. "And it made me realize something—no matter how hard I tried to protect her, life's got its own way of bringing pain. Whether they marry or not, if something happened to Garret, she'd mourn him just the same. Only difference is, if I stood in their way, she'd be grieving a lot more than his loss. She might hate me for taking away her chance at happiness." He reached up for her hand, and she gave it. "That's when I knew I had to let her make her own decisions." He shifted and narrowed his eyes at Garret in a mock threat. "But if you ever do anything to hurt her, I'll hunt you down and gut you like a hog."

"Yes, sir." Garret's serious eyes held his future father-in-law's. "And I want you to know it'll be my honor to do everythin' within my power to make Agatha the happiest woman alive so long as I live." He faced the rest of the room with a somberness Heath rarely saw on the younger man. "Waitin' wasn't easy, but I wasn't about to give up either of my dreams. I've known since I was a boy that I wanted to marry Agatha, but it wasn't until I helped bring my pa's murderer to justice that the dream of being a lawman who could make a difference was born." His loving gaze locked with Agatha's. "From then on, I couldn't imagine my life without either one, and I was blessed that Agatha not only understood but supported my callin'." Garret drew his arm from around Agatha and lifted his glass from the mantel behind her. He held it high, his hand steady despite the crutch he leaned on. "To never givin' up on our dreams!"

"Hear! Hear!" The people cheered, and everyone clinked glasses before taking a drink and resuming their conversations.

The weight of Garret's words settled deep in Heath's chest. The young man's determination to fight for both his dreams resonated, a sharp contrast to the quiet hollowness Heath had been carrying for months. What was he holding onto these days? Passion for upholding the law had once burned in him with the same fire Garret carried, but that flame had dimmed, leaving him with nothing but embers.

But Ginny—his love for her still flared bright as the sun, even if gaining her love in return seemed equally as distant.

Heath swirled the amber liquid in his glass, staring at it as if the answer would appear at the bottom. With men like Garret, Jeb, and Ross in Alameda, was Heath even needed here? Or had his wounded pride been the true drive behind his desire for reelection?

Cole's hand settled on his shoulder, startling him. "What are you still doing here?"

Heath jerked back. "What do you mean?"

"I haven't forgotten the way you looked at my Susannah." His father-in-law gave him a knowing look. "I wasn't sure I'd ever see that look again...until I caught you watching Ginny over the campfire not long before we got ambushed."

Guilt about choked him. "No one could ever replace Susannah."

"Of course not." Cole lifted his chin, his eyes sparkling with pride. "She was one of a kind, that girl. But, Heath." He leaned forward. "Your heart's too big to keep to yourself. I trust you can keep my Susannah's memory alive and still have room for loving Ginny." His gaze moved pointedly from Garret to Jeb to Enrique and finally to Turner, who stood at the other end of the room laughing with Jeb's sister. "We're all back home, safe and sound, if a little worse for wear. Landa and Bicuna are locked away. Chavarria's death has been confirmed. The Valadez gang is no more." He nodded to Heath. "Your job's done here. Go find some happiness for yourself."

Heath's throat was so full of emotion, he had to swallow twice before he could speak. "What if she doesn't want me?"

Cole barked a laugh. "Oh, trust me. That woman wants you. It may just take her a little longer to admit it. From what Jeb told me about her friend Gabriella, Ginny has reason to be cautious. But I believe you're clever enough and stubborn enough to find a way through her defenses."

Heath wanted to ask how the man could be so confident of

Ginny's feelings but decided the question sounded too close to a pup begging for scraps and kept his mouth shut.

Cole was right. Heath's time as sheriff had served its purpose, but the job wasn't what his heart was set on anymore. Ginny was. A future with her was worth the risk of rejection. But how could he convince her to trust him with her heart and her future?

CHAPTER 24

April 15, 1876
Lupine Valley Ranch
Eastern San Diego County, California

*G*loomy clouds blocked the late-morning light, and a light drizzle began as Ginny set the final stick of dynamite in place in the mine, the moisture making dirt cling to the soles of her boots.

Lord, please don't let the weather interfere with my plans.

Praying had become second nature since she'd turned her life over to God in the months since Heath's departure. Rather than avoiding Biddie and Gideon's nightly Bible readings, she looked forward to them. The three of them even spent long Sunday afternoons talking about God.

Ginny smirked as she stepped back from the cave. Biddie was delighted, of course. But Ginny couldn't begrudge her sister a touch of gloating. She'd been right. Trusting God with her worries hadn't erased them, but it had given Ginny a peace like she'd never known existed. It was strange. She'd always thought of peace as the absence of problems, but now she knew

God's peace existed alongside the problems. Because no matter what happened, she could have assurance that God would eventually work things out for good.

Such as how He'd worked things out for Garret. His letter had come as a surprise. She hadn't expected any of the men from the posse to give her a second thought once they'd healed enough to travel home. But Garret had written to invite her to his upcoming wedding. Apparently, he'd told Agatha about Ginny's advice to let Agatha make her own decision regarding what she was willing to sacrifice to marry Garret. Even though Cole had come around after their near-death experience and given his blessing, Agatha still appreciated Ginny's words, and they both wanted her as a guest on their special day. Of course, it was a long distance to travel, and they'd understand if she couldn't make it, but they wanted her to know she was welcome.

The sentiment had caught Ginny completely off guard. She'd had no notion Garret felt any sort of connection to her, and it was right nice of him and his fiancée to invite her. Still, that wasn't the part of the letter that lingered in her mind. No, it was the part about letting Agatha make her own decision that had hit Ginny like a punch to the gut and kept her from sleeping.

Ginny, in her arrogance, had not given Heath the same chance she'd told Garret to give Agatha. Instead, she'd kept her feelings to herself, hiding behind silence and making the decision for them both. Ginny was heartily sick of discovering she was a hypocrite.

She struck a match, and the sharp tang of sulfur mixed briefly with the scents of wet stone and juniper. The weight of the moment pressed heavy on her heart, and she hesitated. It wasn't just the mine she was sealing today. It was the past—every scar left from the day of the attack, both visible and invisible. Jaw tight, she took one last look at the yawning black tunnel ahead of her before setting the fuse alight. And dashing through the juniper bush to safety.

Lupine Valley was cloaked in mist, softening the familiar rocky slopes. She turned her face toward the gray sky. The light drizzle kissed her cheeks, mingling with the sweat and dust that clung to her skin.

The explosion rumbled through the earth beneath her, a muted roar that reverberated up her legs and into her chest. She didn't flinch, just waited as the tunnel entrance caved in, rocks tumbling with a final exhale, sealing away the played-out garnet mine—and everything it reminded her of.

She stood still as stone as the dust slowly settled. When at last the air was clear once more, she smiled. It was done. A great weight lifted from her shoulders. She wasn't tied to this place anymore, not in the way she had been before.

Gabriella's face flashed in her mind. Jeb had sent word that another posse had been sent to the hideout, but the place had been abandoned. According to both Bicuna and Landa, on the morning of the Campo raid, the Torres siblings had been ordered to drive two wagons carrying at least nine more men to aid in the attack, but they'd never arrived. There'd been no sign of Gabriella or her brother since the failed robbery. In his letter, Jeb had speculated that the two might have run off to restart their lives apart from the gang, likely under new names.

Ginny prayed it were true for Gabriella's sake. She swallowed, the bitterness of regret catching in her throat. "I forgive you," she whispered, the words carrying no anger, only quiet release. As sprinkles dampened her cheeks, she prayed that one day she'd see Gabriella again. That she could look her in the eye and share her forgiveness—apologize for not understanding sooner, for letting the hurt fester. To thank her properly for saving Ginny's life, as well as Jeb's and Heath's.

She brushed her hands against her moist trousers. With everyone else in town, the ranch was quiet, the only sounds the soft patter of increasing rain on the thirsty earth and the distant sigh of wind through the shrubs. She turned to soak in the sight of her land, her ranch—the symbol of her freedom.

She'd been holding on to this land and her independence as though they were all that mattered—all she had left. But that wasn't true, was it? Heath had been in her heart every day since he'd ridden away, every minute. She hadn't let him go—not really.

She'd made the wrong choice in Campo. She should have told Heath she loved him, instead of pushing him away. Should have been brave enough to reach for a future with him.

She squared her shoulders and turned toward the ranch buildings. It was time to stop making choices to prove she could live without him. Because, of course, she could. She just didn't want to. She didn't want to live another day without his breathtaking generosity, his humble strength, and his unflappable integrity. She refused to keep living in this empty space between love and fear.

Her mind was made up. She would pack her bags and head to Alameda. Tell Heath what she'd been too cowardly to say before. That she loved him, that she'd missed him with every breath since he'd left. She didn't know what their future would look like—whether they could build a life together in Alameda or if they'd find a way to make this land, her land, their home. All she knew was that wherever he was, that was where she wanted to be.

Even if it meant giving up this ranch she'd fought so hard to keep, she'd find a way to make things work. For him. For her. For them.

A cool drop slid down her cheek, and she wiped it away. She'd tell Biddie and Gideon as soon as they returned. The thought of leaving them layered sadness over her hope, but there was no more doubt. It was time to break down the walls of the fortress she'd built around her heart and instead, let herself believe in the strength of love to heal what fear had broken. She prayed Biddie and Gideon would understand her decision.

~

*G*inny gazed out a small window from Biddie's front room and ignored the quiet protest of her tight scars as she shifted her weight from one foot to the other, gently rocking her four-month-old nephew in her arms. The earlier drizzle had long since passed, and the misty fog clinging to the mountains had burned away under the afternoon sun, leaving behind crisp, cool air.

Biddie hummed as she stirred a pot over the stove, the scent of simmering broth mingling with the soapy smell of freshly scrubbed floors and the leather oil Gideon was rubbing into his boots by the door. The soft crackle of the fire in the hearth filled the comfortable silence between them, punctuated only by the rub of Gideon's cloth and the baby's occasional gurgle.

Ezekiel clutched the fabric of her shirt in his tiny fist, his tug drawing her attention to his happy hazel eyes. A pang hit her heart, wondering how this little boy would grow up surrounded by horses and cattle but no men aside from his father. Clyve would probably stop by now and then, but it wouldn't be the same as having other men working the ranch. She recalled the feeling of being the only female on the ranch until Gabriella had arrived. *Rotten* didn't begin to describe it. But the women of Lupine Valley Ranch couldn't be compared with the ilk Oliver had gathered. Still, would Ezekiel feel lonely surrounded by mostly women?

Ginny had expected to be here, watching over him, teaching him as he grew. But now...she wasn't so sure. She might not see Ezekiel toddle across this room or hear his first words. She brushed a thumb gently over his soft cheek, swallowing hard against the lump forming in her throat. Her chest tightened with the thought of leaving Lupine Valley—and yes, the people living there—behind.

"I've decided..." Ginny said, her voice softer than she intended, though it still cut through the comfortable quiet. Both Biddie and Gideon looked her way. "I'm leaving. I've got to find Heath...tell him how I feel and see if there's any chance for a future together."

Biddie set the spoon aside and turned fully from the stove, a sadness in her eyes. "You're leaving?"

Ginny's announcement couldn't be a total shock. During the weeks stuck in bed post-shootout, she'd been at Biddie's mercy. Eventually, her sister had wheedled the truth from her. Ginny had expected scolding or laughter at her cowardice, but Biddie had shown nothing but compassion and grace, as always.

Ginny nodded, forcing herself to keep her gaze steady. "I have to know, and...I might not be coming back." She felt the weight of those words settle between them. When they'd first reunited, Ginny had assumed Biddie's childhood with her adoptive family, the Davidsons, had made her so soft and loving. Now Ginny could see that Biddie's love for the Lord had more to do with it. Ginny would miss their nightly discussions. "If he asks me to stay in Alameda...if he asks me to marry him, I don't know what I'll do. I just know I want him in my life."

"What would you even do there, though?" Biddie nibbled her lip as she always did when worried. "While he's out fighting crime, would he expect you to be waiting at home wearing skirts and sipping tea?" She shook her head. "I can't picture it."

Ginny laughed at the notion. Then she sobered. Would Heath expect her to start wearing skirts and acting more...like Biddie? Did she even know how? Since Heath was an elected official, his wife's behavior would likely have an effect on his reputation.

"Nah." Gideon smirked. "She'll get herself made deputy and help patrol the town."

For a heartbeat, hope lifted her spirits.

Then Biddie whipped a tea towel in his direction. "Be serious."

She was right. No civilized place would accept a woman wearing trousers, let alone one wearing a badge. Ginny swallowed. The ache for Heath's presence pressed against her chest, but how much could she truly give up to be with him?

Biddie strode across the room, her eyes glossed over and hand trembling as she wrapped her arms around Ginny, squeezing Ezekiel between them. "You're wonderful. Don't let anyone tell you any different, no matter where you live." Ginny stiffened, still unused to her sister's physical affection even after three years. Thankfully, Ezekiel squawked in protest, and Biddie backed up with a tearful chuckle. "Heath's a good man. He'll see your worth, even if the rest of them don't."

Ginny's shoulders relaxed at her sister's words. Heath *was* a good man. She'd put off worrying over what might be until she spoke with him and heard what he had to say. There was every chance he'd forgotten her in the months that had passed and a slim chance he'd consider moving back here with her. She wouldn't assume her future was in Alameda or worry about the problems that might cause until she had to.

The lowing of their newest calf brought her gaze back to the window. "What about the ranch? How will the two of you handle it all with a newborn underfoot and me not here to keep things running? Carmen and Josie may be at Rowland Ranch now, but Lei Yan, Esther, and little Deborah still rely on this place." She turned back to Biddie, who'd returned to stirring her broth. "Maybe I ought to wait until you hear back from your parents about more women coming from their charity house. What if they don't have anyone who wants to move here? What if whoever they send ain't any good? We got lucky with the first bunch, but that don't mean—"

"We'll manage." Biddie glanced at Gideon, then back at Ginny. "We'll be fine. But..." Her voice cracked, and she brought a hand to her mouth as the tears spilled over. "Oh, Ginny, I'll miss you terribly. I can't imagine this place without you."

Not more tears. Ginny shifted. "You'll get on fine," she said gruffly, glancing toward Gideon. The baby stirred again, letting out a soft whimper. Ginny crossed the room and handed the boy to his father. "Here, take him before he gets fussy."

Gideon cradled his son with a smile as Ginny stepped back. Biddie's sobs were quiet, muffled, but they lingered in the air as the last of the smoke from the hearth did. Good grief, her sister had been a regular leaky bucket since getting with child. Ginny should've known this conversation would bring on more blubbering.

"I should go." She turned toward the door. "I got to start packing."

And with that, she slipped outside, the cool desert air a welcome relief against her skin.

~

Ginny folded another shirt and laid it carefully in her saddlebag on the table, her fingers lingering on the rough fabric. After drying on a line in front of the fire, the faint scent of wood smoke clung to the cloth. She glanced around her stone-built home, the walls as sturdy and unyielding as the land outside.

The three beds at the back of the only room lay empty. First Biddie, then Lucy had left. Now she was leaving. Would Esther and Deborah move in here if she didn't come back? The thought gnawed at her, though she knew they'd care for the house just fine, and it wasn't as if she could stop in for a visit any time she liked.

Alameda was a long way from Lupine Valley.

She firmed her jaw and focused on folding a pair of trousers.

She should visit the Davidsons, Biddie's adoptive parents, while she was up north—San Francisco was close enough to Alameda. That way, she could size up any potential ranch hands. See if they were really up for the job of handling her land. She wouldn't accept anyone who didn't thrive on hard work. Ranch life wasn't for the faint of heart. Especially in the remote desert so close to the Mexican border.

She lifted the folded trousers from the table. If she didn't come back, the decision of whom to hire would be in Biddie's and Gideon's hands. Not hers. Air whooshed from her lungs as her throat tightened. The land she had bled for, fought for, broken her body and starved herself to keep—it might soon belong to someone else. Sure, she'd given Biddie and Gideon a small stake in her ranch when they'd decided to stay on, but this would be different. She couldn't ask them to take on all the work while she selfishly clung to ownership. Besides, if she married Heath, anything she owned would automatically become his. It was the law. It was why she'd never planned to marry.

She crammed her trousers into the bag and reached for another, then paused. Should she be packing a dress? Foolish thought since she didn't own one.

She moved to the trunk at the foot of the bed and pulled out her leather vest, leather chaps, and her woollies. Would she even need them in Alameda? She snorted and rolled them up before packing them into another bag. Of course she'd need them. She may not be rounding up cattle, but she'd still be riding through rough terrain. Or would she? She tried to picture herself as Biddie had described, wearing a dress and sipping tea in a fancy parlor.

Tried and failed.

She couldn't imagine sitting still all day, stitching frilly flowers and such on pillows or whatever city women did. Surely, Heath wouldn't expect such nonsense of her. He knew her. Knew she thrived on hard work. If he still loved her, as he'd claimed in December, he wouldn't expect her to change who she was. They'd just have to figure out how she could belong in his world.

Or he might come back with her. Then he'd need to figure out how to fit in her world.

That notion sat much better than the other, if she was honest. But spurs and saddles, here she was worrying again. The other night, Gideon had read Scripture that said she needed to *cast her cares on God*. She wasn't exactly sure what that meant, but she'd gathered enough from Biddie to know she wasn't supposed to worry. With greater determination, Ginny focused all her thoughts on packing everything she would need for the long journey north.

By the time her saddlebag was full, the air inside the house felt thick, heavy with memories she wasn't sure she could carry. With a sharp exhale, she fastened the buckle on the bag. Leaving felt like cutting out a piece of her heart.

The hours crawled by, her churning thoughts as unrelenting as a dust storm charging through the quiet of the night. She asked God to bring her peace and eventually, sleep took hold.

But morning came too soon. Forcing her tired muscles to move, she dressed, grabbed her bags, and headed for the barn.

Less than thirty minutes later, the chill of dawn seeped through Ginny's coat as black of night gave way to a pale, creeping gray. She stood in the half circle of light from a lantern she'd hung on a nail outside the barn door. Beside her, the pack horse she'd chosen to follow Mr. Darcy waited, heavy with her supplies. Ginny scanned the empty yard. Had she forgotten anything?

Mr. Darcy stamped his hooves impatiently, puffs of white wafting from his nostrils.

"All right, all right." With a heavy heart, Ginny turned out the light and mounted, the familiar creak of her saddle feeling like home and a stranger all at once. With the click of her tongue, Mr. Darcy ambled into the fading darkness.

Minutes later, she reached the rim of her valley. The wind stirred, carrying the scent of sagebrush and earth, and she pulled the brim of her hat low against the breeze.

She turned in the saddle, her eyes sweeping over her home one last time. Below, the stone house stood as strong and safe as a dark fortress. When Biddie had arrived after the first attack three years ago, this valley had been Ginny's whole world, her reason to keep breathing. She swallowed hard, blinking back the sting of tears.

"Bye," she whispered, her voice barely audible above the soft rustle of the desert wind.

With a final glance, she nudged Mr. Darcy into a trot, his hooves thudding softly against the earth. Ginny rode briskly down the outer western slope of her mountain, her heart torn between the love she was leaving behind and the love she prayed lay ahead.

CHAPTER 25

APRIL 16, 1876
CAMPO, CALIFORNIA

*H*eath leaned against the wooden counter in the Gaskills' store, his fingers tracing the rough grain as he listened to Silas Gaskill talk. The last light of sunset came through the windows, painting the store's shelves in orange hues. Sacks of flour, beans, tobacco, and lantern oil lined the wooden planks. The air inside carried a muddled mix of store goods—spices, leather, and something sweet—blended with the lingering dust kicked up by the day's comings and goings.

"Luman's doing well, Sheriff." Silas's voice was tinged with the weight of the past few months. "Doctors in San Diego say he'll make a full recovery. Can you believe it? After that shot through his lung, most thought he was done for." He puffed his chest. "But my brother's as tough as they come."

Heath nodded, arms crossed, the warmth of the store a welcome contrast to the swiftly cooling desert air. Staying the night in Campo hadn't been his plan. But he'd been forced to wait out a thunderstorm the night before, delaying his start this morning.

Welcome as the news of Luman's recovery was, thoughts of his last visit to this town haunted him. He could almost hear the echo of gunfire, the memory of that bloody December day still fresh. "Glad to hear it. You're no cotton puff yourself, Silas. The way you fought off those bandits...not many men could've done that."

"Well, sure." Silas gave a rueful smile, tapping a rhythm on the counter. "That raid's got me thinking, though. Wondering if we ought to find some way to make this place bulletproof." His gaze swept the wooden walls, patched here and there where bullets had left their mark.

"You thinking of rebuilding?"

Silas scratched his chin, glancing out the window. The sun dipped lower, casting the landscape in a burnt hue. "Maybe. Don't want to make any decisions until Luman's back, though."

Heath remembered the trickiness of driving Landa and Bicuna out of their boulder cave without taking a hit from a ricochet. "What about using stone? Any bullets shot at a rock wall have a good chance at returning to the man who shot them."

"Not a bad idea." Silas grinned, then cocked his head. "Didn't I hear Ginny rebuilt everything out of rock after Valadez and his men torched her pa's place a couple years back? You were out there last year, weren't you? Did it seem to be holding up well?"

"It did." His chest tightened with the mention of Ginny. Just one more night. He'd present her with his plan and...well, then at least, he'd know where he stood.

Silas rubbed the back of his neck, eyes narrowing at the ceiling as he considered. "Might build a cellar too. Dug into the hill. It'd be easier than storing our cold goods in the creek like we do now."

Heath nodded absently. Would Ginny welcome his appearance? Had he been a fool to quit his job and sell everything he owned before speaking with her? Ross had thought so. Though he'd been too eager to take over as interim sheriff—something he expected to increase his odds of winning the election—to put in any real effort to change Heath's mind.

Silas clapped his hands and rubbed them together. "Right. Was there anything else you needed? If not, I think I'll lock up and head over to my shop. Taking on Luman's responsibilities has me running behind with my smithy work."

Heath took another look around the store, then turned back to Silas. "No, I think I'm set. Thanks."

A gasp from behind had Heath spinning toward the door.

Ginny.

As she stood in the doorway, her hat shadowed eyes wide with surprise.

His breath caught in his throat. So much for his plan to rehearse his speech on the ride to her ranch. Still, he couldn't muster a drop of regret that she was there. Now, if she would only hear him out, he might stand a chance.

~

Ginny froze in the doorway, her heart thudding. Heath was here. Leaning against the counter, talking with Silas Gaskill. How? Why? After weeks of battling her heart, she'd finally decided to go to him, and he was right here. Was he there for her, or was he chasing another criminal?

His lips parted, but then he glanced back at Silas, who watched them with curiosity. Heath clamped his mouth shut and strode toward her. "Come on." His warm hand grasped hers, and she let him lead her outside.

Taking her hand was a good sign, wasn't it? Not that she knew much about honorable men like Heath. But he *had* seemed pleased to see her. Or was she misreading a polite smile? Etiquette didn't require him to hold her hand, though. She was almost positive of that. Almost. If only Biddie were there to give a nod or shake of her head—anything to guide the emotions crashing around in Ginny's chest, as lost as a miner without a lantern.

This late in the day, the town was empty. Their boots crunched loudly across the dirt.

Ginny finally found her voice. "Where are we going?"

"To the creek. I've got something to say, and I don't want Silas—" Heath stopped abruptly, his eyes falling on Mr. Darcy and her pack horse waiting near the post. "Where are you going, Ginny?"

She opened her mouth, but the truth stuck in her throat. What if he didn't love her anymore? *Don't be dimwitted. Why else would he be here?* She swallowed hard and squared her shoulders. "I was coming to find you."

Heath lifted one brow, his intense expression unreadable. "Why?"

She stared into the hazel eyes she'd been dreaming of for months and dared trail her fingers over the stubble on his jaw. "Because I love you."

Heath knocked her hat free, cupped the back of her head, and wrapped his other arm around her waist, drawing her into his arms. His lips pressed against hers in a kiss that chased away every thought, every worry, leaving only a warmth that radiated through her, powerful and consuming. She wrapped her arms around his neck, returning his passion. The scent of sweat, leather, and horses clung to him, filling her senses, reminding her of home.

When they finally pulled apart, Heath's eyes shone. Breathless, he pressed his forehead against hers with a laugh. "Ginny Baker, you are like no other woman."

She smirked. "And don't you forget it."

"Never," he promised and kissed her again.

Enjoying the affections of a man had seemed out of reach for as long as she could remember, yet she more than enjoyed Heath's arms around her—she *craved* his touch. The reassurance that her mistake in pushing him away hadn't totally destroyed the love he'd once declared for her. The reassurance that he was truly there and not a trick of her mind.

Eventually, she drew back. "How are you here? Shouldn't you be chasing criminals or something?"

He grinned down at her. "I quit. Sold my home in Alameda. I came back to win your trust, and I hoped, someday, your heart." His voice wavered as he brushed loose strands of hair from her forehead. "I never imagined this." He gazed down at her with a look of wonder.

It seemed foolish, considering his kisses and what he'd just said, but she had to ask. "Then you...you still love me?"

He clasped her face between his hands, hazel eyes staring straight into her soul. "I will always love you."

This time, she couldn't stop the tears, and he wiped them with his thumbs. "Oh, darling, don't cry." He kissed both her cheeks, then wrapped her in a hug so fierce, it nearly stole her breath.

She'd never felt safer. "These are happy tears," she said into his chest.

He pulled back, searching her gaze. "You're sure?"

She nodded. "For the first time in my life." She'd seen Biddie cry on her wedding day and when Ezekiel was born, but it hadn't made sense to her until now. This feeling that her heart was so full of joy it overflowed was entirely new and not at all unwelcome. Because she knew Heath didn't judge her for her tears or think her weak. Instead, Heath saw her for who she really was—broken yet strong, terrified but determined not to let her fears keep her hidden away anymore. Because now she knew true love was worth the risk of getting hurt.

"Good." He pressed another quick kiss to her lips. "I would've been here sooner, but I needed to see a lawyer first and have something drawn up."

Reaching into his coat, Heath pulled out a folded piece of paper. "This is for you. If you sign this with me before we marry, it'll ensure Lupine Valley stays under your control—completely—no matter what happens." His eyes softened as he unfolded the document. "I wasn't planning on showing you this yet, but now that I know you love me...I don't want to wait." He handed her the parchment.

Ginny's breath caught as her eyes scanned the paper. Several of the words were large and unfamiliar, but she understood enough to see he'd spoken the truth. Her chest tightened, not with fear, but with overwhelming relief. Heath wasn't asking her to give up her home, her people, or her independence.

Heath pulled his hat from his head and held it over his heart. "Ginny Baker, would you do me the enormous honor of marrying me? I promise to do everything in my power to make you happy and to never betray your trust."

Her fingers trembled as she shredded the precious document he'd given her and tossed the pieces to the ground. "Heath, I don't need this. Not anymore. I trust you completely, and I love you with everything I am." She wiped at her eyes, smiling through the tears. "How soon can we be married?"

Heath whooped and tossed his hat in the air before wrapping his arms around her again, pulling her close. "As soon as you're ready, Ginny. As soon as you're ready."

Her heart soared as she pressed her lips to his once more. The last of the sun's rays disappeared behind the hills, leaving them standing together in the twilight, the promise of their future ahead.

CHAPTER 26

APRIL 5, 1878
LUPINE VALLEY RANCH
EASTERN SAN DIEGO COUNTY, CALIFORNIA

*T*he bright afternoon sun baked the valley, sending rivulets of sweat down Ginny's back as she crept beside Heath through the desert shrubs, darting from rock to bush. Her muscles tightened with each step, every movement purposeful as she pressed on, eyes locked on the figure sneaking around a boulder.

The thief thought he'd gotten away.

He'd soon know better.

Wordlessly, she and Heath split—she went left while he went right around the boulder.

The faint scent of desert lavender clung to the air, mingling with the earthy tang of livestock and dirt as she rounded the rock. Twenty feet away, their quarry wove through the brush.

Now past the boulder, she glanced right. Where was Heath?

A soft, bird-like call reassured her of Heath's presence, just as it had that fateful day in the canyon. Though now, she knew

God was always with her, so she was never truly alone. Following the sound, she spotted her husband darting from rock to shrub.

Heath picked up speed, his long strides closing the distance between him and their elusive prey—a little bundle of energy, quick and determined. Just as the small boy ducked beneath a juniper bush, Heath scooped up their two-year-old nephew and pressed his mouth to the boy's belly, blowing hard.

Ezekiel squealed with laughter, dropping the small cake he'd stolen from the batch Biddie planned to sell the Gaskills for their store.

"Gotcha!" Heath tossed the boy in the air and caught him again.

Ezekiel giggled gleefully as Heath plopped him on his shoulders, and his tiny hands grasped onto Heath's hair while his uncle carried him back to Biddie's house.

Ginny smiled, though a sharp pang gripped her lower belly, drawing her breath short. She'd known this day was coming, but now that it was here, it felt all too real. Her hand instinctively pressed against her protruding belly as she followed Heath and their nephew into Biddie's home.

The smell of roasting meat and fresh bread welcomed them when they stepped into the front room, where Biddie busily arranged dishes on the table. Heath set the giggling boy down, ruffling his hair before turning toward Ginny. She leaned against the doorframe, a flicker of discomfort crossing her face.

Biddie looked up, her hands pausing mid-motion. "Everything all right?"

Ginny exhaled slowly, trying to steady herself. "It's time," she said softly, locking eyes with Heath.

Heath's grin faded, replaced with an intensity that made her feel grounded, safe. He stepped toward her, his hands warm and steady when they found hers. "You're sure?"

"Yes." She gasped as another contraction tightened her abdomen.

Without hesitation, Heath scooped her into his arms, and she let her head rest against his chest while he carried her across the yard to their house. She focused on the rhythmic thud of his boots against the packed earth rather than the nervous flutter in her chest.

Still, he must have sensed her anxiety because he murmured, "Everything will be all right. I've got you."

Inside their home, the soft crackle of the fire greeted them, the warmth of the hearth wrapping around them like a comforting embrace. Heath strode through what was now their front room to the addition he'd built after their marriage and set her down gently on their bed, his fingers lingering at her side.

Biddie bustled in moments later, wiping her hands on her apron. "Heath, you can go—"

"No." Ginny pressed her lips together against another wave of pain, gripping Heath's hand tightly. "I need him here. I feel safer with him."

Heath's eyes, filled with love and a fierce determination to keep her safe, met hers. She could hardly believe she'd once balked at his protectiveness. Before their marriage, she'd confessed everything from her past—making sure he knew exactly who he was marrying—yet he hadn't hesitated to accept every part of her. The love in his eyes had only grown brighter instead of dimming, as she'd feared.

Now, Heath nodded and knelt beside the bed, his hand never leaving hers. Ginny breathed deeply, her heart steady despite the storm her body was about to endure.

Their loving God held her future, Heath was by her side, and her sister had become her closest friend. That was more than she'd ever dared dream of. Yet God was blessing her with more. He was giving her a chance to raise her child surrounded by the kind of loving family she'd once thought only existed in fanciful stories.

CHAPTER 27

DECEMBER 25, 1888
LUPINE VALLEY RANCH
EASTERN SAN DIEGO COUNTY, CALIFORNIA

The setting sun cast a soft golden glow over Lupine Valley Ranch as the chill of December settled into the high desert air. Ginny stood just outside the front of her bustling home. The scent of roasting meat and spiced cider wafted through the breeze, mingling with the sweet smells emanating from the trays Biddie and Lucy carried toward the three very long tables set up in the yard. Laughter and chatter spilled out from the house behind her, where every corner hummed with children, family, and friends.

The long-ago memory of complaining to herself that her tiny stone home was too large made Ginny chuckle. Her home —now three times larger than it had been when she and Heath welcomed their first son—still seemed to shrink in the presence of so many loved ones. If they ever planned to host another reunion like this, they'd need to add more rooms.

Lucy and Preston's family, Daniel and Eliza Clarke's grand-children, plus the Davidsons and their grown son, Charles, with his wife and children, were all staying in Biddie and Gideon's home, which had also been expanded. Three of the ranch hands had moved into one room in the bunkhouse so Fletcher and Katie and their children could share one room, while Everett and Margaret Thompson with their younger children occupied the other. Ginny and Heath's three children were sleeping on the floor in Ginny and Heath's room so that Richard and Clarinda Stevens could sleep in one of the children's rooms and their four youngest children could share the other.

In short, every bed on the ranch was full, and much of the floor space had been covered in pallets. Any offspring who wouldn't fit inside and were old enough to be trusted outdoors had set up tents all over the valley, relishing the adventure of "camping in the wild," as twenty-three-year-old Zane Stevens had put it. Daniel and Eliza Clarke, as well as their grown-and-married children, seemed to agree with the sentiment, since they'd volunteered to give up beds inside and sleep under the stars instead. Their bedrolls had been layered with thick furs and laid around the campfires they kept burning through the night. Thankfully, the weather showed no signs of snow or even rain.

Never in her life had Ginny imagined hosting so many people at Lupine Valley Ranch. Yet it was a merry chaos Ginny hadn't expected to love quite so much.

A pair of familiar, strong arms slipped around her waist, and Ginny leaned back into Heath's solid chest with a happy hum. His warmth was a comfort in the cool desert evening. The soft wool of his coat brushed her cheek as he pressed a kiss to her temple.

"Stealing a moment for yourself, Mrs. Monroe?" His voice was a low rumble against her ear.

"Just thinking." She glanced over at the children racing out of the house, their laughter ringing out as they played.

Biddie approached with a grin, wrapping her shawl tighter against the breeze. "How are you handling all these people, Ginny? This was your idea, after all."

Ginny laughed. "As if anyone would believe that." It had taken Biddie two years to convince Ginny to go along with her wild scheme to invite practically everyone she'd ever met for a Christmas reunion.

Biddie shrugged. "I remember a time you wanted to run this ranch all on your own. You planned to live out here like a hermit."

"I did." Ginny's gaze drifted to the families gathered inside, the glow of lantern light casting soft shadows on happy faces. "But I've come to realize, if you push people away, you can't affect them for good. And if you're not influencing others, you're not leaving a real legacy."

Biddie cocked her head. "I thought this ranch was your legacy."

"So did I." She gave her sister a rueful smile. "But you and Heath helped me see that true legacy ain't the things we collect or even the land we work. All of that will fade someday. What really matters is how our actions ripple through the lives of others. That's the only thing that lasts."

Heath squeezed her waist gently, a quiet affirmation of her words.

"I had no idea," Ginny added, her voice softening with emotion, "that being surrounded by family and friends could bring so much joy."

Biddie visibly relaxed. "Then you don't mind this invasion of your home?"

Ginny reached out to take her sister's hand. "This is *our* home. And I've never been happier."

Did you enjoy this book? We hope so!
Would you take a quick minute to leave a review where you purchased the book?
It doesn't have to be long. Just a sentence or two telling what you liked about the story!

Love Christian Historical Romance?
Looking for your next favorite book?
Become a Wild Heart Books insider and receive a FREE ebook and get exclusive updates on new releases before anyone else.
Sign up for our newsletter now.
https://wildheartbooks.org/newsletter

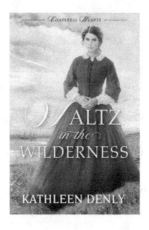

Book 1: Waltz in the Wilderness

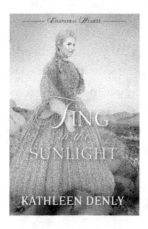

Book 2: Sing in the Sunlight

Book 3: Harmony on the Horizon

Book 4: Murmur in the Mud Caves

Book 5: Shoot at the Sunset

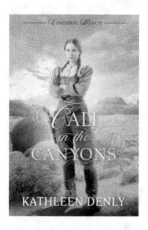

Book 6: Call in the Canyons

FACT VS FICTION, AN AUTHOR'S NOTE

Thank you so much for reading this story! As with every book in my Chaparral Hearts series, *Call in the Canyons* is a mix of both the historically accurate and the purely imaginary. If you'd like to know which was which, please continue reading.

The Gaskill brothers are a complicated pair. According to various historical accounts, Luman and Silas actually shared the role of running the Campo store. They also both acted as doctors on occasion, though neither had formal medical training. However, for the sake of simplicity and clarity in the story, I chose to have Luman be solely in charge of the store and Silas be known for his medical skills.

Because the closest sheriff, court, and judge was in San Diego, eastern territories were assigned a Judge of the Plains as well as a Justice of the Peace. The former handled all livestock-related legalities and crimes, while the Justice of the Peace handled all non-livestock-related crimes. Yes, Luman Gaskill did hold both the roles of Justice of the Peace and Judge of the Plains at various times during his life, sometimes overlapping. Later, when fencing became a widespread practice and cattle no longer roamed freely, the Judge of the Plains became an obsolete position.

The Smugglers' Den is a real location which I hiked to and explored in the spring of 2022. It really was known as a hideout for those attempting to carry contraband across the Mexican-American border in either direction. As for its involvement in the Campo raid, that is a matter of debate. There are many versions of what went down during and following the raid on Campo, and at least one includes the capture of a fleeing bandit at the Smugglers' Den. Most versions also include the posse's discovery of the body of one of the bandits along the road east of Campo with signs that the man had been "put out of his misery."

Speaking of the scene with the Smugglers' Den: You may have noticed that I gave a name to a rather insignificant character in that scene. *McCain* is the surname of a family that had a major impact—for better and for worse—on the settlement and history of the region east of Campo. The McCains were also mentioned in several historical accounts of various posses. Thus, it only seemed fitting to add this small nod to that influential family in this final posse scene.

While there are some variations in accounts of what happened during the shootout, when plotting my scenes, I used the official account given by the current historical society. The movements of the bandits, the Gaskill brothers, and even Jack Kelly are all as accurate as I could make them. That includes the miraculous account of Luman Gaskill being shot in the lung, crawling through the store to fire his shotgun and take down another bandit, before seeking shelter in the river that ran under the store (which straddled the small river) via a trap door in the store. And yes, he really did survive the injury.

Of course, my fictional characters (Ginny & Heath) weren't actually present at the real shootout. So I used the true life unexpected arrival of a French sheep herder who joined in the fray in defense of the Gaskills (and paid for it with his life) to inspire where, when, and how my characters might have taken part in what happened.

Another change I made was in the capture of Cesar Landa (aka Cruz Lopez). In real life, Cruz Lopez was actually shot in the neck and did escape. He was not, however, ever captured. Historical accounts claim that he suffered one miserable year hiding in Mexico before finally dying from "complications of the wound he'd received in Campo." However, I decided it would feel unfair to my readers if both Chavarria and Landa managed to escape. So I let my sheriff capture Landa at the Smuggler's Den.

Chavarria was inspired by Clodoveo Chavez, Tiburcio Vasquez's right-hand man. Chavarria's threat against the Americans living in California and his disappearance are also part of history. It is unknown why, but between the gang's Central California attacks and their eventual raid on Campo, Chavez left the gang. He might have been attempting to start fresh, or he may have been biding his time until his next criminal scheme since the bandits often disbanded and took on regular labor jobs in between attacks. Whatever the motivation, he was working as a cattle hand in Arizona under a fake name when a man he knew from California recognized and killed him. Due to the expense and time required for travel, Chavez's head was severed and preserved so that the man who killed him could bring it to California for identification, which was needed to collect the bounty.

What Heath says about Valadez's family was true about the real Tiburcio Vasquez's family. What Heath said about the relationship between Chavarria and Valadez was also true about Vasquez and Chavez. So, too, was the truth about the relationships between the various gang members. Most of them had more in common than simple greed and a willingness to commit violence. They were usually family, friends, or neighbors. The story about Vasquez returning a watch to a widow is a real part of the historical record also. I think it's important to remember that these bandits weren't just two-dimensional "evil" men. They were complicated human beings created by God with family and friends who cared about them.

Other than the shootout in Campo, all other encounters between the posse and the bandits in this novel are fictional. However, they were inspired by encounters between Sheriff Henry Morse (the real person that inspired my Sheriff Heath Monroe) and Tiburcio Vasquez and/or the men who rode with him (including Clodoveo Chavez, Cruz Lopez, and others).

Miguel's role as a mole is entirely fictional. I am sad (or not, depending on how you view it) to say that there is no historical precedence (that I am aware of) in which a bandit was made part of a posse. *But* he was inspired by the fact that a former member of the gang did once turn against them and join the posse pursuing them. But in that case, everyone on the posse knew about his past affiliation with the gang, and that was why they let him join.

The desert hideout and both Tores siblings were fictional. However, the gang was known to rest and plot at the homes of family and friends between crimes. And it makes sense that Fedoro would take part in the initial raid on Lupine Valley Ranch but not later crimes because the members of the gang were somewhat fluid. There was a core group that usually participated in everything, but it was far from unusual for one or two members to stay behind or be swapped out for different allies depending on various circumstances. Hence why there were only six of them for most of the book, but the expectation for many more during the actual raid. Which, by the way, was also true.

The gang greatly underestimated the Gaskill Brothers (who had been tipped off by a friendly Mexican about the upcoming raid). They expected to easily kill the two men and loot the town without any fighting. It was said that two wagons filled with additional raiders were meant to join the raid on Campo, but when they heard all the shooting, they realized things had gone wrong. Instead of riding in to help, they rode away, saving their own hides.

The description of Campo, California, is historically accurate to the best of my knowledge. (It is interesting to note that as a direct result of the shootout, the Gaskill brothers rebuilt their store entirely from stone and against the side of a nearby hill. They dug a tunnel into that hill for keeping cold goods in place of storing them in the river as they had done before. The Gaskill Brothers Stone Store still stands today as a museum which I highly recommend visiting.)

Carrizo Stage Station was a real stop on the Butterfield Overland Stage route. Today it is little more than an archeological site within the bounds of the Anza-Borrego Desert State Park, but you can still find it on Google Maps.

The unnamed town where the posse spreads their rumors was my biggest historical fudge. No such town existed in that region of the desert at the time of this story, but for the sake of keeping the story moving, I needed a way for my characters to spread their rumors that didn't require weeks of travel time and would keep them reasonably close to my fictional Lupine Valley Ranch (roughly located in the southern portion of the Jacumba Mountains). So I invented a town. But because it was not real, I did not give it a name. Sorry if that disappoints anyone.

Sinfora's ranch was inspired by historical accounts of how some Native Peoples were living in that area at the time—on their own land similar to everyone else, but usually barely getting by. Other Native Peoples still lived in groups, and many worked for local ranchers. In fact, by the 1880s, as many as twenty to fifty Native Peoples worked for the Gaskill Brothers on a daily basis. However, between 1860 and the 1880s, there are numerous accounts of conflict between the Native Peoples and the relatively new settlers. Many of those conflicts involved accusations of theft, and thus inspired the trouble Sinfora faces.

Locations and distances were all based on my best under-standing of the region from both current and historical maps as well as my own multiple explorations of the modern-day region. To view photographs and videos of one particularly adventurous research trip to this region (including pictures of the Smugglers' Den), please join my Armchair Adventure Krew on Facebook and subscribe to my newsletter which will give you access to my Kathleen's Readers' Club Freebie Library. The KRC Library is filled with exclusive short stories, videos, and free printables that are my thank you gift to my readers. Visit www.KathleenDenly.com to find the form for becoming a KRC Member.

If you'd like to learn more about the history that inspired this novel, I offer a list of recommended books in my free book club kit, available through my website or by emailing kden lyva@gmail.com.

If you've read this far, thank you so much. I hope you've been blessed.

ABOUT THE AUTHOR

Kathleen Denly lives in sunny California with her loving husband, four children, two dogs, and ten cats. As a member of the adoption and foster community, children in need are a cause dear to her heart and she finds they make frequent appearances in her stories. When she isn't writing, researching, or caring for children, Kathleen spends her time reading, visiting historical sites, hiking, and crafting.

ACKNOWLEDGMENTS

With the completion of this book, there are now eight novels and one companion devotional in my Chaparral Hearts series. Writing and editing that many stories is no small feat—certainly not one I could have accomplished alone. First, I want to thank my publisher, Wild Heart Books, for taking a chance on an unknown author. Writing this series has been more difficult and more rewarding than I ever imagined, but I will forever be grateful that you helped me accomplish my dream. I would also like to thank my editors who have helped to polish these stories into something that has touched the hearts of readers.

Of course, I would be remiss if I did not acknowledge the selfless assistance of both my beta readers and my launch team. You know who you are and where to reach me whenever you need help. Thank you, from the bottom of my heart!

I would also like to thank the many historians who have assisted my efforts along the way, and the sensitivity readers who have given of their time and energy to help guide my stories. In particular, I would like to thank the Mountain Empire Historical Society for inviting me into their archives and for their assistance in learning the fascinating history of their community. Any factual errors are my own.

Finally, I am so grateful for the continued support and encouragement of my husband and our four children. Thank you for visiting historical sites so I could do research during our vacations. Thank you for acting out scenes with me (especially that tricky one with the bound hands). Thank you for reading complicated excerpts to give me your feedback even after you've finished school and just want to chat with your friends online. And thank you for generally putting up with my absence each time I dive into my "writing cave." You are my first calling, and I will love you forever.

QUESTIONS TO CONSIDER & DISCUSS

- Do you prefer to work as a team or on your own?
- If you heard shots being fired, what would you do?
- Does it take you a while to trust new people?
- Have you ever struggled to forgive someone?
- Have you ever desperately wanted love from someone who was incapable of giving it?
- Have you ever judged someone new based on someone from your past who hurt you?
- What does the Bible say we should do with the pains others cause us?
- Ginny never has a clear "come to Jesus moment" and instead has several experiences that gradually draw her closer to God. Do you know anyone whose spiritual journey has looked similar?
- Have you or someone you know experienced abuse of any kind? How did you cope? What brought you hope?
- Have you or someone you know experienced clinical PTSD (Post Traumatic Stress Disorder)? What was

your experience like? Do you have any advice you'd
like to share with Ginny or Heath?

- Which scene caused the strongest emotional
  reaction in you?
- If you had to live in 1875 and must choose between
  living in Alameda or the desert east of Campo,
  which would you pick and why? What do you see as
  the pros and cons to each location during that time
  period?
- If you could have a conversation with just one
  character from this novel, who would you talk to?
- Which part of this novel surprised you the most?
- What do you think about the ending of this novel?
- Which character did you relate to the most?
- What most appeals to you about the book's cover?
- Which of the Chaparral Hearts novels is your
  favorite and why?

Did you know that Kathleen Denly is available for live book
club discussions? (No charge!) Email her for details at: Write
KathleenDenly@gmail.com. Use Subject Line: BOOK CLUB
REQUEST

Want more?

If you love historical romance, check out the other Wild Heart books!

A Christmas at Hotel del Coronado

When death visits Coronado, will secrets of the past keep them from uncovering the truth?

Her entire life, Eleanore Wainright has been molded to fit the ideal society wife in the glittering world of New York's elite. Her father's aspirations for her are clear: marry a man of wealth and status, and secure their family's future. But when she arrives at the Hotel del Coronado with intentions to do just that, Eleanore's carefully laid plans are thrown into disarray when she comes face to face with Thomas Harding, the man who shattered her heart and disappeared without a trace.

Working as a bellboy at California's newest and most prestigious resort, Thomas never imagined crossing paths with Eleanore again, let alone amidst the backdrop of a suspicious death.

As the investigation continues and tensions rise, Eleanore and Thomas are forced to confront not only the ghosts of their past but also the secrets that threaten to destroy their future and the futures of those they hold dear. With the eyes of New York's elite upon them, they must choose between the responsibilities they're expected to fulfill and the love they've always yearned for, risking everything in the process.

∿

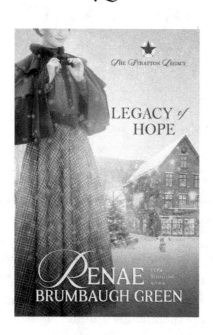

Legacy of Hope by Renae Brumbaugh Green
    She's struggled her entire life to overcome her parentage.

Skye Stratton is nearly perfect. Or at least, she tries to be. She carries the Stratton name, but everyone knows her true half-breed heritage. When she completes her education and is hired as a teacher at the local school, she hopes to finally find acceptance in the town. But when most of her class elects to stay home rather than be taught by an Indian, she knows things will never change.

Alan McNaughten went to Washington, D.C. to make a difference. Instead, he finds himself entrenched in political lies, manipulation, and deceit. When he finds a way to return home to Texas as an Indian Agent, he leaps at the chance. Even if he must hurt an innocent woman to secure his position.

But when the lovely Miss Stratton agrees to teach for the Alabama-Coushatta Reservation, Alan knows he's gone too far. He'll do anything to protect her from further heartache and harm. But what will happen when she learns the truth about her position...and the truth about him?

∾

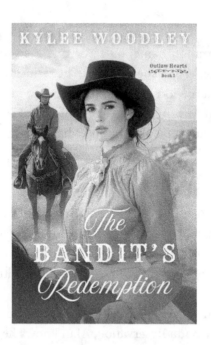

The Bandit's Redemption by Kylee Woodley

A holdup gone wrong, a reluctant outlaw, and the captive she's sworn to guard.

Life in the American West hasn't been easy for French refugee Lorraine Durand. She has precious few connections and longs to return to her native land. So when the man who rescued her from a Parisian uprising following the Franco-Prussian War persuades her to help him with a deadly holdup, she reluctantly agrees. Despite his promises otherwise, the gang kidnaps a man, forcing Lorraine to grapple with the fallout of her choices even as she is drawn to the captive she's meant to guard.

Jesse Alexander must survive. If not for himself, then for the troubled sister he left behind in Los Angeles. At the mercy of his captors, he carefully works to earn Lorraine's trust, hoping he can easily subdue her when the time comes. But as they navigate the treacherous wilderness and he searches for his opportunity to escape, he realizes there may be more to her than he first believed.